A SHTETL AND OTHER
YIDDISH NOVELLAS

A SHTETL AND OTHER YIDDISH NOVELLAS, *Edited, with introductions and notes, by* RUTH R. WISSE

WAYNE STATE UNIVERSITY PRESS   DETROIT

Library of Congress Cataloging-in-Publication Data

A Shtetl and other Yiddish novellas.

    1. Short stories, Yiddish—Translations into English. 2. Short stories, English—Translations from Yiddish. I. Wisse, Ruth R.
PJ5191.E8S54 1986 839'.093'0108 86-15794
ISBN 0-8143-1848-7
ISBN 0-8143-1849-5 (pbk.)

ISBN-13: 978-0-8143-1849-2   ISBN-10: 0-8143-1849-5

For
Masza and Leo Roskies,
my parents

CONTENTS

PREFACE

FOR THREE YEARS, 1968–71, as part of the Jewish Studies Program of McGill University, I taught a course, in English translation, on the Yiddish narrative. By some great good fortune, the course attracted a disproportionately high number of excellent students whose curiosity exhausted the available materials and left us wishing for more. The present volume was prepared with their standards and questions in mind.

The five short novels that comprise this book, here translated for the first time into English, were all written between the turn of the century and World War I, giving some indication of the thematic and stylistic scope of Yiddish literature in that brief period. They also share a common setting, the Eastern European Jewish town, or shtetl, then in a crisis of dissolution. It was thought that by bringing together these five similarly located and almost contemporaneous works in a single volume we might offer the reader a sharpened sense of the interpretive variety of the literature and provide substance for comparative analysis and appreciation.

Each of these works deals in a different way with a single topic: the Jewish confrontation with modernity. The turning point in the confrontation was the abortive Russian revolution of 1905, when Jewish hopes for political liberalization reached a stormy climax, and then shattered in anger and despair. I. M. Weissenberg's novella, which opens this book, was an immediate response to that historical moment; its harsh emphasis on class warfare, vivid descriptions of brutality, and unmistakable pessimism, introduced a new tone and new literary idea of "reality" into Yiddish literature. Bergelson's short novel is no less concerned with the economic underpinnings of society and no less despairing in its vision, but the rhythmic, impressionistic prose and the slow probing of individual sensibility make this a realistic work of quite another kind. The short novels of Opatoshu and Ansky. present the shtetl at somewhat greater remove. Both are actually romances, the emotional tendency heightened in the one case for the telling of a love-tale, in the other for a bitter drama of hate. With the single exception of Mendele's memoir, *Of Bygone Days*, the selections have been placed in their original order of publication, though it should be noted that a period of no more than two or three years separates any one from the next. Mendele's work, written before 1905, is here placed at the end as a kind of elegy, a harmonious portrait of a world the author knows to have passed.

Despite the variety of literary modes, each of these works makes an earnest claim to be telling the truth. And to be sure, they do, in fact, enrich our understanding of East European Jewish life with their vivid descriptions of places, people, and events. Yet this is primarily a *literary* anthology; fact has been filtered through fiction, and the bias of the mediating imagination must be clearly understood. It seems necessary to make this standard admonition only because, in an understandable hunger for sheer information about the shtetl and the East European "roots" of modern Jewry, the reader may be led too hastily to accept interpretation as fact, to read a story as sociology or anthropology rather than as the work of fiction it is. Even though they are "about" the shtetl, these stories are really primarily about themselves, their truth the self-referring truth of literature.

The intrinsic merit of these works has earned them a favored place in the Yiddish canon and recommends them to a wider readership. With the decline of spoken Yiddish in the United States, there is an understandable desire to have the major works made available in English, a desire this book hopes to satisfy at least in part. Introductory comments are sparingly included. For a broader introduction to the field of Yiddish, the reader is referred to the bibliography; for more intensive enjoyment—to the original texts.

I would like to thank my brother, David G. Roskies, and my colleague, Raymond P. Scheindlin, for undertaking the translations of Opatoshu and Mendele, and Abraham Igelfeld for the first draft of Ansky's *Behind a Mask*. The results bear witness to their sensitivity and skill.

Louis Tencer seemed to welcome my weekly list of questions, and I certainly welcomed the precision of his information. I have also received, through the years, unstinting help from Shimshon Dunsky, Hertz Kalles, Rochel Korn, Melech and Rochel Ravitch, Shloime Wiseman, the staff of the Montreal Jewish Public Library, and many other friends in the Yiddish sector of the Montreal Jewish community.

Like everyone else in the field of Yiddish, I am deeply indebted to Professor Khone Shmeruk of the Hebrew University for the standards he has set himself and those who work with him; beyond that, for the kindness he has shown me.

Dr. Yudl Mark was kind enough to read critically the general introduction.

My gratitude to my immediate family is deepest and most difficult to define. Jacob and Abigail Wisse often helped by interfering with work. Billy Wisse contributed some graceful phrasing to the Bergelson translation. My husband, Leonard Wisse, has always corrected my "greenie" usage, and supported my work in subtler ways.

To the scrupulous, exacting editor, Neal Kozodoy, belongs credit for much that is good in this book.

INTRODUCTION

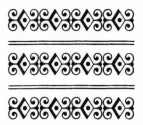

THE FLOWERING of Yiddish literature in Eastern Europe during the latter half of the nineteenth century was part of a larger, more generalized phenomenon: the effort, undertaken by many Jewish writers and thinkers, to create modern, secular forms for a culture that had been conceived and nurtured in religious faith. This effort, itself a response to developments in the world at large as much as to changing internal needs and pressures, was aimed at redefining the religious basis of Jewish life and finding new vocabularies of self-identification and self-expression. From western Europe there beckoned the model of "successful assimilation," and even those who did not look forward to the complete absorption of the Jewish people into Gentile society were impressed by the obvious advantages of partial acculturation, the adoption of the state language, local dress and manners, modern educational methods, and so on. At the same time, East European Jews had to reckon with a competing trend in their host countries in the form of the various nationalist movements, which, though they may have had a stimulating effect on the Jews' own quest for identity, often enough defined themselves in openly anti-Semitic terms. Physically as well as philosophically, East European Jewry was spun into turmoil. Nor was the threat only from the new and the emerging. Throughout the lands of the Pale, Jews continued to suffer from age-old geographic and economic dislocation as well as from the abrupt, unpredictable curtailment of rights which was the hallmark of their existence under the Tsars.

In memoirs, stories, essays, plays, and poems, Jewish writers of the time recorded the breakup of the established tradition and the search, often painful and nervous, for its reconstruction. Literature, at first part of the quest for new socio-cultural forms, gradually became one of the most important of those new forms, a clear testimony to cultural vitality and a growing monument of national identification, if not cohesion. Under the liberal reforms of Alexander II's regime (1855–1881), censorship was relaxed and a steady trickle of young men, no longer willing to consider a traditional rabbinic career, yet barred from the professions, found in literature a calling in harmony with both their own spirit and that of the times. Often penniless, they eked out a living as tutors (*melamdim*), while expressing their innermost selves in writing. Yet so similar were their situations and the problems with which they dealt that the private musings of these young men mirrored perfectly the national concerns. In this sense, although it may seem odd to speak of any modern literature in such terms, modern Jewish literature, especially modern Yiddish literature, erupted from a national, not merely a personal, reshuffling of identity, and even down into the twentieth century was a force for group survival.

In contrast to writers in Hebrew, who knew that they were communicating with a small elite, Yiddish writers addressed themselves to the consciousness of the folk. Of course, by his own admission, hardly any nineteenth-century Yiddish writer would have *elected* to write in Yiddish did he not feel it to be necessary— the necessity being that of the audience, never of the author himself. Those writers who condescended to Yiddish did so in a spirit of self-sacrifice, in order to serve a reading public that was held to be in need of instruction and unfortunately beyond the reach of Hebrew or any other "cultivated" tongue. Hebrew, the critic Dan Miron has observed, was perceived by these writers as the Ariel of languages, Yiddish as the Caliban; no one would have demeaned himself were there not a people in need of the sacrifice. Of course, Yiddish offered its writers at least two very large compensations for the linguistic "bestialization" it appeared to demand of them: the possibility of a readership in the tens of thousands, and, perhaps more important, the sizable artistic resources of a spoken vernacular. But initially the choice of Yiddish was felt as an obligation—undertaken, willingly or not, in deference to the needs of the folk—and hence for a long time the literature continued to reflect an uncommon sense of national responsibility.

On October 11, 1862, Alexander Zederboym, editor of the Hebrew newspaper, *Hamelits,* initiated a weekly supplement in Yiddish called *Kol mevasser* (Voice of the Herald) which became the first durable Yiddish publication in Eastern Europe. The potential of Yiddish as a language of serious communication was as yet barely realized. There were published collections of homiletic stories and compilations of ethical instruction, intended mostly for women; *tkhines,* or personalized Yiddish prayers; tales of Hasidic rabbis, often in satirical form; and some popular novels.* There was also a stirring of modern literary talent. Shloyme Etinger (1799–1855), for example, was a gifted fabulist and comic dramatist who gained a reputation in his immediate vicinity of Poland that was based entirely on circulated manuscripts and oral transmission of his work; by the time of his death not a word had found its way into print. With the inauguration of Zederboym's weekly supplement and the subsequent appearance of other, similar publications, the groundwork was laid for a Yiddish literary renaissance.

In its time, every vernacular has had to prove its worth against the linguistic superiority of its aristocratic rival, and Yiddish is no exception. An early issue of *Kol mevasser* contained a comic dialogue between Yidl, the Jew, and his wife Yehudis, Yiddish, in which the poor homely woman defends herself against her better-looking older sister. As for other (European) rivals: "Dress me up just as brightly/ And I'll prove just as sightly." Yet even the arguments in defense of Yiddish seemed to provide ammunition for the opposing side. When asked why he preferred Yiddish to Hebrew, Isaac Meir Dik, the very popular and prolific Haskalah novelist, replied that an old building could only be demolished by

*For an account of Yiddish literature in earlier periods, see N. B. Minkoff, "Old Yiddish Literature" and "Yiddish Literature in the Past 200 Years," *The Jewish People: Past and Present,* pp. 145–220; Yudl Mark, "Yiddish Literature," in *The Jews: Their History, Culture, and Religion,* II, pp. 1191–1233; Khone Shmeruk, "Yiddish Literature," *Encyclopaedia Judaica,* XVI, pp. 798–833.

the blows of a crude hammer, not by the delicate prickings of a golden needle. And Zederboym himself, in a truly astonishing "defense" of Yiddish, insisted that no other means would be so effective in demonstrating the ugliness of the language and hence in convincing its speakers of the detrimental influence it had upon them. *

Yet however tentatively they chose to write in Yiddish, and whatever the reasons they gave, writers who made the decision were immediately claimed by the challenge of the task. Indeed, the initial choice of Yiddish seemed minor when compared with the looming problems involved in creating a literary out of a spoken language. What level of the vernacular was the most appropriate for literature, which dialect, which mode of orthography? A comical prose would suit the folkish depiction of fishmongers and fruit peddlers, but what of the omniscient narrator? In what tone ought he to address his readers? Though linguists had not yet distinguished among Lithuanian, Ukranian, and Polish Yiddish, basic regional variations were widely recognized.† Should the author write in his own dialect, thereby enriching the flavor of his prose but perhaps limiting its readership to his own immediate area? The advantage of Yiddish was its vibrancy, but too much local color might make a work provincial. And what of the spelling? Yiddish was written phonetically, but if each writer adopted the sound patterns of his region, "father" in one usage (futer) would come out "fur coat" in another. A literary tower of Babel was a distinct possibility.

The struggle for some sort of standardization was undertaken sometimes haphazardly, at other times in a highly self-conscious manner. Even the pages of Kol mevasser, which was hardly interested in the problem of style, reflect the gropings of both the editor and his contributors for an acceptable norm. Each of the three classic Yiddish masters—Mendele Mocher Sforim, Sholom Aleichem, and I. L. Peretz—devoted much energy to the task of creating a suitable Yiddish literary prose style—suitable both for his own particular

---

*There is an interesting account of the beginnings of the Yiddish press, particularly of the publication, Kol mevasser, in Sh. L. Tsitron, Di geshikhte fun der yidisher presse (The History of the Yiddish Press, 1863–1889), Vilna.

†Yiddish dialects are well defined in Uriel Weinreich, "Yiddish Language," Encyclopaedia Judaica, XVI, pp. 790–798. A seminal work on the development of Yiddish is Max Weinreich, The History of the Yiddish Language, Chicago, 1980.

needs and as a guideline for the literature as a whole. In Mendele's case, as even a superficial study of his manuscripts reveals, the effort was bitterly painstaking.* Between one revision and the next, Slavicisms were eliminated, a combination of northern and southern dialect was distilled, and elements of "high" and "low" usage were blended to create a middle style: folksy, yet controlled. Sholom Yakov Abramovitch, the intellectual, invented the persona of Mendele the bookpeddler, whose voice was the ideal vehicle of an intimate narrative style and an "average" diction. The speech of the bookpeddler, a man who was constantly on the move, was not required to exhibit regional peculiarities. Brought into unremitting contact with books and with men of learning, the bookpeddler enriched his essentially homespun language with Biblical and Talmudic phrases. A simple man, marginal, yet familiar, the bookpeddler was clearly a handy sociological choice as a literary persona, but his greatest merit seems to have been that of projecting a believable and authentic folk style.

Sholom Rabinowitz, whose nom de plume, Sholom Aleichem, is synonymous with spoken idiomatic Yiddish, was similarly intent on stabilizing the written language while retaining its oral vitality (his task had of course been much facilitated by the man he called *zeyde*, grandfather—Mendele himself). In an early novel, *Stempenyu*, which recounts the unhappy love of a talented fiddler for a young housewife, Sholom Aleichem sets out to record the musicians' jargon, a slang that caught and fascinated his ear. Passages in which musicians speak among themselves are carefully footnoted for the "square" reader, but in the body of the book the author uses only such vocabulary and idiom as are *widely* known. Sholom Aleichem's prose appears to adapt itself utterly to each of his monologists, yet there is actually a carefully selected "standard folk usage" from which a speaker is allowed to deviate only slightly, usually for purposes of humor. It is only because he had first set up a standard that lapses and quirks were recognizable as such in Sholom Aleichem's fiction.

The same concentrated effort, though toward quite different literary ends, is to be found in the work of I. L. Peretz, and in the patient instruction he gave to young writers who visited his Warsaw

*The Mendele Project of the Hebrew University in Jerusalem is about to begin publication of a Variorum Edition of the complete works in which the process of Mendele Mocher Sforim's literary development will be clearly shown.

home. Peretz was an intellectual, and he tried to smooth out the language in order to make it resemble the narrative tone of contemporary European literature, ceasing to draw attention to itself in any peculiarly folksy way. Do not combine Germanisms with Hebraisms in the same phrase, he warned one correspondent, not *"dem poet's yiesh"* (the poet's anguish, possessive Germanic, subject Hebraic) but *"dem poet's fartsveyflung"* (both Germanic), an admonition emphasizing a desire for evenness that the next generation of Yiddish writers would delight in defying. Stylistically, Peretz is less interesting than his predecessors to those modern readers who enjoy a flavorful Yiddish, but there is no doubt that in making the language into a fluid European literary instrument Peretz had the most profound influence on its future.

The pioneering efforts of the three masters, though extraordinary, were not sufficient in themselves to bring about the full regularization of literary Yiddish. Every subsequent Yiddish writer, including those represented in this volume, remained engaged in this basic task. Of his own beginnings in literature, about 1896, the short-story writer Lamed Shapiro (1878–1948) writes:

> At that time Yiddish was still "jargon." We did not yet understand that every language is a jargon—a blending of indigenous formations with sounds and expressions from other languages. We did not yet have a grammar, that is to say, no grammarian had yet put together a textbook explaining how Yiddish should be spoken and written based on the manner in which Yiddish *was* spoken and written. . . .

Looking back at some of his early stories, Shapiro accuses himself of having twisted Yiddish to fit the rules of Russian syntax:

> I pushed our poor language into Russian syntactic structures that suited it about as well as a uniform suits a bellboy. While I was torturing our etymology and syntax, the easy natural flow of our language, I lay awake nights over the lexicography. . . . The Slavic elements didn't seem to fit well into the German basis of the language. Hebrew with its wonderful innermost pathos sounded like a quotation from somewhere. The only choice appeared to be German, that is [to write] Germanically. There

was an obvious danger of being drowned by foreign words, and this in fact was the source of my exaggerated purism.*

Shapiro's dilemma, as well as the method he chose of solving it, was symptomatic of the dilemma facing Yiddish literature as a whole in its relation to European culture, especially as that culture was represented through the figure of the *maskil,* the young Jewish reformer with Western ideas of enlightenment and progress who was featured prominently in Yiddish prose and drama before 1881, usually as the author's spokesman and sometimes as a romantic hero. Since, "in real life," such a young man would have abjured Yiddish, he was usually depicted by a Yiddish author as speaking German. Thus, Shloyme Etinger's social comedy, *Serkele,* has as its hero a young medical student who speaks near-perfect, transliterated German. Similarly, in Mendele's maiden efforts and even in Sholom Aleichem's early story, "The Penknife," the wise characters speak Germanically to signify their higher intellectual level and purer ideals.

It is difficult to imagine how a rich literature could have developed with all its "good guys" speaking a foreign tongue. But in fact, as the Haskalah came to be progressively discredited during the 1870's and 1880's, the German-oriented enlightener ceased to serve as a positive model, and the language of Moses Mendelssohn lost its intimidating power over the "jargon" it had spawned.† It is in the changing relation between Yiddish and German, rather than between Yiddish and Hebrew, that the pattern of national vernacular emergence can be perceived. As soon as Yiddish speakers and spokesmen accepted the legitimacy of their own language, instead of judging it an inferior distortion of a perfect tongue, the literature became freed to occupy its own ground. Thus in S. Ansky's *Behind a Mask* (see p. 218), the young *maskilim* speak Yiddish, the same

*Some of Lamed Shapiro's short stories may be found in *The Jewish Government and Other Stories,* ed. and trans. by Curt Leviant, New York, 1971. The quotations are from Lamed Shapiro, *Der shrayber geyt in kheyder* (The Writer Goes to School), New York, 1945.

†Moses Mendelssohn's translation of the Bible into German, with his accompanying *biur,* or commentary, had been responsible in a direct way for the decline of Yiddish as a language of instruction. Mendelssohn, and the entire German Haskalah, regarded Yiddish as a degraded version of German, and actively sought to turn all Jews from its use.

language spoken by those they seek to reform, and in Mendele's *Of Bygone Days* (see p.254) even the Polish nobleman, within the context of the story, converses in Yiddish. German, or Germanic Yiddish, which previously had connoted moral superiority, inevitably became the mark of pseudo-sophistication and moral corruption. In the stories of I. L. Peretz, as today in those of I. Bashevis Singer, it is the devil who speaks Germanically.

The Yiddish writer's quest for a regularized language was accompanied by vigorous experimentation with all known forms of writing, an effort to ascertain by trial and error what could be done successfully in Yiddish and what could not. The Yiddish moderns saw themselves not as the heirs of an earlier *Yiddish* literature, of the epic Yiddish romances of the fifteenth and sixteenth centuries, but of their nineteenth-century European contemporaries and *their* predecessors. Yiddish authors were well versed in the best of German, Russian, and/or Polish literature and were familiar with whatever French and English works had been translated into those languages. The artistic standards they sought to emulate were those upheld in the writings of Gogol, Schiller, Dickens, Heine, Hamsun, de Maupassant.

The degree of reliance on foreign models varied; drama, written where there was neither memory nor promise of a stage, was often highly derivative, whereas short stories based on folk tales, jokes, and other indigenous material were far more independently conceived. Rare was the Yiddish author who did not try his hand at every species of prose and poetry; indeed, it is considered noteworthy that Peretz did *not* attempt the writing of a novel.

Variety and tightened artistic control characterize the two volumes of *Di yidishe folks bibliotek* (The Jewish Folk-Library), a collection, edited by Sholom Aleichem, of fiction, satire, poetry, memoirs, and criticism that marks a milestone in the development of modern Yiddish letters. Determined to raise Yiddish literary standards, Sholom Aleichem had decided to put out at his own expense a yearbook containing the best materials he could solicit from prominent and promising writers throughout Russia. He edited more ruthlessly and paid more handsomely than any Jewish publisher of his time, so it is not surprising that his two volumes

(1888 and 1889) testify to a vast improvement in the quality of Yiddish belles-lettres since the 1860's. The two annuals—bankruptcy prevented a third—bring together the older generation of satirists with a younger crop of poets, and include at least one outstanding work in each category, Mendele Mocher Sforim's novel, *Wishing Ring,* and I. L. Peretz's maiden publication in Yiddish, the neo-ballad, *Monish.*

When Sholom Aleichem solicited a poem from him, Peretz was known only as a writer of Hebrew verse. In accepting the invitation, Peretz praised the undertaking but admitted to having read Sholom Aleichem's work only in Polish translation; yet he thereby betrayed a far greater ignorance than he realized of the world of Yiddish letters, since the work he referred to had actually been written not by Rabinowitz (Sholom Aleichem) but by Abramovitch (Mendele)! This small exchange reminds us how tentative and fragile Yiddish letters still were at that juncture and brings home the significance of Sholom Aleichem's decision to create for Yiddish culture a respectable central forum, what is still known in Yiddish circles as *"an adress."*

Di yidishe folks bibliotek stands at the crossroads between the first and second phases of the Yiddish renaissance. Thematically, the works included in its two volumes hark back to the Haskalah, with their determination to educate by entertaining, to improve by exhortation. Authors tried to alleviate the worsening condition of Jewish life by dressing their work in "fantasy, poesy, and optimism." Aesthetically, in their consciousness of artistic responsibility, the anthologies herald a new literary sensibility. But the volumes are in fact characterized by a naive will to goodness; they are innocent of political thought or even political vocabulary, and they offer no hint of the coming storm in Jewish life.

Within the decade, however, revolutionary ferment had intensified throughout Russia, and the pulse of Yiddish writing quickened. The Jewish masses became actively involved in a social struggle that soon crystallized in the formation of national and political movements. In 1897, a year that seems to have been selected for the convenience of Jewish historians, the frameworks of Jewish socialist and Zionist activity were both officially established. The Jewish Workers Bund of Lithuania, Poland, and Russia was founded in Vilna, and the first Zionist Congress convened in Basle. In the same

year, the noted historian, Shimon Dubnow, published his first
Letter on the Old and New Judaism, laying the groundwork for the
politics of Folkism and Autonomism.*

Yiddish songs of the period rapidly adopted the militant
language and ideology of the burgeoning labor movement. More
subtly, but to the same purpose, formal literature mirrored a growing class consciousness and a mounting anger. One of the several
publications edited by I.L. Peretz in those years was called, decep-
tively, *Yontev bletlakh* ("Holiday Issues"). Ostensibly published in
celebration of the Jewish holidays (in order to be gotten safely past
the censor), the periodical was filled with irate exposures of injustice
and little, if any, holiday cheer. The sketches and stories that filled
its pages described the plight of the Jewish woman, the unorganized
Jewish worker, the yeshiva student whose Talmudic training
doomed him to a lifetime of unproductivity. Naturalism and social
realism became the dominant literary modes, replacing the satire of
previous decades. The novel—up until then a relatively unsuccess-
ful form in Yiddish—began to take root and grow; the longer form
alone seemed to provide the necessary scope and depth for depicting the growing stratification of Jewish society. As the gulf between
manufacturer and laborer widened, and an awareness of class
distinction penetrated the culture, the novel took hold and developed.

The sharpening conflict among the proponents of various ideological positions, each intent on winning as many adherents as he
could, alongside the less sharply defined but no less severe tensions
between assimilationists and nationalists, traditionalists and freethinkers, sought expression in the pages of numerous newspapers
and periodicals that sprang into being despite rigorous Tsarist con-
trols. Since political gatherings were explicitly outlawed, the circu-
lation of printed matter became the favored means of spreading new
ideas. *Der yid,* an important Zionist weekly, was launched in Warsaw in 1899 with distribution in Russia where permission to publish

---

*According to Dubnow, the Jewish people should be regarded as a spiritual
community "held together by historical, cultural, and religious ties." Jews should
seek to live autonomously among other nations, preserving their national existence
in the diaspora by use of a separate language, Yiddish; by the achievement of such
political autonomy as might be possible within the diaspora framework; and by the
development of their own cultural heritage. See Simon Dubnow, *Nationalism and
History: Essays on Old and New Judaism,* ed. with an introductory essay by Koppel S.
Pinson, Philadelphia, 1958.

had been denied. In 1903, *Der fraynd*, the first Yiddish daily in Eastern Europe, began publication in St. Petersburg, to be followed shortly thereafter by the dailies *Haynt, Moment, Veg*, in Warsaw, then the hub of Yiddish creativity. Altogether some 300 major and minor Yiddish newspapers and periodicals appeared in Europe between 1900–1914; in the United States, where censorship was not a problem, the Yiddish press was all the more active and more effectively organized.

This sudden burst of expression had an immediate, though not easily assessable, effect on formal literature. More and more young people were attracted to writing as a career, as the literary calling began to assume an increasingly professional character. Some of the many Yiddish writers who broke into print about this time include Yehoash (Solomon Bloomgarten, 1872–1927), Abraham Liessin (1872–1938), David Pinski (1872–1959), Abraham Reisin (1876–1953), Hirsh Nomberg (1876–1927), Lamed Shapiro (1878–1948), Sholom Asch (1880–1957), Peretz Hirschbein (1880–1948), Jonah Rosenfeld (1880–1944), I.M. Weissenberg (1881–1938); and soon afterward David Bergelson (1884–1952), Der Nister (Pinkhas Kahanovitch, 1884–1950), Moishe Nadir (Isaac Reis, 1885–1943), Zalman Schneour (1887–1959), Joseph Opatoshu (1887–1954), and others who, like Opatoshu, became known as the American Yiddish writers; Mani Leib (Brahinsky, 1884–1953), Reuven Eisland (1884–1955), David Ignatov (1885–1954), I. I. Schwartz (1885–1971), Moishe-Leib Halpern (1886–1932), H. Leivick Halper, 1888–1962), Zishe Landau (1889–1937). At the beginning of the century Chaim Nahman Bialik (1873–1934) was noted as both a Yiddish and Hebrew writer, as were Berdichevski (1865–1921), Nahum Sokolov (1860–1936), and others, while many Yiddish writers were also prolific in Hebrew. Russian-Jewish socialists were likewise drawn to Yiddish: some, like S. Ansky (Rapoport, 1863–1920), because of their genuine love of the masses, others, like Abraham Cahan (1860–1951), out of a frank desire to mold them in the image of socialism.

The appeal of Yiddish was at no time wider than in the period before World War I. It was the language spoken by more Jews than had ever spoken a single Jewish language at any one time; moreover, in the wake of unprecedented migrations, it became the only effective lingua franca among Jews in distant lands. For the budding writer, the body of work that had already been produced demonstrated impressively how variously the language could be used,

while its newness was an open challenge, inviting him to take the
literary experiment a step further into the future.

But just as the expressive possibilities of Yiddish were becoming
manifest in all their richness and variety, the language fell captive to
the intensifying political polarization within the Jewish community.
Yiddish became a banner in a political struggle. The Jewish labor
movement seized upon Yiddish as a weapon of secularism and
socialism and proclaimed it a badge of identity, as though the
language were not equally the property of bourgeois householders
and earlocked Hasidim. Professor Khone Shmeruk has drawn a
parallel between this development and the earlier association of
Yiddish with the programmatic aims of the Haskalah:

> Despite the great achievement of Yiddish literature in the 19th
> century, it did not deviate very much—at least not programmat-
> ically—from the fixed positivistic-Haskalah views. The Haskalah
> regarded Yiddish primarily as a means of spreading knowledge
> and education, and as a useful weapon in the battle against
> Hasidism and all other manifestations of Jewish life that, in its
> judgment, required reform. Actually, Haskalah literature in Yid-
> dish exceeded these narrow expectations and broke through its
> programmatically-defined limits. But before there was even a
> chance to determine new areas and opportunities, another social
> movement placed its demands before this literature and declared
> itself to be the chief guardian of Yiddish. The newly-formed
> Jewish labor movement, whose pedigree really goes back to the
> Haskalah, looked upon Yiddish literature more as a propaganda
> tool than as a value and end in itself. And it was from this point of
> view that the labor movement evaluated Yiddish literary creativi-
> ty, extolling those works that accorded with its general aims. *

The height of factional fervor was reached at the Czernovitz Conference of 1908, which passed the seemingly tautological resolution
that Yiddish be declared a national language of the Jews. The
Conference narrowly avoided chaos by defeating a counter-resolu-
tion declaring Yiddish to be *the* national Jewish language, an obvious intended insult to religious traditionalism and "Hebrew-Zion-

---

*Khone Shmeruk, *Peretses yiesh-vizie* (Peretz's Vision of Despair), New York (YIVO
Institute for Jewish Research) 1971, pp. 197–198.

ism," if not to the very idea of Jewish history. The heat of the discussions made it clear, despite the victory of the milder statement, that some delegates regarded Yiddish as the ideological cornerstone of a secular diaspora Judaism.

Its new political garb boosted the prestige of Yiddish among those sectors of the Jewish population that were in accord with the ideas of organized labor, but to cut the language loose from the religious tradition altogether would have meant abandoning a vast referential base, for artists a major source of imagery and resonance. Ultimately, of course, modern Yiddish writers could no more be contained by the ideological movements that claimed them than writers of the previous century had been confined by the Haskalah ideas in whose name they wrote. There grew, alongside a compassionate concern for the people, a quite independent concern for literature, a desire, at once personal and national, to create works of excellence and a major body of art. Whereas in the previous century the main focus of experimentation had been linguistic, writers now grappled with untried subjects, styles, and themes. With astonishing rapidity they moved from satire and naturalism through all the various phases of romanticism in an effort to "catch up" with contemporaneity. Peretz, the most restless of moderns, first wrote Hasidic tales like *Dos shtrayml* (The Rabbinic Fur Hat), harshly critical of Hasidic superstition, stupidity, and insularity. Later, in the face of what he regarded as a dangerous tendency toward total assimilation, he plucked Hasidic figures out of history to serve as models of humanism, bathing them in a tender, romantic light. In one of his mature works, the much re-written symbolic drama, *Di goldene keyt* (The Golden Chain), Peretz uses the Hasidic dynasty as a vehicle for asking a number of searching and deeply pessimistic questions about the rising religion of science, the relation of democracy to the possibility of spiritual greatness, the inexorability of generational decline. Peretz discarded his own literary fashions as quickly as they were adopted by his disciples.

Writers hastened to try out imported tonalities. Poetry, which had been slower to develop in Yiddish than had prose, blossomed forth in the United States, where a self-styled group of *Yunge* (Youngsters) declared itself independent of social and national motifs; in musical, impressionistic lyrics the members of this group sang of their quivering isolation. Innovation was everyone's ideal: the magazines of those years boldly declare originality in their titles—*Dos naye lebn,* 1908 (The New Life); *Di naye velt,* 1908 (The New World); *Dos naye land,* 1911 (The New Land). There was a keen awareness of what was happening in other cultures and a need to get beyond one's own by exposing it to all that lay around. The wide market for translations into Yiddish testifies to the hunger of writers and audiences alike for a taste of worldly goods. There were translations of Karl Marx and Karl Kautsky and *The Arabian Nights;* of Dostoevsky, de Maupassant, Oscar Wilde, and Sir Walter Scott. Mendele had translated Jules Verne; Moishe Leib Halpern, Zishe Landau, and others, translated Heine; Yehoash translated Longfellow; Der Nister translated Tolstoy; Moishe Nadir even translated "Old King Cole," which achieved instantaneous fame in Yiddish as *Der Rebbe Elimelekh.*

This last, half-humorous, example may suggest why, for all its ostentatious borrowing (or theft), Yiddish literature did not stand in any real danger of becoming unduly derivative—so powerful was the centripetal force of the historical community, especially upon any artist who chose, by the language he employed, to remain within its sphere. The mocking, affectionate parody of the Hasidic Rebbe Elimelekh, as he moves from the restrained atmosphere of the Sabbath to the boisterousness of the weekday world, is obviously indebted to the English folksong, but the material and even the melody have been so thoroughly assimilated that a footnote is required to remind the singer of his source. For most Yiddish writers, the center continued to hold (sometimes despite even their most valiant efforts to escape outward). Marginality may have been the Jew's archetypal experience, as well as his characteristic literary assignment, in the cultures of England, Germany, Russia, or France; within the Yiddish world the classic situation of both characters and authors was that of the insider trying to get out.

Not accidentally, the shtetl is the setting or the subject of all the works in this volume. Although in the early years of the century Jews were swarming more rapidly than other sectors of the population to urban centers in both Europe and America, the shtetl continued to dominate the artistic imagination of Yiddish writers at least until the outbreak of the first World War. It was, first and foremost, native ground. Most writers came from the small Jewish or half-Jewish towns of Russia, Poland, and the Ukraine, and in the

manner of writers everywhere they drew upon what was most familiar to them. The shtetl was also a distinctively *Jewish* form of
settlement, with a unique sociological and anthropological character that could be exploited in literature to various mythological
ends.

It would be a mistake to assume, as some readers do, that the
shtetl as it appears in literature is always that homey, beleaguered,
comforting place where "life is with people" and all is with God.
Sholom Aleichem did indeed populate his fictional Kasrilevke with
jolly paupers whose indigence merely disguised a profound spiritual
resourcefulness. Writers before and after Sholom Aleichem,
however, saw with different eyes. Depending in large measure
upon when an author wrote, the shtetl might resemble seven-
teenth-century Salem, where a handful of enlightened heroes
grapple with the reactionary witch-hunting force of religious fanaticism, or a hallowed never-never land of neighborly lovingkindness,
with but a fool or mischief-maker for comic relief. As long as the
reformist belief persisted that the social and moral improvement of
the Jews could be achieved through applied effort, the shtetl
continued to be ridiculed for its ignorance and intransigence. *Di
behole* (The Panic), a short "historical" story by Isaac Meir Dik,
makes fun of a town for responding to a discriminatory Tsarist
decree by marrying off its children, down to the smallest toddlers in
cheder. Characteristically, the author focuses not on the brutal
intentions or possibly brutal consequences of such Tsarist edicts,
but on the backwater spirit of the shtetl, which can only be saved
from its own worst tendencies by a new spirit of rational positivism
and an energetic program of reform.

Not until the end of the century did Yiddish literature begin to
deal adequately with the many varied forces pressing from without
upon the Jewish towns and villages of Eastern Europe; before then
the community was almost always held responsible for its own
condition—as though it were a wholly independent political and
socioeconomic unit. Reformers admitted that some of their sallies
would draw blood, but then, as one of them put it, the social critic
"was like the physician who operates so as to heal, or better said, like
the pathologist who dissects a corpse so as to determine the cause of
death and thereby save others who may still be curable. . . ."

The cause of death was sought within the patient; this optimis-
tic theory of pathology did not admit of the possibility of plague.

Even sentimental novels, with their complicated but predictable romantic involvements, were steeped in Haskalah convictions. Thus, a progressive doctor and his lovely daughter are persecuted by a shtetl that suffers under the malevolent influence of its reactionary rabbi. The town vigilantes intend to punish the "freethinkers" in a ceremonial public beating. Fortunately, the wealthy son of the evil rabbi's chief supporter, a recent convert to the doctor's rationalism and the daughter's charms, intervenes to turn the intended punishment against its perpetrators. The novel's readers, servant girls and their mistresses, even as they wept over the fortunes of the lovers, were being schooled in the new fashions of thought and transferred from one set of prejudices to another. Because the conflicts portrayed were so clearly conventional, there was not much concern on the part of the authors of such works for precise characterization. Figures are typical: the *feldshers* (barber-surgeons) are all *felshers* (shams) while the doctors are selfless and idealistic. Beadles are conniving, though often comical, sycophants; innkeepers are lusty and expansive; water-carriers and porters, pure of heart. Even the most gifted of such works adhered to the basic ideological formula: certain prescribed changes must now affect the timeless complacency of shtetl society. And inevitably, like so much of topical fiction, these stories and novels became quickly dated. Only the negative pole of the plot, the chronicle of local superstitions, customs, curses, retained its freshness and literary force.

Yet time, as we know, did intrude on the shtetl, and with far greater rapidity than the reformers anticipated. A way of life that had seemed impregnable suddenly gave way, as though the institution they had set out to topple were touched by a cultural avalanche, leaving only ruin and memory behind. It was not that the shtetl or its inhabitants disappeared—only the Nazis would accomplish that—but pogroms and economic crises, the resultant waves of emigration, the magical lure of socialist, Zionist, and assimilationist dreams—the worst kind of external pressure combining with the rosiest of promises— drained the traditional society of its inner resources and of the strength to resist. Within a great deal less than a lifetime, in some places within no more than a decade, writers saw the erstwhile object of their hatred transformed into an object of pity, and many felt compelled, like Mendele in his memoir, *Of Bygone Days*, to exalt what they had once excoriated.

The breakup of the shtetl thrust the writer rudely into the

modern predicament and, not surprisingly, became the obsessive theme of his writing. Nineteenth-century Yiddish satire had really been an eighteenth-century form, based on an all-too-stable-seeming environment with binding norms and stifling restrictions. With the disintegration of the shtetl, the writer fell with a thud into the twentieth century. The breakup of his former world was both a fact, reality, and a stunning correlative to his own psychological, not to say metaphysical, fall from grace. The subject, in fact, was ready-made for fiction.

In older writers the necessary adjustment of form and vision took place gradually. Sholom Aleichem, for example, who called himself a realist, had protested in his early fiction against the convention of the sentimental romance: it was inappropriate to serious Jewish literature, he argued, because Jewish life had no use for the ideals of romantic love which had inspired Christian Europe since the Middle Ages. For traditional Jews, love was the result of marriage, not vice versa, and an author was being false to the facts if he portrayed shtetl characters driven by passion to commit adultery and/or suicide. Thus Sholom Aleichem wrote one *"roman on a roman"* (novel without a romance) and another in which the Jewish wife pointedly refuses to be separated from her home despite her attraction to another man. As the Sabbath draws to a close the young housewife sneaks out to a rendezvous with her beloved, but the pervading atmosphere of sanctity in all the surrounding homes triumphs over her passion, and she flees from the long-awaited embrace.

Yet Sholom Aleichem's later and best-known work, *Tevye der milkhiker,* written in installments between 1895 and 1916, gradually comes to the opposite view. Tevye's oldest daughter, unwilling to submit in the accepted way to an arranged match (in this case with a prosperous butcher), selects her own heart's desire, a poor tailor lad. This seemingly modest rebellion, as both the author and his character perceived, was not simply a rejection of the outmoded custom of arranged marriages, but confirmation of a crumbling social order. In the book's progression, the second daughter marries a revolutionary for whom universal ideals have usurped "narrow" Jewish concerns, and the third daughter, a Christian. According to the supreme dictates of love, Chava may marry whom she adores even if she must convert to Christianity in the process. Here, as in many later Yiddish novels, the absolutism of love successfully challenges the sanctity of peoplehood. Form *is* content, the love story itself a decisive blow to traditional Jewish ideals. *

The theme of disintegration emerged still more forcefully in progressive literature. Even before the rise of socialist ideologies, the shtetl's inequitable distribution of poverty had come under strong attack, but it was not until the organization of labor at the end of the century that class lines were recognized as such. Previously only the vulgar and greedy among the "rich" were singled out as villains, while the learned and generous man of property was seen as embodying the double values of material and spiritual achievement. If there was an operative theory of shtetl economics, it was based on the wheel of fortune, which spins "today to you, tomorrow, maybe, to me." Typical of this earlier attitude is Yakov Dinesen's short novel, *The Crisis,* which traces the road to bankruptcy of an honest cloth-merchant whose business collapses through no fault of his own. The villain here is simply fate, that staple of non-ideological literature which has long been known to favor injustice or "irony." There is, in this pre-socialist writing, no necessary equation of money with immorality, and the reward for goodness, when there is one, is the reward of the folktales: wealth.

As small- and large-scale industrialization widened the gap between shtetl rich and poor, however, and a new economic vocabulary drew attention to the breach, literature adopted the terminology of exploitation and a simplified polarization according to class affiliation. As has already been noted, prose writers (like David Pinski and Abraham Reisin) and poets (like Morris Winchevsky and Morris Rosenfeld) decried the shameful degradation of the working man at the hands of avaricious employers. Weissenberg's *A Shtetl,* the most brilliant literary study of class struggle in the Jewish Pale of Settlement, dramatizes the growth of a labor consciousness in an atmosphere of vicious enmity. Weissenberg deliberately inverts the idea of folksy solidarity to reveal in its stead a fatal division along economic lines that must lead to armed conflict. The accepted Jewish notion of national unity is demonstratively crushed by the emergent loyalty to class.

*In the romances of the fourth and fifth daughters, Sholom Aleichem follows the standard plotting of the bourgeois novel: one drowns herself after having been jilted by a wealthy suitor who dares not marry beneath what his mother considers to be his proper station; the other, committing the most heinous of literary crimes, marries for money.

Yet Weissenberg's story is caught in an interesting and typical cross-fire of visions. However necessary or just the economic battle within Jewish society, it assumes a pitifully small and almost foolish aspect when considered against the backdrop of Tsarist might. Unlike the older Yiddish novelists, Weissenberg *does* raise his eyes from the shtetl foreground to take note of the larger political facts that dwarf his internal squabble. The peasant procession weaving its mighty way through the center of *A Shtetl* and the Tsarist police convoy that terrorizes the town at the end reduce the local conflict to a mere "smudge on the horizon." If the economic interpretation of history now called for literary realism in defining the splintering Jewish world, intimations of the shtetl's vulnerability complicated the genre's normal themes. Many a Yiddish writer, far removed geographically from his native setting, found his vision softening as the distance increased. It is not unusual to find works in which the strident social message is undermined by romantic lyricism of style, the writer himself caught in apparently irreconcilable tension between estrangement and attachment, between dislike and disapproval of the shtetl on the one hand, and, on the other, an unwelcome intimation of its mortality. So Weissenberg's harsh naturalism is undercut by a contradictory sense of impending danger; Bergelson's satire in *At the Depot* is counterpointed by a mournful, almost nostalgic lyricism; Opatoshu's novella, written in distant New York, aims at exposing old-world injustice, but the title promises *Romance*, a work that bathes its characters in sunlit memory.

The shtetl continued to engage the Yiddish writer during all the pre-war years, even while he was most eagerly courting artistic modernism. It has been rightly said that Yiddish writers of this period were not given to the "endlessly minute exposure of motives and manners"* so characteristic of the time. Instead, there was an unyielding preference for group characterization, a growing interest in various modes of symbolism which could be used to magnify and interpret collective experience. Yiddish literature of the first decade of the century, unlike the writings of Jews in other languages, seems less concerned with individual normal and abnormal psychology than with the nature of the group, or the individual's struggle within it. In fact, Yiddish writers developed considerable skill in collective

*Irving Howe and Eliezer Greenberg, *A Treasury of Yiddish Stories*, New York, 1953, Introduction. This is probably the single most interesting essay in English on the contours of Yiddish literature in the modern period.

portraiture, a skill that may be considered an independent achievement of the literature as a whole. Kasrilevke, the fictional town that burns to the ground and then reconstructs itself, ranks alongside Tevye, Menahem-Mendl the speculator, and Motl-Peysi the cantor's son as one of Sholom Aleichem's major "characters." Sholom Asch's *Shtetl*, a little too richly romantic for some contemporary tastes, is a tender sanctification of the author's native town. Weissenberg's use of collective nouns creates the effect in *A Shtetl* of the town as a grammatical entity, less the sum of its residents than the shaping power of their lives.

As the actual world of the shtetl passed ever more completely into history, depictions of it in Yiddish fiction bordered increasingly on the mythical and metaphorical. Ansky's *Behind a Mask*, like his famous drama, *The Dybbuk*, uses the heightening effects of symbolism to project a local struggle in the haunting, archetypal terms of myth. In this he foreshadows some of the work of I. J. Singer and the latter's younger brother, Isaac Bashevis Singer, whose towns of Goray and Frampol only appear to be grounded in history and fact but have actually passed over into the metaphysical domain. The disappearance of the world of the shtetl doomed and freed the artist to make of reality a metaphor.

World War I marked a turning point in the development of Yiddish culture. Within a year of each other, the three classic masters —Mendele, Sholom Aleichem, Peretz—were laid to rest, and the literature, accustomed to a youthful image, suddenly found itself mature. The war hardened the geographic boundaries between American and European Jews; the Russian Revolution had the further effect of dividing writers into those who chose to live physically and politically within the Bolshevik sphere, and those who remained outside. Before the war there had been a great deal of interaction—including travel—among Yiddish writers in various lands, and it was fashionable for a publication to bear a Warsaw-New York imprint. In the upheaval of World War I the three major centers of Yiddish creativity began to go their separate ways, with the Soviet branch moving eventually into virtual isolation.

This anthology limits itself to short novels of the pre-war years, the period when Yiddish literature tried to carve out its own place within European culture without sacrificing too much of its Jewish specificity. The genre represented here, the short novel, or novella, is itself a kind of halfway house between the short story, in which Yiddish was at home from the beginning, and the novel, to which it only gradually came to aspire. The popularity of the middle genre indicates the relative degree of security felt by Yiddish authors at this point in the evolution of their literature. Jewishness, many writers, critics, and readers thought at the time, could survive the apparent dangers of modernism by adopting rather than abdicating to its ways. Events in the ensuing years were to render a crushing verdict on the social and political aspects of this experiment; but as for its literary fruits, these the reader of today is still capable of enjoying and evaluating on their own.

A SHTETL

I. M. WEISSENBERG

INTRODUCTION TO A SHTETL

In 1904 the young Sholom Asch made his literary reputation with The Shtetl, an idyll of the Jewish small town in Poland. Published when the shtetl was already going to seed, or its inhabitants to America, Asch's novella captures what was, or is imagined as being, its golden age, a time when Jews were rooted in their own traditions and in harmony with both the Polish peasantry and the aristocracy. Asch describes a season in the life of the town's leading citizen and his household. Chapters are arranged by holiday, from Purim in spring to Simchat Torah in the fall; each occurrence in the life of family and town, set into the Jewish calendar, is hallowed by its sanctity and exalted by the imagery of ancient ritual. Critics hailed the work as "the first yea-saying in modern Yiddish literature."

In sharp, angry reaction to the romanticism of Asch, Weissenberg published his literary rejoinder two years later, flaunting a title as close to the original as parody would allow. A Shtetl deliberately limits its focus to the socioeconomic struggle of the Polish Jewish town, in particular to the growing friction within the Jewish community between the emergent proletariat and the wealthier Jews, newly dubbed the bourgeoisie. Weissenberg follows Asch's calendar, but the festivals, shorn of sanctity, are now regarded as occasions for social protest. In place of the communal harmony that Asch locates in the shtetl of memory, Weissenberg offers the mounting violence, even the brutality, of the contemporary town, rent by class dissension, united only by its common impotence in the face of Tsarist or peasant might. *

"It was," as the story begins, "between minkha and maariv," that interval between late afternoon and evening prayers that is here suggestive of the transitional nature of East European Jewish life itself in the first decade of the century. Slowly and clumsily, over the spring and summer of 1905, the year in which the book's action occurs, the artisans and small factory workers of a town in the vicinity of Warsaw discover their collective power and forge a "union."† Sorrowing ballads of unrequited love give way to rhythmic hymns of political allegiance. ‡ The first tentative and ineffectual outbursts against traditional community leadership evolve into organized strikes that actually achieve at least some of their aims. But once its youthful workers are organized, the town becomes the object of the political designs of two large political parties, each seeking to expand its influence in the area: first the "Bund," the Jewish Social Democratic Union, whose socialism included provision for Jewish cultural autonomy; then the Polish Socialist Party, in which similar socioeconomic ideals were combined with an appeal to Polish national aspirations. The process of radicalization as it is chronicled in A Shtetl was repeated in hundreds of similar towns in that year when political and economic strikes together are said to have involved some three million men. § Within the story, however, the larger historical context is blurred, and lines of political demarcation appear as clouded as they are in the consciousness of the characters. For Itchele the bootmaker, there is no appreciable difference between the contending parties, nor can he easily distinguish between a Polish religious procession and a would-be workers' march. The shtetl is both place of action and confining point of view.

*An outstanding interpretation of the novel is available in Yiddish: Uriel Weinreich, "I. M. Vaysenberg's nit-dershatst Shtetl" (I. M. Weissenberg's Unappreciated Shtetl) in Di goldene keyt, XLI, pp. 135–143.

†Weissenberg's compression of a lengthy social process into a single fictional year may be compared with an excellent historical account of very similar events in Ezra Mendelsohn's Class Struggle in the Pale (Cambridge, Mass., 1970).

‡It may be interesting to note that the "hymn" sung by the shoeworkers in this novel is "Di shvue," (The Vow) the Bund's anthem, composed by S. Ansky whose novella, Behind a Mask, appears elsewhere in this volume.

§Leon Trotsky gives the count as 2,863,000. See The Russian Revolution, ed. F. W. Dupee (New York, 1959), p. 32.

The novella's most interesting technical achievement is its creation of a collective hero. Some Yiddish writers, Sholom Aleichem among them, had used the Jewish town as a national and cultural unit, allowing the shtetl to speak in their stories with a single voice, as though it were but a single being. The socialist literary quest for a collective hero (instead of an individual hero who would represent the collective) is well served in this work which stresses those features of solidarity and cohesion that both inhere in the traditional Jewish enclave and are the desired traits of the new society represented by the union-men. The thrust of the prose is to subsume all particulars in a collectivity: nouns are more often collective than plural—the gang, the mob, the congregation, rather than boys or men; things get done not by individuals, but by a group that has absorbed its individuals into a functioning whole. Action is impersonal—hands are raised and lowered, heads are bloodied or hung. Individual men are identified, when they must be at all, by their trade or social role, and their personal effect on the course of events is often tempered if not subverted by the independent force of the crowd.

Almost alone among Yiddish writers, Weissenberg was a worker and the son of workers, and he was determined to bring a genuine working-class voice into the literature. He fought the dominance of Lithuanian, or literary, Yiddish by introducing many localisms and regional linguistic traits into his writing, a characteristic of his prose that is obviously uncommunicable in translation. His style is blunt and sometimes deliberately crude. The graphic descriptions of violence signify an almost conscious effort to shock, to jolt the reader into a new awareness of a milieu whose literature was previously given to gentler stuff—satire of communal abuses, perhaps, but hardly murder. Weissenberg's class consciousness is complemented by a fine awareness of age differentiation as well: everywhere the raw, unreflective energy of the youthful revolution is contrasted with the sly manipulative skill of prosperous, older householders, so that its youthfulness becomes in fact the dominant feature of the new shtetl force—arrogant but easily humbled, strong but untried, fervent but fickle, the hope of the future but perhaps also its scourge.

In the foreground, A Shtetl delivers a forceful study of radicalization and its spiritual and social costs. Only the two processions that weave their way through the town, one a folk mass, the second the Tsarist militia, recast the shtetl subject in a different, larger perspective. In the very last sentence of the novella the shtetl is set back into the East European map, its internal transformation, which had loomed so large, finally viewed against the great political reality. The radical movement has been squashed like a gnat, a "smudge," albeit still a collective one, on the landscape.

A SHTETL BY I. M. WEISSENBERG

IT WAS between *minkha* and *maariv.** The men were in the study house. Candles were burning in front of the pulpit and in the overhead chandeliers, their flames bobbing and flickering in the dense cigarette smoke as if in a fog. The men huddled in conversation; one, the speaker, stood in the center while the others, with brows furrowed and heads bent forward, strained to hear what he was saying.

The air was filled with anticipation of the approaching holiday. It would arrive with the spring thaw, when the ice cracked and the river overflowed the fields and meadows, dragging logs and fence-posts along with it to some unknown destination. Everyone was busy preparing. The shopkeepers wouldn't even have noticed if their caps were on back to front: there was still so much to be done, orders to be filled, raisins to be unpacked and weighed. . . . The artisans, especially the tailors, were red-eyed, their faces drawn. Standing motionless now in the study house they looked like hens in

---

*Between *minkha* and *maariv:* between late afternoon and evening prayers; since the interval was short, the men usually remained in the synagogue for both sets of prayers.

the evening, with sleep settling over the tips of their noses. Of the shoemakers, those who worked in the shops turning out ready-made boots for the city trade were no more harried now than at any other time of the year. They stood around in small clusters, gossiping about the wholesalers—Yekl Brisker and Nahum Homeler—who would descend on the shtetl right after Passover and buy up every boot in sight. The butchers, beefy red-faced Jews wearing fur caps pulled low over both ears and greasy gabardines with green sashes, had their own study-table facing the teamsters. They sat leaning back against the wall, their eyes flashing under their caps. This being the final week before the holiday, there wasn't much demand for their skill; the housewives were so busy they didn't know which world they were in—meat was the last thing on their minds. The teachers, for their part, put their time in the synagogue to good use: some looked up a passage in the tractate dealing with Passover observances; others were satisfied to wander along the bookshelves studying by candlelight the titles on the frayed spines. At the far end of the room, in a dim corner behind the stove, stood a knot of young men. Caps pushed to the back of their heads, oblivious to everything around them, they looked up with glowing admiration at Yekl the carpenter, a tall fellow who was calmly holding forth with the aid of a gesticulating hand.

The hubbub in the study house increased. The babble of voices filled the corners and rose to the ceiling. Candles dripped from the chandeliers onto the heads below, but the men were too engrossed to notice. Suddenly there was a bang on the table and everything came to a halt. All eyes turned toward the sexton who was about to make an announcement from the lectern. The young men, Yekl the carpenter in the lead, hurried forward from behind the stove and surrounded the sexton as he began to speak:

"Gentlemen," he swayed back and forth with his eyes on the ceiling as though his text were inscribed on the rafters, "Gentlemen! On behalf of the rabbi and community leadership, I want to inform you that no rabbinic approval will be granted to any Passover flour brought in from other towns or cities. It is considered *khomets.* *
Passover flour is available this year at Reb Avrom's at three and a

---

Khomets: The term is used to denote all food which is not permitted during the week of Passover; in this case, the community leadership is affirming its exclusive control over Passover flour by forbidding its importation from competitive Jewish centers.

half zlotys a pound, and free Passover supplies for the poor and needy will be handed out at Reb Elye's."

Having had his say, he lowered his head until the tip of his beard rested on his greasy lapels, and started down the platform steps.

The assembly came to life again. Faces flushed in surprise. The men tugged or chewed at the tips of their beards and waved their arms excitedly. The synagogue seethed like a cauldron. Then suddenly there was a second bang on the table and another voice was heard, a voice so low that it seemed to emerge from underground:

"Gentlemen!"

The congregation gaped. Yekl the carpenter, looking pale and frightened and blinking his eyes, was on the platform with his gang around him.

"Gentlemen, it isn't right. We don't agree to it. The money of poor workers. . . . Flour may be brought in from anywhere . . . there's no monopoly!"

For a moment the congregation simply stared, open-mouthed. From the wealthy section, along the east wall, a cracked voice cut the silence:

"Get down, you impudent scum!"

"Get down, get down!"—there was shouting from all sides and the butchers made straight for the platform. The place suddenly became a jumble of blazing faces, a riot of entangled arms and heads. The shouts blended into a roar. Yekl was sent flying from the platform; he fled the study house bareheaded, his nose running blood.

He was laid up until the day before Passover. That morning, the windows were thrown open, birds could be heard chirping wistfully out of doors, and the sun brightened his room with a soft refreshing light. Yekl left his sickbed and went outside.

The same soft sunlight shone over the marketplace. Shop windows sparkled invitingly. Here and there the ground was already dry and sandy, but in the ditches in front of the stoops thin rivulets of water still trickled and then joined together to run down the street. Where the waters joined they made low murmuring sounds like children being lulled to sleep. They seemed to be inviting the youngsters in split trousers to come and dig their red little hands into the mud.

Doors and windows had been flung open. From attic windows

clean white sheets and women's holiday attire had been hung out to be ruffled and stroked by the wind. Freshly whitewashed chimney stoves could be seen through the open windows as if peeping furtively at the marketplace and then ducking back into a corner, like eager brides when the groom has pulled up within sight of their windows. In the open doorways women, already half-dressed in their holiday finery, stood scouring yet another bowl or chopping block. Their tired smiles said, "Thank God, we've come this far already."

Monish the glazier brought home some new tiles to cover his red work bench. Khaim Yoyne the teacher, who seemed to have straightened up for the first time since winter, carried home, as was his annual custom, freshly washed wine glasses wrapped in a new red cloth. *Cheder* boys, some wearing their new gabardines, greeted one another with a grin and slapped their trouser pockets bulging with nuts. Even the barmaid had braided her hair with a blue ribbon and was on her way home with a pestle to prepare the matza-meal. The old janitor who looked after the shops around the marketplace, shuffled about with his long broom sweeping up bits of straw and shucks that had been dumped outside during the morning cleanup and burning of the *khomets*. * He paused to fill his pipe, and leaning on the broomstick, blew puffs of smoke over his head and watched them rise into the air. He was somehow pitiable. For him, in his heavy overcoat and fur cap, there was to be no spring: his winter endured forever. . . .

Everywhere the warm weather beckoned. A fresh breeze carried the sound of birds twittering and hopping along the rooftops, raising their heads cheerfully to the distant skies. Down below, the waters trickled, then gushed into the river, swelling the waves that heaved and strained from bank to bank. One after another the waves rose and fell, sparkling in the sun that beamed down lovingly like a mother doting on her playful children. Downstream, under the bridge, spray flew as the waves crashed against the pilings sending thousands of gleaming white drops exploding into the air. Everywhere the water surged and foamed. For miles around the countryside was flooded. The tops of submerged

*The laws and customs governing Passover food demand that every crumb of *khomets* be removed. A symbolic "burning" of the final bits of *khomets* is customary on the morning of Passover Eve.

fenceposts, like heads of drowning sheep, looked out over the water to plead dumbly for mercy.

Meanwhile the sound of wheels was heard along the road, and soon a carriage from Warsaw came to a halt on the bridge. At the sudden stop the horses threw back their heads, showing white teeth through foaming lips. Jolly young voices rang out from the carriage, and glowing faces beamed under dashing caps. Then one after another the passengers jumped down—visitors from Warsaw! Their collars were fiercely starched, and their eyes sparkled mischievously, almost wantonly, under the peaks of their caps. No matter, their homecoming would be welcome all the same.

Snatching up the parcels and baskets they had brought with them, they started for home at a run, looking ahead eagerly toward the little houses where more than one mother dropped the board or bowl she had been scrubbing and ran inside with the glad tidings.

And so the holiday arrived.

The first day of Passover. It was still early. The sun had just appeared in the blue sky, and its fresh rosy face looked down at the quiet streets below. The windows dozed in blissful stillness. Their white curtains, like decorous little aprons drawn to protect the sweet peacefulness inside, winked at the street in conspiratorial silence.

But it wasn't long before Fayvl "the Big-Shot" appeared in his doorway in a white linen shirt, with his hands in his pants pockets —new pants to go with the new boots and new hat. The moment he threw back his head and uttered a loud yawn, the street was sure to awake from slumber. Before long a group of neighbors had gathered around him—a circle of respectable householders. Fayvl entertained them with his stories, inviting his listeners every so often to confirm their accuracy. If anyone challenged him, he simply threw back his head and gave a mocking laugh. No matter where he started out, he always came around eventually to travelers' tales —stories about holdups in the Milosz forest, at a crossroads, or in an ancient village—stories to make your hair stand on end. When he began to speak of the merchants of Praga,* his bearing became respectful. His stomach swayed, his neck seemed to stretch, and

*A suburb of Warsaw, famous for its fairs.

even his voice grew deeper. He could go on for an hour or even two. Some of his listeners might leave and others take their place, but Fayvl went on with his performance. Finally his wife, in a white ribboned cap, appeared in the window and rapped at the pane: "Enough! Enough! The tea is getting cold." If this failed, his eldest daughter, a girl with cheeks like red beads and a bunch of keys at the belt of her new pleated apron, stood astride the doorstep, arms folded across her chest. She looked capable of laying a man out at a single blow. But she merely waited, grinning slightly, until her father paused to catch his breath, and then she grabbed him: "Well, father, don't you think that's quite enough?"

The householders went their separate ways.

Little by little, the street began to fill with younger men in loose jackets and broad white collars, trouser cuffs worn over their boots and earlocks neatly trimmed. They greeted one another with a smile and a nod and stopped to chat. Before long there was quite a circle of them, made livelier still by the arrival of Itchele the bootmaker, a clean-shaven young man in a tan jacket and patent leather shoes, with twinkling eyes under the narrow peak of his cap. They began to spar playfully, wrestling and comparing their flexed muscles. Just then the young wives walked by on their way to the synagogue, all decked out and carrying ivory-bound prayerbooks carefully wrapped in white kerchiefs. The fellows ogled and shouted, the women blushed and lowered their eyes, scurrying past as if through fire. As the horseplay reached its height, Yekl the carpenter sauntered up, dressed, like the others, in his best jacket, his face still pale but head erect, and his black eyes fixed on the crowd like someone always ready for new developments.

"Happy holiday, friends!" He exchanged greetings, and joined the crowd. "Well, what's happening in Warsaw?"

"Things aren't bad. There's a lot of action. It's beginning to move," answered some of the recent arrivals with a grin.

"Are there demonstrations?"

"And how! The cafes are full. People are talking up a storm."

"And strikes?"

"Sure. Lots of strikes. Everything you could ask for."

Probing steadily, Yekl was able to find out everything about his beloved Warsaw. He was especially eager to know whether many government spies had been knocked off recently: were it not for them, he wouldn't have to stay in this shtetl to be, as he put it, "persecuted by the fanatics."

But in his usual manner, Itchele the bootmaker broke up the serious talk. "Come on, gang," he called, "Let's drop in to Motl's for a glass of holiday cheer."

So the crowd obligingly pushed its way into Motl's place, past the tin sign on which a teapot, a slice of lemon in a glass, and a teaspoon had all been painted in the same shade of yellow. Before long the street resounded with song:

> O, Brothers and sisters of toil and privation
> All ye who are scattered in every nation. . . .*

The song, which the boys had just brought back from Warsaw, was one that Yekl had never been privileged to hear before. The new songs, he decided with a happy smile, were even better than the old ones: slowly, but surely, the "movement" was growing.

The householders on their way home from the synagogue, with their prayer shawls under their arms, stopped in alarm at the sound of the singing: had the militia been moved into town? Yekl stood watching them through the glass door of Motl's place, with hope in his eyes and a triumphant smile on his lips: "Just you wait, you old fools, you'll find out all about it soon enough." But one thing bothered him: there was no one to educate the workers, to explain their condition to them. If he could only make the right speech, that would do the trick.

The problem gave him no rest. He thought about nothing else through the holiday, and was finally able to put some words together. On the last day of Passover, he let it be known among the "masses" that he, Yekl, would address them that night at the foot of Potter's Hill. At the appointed time, a crowd gathered at the bottom of the hill. Yekl stood at the top, a slight flush spreading over his pale face, and his eyes shining as if lit from inside by two memorial candles. Pulling out a sheet of paper covered with his large handwriting, he looked down at the crowd and began to read his carefully inscribed words. They ended with a bit of a rhyme:

"Down with capitalism!

Long live socialism!"

The crowd caught up the cry and burst into shouts of "hurrah!" Yekl came down the hill and joined the procession back to town, which was accomplished with faces aflame and mouths bursting with song. Young girls, prettily dressed, their hair freshly brushed,

---

*The opening lines of di shvue, the hymn of the Jewish Workers' Bund.

were at that moment heading toward the outskirts of town, carrying glass pitchers in their hands. In keeping with local tradition they were fetching some fresh spring water to mark the end of the holiday. When they caught sight of the approaching crowd, they climbed up on Yosl the soapmaker's porch, and stared in wonder. The men dropped their heads and stopped singing.

This was more than Itchele, who was holding up the rear, could tolerate: what kind of idiots were they, anyway? Hadn't they ever seen women before? They had no ready answer for this, and Itchele, without waiting for any, leered at the girls on the porch. He threw out his chest, raised his head pompously, and strutted ahead. All he needed to complete the picture was a set of spurs.

But the holiday drew to a close, and the gay blades returned to Warsaw. The shoe wholesalers arrived, and the local manufacturers set out huge empty sugar barrels to be packed with finished boots. All had been forgotten. The young men were back in the workshops, twelve to fifteen in a room, sleeves rolled up over their elbows, faces red and dripping with sweat. Their hammers tapped steadily against the soles as they took up the old familiar strains:

> Once I loved a pretty girl
> Vienna was her home
> Vienna was her home
> She went back to her mother and dad
> To see what they were doing
> To see what they were doing.

First they mourned the girl who had gone home, then they lamented the golden bird, "famed for its beauty but more for the heights it flew to," the bird that "brought a letter from Vienna, from the girl he had been true to," and more and more of the same until God himself should have been moved to mercy.

But it happened one day that a young stranger came down to spend a Sabbath in the shtetl, the sort of fellow about whom it was impossible to know anything because he did not stop over at Hershl Menashe's inn where all the shoe wholesalers stayed. An odd creature this was—frail and pallid, wearing a blue shirt belted with red sash, a collar pin at the throat, a soft black hat on his head and long black curls hanging loosely over his shoulders; he flitted down the street as lightly as a bird. It was the Sabbath, and a sunny day besides, and the street was full of young people milling around in a state of excitement. Young matrons and girls in their Sabbath dresses and aprons sat on their stoops after the mid-day meal; they knew this person was someone special. The young men swarming through the street followed him closely with their eyes, from time to time exchanging knowing glances among themselves. Yekl the carpenter stuck conspicuously close to the stranger, flying back and forth to drop a few whispered words here and there among the crowd, until gradually everyone had disappeared leaving the street completely empty.

By the following morning, the entire shtetl knew that the young man had been no itinerant magician, but one of those revolutionaries from Warsaw. In the workshops the youths were more subdued, daydreaming over the unfinished boots they held on their laps. They couldn't tear their minds away from the pale face with the soulful eyes. Each of the dozen or so apprentices and journeymen sat with his head bowed, staring fixedly down at his own work, without looking at his companions. Sometimes a hand would stop in midair, letting the hammer fall and lie on the sole like a fish with an upturned belly. Its owner, holding on to the edge of his bench, would stare straight ahead with the rapt expression of a child holding a bagel in his hand.

"Why are you sitting there like a dummy?" an older worker interrupted.

The youth sat up with a start, gave a foolish smile, and let fall a few words by way of explanation. "Ay, how can you explain to someone who hasn't seen . . . ?" But what it was that he had seen, or when, he would rather have let them chop off a limb than reveal, at least not before he had looked around to make sure that the boss was out of the room.

Sometimes the mood was very different; eyes would suddenly flash and foreheads crease as if from the force of rushing waves. The men would speed the nails into the torn soles—tac-tac! tac-tac!—as though in hot pursuit. At such times someone always burst into song:

> What good is this life to you, brothers,
> A life full of hunger and pain? . . .

The whole shop would join in the chorus, shooting tacks into soles like bullets into a deadly enemy, and the song, loud and mighty, would pour through the open windows into the street.

If Yekl the carpenter happened to be passing just then, a smile would steal into the corners of his eyes and his face would radiate joy as he looked toward the open windows.

In the evening, work was laid aside and the youths strolled quietly through the street, walking along in pairs or dropping in to Motl's teashop for some talk—and singing too, if the occasion allowed. On Saturdays there wasn't a young worker to be found anywhere in town. The streets were empty, the shutters closed, and the only sound was that of snoring. The young men were with Yekl behind the new cemetery grounds. There they stayed until the sun began to set, its red flames mirrored in the river water. Only then, as the better-off young men of the shtetl, with their delicate faces and their hands thrust into the belts of their caftans, were taking their last proper Sabbath stroll down the main street, did the gang return to town, their arrival heralded by the strains of song.

It happened that on one of these Saturdays, the Police Chief, in full regalia, replete with tin epaulets and badge on his cap, hid behind a corner of the slaughterhouse to watch the proceedings. As the group reentered the town it passed the white-shuttered house of Isaac Feyge-Libes, the largest local shoe manufacturer, who stood in front with his son-in-law, Hershele, both with their jackets unbuttoned and watch-chains looped over their green velvet vests. They watched the crowd in tight-lipped silence. But the men lowered their heads as they passed, and Isaac and his son-in-law exchanged a sly and knowing smile. When the Police Chief emerged from his hiding place behind the slaughterhouse, they invited him in for some *khala* and a piece of Jewish fish.

The son-in-law drew up a chair for the Chief, while Isaac busied himself brushing off and straightening the tablecloth. His wife, Chavele, wearing the solid gold necklace that a Lublin goldsmith had made to order for her, took a decanter of brandy from the breakfront and urged her daughter, a young woman sitting on the couch, to serve it to their guest. "Sometimes it's important to please the Gentiles," she said with the smile of an affectionate mother who knows and fulfills her duty.

Yekl the carpenter believed that it was *his* duty to continue these clandestine gatherings, just as it was the Police Chief's duty to spy on the crowd from behind the slaughterhouse. Before very long, the Chief's notebook held the names of all the union-men, with Yekl's at the very top of the first page. But no one cared. The crowd at the teashop grew steadily, and by evening the back room was invariably packed. Every worker or artisan in the shtetl eventually found his way to Motl's and after an hour or two joined the gang. Yekl was in charge, even to the point of keeping the normally high spirits in check: no jumping on the tables and benches. He maintained a steady correspondence with Warsaw, and his regular public reading of the letters he received in reply helped to swell attendance. Each night, the house became more crowded and animated.

One evening Yekl began to distribute a stack of workers' proclamations, just as was done in the cities. But the men, as Itchele the bootmaker put it, were a little backward in their letters, and Yekl himself had to admit that they were "Talmud Torah cripples." So he was obliged to read the document aloud. Everyone crowded around, climbing on top of one another, over benches and tables.

Yekl held the proclamation up to the light:

"*Genossen* and *Genossinen!*" he began, in the Germanic style of these proclamations.

"Translate!" cried Itchele.

"Brothers and sisters," Yekl continued.

"What sisters?"

"In the cities," he explained, "the girls also take part."

"You mean they actually have a hand in it?"

"Yes, of course."

"Everywhere but here," smiled Itchele. "What a town this is!"

"Let's get him a couple of girls," came an offer, and everyone laughed. Itchele pounded his friend on the back, and the merriment spread. Soon they were jumping over benches. Caps flew through the air, voices resounded off the ceiling. Someone accidentally stepped on a child's foot, and the baby set up a howl. Taybele, Motl's wife, rushed out in alarm, snatched up her son and tried to soothe him. Meanwhile the crowd began to settle down; the boys sprawled across the furniture, heads propped up against the wall and stomachs up, like a school of carp. Once again Itchele shattered the calm by crawling over the bodies on his knees; the ensuing fight was enough to send everyone scurrying for cover. Yekl scolded, and tried to restore order: there was a proclamation to be read! But no one was listening. They were enjoying the fun. Besides, they knew all about "Union" without being told. As Itchele said, "Union meant agreeing to what everyone agreed to." At last Yekl gave up.

"Go home, fellas, and get some sleep. Tomorrow is just a regular workday."

Before long the shtetl was thrown into even greater turmoil by the arrival of a second character very much like the first, but with the added distinction of a thick walking stick that he carried at all times. His stay was brief, and right after his departure some of the youths began to let their hair grow and to sport the blue shirts that were the trademark of the Jewish Labor Bund. Suddenly, before anyone knew what was happening, a strike had broken out at Isaac Feyge-Libes. Only a single obstinate shoeworker remained in the shop, refusing to budge. One of the apprentices hid outside the window with a green bottle of kerosene, then leaned in and broke it over the worker's head. After that, Isaac's place was deserted. The youths hung around the marketplace all day, hands in their pockets. Their fathers tried to shoo them back to work, and their tearful mothers followed them around like shadows, pleading with them at least to go to the synagogue.

"What do you want of the few years I have left?" a mother would beg, following close at the heels of her son. "Don't take after Yekl the carpenter! Don't forsake our living God!"

But neither their parents nor the Police Chief, whose name Isaac Feyge-Libes invoked as a threat, had any effect, and concessions had to be made. The youths were promised the shorter working day they had demanded. But as soon as the shoemakers returned to their jobs, other workers went out on strike; they swarmed through the marketplace as the others had done, with their hands in their pockets, or huddled in clusters, whispering ceaselessly. Not for a moment that summer was the marketplace empty. One strike followed another; not a workshop or factory was spared.

Saturday mornings, when the weather was fair, youths in their best jackets and boots carried on in the street while the synagogue stood silent as a tomb. The sexton complained that there was barely a minyan,* and when Yoyne the scribe, returning home from the Hasidic prayer-house with his followers, caught sight of the young men in the street, he was overcome by a terrible sadness: "Lord of the Universe, I, for my part, forgive them . . . ," he sighed. After

---

*Minyan: the ten-man minimum required for Jewish communal prayer.

the Sabbath midday meal the street began to buzz again. The teashop filled to bursting. Even the tanners, older men with beards, were asking to be delivered from the capitalists' hands. They all sat around the table, with the proprietor, Motl, in his skullcap and shirtsleeves, at the head, bouncing his baby on his lap while his wife Taybele served. The rest of the crowd wisecracked until they had to hold their sides from laughing.

A young boy of about sixteen stood with his father, a man with twinkling eyes and a trimmed reddish beard that looked as though it too would laugh at the slightest tug. The son had buttonholed his dad and was trying to convince him of something. He jabbed a finger in the air, arguing heatedly, trying to give the poor man some idea of the problem. But just then someone grabbed his father by the shoulder:

"I see you're in pretty bad shape, Yo'el my friend! Your son has to teach you what's what."

"He's all right, my boy. He knows what he's talking about," winked the proud father, the brim of his cap seeming to wink along with him.

"Well then listen to me," insisted the boy, pulling his father by the beard, but the other man broke in: "What about us, Yo'el, when we were his age?"

"Ha!" exclaimed the father, throwing up his hands, "at his age I was already married. The wife was expecting . . . this one here as a matter of fact," and he winked in the direction of his son.

Yeshaya, a shy young man in a wide brimmed satin hat, who was still being supported by his in-laws, sat staring at the table like an ox into a trough. Some of the boys began taunting him.

"You've been elected to remove the candlesticks from the table," someone informed him, knowing full well that it was a job reserved for a Gentile, and that no traditional Jew would desecrate the Sabbath by such a deed.* "If you refuse, you'll have to stand us all to a beer."

Yeshaya found the choice difficult, and not knowing what to answer he alternately tugged at his sparse yellow beard and scratched his curled sidelocks.

"I'm ashamed to answer," he finally stammered, and the room rocked with laughter.

*According to custom the candlesticks in which the Sabbath candles are lit must remain unmoved until the conclusion of the Sabbath.

Nevertheless, a barrel was rolled in and tapped, and everyone had a beer. By the time Itchele arrived, the place had grown very lively. More beers were downed, and faces began to flush. Suddenly, someone pounded on the table:

"Friends! Let's take an oath! Let's swear to teach the bosses, those dogs, a lesson they'll never forget!"

"Friends!" another took up the cry, "May the plague take them all, one at a time!"

"Listen," shouted a third, "my boss is a gangster the likes of whom you've never seen."

"You've only had to deal with factory owners," said Itchele, jumping into the fray, waving a mug of beer in his hand, "isn't that so? But I've had different luck from the rest of you. For the whole two months that I spent working at Shmuel-Toybes I was a full partner . . . to his wife!"

"Oh, come off it," a voice protested, preferring the earlier subject, "the leather manufacturers are in a class by themselves. Take my boss for instance. One night this winter I wanted to take home a stick that was lying in a corner by the stove. I needed something to chase off the dogs. But the boss comes over to me and says, 'No, you don't!' and takes the stick from me. He says his wife needs it as a poker for the fire. I thought I'd drop on the spot!"

"Let me tell you about *my* beauty," cried an older black-bearded Jew bringing his fist down on the table with a loud bang, "What a sneak! He looks so gentle standing in the doorway at dawn every morning, waiting to greet his workers. If I happen to arrive first, he returns my 'good morning.' But if I don't, he turns his back on me. Now I'm only human, and when I look over and see that the other guy has already finished a pile of work, I feel rotten. So I make up an excuse about so-and-so who was having such a fight with his wife that the whole town came running, and I went along too. You can imagine all the good it does! The next day I feel that I've got to make up for it by coming in a half hour earlier than anyone else, and naturally I get the big hello. He treats me like an old buddy. He tells me all about his business headaches, and how I'm his best worker. The other guy isn't worth a damn; he can't wait to get rid of him at the end of the season. . . . Yet when the other guy comes along, he gives him all the lighter pieces that go faster so that he can catch up with me while I'm trying frantically to stay ahead. The man's a slavedriver!"

"We have to teach them a lesson!" several voices cried in unison, "Let's strike! Strike!"

And this was like a signed declaration.

The next morning when a message came from Reb Oyzer, owner of one of the largest tanneries, Yekl went over to pay him a visit.

Reb Oyzer, a tall Jew with a long face and a two-pronged beard, was just finishing his morning prayers when Yekl entered. His prayer shawl was drawn so far over his forehead that the heavy ornamental band fell halfway down over his pointed nose, and. following the custom of the most pious Jews he also had on two pairs of phylacteries.* When he noticed Yekl at the door, he motioned him to a chair:

"Well, what good news do you have for me?" Reb Oyzer began, drawing his hand down his face from the forehead to the tip of his beard.

"What can I tell you?" replied Yekl with a shrug.

"They tell me you're the leader. And they say you're no fool. Do you really think this is the right way to do things? I'd like to know, maybe I've done something to deserve this."

"It makes no difference whether you deserve it or not. This is the way it's done in Warsaw and everywhere else in the world. When there's a strike, there's a strike."

"All right, so a strike is a strike. But why did you have to take the *goyim* out of my factory as well?"

"What do you think a strike is?"

"No, that's not what I mean . . . I mean why do you have to use force? Did you know that they threatened my *goyim* with iron bars! So help me, they even brought Mikhl's workers into my yard, to scare mine! In a Jewish establishment you don't do things like that."

"Whose fault is it if the *goyim* refused to go out on their own?"

"Exactly what I've been trying to say! Only the Jews are to blame . . . no one else. Jews are good company for going to the synagogue. . . ."

"And for going into battle, too."

---

*Since there was a controversy between Rashi, Rabbi Shlomo Yitzkhaki (1040–1105) and Rabbeynu Tam, Rabbi Yakov Tam (1100–1171) on the subject of phylacteries, very pious Jews prayed with two pairs, following both sets of injuctions.

"What battle? Oh yes, when I read *Hatsefirah** I see that expression in italics. But I still don't know what you're after . . . excuse me but what did you say your name was? It's slipped my mind. . . ." Reb Oyzer knit his brow and repeated the downward motion of his hand over his face.

"Yekl."

"What are they after, Yekl?"

"They want a shorter working day, from seven to seven with a two-hour break in the middle."

"Very nice, very nice," drawled Reb Oyzer, "but I don't know if you are familiar with my business. We don't use high-quality Russian cowhide, only the cheaper stuff, green sole leather. So what happens if I need two or three men to stay after hours at night to smooth it down with the roller? What do I do then?"

"You hire other men for night work."

"I see." Reb Oyzer seemed to hesitate for a moment, and then started on a different tack. "There's only one thing that troubles me, about the workers I mean. As you say, this sort of thing is happening all over the world. There must be people, real human beings, behind it. I'd just like to know whether they ever considered the other man's position . . . suppose that their demands are impossible, for instance, like this one! Why I'd be forced to shut down the whole factory if I did what you're asking."

"Go ahead and shut it down then," nodded Yekl.

"I seem to have missed something," continued Reb Oyzer. "Am I such a tyrant, God forbid, that the workers want to put in only the exact time required, to the minute? They're not doctors, they don't need to consult their watches all day. After all, their time isn't all that precious. . . . You want to know how I treat my workers? I'm not like the rest, you know. I'm a man who studies a *shiyur** every morning and then I have to pray, so I'm certainly not busy keeping watch over them. Who knows whether they're fooling around at work? And I mean really, who cares anyhow? So is it fair of them to count the minutes and seconds?"

"There's no other way it can be done."

"Believe me, I could split a gut eighteen times a day when I see

---

**Hatsefirah: The Dawn;* a moderate Hebrew daily newspaper, edited by Nahum Sokolow, in Warsaw.

* *Shiyur:* a lesson. Usually a portion of the Talmud, which is studied daily.

them pretending to take a leak behind the fence . . . that's their excuse, you understand. Or the way Velvel carries the empty water can at a snail's pace to the well and back . . . I'm ready to jump out the window and fill it for him! Here, take it and go: just so as not to have to see him inching along. And have you ever seen the men stop all of a sudden and start rolling their cigarettes? It's enough to turn you green. But I just pull out my cigarette case and pass it around—you want to know why? Because to me a worker is a man too, I like to treat him as an equal. But when they begin to act like this, then that's it! They won't get anywhere with me!"

"Then I may as well go," said Yekl rising from his chair. Buttoning up his coat, he said goodbye and left.

On a seasonable Saturday morning, Itchele decided that the time had finally come to get even with the butchers for their bloody triumph before the holiday. He got together a bunch of young toughs and stormed the tiny synagogue where the butchers held their services. The congregation was right in the middle of "God is the Lord of all Creation." When they saw what was in the doorway they began to feel a little uncomfortable, and pulled their prayer shawls further up on their heads, repeating the chanted phrases of their leader with feigned, but deliberate, fervor. The gang stood by the door, waiting vainly for some provocation, until finally Itchele marched up to Zelig Shinder, the most powerful of the butchers, and punched him right in the face. For a moment the congregation stood paralyzed. Then in a flash, arms reached to the chandeliers, ripped apart the curved sections and brass bars and the whole roof seemed about to crash in. Boys leaped on the benches and tables. There was a wild tangle of arms and heads; the only sounds were the rustle of prayer shawls and the grappling of arms. Everyone was tearing at someone else's hair, trying frenziedly to sink his fingers into the other's throat. Then there was a sudden thud. Itchele, with the fury of an enraged beast, tore a leg from the table and brought it down on the head nearest him. Someone had pinned Zelig Shinder against the table, and lay on top of him forcing his neck back until his head fell over the edge. A body in a prayer shawl was being kicked around the floor. The mass of heads locked together by teeth and clutching fingers was like a single clumsy massive beast with a thousand moving limbs, heaving and stumbling from one side of the room to the other. Those who fell were dragged along until they clawed their way back into the human mass by clutching at someone in the tangle. Gradually the pummeling grew more rhythmic as one side slowly gained the upper hand. A few sighs began to escape from the dark corners. Fists were methodically raised and lowered, and those who had been tearing at a headful of hair now merely held on, as to a pawn. The bated breath of the combatants was finally released, and the very air seemed to quiver, as around a spinning top that is about to topple. As if at a given signal, everyone lowered his hands and looked dazedly at the person nearest him. The sight of blood brought them back to their senses. In a moment Itchele was at the door, with his gang all around him and the table leg still in his hand. He stood there hatless, hair rumpled, smiling at the congregants in their tattered prayer shawls. Then someone handed him his cap. He put it on, dropped the stick, and left followed by his boys, their faces scratched, caps and hair a mess, and hands bloodied.

In the street outside they met Yekl the carpenter and surrounded him, their bruised faces suffused with joy. He too smiled wanly at the sight of the young warriors and nodded his head approvingly: there were times when a bit of terror-tactics could do no harm.

That same evening the butchers joined up with the teamsters in the synagogue courtyard and swore they would break the bones of every union man they found. The shtetl was in a panic; how would it all end? But the very next time the teamsters made their regularly scheduled run to Warsaw—no one knew how it happened or who was responsible—they came back with empty wagons and faces so badly bruised they were hardly recognizable. They told of being set upon at the inn, and driven away with their wagons empty. The whole town hung its head. And then Mendl-Leyzer who ran the dry goods store was stabbed below the arm . . . it was doubtful he would live through the night.

Women began to curse softly under their breaths, and the men grew ill-tempered. But the young men grinned and looked everyone straight in the eye.

There were meetings almost every night, behind either the Jewish or the Christian cemetery, and Zelig Shinder with a bunch of butchers and teamsters, real slobs, began showing up at these gatherings. The way they lowered their heads and gnawed sheepishly at the tips of their blond beards showed their readiness to go along with the "union-group."

And so the shtetl became known throughout the surrounding region for its powerful organization, and communications were also established with the larger towns of Sedletz and Radom. Not a week went by without visits from two or maybe three revolutionaries, members of the Jewish Labor Bund.

But as soon as the Polish Socialist Party learned of the spreading influence of its chief rival, the Bund, they sent down a permanent organizer to do something about the situation. The shtetl was now blessed with its own resident PPS man, a sickly-looking lad who seemed to belong in a bathrobe. A new round of meetings began, this time on the lawn behind the church. For a time Itchele danced at both weddings; but when the Bund people in Sedletz got wind of the danger, they sent down two of their men for a public debate.

News of the debate sent the young men scurrying about like headless chickens. Everyone looked expectantly to Yekl the carpenter and waited impatiently for nightfall.

When it came, the night was actually clear and lovely. The moon shone on the crowd that had gathered in the meadow beside the river. Even Reuben the wheelwright, a man in his forties with a round black beard, whose only concern was the livers and kidneys he picked up each day at the butcher's and took home to broil—even he was out in his shirtsleeves and skullcap to watch the proceedings. And what a sight it was! In the middle of the meadow stood a huddle of men like a black mound or a shadow cast by the moon. The mound was silent, straining toward the center where the debaters were holding forth. First one, then the other of the Sedletzer Bundists faced off against the Warsaw PPS man, and the crowd stood on tiptoe, necks craned, wedged together in a thick silent mass that blackened the field around. The debate went on and on, argument against argument, ever more spirited and biting. Words flew back and forth whistling like fiery bullets.

There'll be no end to this, decided one of the Sedletzers, and suddenly called aloud: "Brothers, friends! Are you with the Bund?"

"Yes! Yes!" cried the crowd.

"Friends, brothers," countered his rival, "Are you with the PPS?"

"Yes! Yes!" came the answer, even louder than before.

For a moment things appeared to be at an impasse. Then Yekl the carpenter ranged himself alongside the two Sedletzers and cried: "I'm with the Bund!" The whole crowd had already begun to move in his direction when the PPS man called on the people to join him instead. The crowd split in two. Itchele found himself alone in the middle and began to run back and forth protesting: what was the difference? When one side burst into song, the other side sang even louder, until local farmhands and barefoot peasant girls in white kerchiefs came running out to see the amazing sight. The Sedletzers soon realized that the others could sing as long as they could, and nothing more was to be done. One of them drew his pistol and pulled the trigger! There was a flash and a puff of smoke, the peasant girls clutched their heads and wailed: *"Olia Boga—O my God!"*

That was the first Jewish shot ever fired in our shtetl.

From then on shutters were closed at the very first sign of nightfall.

The Police Chief strapped on a holster alongside his customary sword. The ready-to-wear tailors, who had previously resisted the union organizers, now gave in and organized a strike of their own . . . much to their regret. They had to stop taking work home, and instead had to carry their machines on their backs to the boss's shop. They were loath to part with these machines, especially those who had marriageable daughters at home; soon they would be receiving prospective bridegrooms and their fathers, and their houses would look emptier of possessions than ever.

And so it went. If a mother had trouble putting her child to bed, she would threaten to call the strikers. When two market-women got to quarreling, one would throw a scare into the other by saying, "Just you wait! All I have to do is tell my Khaiml, and your stand will be dumped upside down!" A young man who for the past year had been courting a girl from a Hasidic home, in summer behind the cemetery, in winter on the pharmacist's porch, and with countless love letters to his "virtuous" Feygele Greenblatt, now accosted her father with a brazen demand for the daughter's hand. When a certain Pinchele, who considered himself a "unionist," found himself temporarily unemployed or just too lazy to get a job, he set himself up in "business" by buying up whatever produce a village Jew brought to the shtetl—fruit, honey; if anyone was reluctant to sell, Pinchele had only to press his finger against his nose and hint darkly that the organization . . . and the deal was concluded. If a Jew tried to laugh off the threat, the bystanders clutched their heads, crying: What are you doing? You're digging your own grave! You won't be able to show your face in this town anymore! Eventually it got so that if anyone bore anyone a grudge, he would come to the teashop with his complaint. There, Yekl the carpenter, whose soft heart could tolerate no injustice, tried to put everything right. He sat at a table in the back room, surrounded by some of his own boys, while several outsiders, not the "local membership," stood against the wall, waiting to air their little problems.

"What do you want?" asked Yekl of a Jew who had been tugging at his beard and trying so hard to catch Yekl's eye that both his cap and skullcap had slipped over one ear.

"Yekl'she," the man approached with his plea, "I need a permit to add a room to the back of my shop. I fixed it with the Police Chief, but now I'm afraid of interference at a higher level. Please see if you can arrange it for me, Yekl'she. . . ."

"All right," nodded Yekl, bestowing a look of such dovelike kindness that the man was certain the favor was as good as done.

"And why did you come?" he asked a young housewife, still almost a child, who was standing in the corner bundled up in her shawl.

"I'm from Stotsk . . ." she lowered her eyes in embarrassment, "my husband is a Hasid. He doesn't really do anything. I work all day as a seamstress and I have to cook for him besides. It's not a marriage at all. I've been trying to get a divorce for a year and a half, but since there's no river with an official name near our town, the local rabbi can't write out the bill of divorce and my husband keeps putting off going to another town . . . he just keeps putting it off. I have no friends, no relatives, no one to turn to. . . ."

To this petitioner Yekl was more attentive. Here was a seamstress, a productive worker, a "useful member of the social organism." He questioned her in detail to determine whether she had read up on any of the new ideas, and whether there might in fact be some chance for reconciliation between her husband and herself. When he had satisfied himself that they were "of two worlds," he nodded in the same kindly fashion as before. Then the boys who had been standing by, staring openmouthed at the young woman's blushing face, stirred with excitement and offered to accompany her home to settle the matter once and for all.

Once even a woman rushed in from the street, her wig in disarray, her face aflame and her eyes flashing, with a piece of raw liver held aloft in each hand. "Take a look," she cried, trembling with rage, "they turned the cat loose on purpose so she would stuff herself with liver from my basket and drag the rest through the dirt."

To this Yekl had no reply. But at least the woman had unburdened herself of her complaints . . . she felt a little better for it.

Yekl gave everyone a sympathetic hearing and listened to all complaints. The shtetl grew to love him. Sometimes he was called Reb Yekl Dayan, as though he were now the official rabbinic authority. He was praised openly for his kindness and wisdom. He even won the approbation of the Police Chief who called him "The Jewish Ruler." The district judge, who came down once a month for a couple of days to hear local grievances, could not contain his surprise: how pleasant the shtetl had become! There were no more complaints, no more petitions, nothing.

Only one person disapproved strongly of the new turn of events —Dovidl Rosenzweig, a busy little man with darting eyes and a non-stop tongue, who had a reputation as a shrewd pilpulist and a bit of a lawyer. When a Jew came to him with a problem, he would first turn up the lamp, then hurry over to the bookcase, take down a volume of tiny print with numerals in the margin, leaf through it till he came to the right page, run his eyes rapidly down the lines, mop his brow, and look up, motioning the visitor to a chair.

"Ahem, have a seat please. You've got quite a complicated problem here, but luckily you've come to me . . . so we'll find a solution. Now we'd better start with a petition referring to paragraph 345 . . . I've just looked it up here, as you can see. With this reference, the whole thing will be straightened out much faster."

"Yes, Dovid'she, yes," crooned the Jew, melting with pleasure. "You've got such a good head. . . ."

Then Dovidl Rosenzweig would ring the porcelain bell on his desk, and in would run his son, a young dandy with ears pricked up like a rabbit's and narrow squinting eyes.

"Did you call, father?"

"Here's the pen and write what I tell you: 'Your honor'" . . . Dovidl Rosenzweig began to dictate the letter to his son, who sat with the pen poised over the paper, then gave it a tentative flourish and started scratching across the page. The father continued to dictate, pacing the room in his calico bathrobe: "'And the said Levi Greenstein caused me, Menashe Khoymer, such and such, and therefore I . . . I have the great honor . . . and refer you to paragraph such and such. . . .'"

When it was done, the client signed, confident that all would be well.

And if the "said Levi Greenstein" came in a little later with the very same request, Dovidl would pull out the code and look up a similar paragraph on his behalf, number 346 this time. . . . The applicant would leave with the same assurance that all would be well.

So it was obvious that Yekl's judicial practice displeased this humbug. Dovidl went around looking very grim, and whenever he caught sight of Yekl in the street he turned visibly green.

But Yekl continued with his work. He spent a few hours of each day in the teashop, straightening out all the "legal problems" of the town and surrounding district. It was all done in the name of the organization: the organization, in other words, had rendered its verdict, and everyone knew what that signified.

One day Pinchele came into the teashop, the same blackguard who extorted produce from Jewish villagers and sold it in town at inflated prices. He told Yekl a phony story about his grandfather who, he said, was owed a thousand rubles by a certain Lazar, one of the local shopkeepers. Yekl listened patiently, as he would to any ordinary tale; but as for Pinchele, no sooner had he finished than he made tracks for Lazar's grocery store.

"Listen, Reb Lazar," he threatened the elderly grocer, "the organization says you'd better pay up those thousand rubles you owe my grandfather." "My dear fellow," pleaded the grocer, "you don't know the whole story. It all goes back over fifteen years. . . . Your grandfather was a supplier to the army. He brought me a crate of plums that was rotten through and through. I didn't want the stuff at all, but even so, I settled with him on the spot."

Pinchele was unmoved: "If I don't get the money, your guts will be dragged through the street!"

And although Pinchele left at once, the word *organization* lingered. The shopkeeper trembled and his wife was sick with fear.

That same Friday afternoon, after returning from the ritual bath, Lazar was at home alone while his wife and children tended the shop. Fresh *khala* lay on the table before him, beside the polished glass cover of the kerosene lamp and his freshly laundered red handkerchief; Lazar himself sat sipping a glass of tea. Suddenly he saw the door opening slowly and a pair of eyes, Pinchele's eyes, glancing furtively around. Lazar felt sick. The blood rushed to his face, his eyes bulged, the hand holding the teaglass trembled, and he fell to the floor in a heap. With a confused look on his face, Pinchele sprang forward and began to holler. He dashed a ladle of water into the man's face and went on shouting until the house filled with people, all pushing, screaming, peering to see what had happened. They fell all over Lazar, rubbed his temples, and raised a cry, but to no avail. Finally someone poured a whole glass of water over his face; Lazar's eyelids opened momentarily, revealing two stark bulging eyes, and then dropped shut. The doctor arrived and moved the crowd back a little. He ordered the window opened, and examined the man. Lazar lay in the middle of the floor; his face had gone quite yellow. Finally the doctor turned aside without a word, took the patient's pulse, gave him some drops, and ordered him lifted onto the bed. Before leaving he said softly to those at the door: "*Tak. Tak. Apopleksia.*" Then spreading his palms in a gesture of helplessness, he lifted his shoulders and shrugged.

So it was. That very Saturday night, in great secrecy, the funeral was conducted. Lanterns like glowing eyes moved through the still black night in the direction of the graveyard and disappeared in a distant clump of trees.

A deadly fear gripped the shtetl. Yekl the carpenter and the PPS man kept their heads lowered as they walked the street, where they were haunted by the faces of men and women with dumb, lifeless eyes. Even Itchele was broken and dispirited:

"God Almighty!" he complained to Yekl and the man from Warsaw, "How could you let this happen? Why wasn't it prevented?"

They stared back at him without answering, but Itchele's eyes flashed like an outlaw's. "If you couldn't control it, you shouldn't have undertaken it," he said.

Still they didn't answer. Itchele glared at them with contempt, spat at Yekl's feet, and strode away.

Meanwhile the news coming from Warsaw and the other big cities was not good—Baku was in flames, Tatars were slaughtering people in the streets, and even in the immediate area there was talk of something in the wind . . . something planned for "this Sunday."

Sunday came. Red-faced peasants in coarse woolen coats, dark caps with shiny peaks, and high-heeled boots, poured in from all the surrounding villages. Priests from neighboring parishes came with their flocks. Heavy chanting and deep organ tones issued forth from the high arcades of the church and spilled over the silent shtetl rooftops, filling the air with a fearsome sound.

At noon, the churchgoers emptied into the enclosed yard. First came a holy icon topped by a golden orb that flashed in the sunlight, dazzling the eye with millions of tiny golden darts. It was followed by a banner depicting a white-headed eagle that older folks remembered having last seen some thirty years before. Then a red and white striped flag, and further back another banner showing a crèche. The banners could be seen fluttering above the wall as the procession moved around the churchyard, like Jews circling the synagogue on Simchat Torah with the scrolls of the Law. A soft, muted chanting was heard. Gradually the banners neared the open gates and a moving mass of faces appeared, row upon row of people walking shoulder to shoulder, the men bareheaded, the women with red and white kerchiefs tied under their chins. They swarmed through the narrow gates and onto the wide gravel road that led through the verdant fields.

Row upon row of shoulders and heads moved into the distance, while more and more kept emerging from the open gates in a seemingly endless flow. A light dust rose from beneath the thousands of shuffling feet as the sea of rustling gray coats flowed steadily onward. The rows of heads rose and fell like waves along the strand. Banners waved. Ahead walked the priests in their white breastplates and square black velvet miters. Behind them came the folk, a submissive multitude of thousands, moving with bowed heads to the strains of a deep and steady chant. The long procession drew farther and farther away toward the spot on the horizon where the banners waved and beckoned across the field.

Then Jewish women and girls began to appear on the hilltop outside the shtetl where they used to gather yellow sand to sprinkle on the floors for the Sabbath. Shtetl workers in their shirtsleeves came too, to observe the goings-on: at least they, thank God, were not the target! The women praised God for His great bounty, of which they were undeserving, and cheerfully watched the receding procession: let there be banners, idols, stones, bones . . . as long as Jewish children were left in peace. Blue skies sprawled overhead; nature itself seemed to have declared a holiday, opening every door and gateway to summon the world out into the fields.

Itchele, Yekl, and the PPS man were out on the hill with the others watching the distant happenings. They saw only a sea of men's bare heads and red and white kerchiefs scattered like flowers among the flowing multitude. The banners fluttered and unfurled and finally came to rest before a tree where the entire peasant mass stopped. There, where the roads parted, a cross stood under the tree, deep in the shadow of its branches. The chanting grew deeper and the people grew still. And then they kneeled. The entire multitude, from one end to the other, sank to its knees like grain in a great field when the wind bends it groundward. In one sweeping motion all their backs bent over, and their faces bowed to the ground. The chanting seemed to soften, to grow more hushed as though soon all the motionless heads would be lulled to sleep. A sweet rapture embraced the countryside. The fields were bathed in a sea of light, and the golden sun shone steadily on the silent congregation below. A soft breeze caressed the blond hair of the silent bowed heads. Banners waved, the golden orb glittered, piercing the sunlight with its thousands of fiery darts, but the sun sat unperturbed, staring thoughtfully into space.

Abruptly the chanting ceased. At the far end, people were beginning to stand up. Then the chanting was resumed as the congregation surged forward along the road into the green field. And all the while the housewives and girls and some of the young men of the shtetl stood watching from the yellow sandy hill. The procession receded farther into the distance, where the broad gravel road was no more than a narrow path slithering and snaking uphill and down among the green fields. Soon it was almost out of sight, a thin black stripe across a green landscape.

The spectators started back to town, but Itchele stayed, gazing thoughtfully into the distance.

"Let's go back," suggested the PPS man.

"Tell me," Itchele asked, snapping out of his reverie, "what sort of a march was this?"

"A procession," replied the PPS man.

"A religious procession," added Yekl for clarification.

"Didn't you tell us that a Christian was coming down from Warsaw to make a speech, and that we would all march together?"

"Shoulder to shoulder," added Yekl.

"Oh yeah," shrugged the PPS man, "But this was something different. These are the 'Narodovtsi'. . . ."*

The explanation was irksome. It seemed to Itchele that the PPS man had deliberately used a fancy term like "Narodovtsi" to avoid answering the question.

"Liar!" he cried, "You know very well you're lying!"

The PPS man laughed aloud. This only angered Itchele the more, but he decided that it hardly made any difference. Since the death of Lazar the shopkeeper he had lost all interest in this business.

He started back to town, heavyhearted, but once back in the shtetl he felt even worse. Looking around the marketplace at the peaceful little houses with their windows half open, he sensed something he had never sensed before: there, beyond the shtetl, lay such a vast multitude, and here everything was so small, so puny, held together by just a dab of spit. . . . It occurred to him that if the thousands out there suddenly decided to have a bit of fun—just a simple bit of peasant fun—if each of them took from the houses of the Jews no more than a couple of rotting floor boards apiece and carried them off under his arm, nothing would remain of the shtetl but an empty plot of land.

After that Sunday, the young men wanted a banner of their own. The PPS man, when he became aware of it, was afraid that Yekl might take the initiative, just as Yekl was afraid that the PPS man might do the same. Overnight in the teashop two flags were readied, and by morning a crowd had gathered in front of the glass door—handsome scrubbed youths with freshly brushed caps and a festive sparkle in their eyes. The crowd grew until the street was black with people. Where was the PPS man, they wanted to know.

*Narodovtsi: from narod, the people. A right-wing Polish populist movement, at times aggressively anti-Semitic.

All at once he arrived, carrying a flag with Polish letters embroidered in silver. His face was drawn and his eyes were bloodshot from lack of sleep, but the flag fluttered and waved overhead to the great joy of the crowd. He was greeted excitedly and surrounded by a circle of upturned, eager faces.

Soon after, Yekl appeared waving a second flag just as lovely and every bit as bright as the other. He walked steadily, looking straight into the crowd with a serene and devout expression, but Itchele, who waltzed alongside him, grinned broadly at everyone. They stopped in front of the crowd and Yekl nodded:

"Good morning, friends."

Then he stood quietly, his flag facing the PPS man's. This was not at all as he had foreseen. He had intended to lead his followers separately behind their own banner. But now that everyone was standing together it was too late. The PPS man hadn't anticipated this either. So the two men stood glumly face to face, raising their heads occasionally only to drop them again.

The youths craned their necks to get a look at the flags, Yekl's too, with its simple, homey Yiddish words in the familiar alphabet: what a thrill it was to see both flags waving together!

"Well, why are we standing here?" Yekl asked after a long silence.

"Go ahead, what do you want of me?" countered the PPS man, shrugging off the question. Though Yekl made no reply, Itchele was not to be cowed:

"Listen, you blockhead! Don't take us for a bunch of suckers."

"Who said anything like that?" the PPS man protested. "The only reason I'm standing here is because I sent some men out to cut the telegraph wires and I have to wait for them to come back."

"That's different," conceded Itchele. But the explanation made Yekl even glummer: the PPS man always seemed to be taking the initiative. Yekl had the feeling that he too had meant to do something of the kind, but it had slipped his mind.

A couple of youngsters came running up, breathless with excitement, their caps askew. They pushed their way into the circle and whispered into the PPS man's ear.

"So where are they?" he asked.

"They're on their way. They'll soon be here. They really cut it right through. The wire made a terrible sound. B-r-r-r!"

And soon the youths themselves appeared with smiles of

triumph. Their leader wore a jacket and boots and a red kerchief around his neck and carried a white stick. As he came toward them, he signalled by raising the stick in the air with the curved end upward, then leaped up as though grabbing hold of something. Finally he sliced the air with the edge of his hand and nodded decisively: it was done!

Among the crowd an uneasy murmuring began and faces grew troubled. The soldiers would soon be on their way. The provincial officer would hear of it. But the PPS man was delighted with his deed. Now the work was complete! He smiled to himself and he and Yekl moved forward with the flags, side by side, followed by the rest of the crowd.

The street emptied as though in their honor; all the stores closed down. The crowd marched behind the flags, faces aglow with collective joy. A song started up, growing louder and bolder till it flooded the entire street.

The ranks of the marchers kept swelling as new recruits joined in. Slogans and counter-slogans broke through the singing. Finally, they reached the mayor's garden and the town hall. The crowd came to a stop and the leaders shouted out their demands, which were caught up and repeated by the vast sea of voices. After that, they all moved back into the street. Unnoticed by anyone, the mayor, half hidden by the shrubs, conferred with the excise officer, the Police Chief, and a couple of gray-coated woodcutters with axes in their hands who kept an eye on the demonstrators from afar. The PPS man marched jubilantly out in front but Yekl, right beside him, considered *himself* the leader. The further they marched, the noisier the cheers became, until the street seemed ready to explode. On and on they marched, until they reached their destination—the marketplace!

But the square was empty when they got there. The stands of baked goods were bare. A pale, frightened face peeked out from a crack in a doorway, threw one confused look at the flags and the dense crowd, and shut the door tightly.

In a flash the PPS man was atop one of the stands, waving his flag, and Yekl the carpenter with his flag was on another. The crowd settled quietly around the two stands and looked up expectantly at its leaders. Since Yekl appeared to have nothing to say, the PPS man launched into an oration and spoke with such energy that his hat almost fell off. He spoke at length, tossing his head and flexing

his arms and legs like a horse. The crowd, dazzled by this hailstorm
of words, stared directly upward at the face trembling with emotion
and the eyes burning like torches. Housewives ran out, their sleeves
rolled up above their elbows and their hands sticky with dough.
Girls with tangled hair carrying babies in their arms, and young
children with bagels in their hands, joined the outer circle of the
crowd. As soon as the PPS man noticed these new additions to his
audience, he shifted his tone, like a comedian, and began to call to
his comrades in a higher, sharper voice:

"*Bratshe, tovarishtshe!*"* he exclaimed, his mouth chopping
the words like lettuce for a salad.

Far back in the crowd some of the Gentiles exchanged twisted
smiles under their blond moustaches. One of them pushed in
behind the girls and women at the back, poked his head in toward
the center, feigned an expression of dumb innocence and stammered fearfully: "The soldiers are coming! The soldiers!"

The women nearest him panicked. There was a hushed
moment of suspense; then like an electric charge the message shot
through the crowd and with an abrupt jolt the whole mass suddenly
erupted.

"Stay where you are!" Yekl screamed with all his might. Itchele
jumped up beside him and yelled even louder, waving his arms, but
the pandemonium only spread. The men at the center stood fast,
but at the edges, everyone was already on the run. It was impossible
to restrain the women and the girls; they bolted, tripping and step-
ping over bodies that lay in their way. The hard knot of men at the
center kept shouting: "Stay where you are! Stay where you are!" but
to no avail. The turmoil only increased. Hands and feet and disheveled heads tumbled in a mass on the ground. Each tried to extricate
himself by clutching at someone else: grasping fists and fingers
refused to relax their grip and the crowd melted into a tangle of
protruding arms and legs. At last a path was cleared, and within
minutes the women and girls and many of the youths had fled. Only
the staunchest of the men remained, the elite. The PPS man turned
to them once more and waited for them to settle down.

By this time the woodcutters had nothing more to do. So they
turned into the market lane and walked idly back to the town hall.

By evening the shtetl knew that the telegraph wires had been

---

* *Bratshe, tovarishtshe:* Brothers, comrades!

cut. By morning there were soldiers in town. They arrested Yekl the carpenter and took him off to the provincial jail. His neighbors turned their heads as he was led from his house under guard. Only the tobacconist watched the proceedings with a frown: Yekl still owed him two rubles for cigarettes. . . .

The PPS man, according to one of the local coachmen, had made off by train in the middle of the night.

The sun went on shining anyway. Everything was bathed in light. The upper-story windows of the shops peered out into the marketplace. Householders began to gather: Isaac Feyge-Libes with his son-in-law Hershele; Dovidl Rosenzweig with his cap pulled over his forehead, hands behind his back, and paunch protruding slightly; then little clusters of prominent Jews with beards. The largest group gathered at the water pump where Dovidl was holding forth, gesticulating wildly and talking very heatedly, probably about the union men who were nowhere to be seen. Presumably they were all lying low.

But suddenly Itchele the bootmaker appeared across the marketplace, eyes downcast as though he were fed up with the world and preferred to look at the tips of his patent leather shoes. His hands were folded behind him, making his broad shoulders and back appear somewhat sunken, and his eyes were visibly moist. As he took a quick look at the clusters of householders, his cheekbones trembled; but he kept coming closer. Among one of the groups he recognized Chaim Yosele, a journeyman shoemaker who was now evidently a convert to respectability. Itchele walked by, feigning disinterest, but aware of the eyes watching him. Voices overtook him:

"There's no Tsar, they claim, there's no God either!"

"There are only fighters!" he heard Chaim Yosele titter.

Itchele turned sharply and glowered at Chaim Yosele who only two days before had been one of those "fighters" himself! The blood rushed to his cheeks and his eyes blazed with anger. The onlookers froze. Dovidl hurried toward Itchele with outstretched arms:

"Just look at you now! Look how angry you are! You get angry without even waiting for an explanation. He was talking about the PPS man. . . . You can see his point, after all, you're a clever fellow yourself. If you have to do something like that, at least cover your tracks. You don't have to leave a calling card! If you don't tweak the Tsar's nose, you won't have to go into hiding. The whole thing is so ugly. You know what people are saying now? That he's flown the coop. He just took off and left you holding the bag. He's probably the one who put you up to it, isn't he?"

The shaft hit home. Itchele bit his lips and hung his head. Without saying a word, he shrugged his shoulders and walked away—the plague take them all, and the PPS man too! He clenched his fists but then remembered something he had decided a while ago: what difference did it make? Since the death of Lazar the shopkeeper he was through with the movement anyway.

Meanwhile Dovidl returned to his circle of listeners and began haranguing in earnest:

"I really let him have it! I showed him how stupid their ideas were. Their whole movement's as good as buried!"

"And I was afraid he was going to come over and sock me!" Chaim Yosele giggled.

"Why should he make a fool of himself? He knows we would have made mincemeat out of him. Besides, with a hefty father-in-law like yours, and your father-in-law's two brothers, why should you be worried about Itchele? It's not like before. There are no more Jewish cossacks!"

"Come on. Let's go somewhere we can talk," said Isaac Feyge-Libes the shoe manufacturer, and he moved away, his son-in-law at his heels.

Dovidl agreed, pulling Chaim Yosele along behind him.

At a slow, leisurely pace they strolled along the street single file, their hands clasped behind their backs. Chaim Yosele tried to imitate their gait. One blond sidecurl stuck out foolishly from behind his ear, his cap had slipped dangerously to one side, but he strutted along, jacket unbuttoned, like a real somebody, as if to say: make way for me. All the time he kept glancing around to see whether anyone saw him—there he was, with Isaac Feyge-Libes, the biggest shoe-man in town; with his son-in-law Hershele, a genius who at thirteen had conducted services in the tailor's congregation—the women would peek through the cracks to get a look at

him. There he was in their company, on his way to Dovidl Rosenzweig's house. . . .

The four of them sat down around the table in Dovidl's office.
Isaac Feyge-Libes took a ruble from his wallet and tossed it on the
table with a request for shnapps. Chaim Yosele was about to pick up
the coin and fetch the refreshments himself when Dovidl grabbed
him by the elbow and held him back. He rang his little bell and
immediately the door swung open and Dovidl's son rushed in:

"What is it, father?"

"Bring us some shnapps and a couple of beers," he ordered,
handing him the coin.

Some minutes later, when the bottles and glasses were already
on the table, Dovidl got up to lower the window blinds.

"We'll show them, those ignoramuses!" he remarked, with a
meaningful look at the manufacturer.

"We'll serve them up for stew!" Isaac Feyge-Libes chipped in,
tugging at the twin tips of his beard.

"We'll form an association to oppose theirs!" Hershele proposed.

"We can draw up a list and get all the householders to sign,"
Dovidl added, showing off his talent for organization.

"As for you, my fine young man," Isaac turned to Chaim
Yosele, who was still finding it hard to believe in whose company he
sat, "how is it that you never come to see me, as though I weren't in
the business at all? Some people have all the luck. But when I need a
worker, a craftsman, I have to go begging for one. . . ."

"To tell the truth, Reb Isaac," Yosele puckered his fat lips as
though cooling a steaming plate of kasha, "I've been thinking that
I'd like to go to work for you."

"Naturally! You're like one of us, after all," Dovidl chimed in
with an expressive twinkle for Isaac's benefit, "and your father-in-
law is certainly one of us!"

And so the matter was settled. Chaim Yosele went to work for
Reb Isaac. In the factory, Reb Isaac would slap him warmly on the
back. "You go right on out and strike with the others, Chaim
Yosele," he would say, pointing to the workers with a sinister little
smile, "you be a fighter like the rest of them, do you hear?"

"Chaim Yosele," the clever son-in-law would call out mocking-
ly, in the presence of the other workers, "our district officer is such a

fool. What sort of match are his soldiers for these brave warriors of ours?"

"The 'fighters' are going to get it, all right!" Chaim Yosele declared self-importantly.

Some of the workers lowered their eyes. Others smiled sheepishly at their three "judges." They were well aware that the slightest whisper in the provincial · officer's ear nowadays would be enough. . . .

Chaim Yosele spent more and more of his time conferring with Hershele. One evening Hershele suggested to him, "See if you can take care of that tall beanpole with the red bandana around his neck."

So Chaim Yosele hung around the synagogue courtyard between *minkha* and *maariv* and when he saw the gangling youth he ripped the red bandana from his neck, and provoked a fight.

His father-in-law reproached Chaim Yosele for getting into so many bloody rows. But Chaim Yosele puffed out his cheeks and exclaimed:

"They don't let you earn a living—these strikers!"

Since the captain of the gendarmes had now begun to frequent the shtetl, Dovidl and his son were always to be seen rushing down the street in their Sabbath caftans to pay a call. When someone asked the son why, he was told bluntly:

"Whom else would the captain send for? It's a town of animals, after all. Did the captain have anyone else to talk to when he came?"

The workers now sat at their benches as meekly as lambs. The more resigned they became, the greater Chaim Yosele's daring. Every evening he would beat up the gangling youth and every morning he was greeted by Dovidl with a big hello.

Early one morning when the ground was still wet with dew, and the scattered sawdust and straw of the market place lay bleached in the sun's early glare, Chaim Yosele's father-in-law stood haggling with a peasant and two other prospective Jewish buyers over a wagonload of fruit. Suddenly a woman came running up to him with several others close behind, screaming:

"Help! Come quickly! They're beating up your son-in-law!"

"Woe is me!" the poor man cried in confusion, "so early in the morning?" He set out at a run, still in his apron, and headed straight for the "beanpole's" house. A group of people stood there looking up at the second-story windows; Dovidl too was watching from his own doorstep across the street. In the middle of the crowd stood Chaim Yosele, his face and head smeared with blood. As soon as Dovidl saw the father-in-law rushing up the street, he smiled to himself and turned back into the house.

At the sight of his father-in-law, Chaim Yosele lunged toward the front door. But the father-in-law, who was even more distraught than he, shoved the boy behind him, broke through the door, and started up the stairs. A hail of wooden boards came crashing down the stairs to block his way. The gangling youth stood with his mother behind a pile of wood, frantically hurling down one board after another. Through the open door came the shrieks of small children and the screams of the father who kept running over to the window in a frenzy and then back to the aid of his wife and son. The boards flew in mad confusion down the stairs, but Chaim Yosele's father-in-law continued climbing, shielding his head with his hands. In a flash the gangling youth ran inside, grabbed something from over the chimney, and oblivious to what he held in his hands, rushed out again to attack.

Chaim Yosele's father-in-law felt a single blow under his heart. For a moment he remained motionless, with a dazed glassy-eyed look, staring at his antagonist in a trance. Then he began to stagger, and making a grab for the railing, stumbled weakly down the stairs. At the bottom he shot an uncomprehending look up at the sky, and then opened his mouth wide, in a great gasp for air. Desperately he looked around him, his eyes flickering with doubt. Some hidden force drove him back toward the door. He pushed against it with both hands, and trembling violently, was able to force it open. As he lifted his foot to step over the boards a stream of blood gushed from his boot. . . .

The crowd looked on, dumb with shock. Someone let out a woeful cry and stepped forward with fists raised and teeth clenched as though restraining some fierce emotion.

"Help! Help!" people shouted from all sides. But the man was already spinning blindly in a circle, leaning more and more to one side until he thudded to the ground.

"He's dead!" went up the cry.

"Take off his boot!" someone yelled, and there was a sudden rush for his foot. The boot came off with a jerk; a pool of black blood poured out as though from a butcher's pail.

The dead man's glazed eyes stared upward one final time and the brows trembled slightly. Right in the center of the heart there was a hole the size of an egg. Warm blood still oozed from the wound, soaking the man's body and all his clothing.

The body was lifted and carried off. Someone supported the head, which bobbed behind like the head of a slaughtered goose. The face was waxen, the mouth somewhat twisted and clenched from pain, and the eyes half-open, bulging. The bearers walked unsteadily, a little wedge of men with a body in their arms, and Chaim Yosele ran behind, beating himself on the head and bellowing: "My father-in-law!" But the rest of the crowd remained on the scene, yelling up at the windows: "Down! Down! Bring them down!"

Ladders were set up against the wall.

All at once Ephraim, one of the men who helped carry off the body, came running back in a sweat:

"What is there left to live for? The organization has killed!" he screamed dramatically, then offered himself by the throat, "Go ahead, go ahead and kill me, too!"

"The organization . . . the organization. . . ." sobbed the women, choking on their tears, "a father of eight little children."

Without warning, the Police Chief suddenly appeared. His blond moustache quivered, and his eyes flew over the heads of the crowd to the windows above. The cap with its badge sat firmly on his head, and he kept a tight grip on the sword in his belt as though he were about to draw.

The crowd grew more agitated. Angrily, they glared up at the windows. Ephraim, followed by several of the others, stormed the ladders, screaming upward with blood-red faces.

Shrieks from inside the house pierced the heavens. But several hands were already reaching out to smash the windows. The shattering of the panes was drowned in a roar of voices, as splinters of glass rained down over the sea of blazing faces below. Only black silhouettes were visible in the windows. Some of the men climbed inside; others stood on the ladders trying to get in, while the bottom rungs were being contested by ever greater numbers of volunteers.

At the same time a mob broke through the outer door and rushed the stairs.

"Bring them down! Down!" the cries sounded across the yard. The crashing of boards merged with frenzied human screams and filled the air with madness and chaos. In the narrow doorway the crowd pushing inward was halted by those starting back down. The boy's father, pale and stunned, was shoved through the door by fifty hands. Then the son, his face quite unrecognizable, blood streaming over his hair and face. He was pushed against a wall with his head slumped forward. Boards began to rise and fall over his head, and the mob, like a compressed mass with a thousand flailing limbs, raged and beat him savagely until the boy sank under the blows. He was no longer visible, but a few kicks were added for good measure. The Police Chief tried to force his way through, the veins bulging in his neck, and his eyes fierce with determination as he tried to push people back with his arms. But the mob was a solid mass, united in a single raging passion that burned in every face. A naked sword flashed suddenly in the policeman's hand, held straight up over their heads. The mob fell back as if hit by a splash of cold water. Terrified, they watched with bated breath. . . .

"Move back!" shouted the Police Chief. He lifted the youth who lay on the ground gasping, and shielded his bloody head with both his hands. Supporting the boy under the arm, the officer told those around him to see to the father, who was also stretched out on the ground, tearing at his hair with mournful cries. Some of the men dragged the father along as the crowd set out after the Police Chief and the boy, who huddled against him and tried to bury his head under the officer's arm. But the mob ran loose like a wild herd, brandishing wooden slats and trying to hit the boy anywhere they could. Ephraim threatened the youth with a club, which he held upraised over his head, but each time the weapon began to fall the father would leap forward and pull it away. Ephraim dodged and looked for another opening; when he saw his chance, he took aim at an eye and swung with all his might. The boy pitched forward with a terrible cry. In that same moment the father threw himself over the boy, covering him with both hands and pressing his whole shuddering body over him like a shield. The crowd felt it had had enough. The officer drew his sword again and the boy lurched to his feet, stumbled and staggered onward. His eye fell out of his face, large as a potato, coated in black. Pieces of hair and flesh had been ripped from his scalp, and blood ran down over his neck and shoulders. They barely made it to the town hall.

Now the mob prowled the streets looking for "strikers." Men with blackened faces and matted beards ran headlong down the street brandishing their wooden boot-supports as clubs. They found a boy hiding under the bridge. By the time they were through with him he lay bruised and battered on the soft earth, his face so badly swollen that the eyes could not be seen.

Suddenly word spread that the brothers of the murdered man were on their way! . . . They had been traveling with their partners to Warsaw, but were intercepted at a stop along the way by a telegram from the shtetl. The mob awaited them impatiently: now the action would really begin! At noon a couple of horses came clattering down the street into the center of town, pulling a wagon-load of men. The passengers jumped down; among them were older men in fedoras, and youths in shiny peaked caps and leather jackets, the brothers of the dead man, his partners, and a few who had come along for the ride. Knives and revolvers glinted sharply in their hands as they ran into the marketplace shouting: "Our brother! Our brother!"

Their first stop was the dead man's house. A white sheet covered the corpse, which lay on the floor with candles burning at its head. The widow and a floorful of children lay prostrate around the dead man, burying their heads against his body. The brothers took one look at the scene, a quick look at their brother's face under the sheet, and hurled themselves to the floor. They beat their foreheads, crying: "Our brother! Our brother!" The house resounded with weeping and heart-rending cries. Slowly, with knives bared, the partners began edging toward the door, but the widow ran to block their way:

"Even if you slaughter the whole town," she sobbed, "you still won't bring my husband back to life!"

Out of pity for her, they turned away and stuck their weapons in their pockets. But once back out in the courtyard, they picked up boards and clubs and rushed into the street.

Then blows echoed through the streets for fair, as workers were pulled from their benches and dragged from their lofts. Inflamed and bloodthirsty, the men chased down their victims, and soon blood began to spurt afresh from heads already steeped in gore. The cobblestones were bathed in blood. The sky shuddered. The sun burned red, the air was thick and red. Like a great slaughterhouse, the marketplace lay smashed and bloodied.

It was then that Itchele appeared in the square with an iron bar that he had pried loose from one of the storefronts. He marched across the square with iron-firm steps. Quickly he slid into the lane and turned into a side street where he stopped before the open window of Isaac Feyge-Libes's workshop.

"Where are the boys?" he asked Hershele when he saw the empty workbenches.

"What boys?" the other replied, turning pale as a sheet.

"Have they run away?"

"Run away? . . . yes . . . with their paring knives. . . ." Hershele slowly regained his composure and threw out his arms as though a tragedy had befallen him.

With a grimace of disgust, Itchele threw the iron bar to the ground and took to his heels. But all at once he stopped, turned back, retrieved the weapon, and fled a second time as if someone were tearing him by the hair. . . .

He paused at another window farther along the street, but found no one there either. By now he was a little calmer. Slowly, he strode away, hanging his head, with both hands clutching the iron bar behind his feet. As he passed a house on the next street he heard a scream and a terrible racket coming from behind the front door. He ran over to the entrance and stood transfixed: the whole gang from Warsaw was in the yard with their clubs and revolvers, menacing someone at an upper window. A moment later he saw Tevel, a boy of about eighteen, being dragged from his workbench, his sleeves still black from the dye. The boy shot one desperate glance toward the door to the yard before blows began raining down on him. With a sharp sigh, as if someone had knocked him off balance, Itchele grabbed hold of the doorpost for support. His face contorted with pain as he watched the butchery. Then he staggered into the street, a beaten man, poisoned to the very last drop of his blood.

He went home and threw himself down on the bed, tossing and groaning. His mother and younger brothers and sisters watched from across the room, holding their breath. For a full day and a night he lay in the same spot. The following day his first words as he finally rose from the bed were to ask his mother about Tevel. She told him it wasn't known for certain whether the boy would live. The expression in Tevel's eyes as he looked toward the door haunted Itchele still. Could a living person look like that? As he recalled the scene, Itchele's eyes grew damp with moisture. . . .

But when he stepped outside, Itchele learned from the barber-surgeon that Tevel was actually on the mend. The sun greeted him full in the face. A splendid brightness flooded the marketplace, and Itchele was forced to squint, unable to keep his eyes open. Everything was very still, much too still it seemed to him. The shops were open, and the storekeepers stood in their usual spot in the doorways. But their bearing was stiff, unnatural. The sky too was motionless, perfectly blue and clear. The sun shimmered and glared off the whitewashed walls of the shops. The stillness was ominous, like after a funeral. Suddenly Itchele saw a few tailors scurrying by with their sewing machines on their backs, their heads pressed so low by the heavy load that the tips of their beards stuck straight out from their chests, and the ends of their long coats swept the ground behind them. Itchele turned away from the sight; he was reminded of Menashe the ironmonger's death . . . even before he was buried his daughters were stealing the good china from the attic, behind each other's back. But now, Itchele thought, he would settle for anything—as long as Tevel was all right. . . .

That evening when Itchele sat down for a bite and a glass of tea—after his long fast, his mother insisted on the glass of tea—a boy burst into the house:

"Itchele," he whispered breathlessly, "some fellows are down from Warsaw . . . workers . . . with guns . . . they're waiting just outside the shtetl. . . ."

He slammed the glass down on the table and followed the boy outside.

Before long a bunch of young men had gathered in the market-place—Itchele and about eighteen others. The atmosphere was charged. Storekeepers stood in the entrances of their shops, watch-ful and waiting, with one foot ready to slam the door.

As it happened, there was no trouble that night. The funeral had been held the evening before, and right afterward the men responsible for the beatings had all left town. Only the brothers themselves remained, and as Itchele put it, "They are his brothers, after all. . . ." By the next day not a trace of the Warsaw visitors remained. They were said to have fired some shots into the air before driving off in their wagon.

Things returned to normal, and everyone knew that Itchele was now in charge of the organization. Once again Dovidl Rosenzweig slunk around like an orphan. Sometimes, out of sheer loneliness, he would sidle up to one of the union-men and mention an item he had read in the papers—about the strikers in Bialystok or the revolutionaries who had set the fires in Baku—and praise them to the skies.

The summer dragged on. As the days shortened, people began to buckle down: the year promised to be a prosperous one, somewhat hectic perhaps, but with jobs for everyone. As for military consignments—there was work enough to drown in! Almost unnoticed, the days passed, the sun moved further aslant, and the wind shifted, bringing a fresh new tang to the air and a whisper of strange new secrets. . . . The sun's rays shed a redder, cooler light over the earth with intimations of something cold and unfamiliar. Each day, the sun grew more thoughtful and silent, as though regretting something lost. It took the birds till noon to begin testing their wings and pecking at their underfeathers. Then, stretching their wings, they hopped tentatively over the synagogue roof, no more than a shingle at a time, twittering piteously; there was much longing in that sound.

And the evenings were different too. Night fell ever more abruptly, and before you knew it the sun was setting in a corner of the horizon behind some red clouds that were trying to find a night's lodging in back of the woods. A red glow spread over the synagogue roof with its tiny attic window staring raptly into the distance. Far away, in silent yearning, the sun went down. Shadows stretched noiselessly across the street. The shops looked like dark bakers' ovens. Market-women with their baskets and stools under their arms shuffled homeward, chilled to the bone, their faces pinched and wrinkled, and their lips blue.

The nights kept getting colder.

Lights shone gently from all the houses and stores. The shopkeeper's white face in the doorway stood out sharply against the dark night, and his yawn rolled into the empty marketplace like a hollow echo. Overhead, the sky was a crystal plate decorated with sharp-edged, glittering stars that seemed to be burrowing deeper and deeper into the recesses of the night. One by one, the lights in the windows went out. Heavy footsteps resounded through the square as the watchman made the rounds of the shuttered stores, making known his desire for a new fur coat in a series of strange sounds and endless mutterings. . . .

At dawn thick white dew shrouded the marketplace from rooftop to ground. The cold red sunrise ushered in a ruddy, cold day. The High Holy Days were approaching. Boys and study-house benchwarmers played hide-and-seek with the shofar, and every morning after the first prayers the sexton had to conduct an angry inquiry into its whereabouts. Every morning the well-heated ritual bath hissed with steam. In the early dawn, shutters rang as the sexton rushed from house to house, waking the men for the penitential prayers. Like a demon he flew through the streets and alleys, rapping loudly at each house, then rushing on to the next.

The older Jews became more serious and subdued; the youths, paler and more gaunt. The synagogue courtyard was quiet during the day, the house of study dozed, and its moldy green windows gave off a restful bluish glow in the sunlight. But at night they were ablaze with red. Inside, the congregation prayed fervently; the groans and sighs blended with the heartrending chant of the petitioners, and then flowed into the muffled darkness outside. At daybreak, when skies began to clear, the lights in the synagogue were extinguished and sallow faces appeared in the windows to look out at the sober new morning. Across the square the treetops of the barrel-maker's garden rustled and nodded, as if they had been privy to a secret that night. The sky paled in the east and a bright stripe of clouds stretched across the horizon, but the rest of the sky remained ashen, and in the cool morning air one could almost hear a sigh: "Remember the Covenant." The people recited and remembered, aware that the night of nights would soon be upon them. . . .

And it came—the eve of Yom Kippur.

That morning the roosters wakened not to crow but to lament, with bitter, mournful cries.* "There is no judge and no judgment," their voices called as they were dragged from their roosts, roused from the sweetest of dreams, for the slaughterer in his broad-sleeved smock with the slaughter-knife in his teeth was passing from house to house. There was a flurry of feathers and a flapping of wings against the ground. Stifled cries were silenced, and a final gasp or flickering glance was crushed beneath an indifferent boot.

---

*Roosters used for the atonement ceremony of *kapparot* are slaughtered on the eve of Yom Kippur.

A red morning trembled in the east. Fearsome and blood-stained, it heralded an afternoon more awe-inspiring still. Shops were bolted; the wax memorial candles shining through the windows were enough to fill one with dread. Choked cries emanated from the houses, punctuated by the groans and sobs of men and women. Soon the shutters were closed and the Jews of the shtetl, dressed all in white, their eyes red with weeping, walked down the street in the direction of the synagogue.

After Yom Kippur the sky grew changeable. Winds began to whistle and clouds like runny gray mould chased across the sky, rotting the heavens. The birds awoke in a fright, and quickly banding together flew forth in V formation, like two ribbons stretching back from a single head, until they disappeared among the distant clouds.

The trees took fright and yellowed. A rustling was heard through the woods, and leaves began falling to the ground, blanketing the earth like a yellow shroud. As the wind howled through the trees the branches, now naked, began to beat themselves and groan, deafening the heavens with the sounds of their mourning.

It was almost Succoth, and everyone was busy banging together his booth, hammering boards into the wooden posts under his windowsill. Once again the wagon came clattering over the bridge, carrying visitors from Warsaw who jumped down as it came to a stop, grabbed their parcels, and ran homeward, keeping their heads tucked into their collars against the damp chill wind.

Throughout the entire holiday week the sky remained overcast and it rained steadily. But for Simchat Torah, the holiday of the Rejoicing of the Law, the weather improved. Youths moved into the streets, and staged a stormy demonstration during the procession of the scrolls in the synagogue. It was a demonstration that did them proud; as Itchele said, a real "smash!"

And that was the way things went for the rest of the winter. Since there was a general strike on,* no one left the shtetl. The citified sons stayed home, and the town declared a Sabbath of its own: a local strike was called on a local scale. Only later was it

*The strike was called in October 1905.

discovered from the underground newspapers and proclamations that this was part of the general strike which workers everywhere were waging.

Gangs of young men roamed the streets daily like packs of hungry wolves. The door of the teashop swung open and shut as youths inside and out tried to put the bite on someone—maybe a "brother" would stand them to a meal or lend them a little money to tide them over—anything to still their hunger. Later on, when they were back at work, they would have no use for such behavior, but in the meantime it was either beg or starve. . . . It was in this spirit that some thirty youths set out for Aaron the butcher's.

When he saw the the calamity bearing down on him, the butcher edged back into a corner and blinked out in terror. His wife, a rather chubby woman, got the hiccups and made abrupt crowing noises to the delight of the gang, which imitated her every sound like a cantor's choir. They raised such a row that people came running in off the street and peered through the windows. Meanwhile one of the boys found a very large loaf of black bread in one of the cupboards, and within minutes it was plucked apart like a rooster. At least they keep their hats on while eating, the butcher thought to himself, beginning to breathe a little easier:

"What is it you want, my young friends?" he asked finally.

"What we want," several voices cried in unison, "we'll tell you what we want. You can keep your gizzards and giblets and drumsticks. . . . All we want is bread!"

"If it's only bread you want, that shouldn't be too difficult," said the butcher, coming a little closer. "Tell me, about how much do you want me to give you for bread?"

"Ten rubles," someone blurted out.

"Ten! Ten!" chimed in the chorus.

"It's impossible," the butcher protested, "you want to ruin me?"

"Who wants to ruin you? All we want is enough for a bit of bread and herring for each of us!"

His wife had been standing in the chimney corner, her mouth twisted into an unpleasant grimace, and her lips visibly trembling.

"Yocheved," the butcher summoned her, "these Jews want bread, and we'll just have to get them some. . . . Go borrow ten rubles from the neighbor."

She moved toward the door, but turned before leaving to throw a lingering glance in the direction of her poor husband: to what fate was she abandoning him? In fact her husband was quite capable of rustling up the ten rubles himself, but he didn't want to give the gang any wrong ideas.

The youths received their money in cash and tore into the street, cheering lustily. Afterward the teashop was very lively. Youths jumped over the benches and tables, and Itchele cheered them on:

"Good for you, boys! If you know how to take care of yourselves, that's half the battle!"

From the newspapers and from rumors the shtetl learned more and more about the strikers in the cities. No one cared a damn any more for Victoria's constitutional reforms—why, here, even the railroads were on strike!

And then suddenly there was news of pogroms . . . long lists of towns and cities . . . horrible accounts of the Black Hundreds* cutting open human bellies . . . crushing the heads of suckling babes. The news struck terror into the heart of young and old alike. There were rumors that thugs were on their way, that they were already in Warsaw. Four thousand men were said to have come by the Terespol train. Reb Avrom Feinberg lost no time having his door nailed up with thick iron bars. His neighbors, scarcely one of whom had a door of his own, just a wife and children and a rickety table, wanted to declare a day of fasting. Faces turned black as the earth. Even Itchele was dejected.

Evenings, clouds bobbed in the leaden skies like gray clay pots in dirty water. Windows looked somberly out at the street. Careworn Jews, their heads bowed to the ground, crept toward the synagogue for minkha and maariv.

In the study house one evening, the congregation discussed the latest events. Cigarette smoke rose to the ceiling, and the candle lights flickered as if in a fog. The reader, pausing between prayers, stood facing the congregants with his back to the lectern. At that moment the Gentile bath attendant appeared in the doorway, a fur cap on his head and the corner of his dirty undershift showing under his heavy cotton vest. His eyes glittered like a tomcat's, and his lips, which usually were turned up in a foolish smile, now seemed to be sucking at something. Stach, the bath attendant, had

*Popular name for the 100-man paramilitary units of the League of the Russian People, supported by Tsar Nicholas II to "preserve public order." The Black Hundreds initiated many brutal pogroms against the Jews.

news to report: thugs were on their way. They had been seen on the Warsaw road. The men's jaws trembled.

Later that same evening, Chanele, the women's bath attendant, returned to town from a village near the station where she had accompanied one of the women back home from the ritual bath. She told her neighbors what the woman had seen: Russians in red shirts and long peasant blouses were hanging around the station that morning . . . the thugs everyone was talking about! By now maybe there were as many as a hundred of them. . . .

Her neighbors listened, groaning "Merciful God," and wringing their hands. When they slipped out of the bath-house, one by one, instead of going straight home they dropped in on other neighbors who passed the word along until it reached even the study house of the Blendiver Hasidim. By then it was a grizzly tale: a hundred villainous hoodlums with swords and knives were massed at the station, waiting to attack.

People began closing their shutters. The street remained dark and deserted. Occasionally, someone would run nervously by, stopping at every corner for a frightened look and then fly on with coattails flapping in the wind. Where would such a Jew be running to, unless to the bathhouse, to hide in the loft, under the birchbrooms?

The teashop was still filled with young people, but a mood of silent dejection hung over the room. All at once Itchele burst in like a thunderbolt:

"Why are you sitting around?" he cried. "Don't you know what's happening?"

He was greeted by stares.

"So what are we supposed to do?"

"Who'll come with me to the ironmonger's for scythes?"

They were ready, to a man, to follow Itchele wherever he might lead. He selected a handful and in a little while they were back carrying scythes tied in bundles. Everyone grabbed a weapon. Their faces brightened with excitement as the curved blades of the scythes sparkled in their hands.

But a look around the room suggested there were still too few of them and they sent for the tanners to join them. A moment later the messengers were back with a little girl who seemed to be bursting with joyfulness. It was Yekl's sister, bringing the news of her brother's return. *

---

*A political amnesty was part of the new constitution.

"Yekl is back!" There was a flurry of excitement.

Scythes in hand, the crowd surged into the street and made straight for Yekl's house, where they swarmed around him like bees. Overwhelmed, Yekl raised his hands for silence. Noticing the scythes, he asked what was going on. It took a moment before the men remembered their mission and explained about the thugs.

"Phooey!" Yekl spat, "It's a lie! It's a provocation! I've just come from the station, haven't I?"

The scythes were put away. With a rousing song, Yekl was escorted into the marketplace while some boys ran off to the Charity for Poor Brides to fetch huge red lanterns which they lit and mounted on tall poles to brighten the whole market square. Singing lustily, the young crowd accompanied Yekl from store to store. The lanterns' reddish light flooded the walls, and their reflection blazed in the upstairs windows like fires in the night. The confused sounds of shouting and singing echoed through the shtetl.

From the two householders who came over to extend Yekl a welcome, the town learned, to its relief, that the rumors of hoodlums were utterly false. Grateful to God for His mercy, everyone went off to bed.

By early morning, Yekl was already out in the square near the public wall; the Chief Police Officer was with him, and they were playing a little game: Yekl pasted up copies of a proclamation and the officer tore them down. A lick of the tongue, a proclamation mounted, and then torn down. Another proclamation pasted up, another torn down. They stood side by side, looking one another right in the eye, as if the whole thing had been prearranged, until the pile of proclamations had passed from Yekl to the officer. At that point they looked one another in the eye again, as if to say: Well, how about that? . . .

Men and women stood by and smiled at Yekl's audacity: the Tsar's new Constitution must really be in effect after all!*

Meanwhile the rabbi in his nightcap, with his long earlocks and padded satin coat, was on his way to the study house with a group of followers to recite the psalms. When Yekl saw them, he quickly rounded up some of his gang and marched in behind.

Up front the recitation had already begun. The reader was standing at the lectern, chanting, "A psalm of David . . ." and the congregation was swaying and singing along. The rabbi's cap swayed back and forth against the wall; the other worshippers sat around the

*The Imperial Manifesto of October 1905 granted civil liberties.

tables over their open psalters, wrapped in prayershawls, chanting mournfully, hardly in the usual hasidic manner at all. Yekl and his gang mounted the platform. Startled, the rabbi and congregation raised their heads.

"What good are the psalms?" Yekl shouted with a bang on the table. "This is no time for psalms!"

The congregation was dumbfounded.

"This is the time, not for psalms, but for arms! For fighting with weapons!"

"Help! Arms!" screamed the rabbi, tearing himself by the hair. "Help! Arms! There are no arms . . . only psalms! Psalms!"

"No psalms!" Yekl outshouted him, "only arms, real arms! Pistols! Revolvers!"

"Help! Revolvers!" screamed someone in the congregation, an impassioned Jew with eyes radiating heavenly devotion. He jumped up on the rabbi's table and faced Yekl, his long beard atremble with the emotion of his effort.

"You're just a thief!" Yekl hollered him down, waving a finger in front of his face. "Your scale is false. You put your foot on it whenever you're weighing anything. You short-change the farmers!"

"Jews, kill me . . . I'm ready to die for the sanctification of the Name!" the Jew shrieked in a high quavering voice. He tore open his clothes at the breast and fixed the congregation with a fiery stare.

"Get down! Get down!" went up the cry around the podium. Faces burned in anger and fists rose in the air.

"Psalms! Psalms!" cried the congregation from all sides, and the devout Jew with the long beard suddenly burst out with a cry: "A psalm of David. . . ."

"Quiet!" Yekl's gang pounded on the podium, and then one of them pulled a gun.

"Help!" screamed the crowd. Hands stretched upward to grab the Jew down from the table. The men's faces were contorted with fear as they looked up at the platform.

The gang on the podium made a move for the stairs, and in a flash the congregation threw open the windows and began to leap out. Within a minute the study house was empty. There remained only the rabbi, who sat in his corner with his face to the wall, crying like a small child, and some elderly Jews in prayershawls, sitting at the back tables as if petrified, looking fearfully at their rabbi. . . .

A breeze blew in through the open windows, and sent the curtain of the Ark billowing outward, as if it too were trying to tear loose through the window. Outside there were wild shouts of triumph. Like a stampeding herd, the youths began running through the street. Even Itchele could not hold them back, though he spread his arms and he and Yekl tried to stop them, yelling "Enough! Enough!" But by now the boys were in a fever of excitement. One after another the shops were locked up, but the youths ran headlong, screaming at the top of their lungs.

All at once some boys dashed up breathlessly:

"Listen . . . hurry . . . get down to the courthouse. They're trying to oust the judge . . . there are *goyim* there too, and others. . . . Hurry! Hurry!"

"Come on now, let's put an end to it!" Yekl cried with the rest.

"An end to it! An end to it!"

"Long live the revolu. . . ."

"Hurrah! Hur-r-a-a-a-h!"

And they surged forward.

Like a thick black cloud they descended on the courthouse, where a group of Gentiles awaited them. The two groups merged and stood together looking up at the courthouse windows, until some of the men moved forward to enter the building, and the crowd swept in after. In a short while the judge rushed out, looking quite distraught and glancing back nervously over his shoulder. Uncertain where his safety might lie, he hurried down the street as if driven by a storm, bareheaded, the tails of his coat flying out behind him.

The crowd raised a triumphant cheer and watched him scurry out of sight down the end of the street, where the bailiff lived.

That same night the youths were dragged from their beds; by morning the rooftops were shrouded in fog, and it was quiet, except for the occasional echo of an iron rod against a wall. Householders came out to exchange news about the events of the night. Pale mothers with tear-stained eyes appeared in the street; their sons stood at the town hall, bound in chains, surrounded by soldiers: soldiers in greatcoats with rifles over their shoulders. Itchele and

Yekl were there, with almost all their friends. There were only two who didn't belong: a Jew of about forty with a black beard and an intense expression on his face who had been arrested because he didn't let a soldier inspect the cupboard where his wife's jewelry was kept; and a peasant in a gray coat, with a very ordinary face and big innocent eyes, who had lingered in the tavern till rather late the previous night, and on his way home had indulged in some caroling. . . .

"Pavel," asked one of the locals when the guards had moved slightly apart, "How did you get into this?"

"My dear friend," said the peasant, helplessly, a sour look on his face, "I was enjoying a drink, at my very own expense too . . . and now even that's not allowed!"

Several dozen reinforcements came galloping up. Wagons, driven by peasant-coachmen, drew up behind them and the officer motioned for the youths to climb aboard. They crowded into the wagons. The horses, growing impatient, tossed their heads and pawed the ground until the wagons finally began to move, surrounded by a circle of soldiers on horseback.

As he rode into the main street, the officer in charge signalled to his men. Smartly, they slapped their hands against their scabbards and drew; the glare from their naked swords flashed like a bolt of lightning. The procession ambled through town, the shame-faced prisoners in the wagons and the horsemen swaying gently in the saddle. Everything was hammered shut. But for the thud of horses' hooves and the jangle of spurs the street seemed uncommonly still, silent as a tomb. A dreadful fear gripped the heart; what if the street should die, just so, behind its locked shutters, as they were passing through?

Not until they had crossed the bridge did the soldiers urge their steeds to a trot. Gray morning mist enveloped them as they receded into the countryside. From a distance it looked as though a wandering black smudge had set out to roam the wide gray world.

AT THE DEPOT

DAVID BERGELSON

INTRODUCTION TO AT THE DEPOT

DAVID BERGELSON'S early fiction offers the most fully sustained example of impressionism in modern Yiddish prose. His stories and novels, written between the abortive revolution of 1905 and the successful Bolshevik revolution twelve years later, convey a palpable sense of the tedium and stagnation, the oppressive hopelessness, of pre-revolutionary Russia. Social progress and personal advancement hover just beyond the reach of his characters and their native communities. The shtetl is in decline; its inhabitants are trapped by torpor and unable to pry themselves loose into the beckoning world outside. Like characters in the plays of Chekhov, they will still be longing for Moscow when the curtain falls.

At the Depot, 1909, Bergelson's first published novella, introduces the commercial society of grain dealers and brokers around a railway station in the Ukraine. The agents are classic examples of economic middlemen, buying up produce from large landowners and sharecroppers and arranging for its distribution in the distant urban centers. They are themselves caught in the middle between the shtetl and the city, between a traditional Jewish way of life with its ritual bath and cheder, and the possibilities of Russified assimilation, either through participation in the simmering political underground, or as part of the growing professional middle class.

The main character, Benish Rubinstein, is marginal to the

*already marginal depot society. Still bearing traces of his pampered,
bookish upbringing, he cannot reconcile himself to the competitive
hustle of his own entrepreneurial employment, and indulges vague
notions of escape—through a love affair, by becoming a village
tutor, in suicide. His female counterpart, Avromchik's wife, Clara,
also possesses the dubious advantage of a sensibility which alienates
her from the vulgar commercial atmosphere, while lacking the
corresponding will or ability to transcend it. The two young people
are drawn to one another because of their mutual dissatisfactions,
but their attachment is only transitory; it is characteristic of Bergelson's world that nothing is ever consummated except business tran-
sactions.*

Despite the novella's unfavorable depiction of the life of trade,
it is not quite the Marxist critique of the bourgeoisie that some
Soviet literary critics have claimed.* To be sure, the new "lingo" of
the revolution is in the air, but radical political ideologies are
heard—as they usually are in Bergelson's work—through a wall, and
their proponents are even less engaging of our sympathies than is
Rubinstein, the book's petit-bourgeois, anti-heroic protagonist. The
unseen figures who debate the abuses of capitalism in the home of
Moni Drel are as petty and self-centered as those debating the size
of the crop at the depot, and no less prey to the pervasive climate of
doom that snuffs out all hope and idealism.

For at the center of this short novel, as of the depot, stands the
somnolent station house, a reminder of the essential changelessness
of life despite the illusion of eventfulness. Incoming trains bring
promise of mystery and adventure; shifting seasons elicit eager
speculation; new arrivals at the depot create a stir of anticipatory
excitement. But in the image of the station house, which both
introduces and closes the book, is the spirit of stasis. The seasons,
the fortunes of the dealers, the comings and goings of trains, and all
events in the lives of the characters, recur in repetitive, predictable
patterns. Benish Rubinstein can never transcend the ineffectual
restlessness of his character, nor will the region ever escape its
"deep, eternal gloom."

In Bergelson's vision, the movement of life, hence of the plot
and often even of sentence structure, is not linear and progressive,

---

*A good exposition of this type can be found in I. Dobrushin's critical book *Dovid
Bergelson* (in Yiddish). The author emphasizes the specific relation of events in the
book to the rise of capitalism in Russia after 1905.

but circular and static. His many works of this period introduce a wide range of variations on a theme: there is Burman, the thirty-year old government rabbi of "In a Backwoods Town," who by the end of the first paragraph has grown "drowsy and indolent, has ceased writing to his only sister . . . and has let his blond mustache grow long and his chance to finish at the university go by forever." There are, among others, Joseph Shor, in the delicate story which bears his name, who tries vainly to find a refined big-city match for his provincial wealth; and Mirl Hurwitz, the moody heroine of Nokh Alemen—"After All Is Said and Done"—the title condemning its subject before she even comes on the scene. But the depot with its superficial bustle and allure remains Bergelson's most enduring symbol of illusory existential choice in a life which offers essentially only boredom and futility.

AT THE DEPOT BY DAVID BERGELSON

NARROW roads start their winding way in forsaken little towns of the countryside. Then cutting through sleepy villages, they creep up silent green hills, drop to the valleys, and join far off on a distant rise to bow before the red stone railway station.

The tall, two-storied building has been a regional landmark for years. Petrified and inert, it dominates the countryside like a spellbound sentry, cast by some prankster into everlasting, melancholy sleep. Whoever that sullen magician may have been, he has long since returned to dust, and his bones have grown black in the damp ground. But the station has yet to be released from its trance: somnolently it stands guard over the incoming roads, over the near and distant hills and valleys, and over the pretty village, scattered at the bottom of a long valley, that has spent years clambering up the slopes of two adjacent mountains without ever reaching the top. The old station shares in the silence of the village and countryside; secretly, though, as it stares into the blue, unknown distance, it yearns for a proud and forceful hero to come storming the sleepy hamlets and recall to life everything languishing and dead. But the horizon is imperturbable and glum, and so deeply bored by the sleepy countryside that it too begins to doze. Occasionally its toothless old mouth opens in a weary yawn, and out spits a long rushing passenger train. The train comes from far away and is eager to impart its good tidings to the station and the surrounding countryside. But after hearing the first mournful echo of its expansive merry whistle, it realizes that nothing will ever pierce this region's deep, eternal gloom. The train slows to a dispirited crawl, and comes to a stop with a long heavy sigh of steam. The sigh hangs suspended in the air like a verdict: "Useless, useless, and doomed."

As for the passengers inside one such train, they felt an inexplicable twinge of sadness and thrust their heads out the windows to examine the ancient, sleepy depot. The drabness and tedium were disheartening; no one felt the urge to say anything or stir from his seat. The people on the platform stood motionless, looking as glum and stony as the station itself. Some paced alongside the train, absorbed in fantasies about the brooding strangers aboard. The very unfamiliarity of these travellers, the mystery of where they came from and where they were going, of what they did for a living and what they were concerned with, won the silent respect of those on the platform, who tried in their turn to appear very fine and grand for the occasion. The station attendants drew themselves up to their full height; the porter standing at the bell thrust out his chest; the young salesmen cocked their heads, now this way, now that, in serious appraisal of one or another attractive female passenger. The grain dealers, absorbed in their business affairs, stood looking at the train while chewing at their beards. Further along the platform stood a swarthy little broker with a frightened face, beset by the uncertainties of his recent impoverishment. The strange, silent passengers reminded him of the money he had once had, though he could no longer remember where it had come from or where it had gone.

Sitting alone on a bench was a gray-haired old man, blind in one eye, who tapped his worn cane against the hard stone platform. Once this man had been a messenger entrusted to carry documents and mail from town to town; now, bored perhaps by the sameness of his surroundings, he would have liked to tell someone of his poverty, of his open, unseeing eye, his children in America, and his wife, dead these many long years. But no one took any notice of him. Gradually his mind had grown childish and now he amused himself with the dull thuds of his cane against the stone. When the game lost its charm, he raised his one good eye and saw Pinye Lisak. With the assumed air of a beggar, Pinye was silently appealing to a newly-arrived grain dealer, as if to say: "I am Pinye Lisak. Once I had money of my own, but now I'm reduced to brokerage . . . perhaps there is something you are interested in buying?"

The stranger ignored him, but Pinye's face remained distorted in an obsequious grimace, causing a good deal of merriment among the dealers once the train pulled away.

"As I am a Jew," swore Levi Pivniak, a tall broker with a noticeable stoop and bulging, mischievous eyes, "He looks like a pauper already."

The grain dealers, salesmen, and brokers who clustered around him, bared their tobacco-stained teeth in a hearty laugh that resounded solidly across the empty depot, inspiring in each of them a deep satisfaction in his own future. The only serious face in the place belonged to Pivniak, who stood calmly at the center of the group, arms folded, head at a confident tilt.

As the laughter subsided, the group was joined by Avromchik Kaufman, a thick-set business-like fellow with impressively broad shoulders. His hands folded behind his new jacket, he walked with his head jutting forward and a lazy, self-assured smile on his face as though letting the world know that it could save itself the trouble: no one would get the better of him.

The local dealers knew that Kaufman was wearing an expensive suit, that his father, a miser, was the richest man in the neighboring town, and that he was still single, a successful grain dealer with money of his own. So Avromchik enjoyed an easy familiarity with these men and smiled when they thumped him on the back. After hearing their quips about Lisak, whom he could observe across the length of the platform, he made a solemn suggestion of his own: "He still has that raccoon jacket of his. If he's willing, I'll pay him an even hundred for it and he'll be a rich man again."

They all enjoyed the joke. Pivniak's eyes flickered with mischief and then feigned surprise. "Do you really want that jacket? Watch me arrange the sale," he said, and pretended to rush off in Lisak's direction.

There was another part of the depot, free from the bustle of local dealers, where coachmen sat nodding atop their harnessed buggies, waiting with superhuman patience for their masters to arrive. Upon arrival, the master would climb into his waiting buggy, and pull the driver by the sleeve. The driver would snap to life and raise his whip over the horses. Soon the carriage would be swaying along, rocking the master to sleep. As the horses trotted amid the green fields, past an occasional hill or valley, the little bells around their necks tinkled monotonously; still half asleep, the master imagined the bells were telling the silent fields of all that he had seen on his travels. Then he forgot that he was on his way home, and dozed off again. In some distant town, nestled in a valley, stood a house with windows and doors and rooms eagerly awaiting his arrival. One of his children was running around barefoot, boasting of the gift he was soon to receive. But meanwhile, in the swaying buggy, the master was still fast asleep.

CHAPTER 1

Once, a warm spring day smiled down on the depot and its lethargic grain dealers as though asking brightly: shall I show you a trick? The depot pretended not to hear and went back to sleep. The dealers regarded the bright day as the harbinger of a plentiful harvest and were reluctant to begin trading prematurely. All around them the richly cultivated fields lay resting beneath tranquil skies. Here and there soft winds could be heard whispering confidentially to the grassy hillocks: everything will soon be plentiful and cheap.

In a green valley at the outskirts of a peaceful village, two dealers passed on the road. Drawing to a stop, they shouted questions at one another:

"Where are you coming from? The peasant farms?"

"And you? From the estates I'll bet."

"Where else? I wanted to look over the crops."

"Well?"

"Well what? . . . the guy is begging us to buy."

"Will he have many carloads to sell?"

"No question."

"How do you know?"

"Just look around you. . . ."

The two dealers looked around at the green fields on either side of the narrow road. The grain was busy growing. It swayed in slow and pious worship, repeating its fervent promise of a plentiful harvest . . . a plentiful harvest.

Yet in mid-spring, it suddenly stopped raining, and the grass began to wither. By the time the local dealers realized there was a drought on, dust had begun to gather on the grass and trees. Burning winds bore it through the air, dulling the light of the long hot summer days. The dealers were now sunburned and streaked with sweat, and feverishly busy. With the dust caking their faces and beards, and irritating their blood-shot, sleepless eyes, they bustled around the huge station grounds, arranging whatever sales they could, even if it meant snatching a customer from under someone else's nose. At brief intervals they appeared on the platform to load up, bargain, sell, and buy again to replenish their supply.

Every day the trains brought merchants from the big cities to negotiate with the sweaty, sun-streaked local dealers. Standing on the steps of the departing train they would shout their parting words: "Then it's settled? Tomorrow you'll ship it out!"

The local dealer's shouted reply was drowned out by the wheels of the long railway cars. He nodded his head to indicate, yes: it was settled. Long after the train had disappeared, chased by the wild gusts of wind and dust that darkened the air and sky, his mind was still on the sale. Someone, he felt, had been cheated, but whether him or that city merchant the dustclouds had just swallowed up, he couldn't tell. The other dealers surrounded him and pelted him with questions:

"Did you sell?"

"Really?"

"For how much?"

He was too preoccupied to understand the question. He answered as if out of a deep sleep: Eh?

When the dealers had bought up all the available crops of the area and shipped them to the various distant provinces, the station returned to its former calm. Once again the brokers walked around with time on their hands, time to discuss the unusual reversals and upsets.

Elye "the Merciful," a lanky, freethinking young man with a kind heart and two distinct voices—one manly and thick, the other high-pitched and thin—had netted about ten thousand rubles that summer. He came to the station with his own driver and his own team of horses and took his tea in the first-class lounge.

Shloymke Perl, a young fellow with a shady reputation, who until recently was wearing patched trousers and mooching cigarettes, now traded in the grand manner, buying and selling by the carload.

Then there was Chaim Mendl Margulies, a "big spender" who leased the estate of an absentee count and ran it for his own profit. A man with a delicate, aristocratic face, and aristocratic tastes to match, he had dropped vast sums of money and no one knew whether he had anything left in reserve. He still came to the depot in a new phaeton drawn by a flashy team of horses. He lived as lavishly as ever, and continued to conduct business with the nobility. But it was because of him that Chanina Shapira, a rich money-lender with a chronic cough, came as often as he did to the station, where he would stroll around, stroking his tangled yellow beard under the watchful smile of the dealers. On one occasion, when the depot crowd was in high spirits, Pivniak, who was sporting a new black overcoat, was delegated to approach the money-lender. Pivniak did as he was bidden; he stopped Chanina and asked whether he had not sworn out a complaint against Margulies before the local judge, and whether the case was not to be tried on the sixteenth of that very month. What was the story, eh?

Pivniak's shameless fabrication provoked hoots of laughter from the onlookers, but failed to disturb the slumbers of the tall red station. Chanina was on the point of answering, then thought better of it, and instead gave an audible snort. For want of something to do, he drew a crumpled scrap of paper slowly from his pocket, raised it to his wide, nearsighted eyes, and sniffed at it tentatively, as though it might have been dropped into his pocket, and were about to go off like a bomb.

Benish Rubinstein, a dark young man of medium height, with a narrow, overgrown forehead, deep black eyes, and a sharp, pointed nose, stood in the middle of the platform like a forgotten man. He was well educated, of a good family and of decidedly liberal views, and he had recently remarried, receiving a dowry for the second time. His second wife was a dumpy woman with a greenish complexion, the daughter of a wealthy parvenu. He, on the other hand, was a bit of a miser, with close-shaven cheeks and traces of studyhouse bookishness. He resented the fact that other dealers were earning a profit while he was eating up ready cash, and in his envy he chewed anxiously at his fingernails. From time to time Avromchik Kaufman strolled over casually to give him a playful slap over the shoulders. "Benish," he shouted into the other's glum face, "you're a lucky man."

Benish smiled back thinly, but his eyes glittered, and he was uncertain whether he ought to take offense or not. Before he could decide, Avromchik was already striding off, with his hands behind his jacket and his head jutting forward. He had made a lot of money that summer, and by adding to it the sizeable sum he had managed to squeeze out of his miserly father, he now was able to buy the reservoir near the depot. He gave the impression of having grown stronger; his face seemed more confident, and his smile, lazier. Whenever he ran into his old friend, Itsik-Borukh, at the depot, he grabbed him by both hands, shook him good-naturedly back and forth, and asked: "Tell me the truth, Itsik, does it pay to drive yourself?"

Years ago, when as children they had studied together in the same *cheder*, Itsik was forever playing tricks on Benish, smudging his face with dirt, or sticking a white paper to his back with the word IDIOT printed in large black lettering. Later Itsik had gone off to a big city to study on his own for the external university exams. He was still there when his younger brother was accepted into the university, and even later, when his father, a "Litvak,"* and one of the first dealers to sell on commission, had grown old. When his father died, he quit the big city and returned to the depot for his mother's sake. The station habitues treated the newcomer with respect. They were impressed by his aloofness and by his robust physique and long hair, which bespoke his former revolutionary activities in the distant city.

Shaking himself free from Avromchik's grip, Itsik whispered in his ear: "I feel sorry for you, Avromchik. How can anyone be so strong, so healthy, and so dumb!"

*A Litvak: a Lithuanian. In folk parlance, a cold rationalist, a man of sceptical bent.

Avromchik laughed tolerantly and rewarded him with another jovial slap on the back.

CHAPTER 2

It was during that summer that Avromchik built himself a home: its construction was as lazy and slow as the unctuous ruminations of his lazy brain. And yet, by the beginning of September, a handsome cottage stood near the reservoir at a slight distance from the depot, wearing its flat white roof with becoming modesty, gazing intently at all the passing vehicles as though the four long glass windows of its front wall were huge gaping eyes. Barefoot local peasant children, who tended their geese on the adjacent field, came over to peer through the open windows into the five empty rooms, all painted and wallpapered, and to listen for the echoes of the stones they furtively threw inside. Avromchik would sometimes stand on the handcarved, unfinished veranda, hands folded behind his jacket, nodding cheerfully at the passing salesmen and dealers. The dealers did not wish him well. Nevertheless, the veranda was eventually completed, and Avromchik celebrated with a bachelor's house-warming party which attracted many invited and uninvited guests from the neighboring town.

The guests, including a number of girls in shabby little hats, arrived in two large, tightly-packed carriages amid a great deal of shouting and merriment. But as they drew up to the new and empty house the girls felt suddenly embarrassed because their host was a bachelor and a complete stranger, and they remained seated in their places. Ashamed to go in, they giggled loudly and blushed, nudging one another in the ribs. Then they set out for the station grounds, where they strolled around arm in arm, still a little shyly, nibbling at cheap stale candy.

Among these girls was Avromchik's sister, a strapping girl of about seventeen, with the face and mannerisms of a boy. Her stride was masculine too, and she swung her long arms vigorously as she walked. It was as if someone, long ago, while she was still a child, had put the wrong clothes on her; sooner or later, when the mistake came to be rectified, she would undoubtedly cut off her long braid and don jacket and trousers, as was proper.

The sales agents hanging around the depot exchanged lewd and witty remarks as they appraised the unusual bevy of visitors; Benish Rubinstein, standing slightly apart from the others, fretted and bit his nails. He was annoyed that Avromchik had invited so many blushing young girls down to the station, and when he saw Itsik-Borukh, he asked him, as a like-minded ally, what did he make of all this? He liked speaking cryptically, in unfinished and therefore suggestive phrases.

"That girl over there has a pretty face." Itsik said, pointing to the one of his choice. After studying her a little longer, he added, "Pretty but dumb."

A young salesman, with a face red like a butcher's, tried to engage the girls in conversation, but succeeded only in embarrassing them and in setting them scurrying and giggling loudly in every direction.

"Well, Itsik?" Benish persisted. Receiving no answer, he continued to gaze expectantly at this newcomer from the strange and distant world of the city. Nothing seemed to bother the man. . . .

"You have some fine qualities", said Benish approvingly, adding as an afterthought, "You don't hate anyone, do you Itsik?"

Itsik glanced around and admitted to hating sour borscht, fools, and people who didn't know their own minds.

Rubinstein's close-shaven cheeks reddened meekly in protest: "Come now, Itsik."

But Itsik was already gone. And Benish suddenly felt altogether forsaken. He felt he was drowning in a sea of hatred; someone was choking him mercilessly from behind even as he sank, squeezing his throat a little tighter day by day. Exactly who was choking him he did not—he would never—know; one day, still ignorant, he would turn black and blue, extend a blue-black tongue, and give up his soul—a soul, he felt, as ugly and stupid as the body it had entered and inhabited.

He began chewing his nails ever more vigorously, and tried to regain his composure by computing in his head the money he still possessed. Unwelcome thoughts kept intruding, reminding him of the dealers who had prospered that summer, of Chaim Mendl Margulies who still owed him quite a large sum, and of his own useless meanderings about the depot, which accomplished nothing and seemed only to whittle away at his remaining cash supply. "It doesn't take much work to become a pauper," he smiled wryly to himself.

For a while, he continued to wander aimlessly around the station, then he made his way to the other side of the building where the agents and dealers were climbing back into their carriages for the return trip to their lodgings in the next town. Levi Pivniak leaned out of one of the larger carriages to shout:

"Well, Benish, let's go home to the wife."

But he made no move to go. His wife was a dumpy woman with a greenish complexion and a thick snub nose. Whenever she went to the pantry, she climbed on a stool, fell, and broke something. And with this sickly woman, who could never bear him any children, he had to spend the rest of his life, looking at her green face and snub nose, and watching her break the dishes and glassware.

The sun was setting. For a few final moments the huge red ball hung on the cloudy horizon, setting fire to the yellow leaves at the tips of the acacia trees. Then it slid down behind a bald mountain.

"Does Mr. Rubinstein intend to spend the night at the depot?" asked another voice from one of the carriages.

Benish didn't bother to reply. His eyes were on the little figure of Pinye Lisak skulking forlornly, in an oversized black coat, around the three rented carriages. Having no money for the fare, Pinye was ignored by the coachmen. Finally Elye "the Merciful" invited him into his carriage and sat him up front with the driver, a strong peasant lad with the black hands of a cobbler, who so resented the intrusion he began to poke Lisak and make threatening faces at him. Lisak made himself as small as possible on the seat, his face wearing an expression of mixed fright and gratitude.

The last carriage left the depot, crammed with passengers happy to be on their way home. Benish watched the driver beat the scrawny horses in an attempt to catch up with the earlier departures; the cool evening breeze chased after the carriage, sweeping its dust in the direction of the town.

A tall provincial officer with stiff military bearing emerged from the station house. The door banged shut behind him, resounding loudly, not as in a building with rooms and corridors, but like a hollow, empty barrel. At the sight of Rubinstein standing alone, absorbed in his thoughts, the officer felt he wanted to say something but on second thought decided that this might be undignified. Instead, he set out for home, holding himself proud and alert, as though he were being observed from the station and its tall swaying trees by the thousand piercing eyes of his superiors.

The sight of the distant carriages crawling one after another up the hill and over the cloudy horizon made Benish feel abandoned and forgotten. He could see, as vividly as if he were actually there, the town behind the horizon, the herd being driven home from the pasture through the long narrow street, the women sitting in the open doorways of their homes, waiting for their husbands to return, and complaining about the early autumn chill.

His own house stood at the bottom of the street, surrounded by a low fence, and it had a padlock on the door. Were he now to arrive, he would try the lock, peer through the closed window into the empty house, and then set out to look for his wife. He would find her at her father's house; she would greet him with perfect equanimity, her face as green as ever. But his mother-in-law would undoubtedly bounce up from her chair and say:

"Look who's here. It's Benish. Go, daughter, go home and make him some tea."

And they would take their leave.

Even farther beyond the same cloudy horizon lay another town with a main street that was wide and twisting, and there it was already night. Midway up that street stood his father's house, an old crooked structure with misshapen windows. In that house he had been born, and in the old studyhouse nearby he had spent his youth. At that very moment his father was probably sitting in the studyhouse, surrounded by deferential Jews who still remembered *his* father-in-law's impressive wealth. But he, Benish, stood alone in an empty depot, without a home, and with a lock on the perfectly silent and empty house that was his.

From that day on Benish did not return to town in the evenings, but rented a room from one of the local farmers which he called his "home." This was an act of spite against his sickly wife and another loathsome person, his snooty mother-in-law, who then had to take over his wife's support. But neither his wife nor his stingy mother-in-law took the trouble to inquire why he had stopped coming home. He was apparently so insignificant that his absence mattered no more than his presence. Their lack of interest made him all the more obstinate, and soon he even stopped writing letters.

The days at the depot crept by with steady monotony. In the early morning the grain dealers would arrive. As a result of the drought, there was nothing to do but make small talk with the brokers, or follow the progress of the long passenger trains as they entered and left the station. Benish avoided the other dealers as much as possible because of the loud delight they took in the losses he was sustaining and in the ugliness of his wife. They were all mean and unprincipled, they were all, except for him, earning money, and he hated them all heartily. Nevertheless, when the dealers left for home in the evening, the station seemed an emptier and gloomier place.

After they left, Benish drifted around the deserted station grounds, feeling hurt and abandoned. His thoughts were grim and unpleasant, no matter where they turned: to his empty house standing alone among the friendly homes of the cheerful town, or to the prospect of wandering around forever, silent, lonely, and sad. His presence, moreover, seemed to irritate the station attendants, who, passing the bench where he sat, would throw quick, angry glances as if to ask: why do you loiter here? Even the porter who swept up every night was beginning to find him bothersome: why else did he glare at him and sweep the dust right into his face? He resented this man who straggled about like a dog for no apparent reason after all the other merchants had gone home to their wives and children. As if the air itself were out to get him, the evenings turned cool and autumnal, and soft winds spread about a heavy gloom; the winds were not strong enough to sway the tall poplars that stood in two soldierly rows, upright and at attention, in the field opposite the station, but their leaves turned over and trembled in silent prayer.

Sometimes Avromchik Kaufman made a quick trip to the station to check if the last freight had brought his order of kerosene and lumber, and then he hurried back to the reservoir. In the evenings the lights of his house could be seen shining in the distance, and through the still, empty air, his elderly caretaker was heard absent-mindedly banging a stick against the wooden fence.

At the far edge of the station grounds Itsik-Borukh sometimes could be seen on his way to the pump, where he would try to find someone to go bathing with him. He was so powerful and stubborn that he still bathed regularly twice a day though the water in the lake was like ice and cut the body with knifelike cold. He sent all his earnings home to his mother, but he himself stayed at the depot, aloof from everyone, with an expression that never varied from Sabbath to weekday.

One evening Benish dropped in for a visit, and found Itsik lying on a low couch, staring up at the ceiling. Benish asked if Itsik was bored. Itsik replied no, but continued to stare at the ceiling. On that occasion Benish stayed for a few hours, and thereafter fell into the habit of visiting every evening. Most of the time Itsik merely stared at the ceiling without saying a word, as if he could see in its dark corners those great cities where he had spent his youth. Itsik's unconcern with the profits of the other grain dealers, and his equal unconcern with the heavy losses sustained by Benish, made it agreeable to be in his presence and even to speak freely while he kept silent.

Once, after lingering even longer than usual, Benish spent the night in Itsik's room. He took that opportunity to reveal his deepest confidences, but Itsik maintained his usual silence and looked as if he were pretending Benish was addressing someone else. The lamp, shaded by a red paper hood, cast a reddish glow over everything in the room, the air, the walls, the table with the perking samovar and the full glasses of tea, and over Itsik himself, lying in his usual position with his hands folded behind his head. It was pleasant to sit in the warm stillness, to hear the sounds of a piglet squealing in the dark corridor behind the door and of the landlord who was quarreling with his pretty young wife in the other half of the house. Yet despite the calm, Benish's heart ached and contracted in pain. He spoke in a low voice in a tone of muted complaint:

"Can't you understand, Itsik? They're saying: 'look at us and eat your heart out.' It's as simple as that."

Etched visibly into his face was resentment: against his wife, against the dealers who were making good profits, against life itself. His deep narrow eyes glittered, giving the impression of helplessness and pain. "Everywhere there are scoundrels like Avromchik Kaufman who smile and prosper."

But suddenly Itsik stretched his powerful body to its full length, and yawned aloud:

"Rubinstein, they say your first wife was beautiful and clever."

Rubinstein, his eyes glittering fiercely, wanted to respond that his present wife was ugly and stupid, but held his tongue.

The pretty young wife of the landlord came into the room. She pushed several chairs against the couch and with her round arms exposed, made up their bed for the night. Benish took off everything but his underwear and lay down next to the wall. Then Itsik turned out the lamp, stretched out beside him, and promptly fell asleep. The little pig was heard poking its way into a dark corner where it curled up and stopped its squealing.

Suddenly there was only silence and emptiness and between the side-curtains, the dark heavy September night peered in through the open window. The landlord, bundled up in his sheepskin, passed the window on his way to work; at a distance of at least three *viorsts*, he would spend the night as a lonely watchman. The lantern under his arm bobbed up and down like a gigantic fiery eye, now fading, now disappearing from view, but never extinguished. Benish's heart began to ache again, and his mind throbbed with memories of his departed wife, a very lovely, very gentle girl with soft and delicate feelings, who had somehow loved him, as dark and homely as he was, with his close-shaven cheeks and fingernails bitten to the bone. He must have loved her too. Otherwise he would not have fallen into a frenzy when she died, rushing into the street like a madman screaming "help" for two hours until every woman in the neighborhood came running. No one screams like that without cause, certainly not he, Benish Rubinstein. Yet in spite of this, he returned to his father's house shortly after she died, tore up the lovely photograph she had given him when they were engaged, shoved the pieces under a leaf of the dining room table, and remarried four months later, receiving a second dowry into the bargain. When he brought his second wife home to introduce her to his family, his mother, a decent and clever woman, welcomed her as a fine, respectable daughter-in-law; but his younger sister, an outspoken provincial girl with a mole under her nose, broke into loud sobbing and mourned as though over a corpse: "Some replacement you found!"

The replacement, who was in the adjoining room at the time and heard every word, did not even protest: a leaden, lifeless woman. Once, when the dining room table was being moved, the torn scraps of the photograph fell out. His wife picked them up and studied them. Her eye looked up gently and without reproach from one of the scraps. "Whose picture is this?" Though his face was aflame and his throat strangely parched, he felt obliged to answer. But his reply made not the slightest impression, and at that moment his resentment toward his wife grew stronger. He wished his sister were there to cry out as she had before: "What a replacement! What a replacement you found!"

Just as he began to doze off, a sudden rapping was heard at the window on the other side of the house. He shuddered and opened his eyes. The soft taps rained against the thin glass pane, which vibrated as if confessing a secret to the night air. Then came the sound of a door opening cautiously in the vestibule, a hushed whispering in the dark, and footsteps going out into the hall and then back again.

"There goes the ghost!" muttered Itsik from his sleep, shifting his weight and pressing Benish a little more tightly against the wall.

"Who is it?" he wanted to know.

"Avromchik. He's here every night. . . ." Even as he spoke Itsik fell asleep again; the sound of his strong regular breathing filled the room.

Benish was incredulous, and for a moment his face froze in a grimace of surprise. Later, when he realized it really was Avromchik there on the other side of the house with that pretty young wench whose bare round arms had so recently made up his bed, he began to brood resentfully over the other's good fortune: "A pig knows how to wallow in the pleasures of this life. No wonder he's so pleased with himself."

Assuring himself that it was not envy but merely annoyance that he felt, he lay there sleeplessly, chewing on his fingernails, and wondering why Avromchik should have this too, in addition to his money, his reservoir, and a new home with new furnishings.

Early the next morning he buttonholed Itsik at the depot and blurted out:

"You'll see: Avromchik will even find himself a pretty wife."

Itsik was slow to understand his meaning, but when he saw what Benish was getting at, he merely turned aside and spat.

CHAPTER 3

Pinye Lisak stole away from the depot, looking furtively behind him to see if anyone noticed his retreat. In any case, his presence was superfluous: no one spoke to him any more and he was afraid of them all. As might have been expected, it was some time before his absence was noted, and even then it provoked only mild surprise:

"Come to think of it, I haven't seen him for a while."

They were brought up to date by Levi Pivniak who said: "You want to know about Pinye Lisak? Why, he's begging from door to door." The man was a born meddler. Nothing escaped his prying eyes. In imparting the news, he even raised an astonished eyebrow, as if wondering how anyone could have remained ignorant of so common a fact. When his audience persisted in its disbelief, Pivniak folded his hands into his sleeves, bowed his head to his chest, and magisterially, without looking at anyone, summoned Nahum Piatke to appear at once.

A red-haired young man with a ruddy freckled face, one cheek swathed in a bandage, and pale, bloodless lips, came forth to bear witness: his own mother-in-law had seen Lisak in Odessa, making the rounds and passing himself off as one of the survivors of the Kalibelod fire.

His duty accomplished, Pivniak coughed for no apparent reason and strode away without looking back. Bewildered, the grain dealers smiled at one another quizzically, wondering what to make of the news. Before them rose an image of Lisak's swarthy, frightened face, drifting about some distant place, wincing at the sight of the scorched women who had to smear their bodies every day with mud: "Refugees of Kalibelod. Lost everything in the fire." The red-haired, freckled youth continued to stand there swearing to the truth of his report. It gave one an uncomfortable feeling.

One day several weeks later, after the trains had pulled out of the station and the crowd begun to disperse, the dealers noticed Lisak's wife, a heavy woman made even stouter by pregnancy, with smooth flaxen hair and an equally smooth, sallow face. She was standing with her face to the wall, crying soundlessly. The dealers kept their distance, but the sight of her trembling shoulders reminded them that not long ago, when she used to accompany Lisak to his tiny office to help with his business affairs, her hair had smelled of perfume. Moved by her plight, they decided to take up a collection. Elye "the Merciful" approached each of them in turn, smiling gently and pleading:

"You must shut your eyes and give blindly for a cause like this."

The dealers responded to his appeal. When it came to Benish, Pivniak interrupted long enough to mutter: "Give generously.

When your turn, God willing, comes along, we'll take up another collection for you."

The bystanders enjoyed the joke, but Benish took offense and his deepset eyes flashed angrily. What wrong had he ever done to this broad-boned hunchback? He turned on the dealers and pointing to Lisak's wife, accused them of bringing her husband to ruin: first they forced him into beggary, then they took up collections for him. His insulted eyes surveyed the dealers, finally focusing on Meir Hecht as if to ask: was this as it should be?

Hecht turned toward the sobbing woman. His head with its prominent nose and flaring nostrils was tilted upward as though someone were chucking him lovingly under his black, newly-sprouted beard, asking what he had learned that day in *cheder*. He had recently came to the depot from the province of Chernigov to buy up some bran. As he had little to do with the other dealers, he was dubbed "The Holidayer." The nickname may have been inspired by the fashionable black suit he always wore, or by his heavily inflected speech that was punctuated by leisurely pauses, a little like the study chant of a pious Jew on Sabbath, or by the festive tranquillity of his face, which was smooth as dark silk. This fellow Hecht was a strange creature. His delicate sensibilities were outraged by trade and those who conducted it, and yet he was a tradesman himself. He had a pretty little wife back home in the province of Chernigov. She wrote letters to say that she loved him, and he wrote back that the price of bran was holding its own.

Wrinkled, yellowing leaves fell from the trees. Turning a few somersaults on the way down, they glided gracefully back and forth through the air before coming to their final rest on the station platform, dejected and broken: was this, then, the end?

The answer came in the form of a whisking broom and the cold blast of an ominous evening wind. Swept up from one place to another, they tumbled to the far side of the tracks while other leaves, as wrinkled and yellowish as they, fell to the platform from the semi-naked trees. Mournful evenings descended upon the depot. No one admitted to fright, but everyone fled to the warmth of the bright warm cottages, leaving Benish Rubinstein alone in the cold.

Once inside, everyone calmly drank tea, smiled pleasantly at his host, bounced a child on his knee, made conversation, all to stave off the gloom on the other side of the bright windows. Thus was the gloom driven back to the station, and from there its bleak hegemony extended as far as the eye could see. The straight railroad track and tall telegraph poles stretched to the very edge of the horizon, eventually disappearing into darkness, but traces of gloom lingered in the long row of red lanterns that bobbed and bowed in the direction of the oncoming night. Long, heavy freight trains stood angrily in the station, then began to shunt slowly backward along the track; at the sound of a sleepy conductor's whistle, they jerked suddenly to a stop and resumed their brooding, stationary silence.

The sight of the freight cars bulging with goods filled Benish with envy of those whose pleasure they would serve. The cars were loaded with lumber for Avromchik and many other comfortable Avromchiks who lived near sleepy outlying depots: some people were apparently enjoying their lives.

Only two others remained on the empty platform. Israel Zazoly, a Jew from the country, was engrossed in friendly conversation with himself, in the course of which he cursed himself intermittently with a hearty, "pox on your father's house!" Not far from him the sole lingering student was engaged in a heated argument with the pretty salesgirl at the newspaper stand. He may have been explaining why he was hanging around the station so late, and why she ought to love him despite his snub nose, gangling height, and bulging glassy eyes. It was rather sad to hear.

Benish tried vainly to do a little reading. Time was when he could study for days on end, but now . . . whenever he tried to read he was beset by memories of his boyhood, and of his first wife who liked to nestle her head against his shoulder and close her eyes in contented silence. And all this led him inevitably to thoughts of his present wife, strange and sickly, and of his obese mother-in-law, whose affected voice he thought he heard right now: "Well, if it isn't Benish himself! Go on, daughter, go home and make him some tea." For spite, he resolved not to think about them, and he went to call on Meir Hecht who had also read and studied much at one time, but now smoked cigarettes and ruminated: life, he was fond of saying, was more interesting than any book. As he made this pronouncement his silky, insolent face would grow quite earnest and his eyes open very wide. Then he told a wonderful ancient tale of a man of the Church who had pointed to the natural surroundings saying, "These are my books."

During one such conversation, Benish suddenly thought of his own mean little life which had already made half a pauper out of him and would soon be the object of open scorn. He smiled bitterly: "And what about my own life, eh?" Meir Hecht's eyes widened with pleasure and deepened their glow. Nodding and puffing on a cigarette, he assured Benish with a chuckle that the same held true for his own life and everyone else's. Well, it was all very well for him, for Hecht, to say so. He was earning considerable sums of money, and he had a lively, attractive little wife. When she paid him a visit, she always smiled cheerfully up at him as they whiled away the time by playing hand-slap games. He would slap her small chubby hands so hard they tingled and she would run away shouting: "Go away! I hate you!" In the evenings as she walked beside him, she looked up proudly at his dark silk-smooth face, and told lovely, charming stories about the things that had happened back home in Chernigov. The men couldn't take their eyes off her. They exchanged envious, insinuating remarks:

"Sweet and petite. . . ."

"You said it!"

Avromchik now came to the station every day in his new suit. Once Pivniak teased him publicly by greeting him with the words, "Happy holiday to you, Reb Avromchik!" But rather than take offense, Avromchik only smiled lazily at Pivniak and motioned in the direction of Meir Hecht's wife. Pivniak's roguish eyes inquired whether Avromchik wanted one such for himself. At that point, Benish would have liked to tell Avromchik to his face that Hecht, who was a fine young man with many sterling qualities, deserved to have a fine wife, whereas a fat pig like himself. . . . But then remembering Avromchik's dumb luck, he began to bite his nails. It was now quite clear to him: the others would all live happily ever after, but his own house in the nearby town would remain locked, and his sickly wife would continue to write that she was well, yet unwell, that she had lately fallen off something or other, hurting herself badly and breaking the porcelain vase. And as for his business dealings, it was hopeless even to think about them!

The autumn dragged on. Short bleak days when no sun or sky was visible were followed by twenty-four hour rains that brought fresh black mudholes reminiscent of the dawn of creation. All this meant extra hardship for the coachmen who had to keep binding up the horses' tails and bundling themselves into thick wet greatcoats. They were afraid of the darkness as of death itself. "It's impossible to drive," they complained, whipping their horses forward, "one might as well be blind!"

At one point the dimly-lit and rain-soaked depot was smothered by a thick fog that severed it from the rest of the world. There were fewer people around now, and Benish felt terribly alone. Meir Hecht had gone away for a few weeks. Avromchik had found himself a pretty fiancée and was boasting of getting married on the Sabbath of Hanukah. As for Itsik, his life at the depot remained as solitary and mysterious as in the cities where he had once lived. During the day he busied himself at the depot and in the evenings he strode off with a thick walking stick in the direction of the scattered village in the nearby valley that was still clambering up the adjacent mountain slopes. Whom was he going to see? There were no Jews there except for Chaim Mendl Margulies, the man with the aristocratic face and bearing, who managed the count's estate and occupied the lovely, spacious manor house.

CHAPTER 4

One frosty and overcast evening Avromchik came in on one of the long passenger trains. The local dealers surrounded him with animated curiosity, some tugging him by the shoulders, others by the hands, everyone asking at once:

"Well, Avromchik, where is she?"

Pulled and pushed in every direction, Avromchik grasped the package he was carrying and shouted good-naturedly:

"Don't get so excited! Have patience. Wait a minute. . . ."

When they turned their heads, they all fell silent. A shapely girl of medium height was standing beside Avromchik with an expression that seemed to ask:

"You must be the grain dealers?"

She had an attractive dark face and clever black eyes that glowed with a dreamy, faraway look.

This was Avromchik's wife. The younger men blushed, and the older ones pinched each other behind their backs. Whether accidentally or not, one of the pinches found its way to Avromchik who almost screamed aloud, but was unable to determine whom he ought to repay for the favor. The men all had such serious, responsible faces, and such mischievous, twinkling eyes. Apparently, they were a little ill at ease.

Avromchik was therefore eager to show off his easy familiarity with her; taking his wife by the arm he led her away to their home near the reservoir. The dealers felt a sudden relief, and their roguish, merry eyes accompanied the departing couple down the road. As usual, Levi Pivniak was the first to break the mood of earnest self-restraint. Folding his hands inside the sleeves of his jacket, he pronounced her not quite beautiful, but certainly far from ugly.

"And what a pair of eyes!"

"And what a pair of. . . ."

Their minds were dizzied by the boldness of this, and the conversation grew flustered.

"Seems a little on the thin side, but. . . ."

"Isn't she something!"

"She sure is!" They were talking in broken phrases, with gestures and winks to supplement what could not be said.

"Just wait and see."

This insinuating prediction came from a tall, robust sales agent with a silly florid face and a long curling mustache. The silliness of his face was so well concealed by the black mustache that those seeing him for the first time were struck rather by his awesome height and robust good health. The many successful intrigues he had carried on during the course of his vapid life with women as healthy and silly as himself had made him quite confident and self-assured. Since Avromchik's pretty wife pleased him, he boasted that he would soon be on intimate terms with her. The dealers believed him, and were jealous already.

Within a few hours Avromchik was back at the depot. The dealers continued their teasing, but he was now at liberty to return every pinch and nudge in kind. In the darkness a very young man with soft down on his cheeks, coughed in embarrassment and an older "authority" declared loudly:

"These delicate women are not to my taste."

Everyone was suddenly laughing. Avromchik joined in their laughter as though the delicate and attractive female, the subject of all these remarks, were no more his concern than theirs, as though not he but some unknown stranger had brought her down to the depot and then disappeared with her. Someone gave him an approving thump on the back and soon, over the sound of back-slapping and the noise of departing trains the cry of "molodiets!" was heard, muffled at first, then repeated more loudly and resonantly.

It was at that moment that Benish recalled the comely wench to whom Avromchik had so recently paid his nocturnal visit. His eyes glittered fiercely: hadn't he predicted that this would happen? Someone beside him was shaking his head in wonder that Avromchik could have landed such a beauty, while someone else expressed astonishment that anyone should be surprised. In their excitement the grain dealers became very rowdy. There was much pushing and jostling and Avromchik was finally pulled into the bright second-class salon where a sour-faced Tartar stood behind a bar laden with bottles. As long as he stayed among them, Benish knew he would feel as coarse and mean as the others; but he had nowhere else to go. So he stayed, and heard first the lewd voice of Levi Pivniak, then a second voice estimating the cost of the long drunken night ahead and crying:

"The treat's on you, Avromchik!"

Later, the station was cold and deserted, except for one dark corner where some tipsy grain dealers were arguing among themselves about a sale to a local landowner. The wind carried their haggling voices into the cold night air:

"I hope your doctor's bills amount to at least half of what your meddling has cost me!"

The long row of lamps bore silent witness to the curse. The little flames bobbed and nodded slowly like so many tiny human heads giving testimony to an unseen stranger: "We heard. We heard."

A figure detached itself from the group in the corner, hunched its shoulders like a beggar, and extended a hand for charity. Even as he turned aside, refusing to give, Benish heard the man's nasty and persistent voice mocking him:

"Give or don't give, it's all the same. You'll be a pauper anyhow."

Benish slowly walked away from the depot, chewing on his fingernails. Terrifying thoughts assaulted him: he would soon be a pauper, a miserable beggar like Pinye Lisak. The crowd at the depot would make fun of him, as they did of Lisak, and he would not even be there to hear it. Lonely and crazed with resentment, he would rot in some faraway place while the ancient red station house stared as frigidly as ever at the approaching and departing trains, at the enterprising and cheerful dealers.

The night grew heavier. An intense blackness filled the chilly air, hiding the cloudy skies and smothering the houses, trees, and railroad tracks. Somewhere in the dark a locomotive gave a tentative whistle that broke off in the middle and expired in a hoarse and heavy sigh. Caught by the wind, the sigh was carried to the small grove of trees on the south side of the depot where it disturbed the nocturnal stillness of the sleeping naked trees. For a moment the grove stirred awake, cast a reluctant eye into the depth of the blackness, and then fell back into so sound a slumber that nothing, not even the submissive bending of the staunch naked trees, could disturb its rest.

Rubinstein walked homeward, deep in thought, yet painfully conscious of his own self. This was he, Benish Rubinstein, whose fortune, like his life, was in steady decline, who had not been home, or seen his wife, or spoken to her, in three months.

Behind him in the dark, the great station bell swung back and forth, battling the wind. Its slow, even peals announced the coming of a train that was even now slicing its way across the night in their direction. Two conductors, muffled up against the cold, emerged from the darkness with flickering reddish-green lanterns in their hands. The passage of these two bulging figures intruded briefly on the darkness, which soon closed behind them and became even more intense, as if pleased to reassert its rule. The darkened houses near the depot stood like gravestones in a long mournful row, eager to share the easy, peaceful sleep of their hard-working owners, but kept awake by the blustering wind.

Benish felt very lonely by himself. In the darkness to his left, where there was only the reservoir, he saw Avromchik's bright little house standing alone in the cold black night that stretched endlessly across a frozen expanse of fields and valleys and naked mountains.

Rubinstein was attracted to the house. It was a pretty little place. A thin strip of light escaped through the outer shutters of the first three windows, but the shutters of the furthest two had been left open, and inside them it was dark. All at once the night was startled by a light, and he saw Avromchik's wife standing in the doorway to the bedroom with a candle in her hand. From inside the room the twin beds, twin dressers, and twin night tables stared back at her sullenly. Her slender figure began moving forward, but something startled her and she hastily withdrew. The candle fell from her hand and was extinguished, plunging the room back into darkness.

Benish felt the pounding of his own heart: should he go in? He was ashamed at the thought, until he reminded himself that she had just suffered a fright. Perhaps she had imagined a hideous intruder standing between the beds. Or perhaps the beds themselves frightened her. . . .

Before he could make up his mind what to do, the room became bright again. She was back in the doorway with a candle in her hand as before, looking fearfully into the heart of the room.

Benish thought to himself that Avromchik would soon come home and grin at his wife with the same smug and lazy smile he had lavished on the pretty farmwife with the bare round arms.

Benish was drawn back to the house night after night. The evenings were dark and cold and reeked of loneliness, and the wind howled over the dormant houses at the depot. It was hard to understand why he braved the darkness on such bitter nights or what he hoped to find. But having nowhere else to go, he would prowl around, wondering whether that fat pig, Avromchik, realized how well off he was.

Whenever Avromchik stayed late at the depot and the shutters of his house remained open, Benish could look inside and see the lovely slender female figure with the deep black eyes, smiling occasionally at the maid. Meanwhile Avromchik played cards at the depot with the other grain dealers and bought an occasional whiskey from the sour-faced Tartar. Whenever he ran into Benish he pulled him by the hand—"Come on, Benish, what are you worried about?"—and then nudged him playfully in the ribs. Benish simmered resentfully: why should Avromchik have it all?

On one particular evening, he walked over to the depot and downed several bottles of beer in quick succession. He was a poor drinker; beer alone was enough to make his head spin and his mind churn with greater hatred than usual toward Avromchik and the other dealers. He looked up at the Tartar who was pouring beer into his glass, and asked:

"I guess the dealers are playing cards, eh?"

The Tartar leaned toward him across the bar as though reporting the outcome of an important mission: "Yes, they're in the men's lounge."

This thick-headed bartender was apparently under the impression that he, Benish Rubinstein, wanted to join the card game in the lounge. Benish hastily downed the full glass that had been put in front of him and explained that business was very bad these days: the dealers couldn't cheat one another in trade, so they were reduced to cheating each other at cards. The formulation so delighted him that he smiled at the Tartar and tried to develop it further: a dealer isn't alive unless he's cheating someone. Now, in his own experience, for example. . . .

But the Tartar understood nothing of what he was saying, and Benish began to regret his words. He looked straight into the man's swarthy face and saw that his eyes had an ominous flicker, and his lower lip kept falling open and shut.

"Never mind." He dismissed him with a wave of the hand and left the building. A wave of cold air suddenly enveloped him. He walked along, tipsy from the successive beers. Sad thoughts and hopeful ones were tangled in his mind, and his mood was now gay, now gloomy: Things were not going very well for him . . . but at least he was not like the others, like Shloymke Perl, and Elye "the Merciful," and Avromchik Kaufman, who sat in the men's lounge cheating one another at cards . . . Benish Rubinstein could not cheat, so he would have to do something else. He had to make a living somehow. Maybe he could become a tutor in a village somewhere. . . .

Half giggling and half in tears, he concluded that everything was actually for the best. Pivniak and his mother-in-law and even his wife Frumke would be satisfied by his decision.

By this time he had reached Avromchik's house and was again pacing back and forth, stopping to peer through the window. What was he, a village tutor, doing there? Clara was inside—so he had heard her referred to at the depot—she was sitting at the table facing the window, absorbed in something. It was cozy and peaceful inside. Outside where he stood, the icy wind whistled and blew against his back and shoulders. Tears sprang up in his eyes, perhaps from staring for so long from the intense darkness outside at her calm illumined face within. He saw her rise to turn down the lamp. Her dark and earnest face was so very familiar and dear. It seemed to him that he had known that dark face for a very long time, those serious and clever black eyes, the delicate slender body. He had known her forever, from his earliest childhood. . . .

He was shivering with cold. Why should he, the village tutor, with the closely shaven cheeks and narrow sunken eyes, stand outside in the biting cold, shivering in his skin, while inside where she sat it was so cozy and warm, so clean and homey? And she was lonely by herself. Why not drop in after all? He could always think of a suitable excuse. . . .

Standing on the smooth stone steps, with his hand pressed against the bell, he was suddenly struck by the thought that Avromchik might be home. Even as he rang he was frightened and regretted his action: he had done a foolish thing.

The door was opened by the squat peasant girl whose hair, he noticed, was disheveled and whose feet were bare. Almost sober by this time, he decided that he must ask for Avromchik, and then immediately take his leave. But before he could carry out this resolution, the familiar pretty face appeared in the doorway, with the clever black eyes trained on him. He grew tongue-tied, and felt himself blush. A confusion of thoughts tumbled through his mind as he looked into her dark, earnest face.

"Come in and sit down," she said.

He sat opposite her at the table feeling that his smile was surely gratuitous, and afraid he had completely forgotten his reasons for coming here. When she asked if he had come to see Avromchik, the smile suffused his entire face. Though he had made a determined effort not to spread his hands over the table, there they suddenly appeared. He blushed and stammered:

"Avromchik? No. Actually, no."

He immediately sensed how foolish and unnecessary the word

"actually" was, and in an effort to improve matters he tried to explain that he just happened to be passing by . . . that he just dropped in . . . that he was a grain dealer. . . .

The more he spoke, the more confused he became. His face was crimson and his throat was parched. Meanwhile she sat opposite him leaning her head on her hands like a tired child:

"Are there many dealers at the depot?" she wanted to know.

Her soft, unhurried voice reminded him of something important and brought him back to his senses. He began to explain that he himself was one of the dealers, but all at once he broke off in fear: by tomorrow he would be the laughingstock of the depot. Some loudmouth or other would regale all the dealers, agents, and brokers with the story of how Benish Rubinstein was making overtures to Avromchik's wife.

"Not everyone has an easy life," he sighed.

At these words he saw her head shoot up and her eyes look fearfully into his face:

"Tell me! You must tell me! What is it like here around the depot?"

He responded to the plea in her dark face, and forgetting that he was seeing her for the first time, poured out his aggrieved and heavy heart:

"Some people have a harder life than others, and what's most important is that some people don't even understand the meaning of their lives."

He was thinking of Avromchik and Pivniak and the florid sales agent with the curled mustache and of all those who were playing cards in the men's lounge.

"What is it like, you ask? We live here like pigs, or if you prefer, like dogs. . . ."

He smiled unexpectedly, but whether in bitter regret for the life he had been describing or because someone had just rung the doorbell, it was hard to determine.

Sitting opposite her again the following evening he felt quite comfortable and at ease. He complained about the depot, the dealers, and the life of trade.

"Dealers are a special breed, an ugly breed . . . first they choke a body to death, then they feel sorry for him." They had begun to put the squeeze on him, for example, and he was already

half dead. Since he was incapable of swindling others, he himself
was being swindled.

The interest that showed in her face filled him with a strange
sense of pleasure, and he stayed late into the night.

She had asked him, he began, about life at the depot: well, it
was a wretched and stupid life. His own life was no different from
the others: plodding through the muck, day after day, without
rhyme or reason. Were she, for instance, to try interrupting a
merchant in the middle of his affairs he would tear himself loose
from her and go right back to what he was doing. As for her, well of
course, he didn't know her very well and was only seeing her now
for the third time, but he knew her well enough to understand that
she ought never to have come to the depot. She had no place
among people who thought less of their lives than they did of their
money. By this time she had probably come to realize this
herself. . . .

He sensed that it wouldn't do for Avromchik to discover him
there again, and rose to his feet. He was going "home," he said, to
his present lodgings, a small rented room in a local farmhouse.
Sometimes, unable to fall asleep, he lay awake thinking of the
senseless life that grain dealers led. He tried to think of a way of
escaping the dealers, and of escaping himself. And he had a wife, he
continued, in one of the neighboring towns, a dumpy woman with
strange ailments and a green complexion. Although he hadn't been
home or written to her in three months, she didn't seem to mind,
not in the slightest. . . .

Walking slowly back to his lodgings, he no longer felt concerned with the depot or the dealers, or with being discovered by
Avromchik, or even with the attentions of Avromchik's pretty and
earnest wife. He became a part of the thick darkness surrounding
him, and returned to an unpleasant thought: he hadn't been home
or written to her in three months, but she didn't seem to mind, not
in the slightest.

CHAPTER 5

One day Elye "the Merciful" told Benish in his high-pitched womanly voice that his mother-in-law had stopped him in town to ask

how much the local dealers were earning and whether Benish was making a living. She felt that she certainly had a right to know.

Her shrewd and meticulous inquiry into his affairs seemed to carry with it the message that he was quite welcome to stay where he was. Yet Benish was obliged to smile politely and to thank Elye for the greetings from his mother-in-law. And what if she were a loathsome creature, pretending ignorance of his impending ruin, and asking innocently if her son-in-law was making a living? She could go to the devil, with the dealers and the profits in her wake. If he wanted to, he could throw up the whole thing and become a village tutor.

All the same, he wandered around absentmindedly for several hours, chewing his nails. Later, for lack of anything to do, he dropped in on Itsik-Borukh and watched him carving wood to make a child's wooden sled. He was struck by the care and devotion of Itsik's work, the way he stopped every few minutes to wipe the sweat from his brow, and then returned to his chopping and carving. He was also thinking about himself, and suddenly went over to Itsik to tap him lightly on the shoulder and ask: did Itsik think he could earn twenty rubles a month as a village tutor?

Itsik lodged his hatchet in the wood, and looked at him with such warm affection that tears sprang to Benish's eyes. He was drawn to this powerful and reserved young fellow, who was already bending over the wood again, chopping away. Benish wondered what possible need he could have of a child's sled, but there was no point in asking.

Some time later, on an overcast and frosty Saturday afternoon, as he was passing the frozen lake where the pump stood, he saw Itsik harnessed to the sled, pulling Chaim Mendl Margulies's nineteen-year-old daughter across the ice. It was a very odd sight.

At the depot they were saying that Margulies's daughter was in love with Itsik, and that she was the reason for his nightly visits to the nearby village. But there was still something unusual and baffling about the whole affair, and the dealers scratched themselves behind the ear as they wondered out loud: could it really be as simple as that?

As for Chaim Mendl Margulies, he of the aristocratic face and stately manners, he was so absorbed in his important financial speculations and his discussions with the magnates who passed through the station, he didn't even notice Itsik's presence.

From then on, Benish began to observe Itsik closely, and certain thoughts kept recurring to him: Itsik was a healthy and good-looking young man, without any problems whatsoever. He lived in a marvellous private world of his own, where no grain dealers ever intruded; he loved life with singular passion and had no use for money. It was therefore natural that the dealers should respect him, and that Margulies's daughter, with the curly blond hair and crinkling skyblue eyes, should dote on him and gaze at him with such fierce pleasure and passion and delight.

But he, Benish, had a small face with closely trimmed black cheeks, a pointed nose, and beady black eyes that glittered even in the distance. Try as they might, his eyes could never cry, but smiled back whenever anyone smiled at them. Moreover, he was a little man, and he persisted in doing foolish things such as tying himself down to an ugly, sickly wife so that people might have something to laugh at, and he had reduced himself to loitering aimlessly around the depot, earning nothing but the sarcasm of his mother-in-law who wondered whether or not he was making a living. And where would it all end?

He waited until Avromchik was immersed in a card game with the dealers, and then set out toward the reservoir. There was surely no point to his going! If it was merely to see Clara, why should he? Would it net him any profit? Yet his gloom was so heavy that he felt he had to talk to someone, and at the depot there was no one, except for Itsik who was pulling Margulies's daughter around on his home-made sled somewhere on the lake, and the card-playing grain dealers who mocked him for wandering around, living off his ready cash and despising his ugly and sickly wife. And recently Clara had stopped during her walk to ask whether he would not drop in sometime to see her. She had seemed frightened, and added: "It's so lonely around here!"

So he accepted the invitation, and sitting opposite her now at the table, slowly sipping his tea, he spoke in the weak tones of a helpless sinner. Would she please forgive him, he began, if he spoke a little too freely the previous time. She probably realized that it was hard to keep everything to oneself. Sometimes one said a little more than was called for. . . .

Her friendly glance, and the attentiveness with which she listened to his every word, aroused in him a nagging envy of her smug, self-satisfied husband, who took everything in life as it came,

with that never-changing, lazy smile forever on his lips. She ought
to be told the truth!

He did not, he went on, want to offend her. It was enough that
his own wife and mother-in-law found him offensive. He was an
object of dislike and derision to the dealers and agents at the depot,
and he wanted her, at least, to think kindly of him. . . . Yet he had
to admit that there was a time when people loved him, though it was
a long time ago to be sure. The teacher's eyes that glared so fiercely
at the other children had smiled benignly at him, had winked in
affectionate gratitude at his thorough and proper grasp of the rabbi's
teaching. And elderly, gray-bearded Jews with radiant faces had
rejoiced in him as in an equal. . . . Even Moishe Aaron "the
Grandchild," a querulous, unkempt, consumptive old man, who
had spitefully driven his own wife and children from his home, who
believed in nothing and spoke to no one, had once confided to him
alone how profound and intense was his loathing for his fellow
man. . . . And even somewhat later, when he was grown up, and
was visiting his first fiancee. . . . Well, no matter. Since it was
probably of no great interest to her, he needn't speak of it.

She flushed slightly. Why, she wanted to know, should Benish
think it of no interest to her? She understood him perfectly and even
shared some of his feelings. In fact, though there was probably no
use admitting it, she had been thinking of him that very evening,
and also the previous evening. . . . It was very gloomy sitting alone
at home, listening to the soft, slow ticking of the clock and to the
wind rattling the outside shutters. . . . But that wasn't what she
had started to say. . . . He had gone through such a lot in his life.
What? Was he leaving already? Why the hurry? The evenings were
so bleak and long, and so depressing, and he came so rarely. It was
surely cozier here than back in his rented room. But perhaps he felt
uncomfortable with her. . . . He was free to admit it, it didn't
matter.

Maybe he could tell her before he went, she said, where
Avromchik disappeared to night after night. Was he really at the
depot? Was he playing cards, as they said? Benish ought to know if
anyone did. And if he were not in such a hurry, there was another
important subject she would have liked to discuss with him
. . . but he would surely drop in again soon and it would wait till
then. Good night, good night.

He walked home with his head lowered, pondering the difference between his own wife, Frumke, the clumsy eccentric with the greenish complexion who took no interest in anything except breaking dishes and glassware, and Avromchik's wife, Clara, with those clever eyes and . . . so much else besides. They said at the depot that she even had brought Avromchik a sizable dowry.

If only he had such a wife, he would be sitting with her in a cozy room, with the storm winds tearing angrily at the shutters, telling her about the time long ago when in just such a storm, while he was on his way home from *cheder* by way of the narrow synagogue lane, he had heard someone in the darkened women's section banging slowly against the pane. He would tell her how for a three-penny dare he had once spent the night alone in the cemetery . . . he would not, in any case, be worrying about money.

CHAPTER 6

Hard-packed snows with scattered patches of dirt covered the frozen ground and hid it from view. Snow lay upon the hills and fields and lonely valleys where a solitary sleigh sometimes passed, leaving behind in the air the tremulous echoes of its old copper bell. A hoary mist settled over the region and over the icy trees that like elderly folk bent their heavy backs down to the ground.

Benish sat bundled up in the recesses of the sleigh, watching the blue puffs of steam that issued from the mouth of the driver, who had turned around to face him. Disjointed words flew out of the driver's mouth, froze in the air and then evaporated.

"Moni Drel . . . no fool . . . bankrupt just a year ago . . . built himself a new home . . . opposite the post office in Setrenitz . . . property . . . manager at the sugar factory . . . leased the mill from the count . . . no fool, as I am a Jew . . . giddyup!"

This very same Moni Drel was the object of his visit. The previous year Benish had returned Moni's promissory notes for eight hundred rubles at 20% of their value, and now that he was the one in trouble and Moni was doing so well, he hoped to receive a little help. Admittedly, Moni was not famed for his generosity. It was probably useless to complain to him now, but perhaps there was a slim chance after all. If only the driver, Shloyme the Lip, would keep his secret at the depot.

The sleighbells tinkled monotonously, telling the long sad story of a distant corner of the world where everlasting winter reigned, and great snow mountains slumbered eternally under blankets of fog and cloud. From time to time, creatures muffled up in thick winter clothing passed them on the path, like sleepwalkers oblivious to the white rust that had formed on their beards. The driver shouted at them to look out, but the sounds of his voice froze long before reaching their ears and hung suspended right under his nose. Far off on the horizon along the slope of a broad mountain, the signs of "greater Setrenitz" began to appear: first, a tall upright brick chimney, piercing the fog; then the sharp steeple of a solitary brooding church, then the telegraph poles, and finally an ample spread of low, snow-white rooftops.

Moni Drel's daughter, a girl of about eighteen, greeted him in the dim entrance hall. Her father was in the sugar factory, she said. He would probably go on from there to the mill and would not be home until evening.

He was about to reply that waiting was actually inconvenient, but that since he was already there. . . . Instead, a self-deprecating "Oh well" escaped from his lips, accompanied by a meek little smile. He was instantly ashamed of himself, and blushed.

The girl repeated her message: her father was not expected before evening. He could wait in there if he wished to. She opened the door to an adjoining room, and promptly disappeared.

Had Itsik-Borukh come in his stead, he brooded, the girl would not have scurried off so quickly, nor looked at him as if to say: well, hurry up, don't complain, just make up your mind—staying or leaving?

He sat down and looked around him. The study was nicely furnished. There was a penholder with a marble poodle wagging its tail in the air. Paintings in thick gilded frames hung on the walls. It might all have been bought with his money, who could be sure? Yet there he sat gingerly among these strange objects, afraid to touch them. The house itself, or a considerable part of it, was probably built with his money, yet he didn't even dare lean against the desk or relax on the sofa with his feet up on the cushions.

Voices could be heard in the adjoining room, rising now and then in argument. Girls were engaged in what sounded like an intelligent debate. At one point a girl with a very gentle voice was silenced by a thick male voice:

"Your father, for example, runs a shop. Let's say that he charges ten cents for every yard of cloth that he sells. Since he himself does not produce the cloth, the ten cents properly belong to the worker. In other words, he is living at the worker's expense."

Drel's eighteen-year-old daughter chimed in with her support: "Right! Exactly!"

On tiptoe he crept toward the door of the adjoining room and pressed his ear to the wood. The male voice was speaking again, its easy flow soothing the excited girlish hearts:

"I'll give you an example. . . ."

Perhaps he was a bachelor, a teacher with a high forehead balding at both corners, an intellectual who avoided looking directly at females, but had a habit of flattening his glasses back against his nose. Perhaps Drel's daughter looked up to this man, perhaps she even loved him despite his receding hairline and the two red ridges etched by his glasses over his studious nose, and perhaps that was why she exclaimed each time he would finish speaking:

"Right! Exactly!"

But he was annoyed with the girl. He chewed his nails and smiled sarcastically thinking about her and her father:

"The devil take them! First they cheat and stuff their pockets with someone else's goods, then they sit in comfortable, decorated rooms, looking up fondly at a gentleman-friend, and preaching morality: 'You don't work, yet you live. That's proof that you're living at someone else's expense.'"

The young man was still speaking: "That's what we mean by capitalist, do you understand?"

He was suddenly reminded of a young agent at the depot who had picked up some of the new lingo and asked Avromchik where capital originated. Avromchik gaped as though at a madman, but Pivniak shrugged his shoulders and answered on his behalf:

"What kind of a question is that, you fool? When you get your dowry, then you have your capital."

And yet, where did capital originate? If the fellow behind the door knew, Benish certainly should know. He had the better mind, and besides, he had once had some capital of his own, though he had it no longer.

In the evening, Moni Drel came home. His children ran to greet him crying: "Daddy, someone's waiting for you in the study."

Then someone brought in a lamp, set it down on the desk, and closed the door again.

People were drinking tea in the dining room, and spoons were heard clinking. Surely Moni Drel didn't have to keep him waiting so long. He might have come in to say hello. But then it was Moni Drel's custom to do incomprehensible things, each of which made very good sense in its way: though his hearing was perfect, he would speak very softly, pretend to deafness in one ear, and incline his head toward the person addressing him to inquire, "Eh?"

He finally came into the study to ask what it was that Benish wanted. His short stiff beard looked as if it had just been attached to his chin and from his expression one would have thought he was seeing Benish for the very first time. Benish blushed, and stammered out an introduction:

"You see, last year . . . last year. . . ."

It was such a waste of effort to sit across from that bloodsucker. And it was so difficult to find the right words. Drel regarded him with perfect composure and inclined his supposedly damaged ear to ask, "Eh?"

He explained about his losses: he was failing and sinking into ruin. Since there were really about 700 rubles owing to him he wondered if Drel could . . . there was no way he could take the money by force, but he begged of Drel. . . .

Drel listened attentively as though it were possibly someone else and not he who owed Benish the money. Nevertheless, he would give him a sympathetic hearing and try to suggest some means whereby Benish could recover his money.

"Mr. Rubinstein," he explained softly and patiently, "you are an intelligent young man. You can appreciate even without being told that having grown accustomed to it, I now have to maintain a decent standard of living. My wife travels abroad once a year: she suffers—may you be spared—from a liver ailment. My two sons board in a large city: they cost me at least a hundred and fifty rubles a month between them. For the other children I have to employ a resident tutor who costs me eighty rubles a month plus room and board. Then I have to clothe the children and myself. A man has to keep up appearances in this world. Take my own situation: since I come into contact with people all the time and depend on these contacts for my livelihood, I have to make a decent impression when I show myself.

"Hear me out, Mr. Rubinstein. If there is anything left after expenses, I will repay you before any of the others. I may not be able to pay off all my debts, but yours. . . ."

They were interrupted by the loud shouting of Shloyme the Lip who stood in the outer hall:

"That good-for-nothing! How long is he going to warm the bench? I've been sitting out there all day for his lousy ruble! . . ."

Benish was left with a final hope—that Shloyme the Lip would keep this to himself at the depot.

CHAPTER 7

There was an incident: he and Shloymke Perl made a deposit on a load of scorched corn. The corn netted them a large profit, but Shloymke claimed that Benish had not contributed his share on time and refused to divide the money. After eight consecutive days of litigation in one of the neighboring towns, he came away with about four hundred rubles. This was the first profit he had seen all winter.

On the return trip he smiled happily to himself and decided that people were not so bad after all. He even neglected to bite his nails.

By the time he was back in his own bed that evening he had plans for earning enough to build a house like Avromchik's near the depot. Throughout the night, a strange dream kept weaving in and out of his sleep: he and Avromchik's wife seemed to be on their way home to his father's house for Passover. He took her for a walk through his native town, pointing out the prayer house where he had studied . . . the home of a rich atheist with a huge library who had lent him books to read . . . the valley where during the holidays he used to lie on the grass beside the abandoned mill, looking up at the endless skies. . . .

When he awoke early the next morning, his landlady was
stoking the fire in his room. She told him that Avromchik's wife had
been there on Sunday to ask about renting the garden for the
summer. She had been inside the house too, asking who occupied
this room.

He passed the day idling around the depot, and in the evening
made his way toward the reservoir. He waited until it was quite dark
before nearing the house to peer in through the bright dining room
windows. There were several agents and dealers playing cards
around the table, and he was not entirely pleased to see Avromchik's
wife, at the far end, smiling at the florid sales agent with the curling
mustache. Perhaps she preferred the sight of that handsome agent
to his own scrawny face?

A half hour later, back in his cramped and dingy quarters, he
ran his hands over his pointed nose and closely shaven cheeks and
decided that it was obviously so.

He stopped going to see her and spent his time pacing the station
grounds. He regretted the many wasted evenings, the mooning
around the reservoir, and now decided to turn his mind to other
matters like the four hundred rubles he had recently earned.

And yet one evening he found himself back near the reservoir.
Without making a sound, he stole into the dim entrance hall of
Avromchik's house and stood there for several minutes unobserved
by anyone. Through the open door he caught sight of the curled
mustache that belonged to the handsome agent and, still unnoticed,
made his way back outside again.

Some time later on a very cold and damp day, he noticed her at
the depot, and caught a quick glimpse of her lovely, dark face from
the distance. Dressed stylishly in a short winter coat, she drew
approving stares from the two telegraph operators who ogled her
through the window. Benish turned aside and deliberately began a
conversation with Elye "the Merciful," for no other reason than to
spite the young woman standing somewhere behind his turned
back.

The cold damp south wind splattered mud over the clean
snowdrifts, the trees, fields, and encircling hills. Patches of dirt
peered up at the overcast skies asking mutely: would you kindly
cover us again with that pure white blanket of snow?

But the skies were mute themselves, and it remained for the open wind to snatch up the raspings of vagrant crows and offer these by way of an answer. Melting snows left the station grounds splattered and dirty. The wind rattled the glass of the unlit lamps, spreading a strange sense of desolation over the depot. From time to time someone passed by, with his head lowered against the wind that tugged mischievously at his coattails.

Soft and gentle words poured steadily from Elye's mouth: a certain landowner had sold his crop of oats at a very good price, and Benish could probably buy it now for even less. In his delicate, good-natured way, Elye was trying to render this kindly little service.

But Benish, who was only conscious of her presence somewhere in back of him, and of the two telegraph operators leering at her through the window, was not even listening.

A wet, smoke-smudged passenger train pulled into the station for a five-minute stopover. The wind blew at the windows in playful gusts, bent on some cheerful mischief. But the coaches remained perfectly still, with an air of angry brooding, and no one quit or boarded the train. It was as if each coach held a corpse whose disconsolate relatives were escorting it to some distant burial.

At the rear of the train, where she was strolling around, a young student finally came out on the platform of the coach and stood with his mournful eyes glued to her dark and lovely face. She returned his glances from time to time. Benish wondered whether he ought to go over and speak to her after all.

Then the train pulled out and slithered away rapidly until it disappeared into the tinny, low-lying winter clouds. Only the two of them remained on the wet, empty platform. He stood at one end, wounded and spiteful, she at the other, lovely and all alone.

Again he felt an urge to go over and look closely into her dark face and patiently tell her she ought not to have come down to the depot alone. But just then she walked by without even seeming to notice him. He bit his fingernails and decided that he was wasting his time on nonsense. Why should he be mooning around, doing nothing, and—really—what difference did it make whom she was thinking of: Avromchik, the ruddy agent, or even the student on the platform of the train? It was of no interest to him. . . .

On her way back along the platform, however, she stopped beside him and complained to him with a worried expression:

"It is so desolate here, isn't it?" Her face was strained, but whether because of the wind or the bleakness of the depot, he wasn't sure.

"Dissolute?" he repeated. "Yes, it certainly is." He felt himself blushing and smiling against his will. Why had he suddenly been so rude to her?

She was hurt by his offhand quip, and glared at him with proud and haughty eyes. Suddenly she turned to face straight into the cold, wet wind. She hesitated a moment then decided to retaliate. She would thank him never to say such a thing again. . . . And that evening when he sulked so foolishly in her entrance hall instead of coming in . . . she would have been glad to see him. He could have joined them. And he knew very well that she shared his feelings about the denizens of the depot . . . she hated them no less than he did.

His eyes followed her until she was out of sight.

Why, he wondered, having such contempt for these merchants, had she come down to live among them? And why, if his hatred was even greater than hers, did he not make his escape? What kept him there? Was it the four hundred rubles, which represented his total earnings for the entire year?

CHAPTER 8

At the very end of winter, when the frosts were milder but heavy snows still continued to fall day and night, Meir Hecht returned to the depot to sell his stock of bran. He rented a spacious room in a local farmhouse, made as much money as he had the last time, smoked an endless chain of cigarettes, and had as little to do with the other dealers as possible. His dark, silksmooth face had not changed, except that when he looked at the dealers with his wide-open eyes, his contempt for them and their dealings seemed to have grown much deeper and stronger. Benish studied him like a riddle, and wondered about the unknown distant province of Chernigov where Hecht's contempt had been nurtured: what odd creatures its inhabitants must be.

Hecht himself was certainly an odd creature, with his delicate sensibilities; he hated trade, yet he lived by it. For days at a time he would sit in his room, his nostrils distended, staring earnestly at the smoke rising from his upturned mouth. Of what was he thinking? Of himself? Of his profits? Of the pretty little wife he had left behind in Chernigov? It was impossible to guess.

There were many books strewn under the table and bed of his room, all tattered and stained with food and drink. He never held them in his hand and never spoke of them, but their presence seemed to suggest, to Benish at least, a thought. Since even he, Meir Hecht, with his intense hatred of merchants, could not escape being a merchant himself, of what use were these precious clever volumes and what help could they be to anyone? If he himself was unable to escape the clutches of commerce then all these intellectual trimmings were useless, and one might as well sit comfortably as he, Meir Hecht, was doing, staring silently at the smoke rising from his pursed and upturned mouth.

Benish could not contain himself, and asked a question, though it was admittedly none of his affair. He, too, Benish, that is, hated the life of trade, and he was therefore considering becoming a tutor in a village. But why should Hecht have to be a merchant? For instance, on whose account did he have to come down to the depot?

Hecht's eyes widened in surprise. What kind of a question was that? Why, on his own account of course.

Just the answer you might expect from a Lithuanian rationalist! Benish was dissatisfied, however, and made a mental objection. He had the example at hand of his own clumsy wife. Since she had no use for him, hadn't he simply managed to escape from her?

One day, at Itsik-Borukh's quarters, he met a thin girl with a small, childlike face and bobbed hair. She had fallen in love with Itsik back in the city, and had taken a job in a nearby town to be closer to him. Itsik was then sick with influenza. He lay quietly on a low couch, his throat wrapped in a scarf, his face red and feverish. Although he appeared to have no use for this thin small girl, she pretended not to

notice, and stopped by every evening to chat with his brother
Volodye, a freckled and pimply student who had recently come
home on a visit. The girl spoke heatedly, and her hollow cheeks
flamed with passion. Volodye's pale watery eyes smiled back at her;
he was pleased that he had chosen to come home at this fortuitous
time.

Benish took no part in their conversation. It was all the same to
him, whatever they talked or argued about. His thoughts were on
the sunflower crop in which he had recently invested, and on which
he now stood to lose a hundred and fifty, if not two hundred rubles.

By this time the clusters of dealers at the depot were already saying:
"Some business Benish is doing!"
"That sunflower load will be on his hands for years."
"No, I mean his loan to the gentleman from Batsenets."
"Why even talk about it? The man is an imbecile!"
His mother-in-law ran into Pivniak in town and tore her hair:
"Heaven help us! The whole world knows that the Batsenetser
was on the verge of bankruptcy!"
Pivniak was soon back at the depot. "Take it from me: the man
is an idiot. A full-fledged idiot!"
As far as Benish was concerned, they could all go to the devil.
He had no interest in what they were saying about him. All that
really mattered was that the Batsenetser was into him for five hundred rubles. He was nervous, and chewed on his nails, and his mind
kept gnawing away at one and the same thought: five hundred
rubles was no joke.
When he later ran into Avromchik at the depot he was, for the
first time, happy to see him: Avromchik had just come away from
the Batsenetser with a thousand rubles in hand. What did he think
of his chances? Could he rescue his five hundred rubles?
Avromchik made a sour face and began scratching himself
behind the ear so vigorously that he seemed to be suffering from a
terrible eczema.
"Ay, my dear Benish," he scolded in a shrill voice, still scratching himself behind the ear, "Why didn't you speak to me first, eh,
Benish?"
Benish nibbled at his nails and turned his eyes away to focus on
Avromchik's feet.
In other words, he concluded, the money was gone. Well,

never mind . . . he could always get along with five hundred rubles less. But then maybe . . . maybe there was some way of getting back the money after all? Did Avromchik think it was possible? No? Then to hell with it. He didn't even want to think about it any more. . . .

But when Avromchik made a move to go, Benish detained him. He just wanted a few more words with him. For instance, what about the following plan: he would swear out a formal complaint before the district clerk. Or else, he could pay a visit to the Count of Kilkev, to press his claim. That wouldn't help either? Well, then, there was obviously no point discussing it. No point wracking your brains for nothing.

But his brains continued to wrack themselves.

The sunflower investment, for which there was no client forthcoming and which the mice were steadily eating away at in some dark and dusty corner, and the Batsenetser's stupid bankruptcy following his own no less stupid loan to him, lodged themselves in his mind and gave him no rest. It was painful to keep thinking of them, but impossible to forget them.

If he did occasionally forget himself, it was during a walk around the depot when he remembered the good fortune of Avromchik Kaufman who had no bankrupt debtors, but a reservoir and a lovely home, and money, and above all, a pretty and clever wife of whom he was wholly undeserving. He longed for another stormy winter night with snow swirling in his eyes and blustering winds rattling the shutters, and no one at the cheerful little cottage but himself and its pretty mistress who would look up at him with her clever eyes, listening sympathetically to his heartfelt woes, and saying:

"I understand you, Benish. I know exactly how you feel."

The gossip at the depot began to annoy him. What did they have against him? Why did their jeering faces peer at him from every crack? Why did they have to keep pointing him out:

"There goes Benish. There he goes, as I am a Jew!"

Winter was coming to an end. One of its last evenings was warm and humid, with dampness exuding from the station grounds, the trees, and even from the faces of the bystanders. Somewhere above the chaos of earth, spring and winter were grappling for control of the skies. Spring pleaded gently with the skies to turn blue and clear. But bushy-browed winter bullied and threatened: "Skies, do your worst!" The skies, uncertain, turned first overcast, then clear. The weather prophets of the depot looked up idly and wondered whether the sun would set that day in clouds or clear blue sky. And the gossiping grain dealers were still on the subject of Benish:

"He's almost a pauper by now—it better not be contagious!"

Whenever a passenger train arrived, they put Benish aside temporarily and turned their attention to the students on their way home for the holidays. They singled out an emaciated young extern with a sorrowful expression: "Poor boy . . . what a shame . . . woe to his mother."

But no sooner did the train depart than their conversation reverted to Benish: "Tell me, where is he going for Passover? His mother-in-law is ready to chase him off with a stick."

Elye "the Merciful" walked by with an out-of-town dealer, complaining in his high-pitched womanly voice about the state of their profession. There was a certain dealer, Benish Rubinstein . . . he had heard the story? Well, then, that was a perfect example of how dangerous it was nowadays to part with even a penny.

Standing alone and apart from the others, Benish bit his nails and wondered who but Pivniak could have spread the news around so effectively. But Pivniak pretended innocence. Standing not quite out of earshot, he joked with the other dealers:

"Listen, Merciful. May these Jews be my witness: I've been thinking over your case and I have a bone to pick with you. There is only one way to deal with your kind. You ought to be stopped right here and now and have your face slapped. Do you understand me?"

The assembled bystanders laughed, but the kindly and good-natured butt of the joke smiled in obvious confusion.

"Slapped?" he asked, "But why, Reb Levi?"

Pivniak paused for effect and then explained himself:

"Yes, slapped. You have enough money; your father's reputation is above reproach; you don't touch anyone's wealth or honor; you even insist on doing kind and generous deeds. There is obviously no other way of dealing with such a paragon of righteousness except to provoke you publicly and force you to lodge a complaint with the county judge."

The good-humored laughter and back-slapping that greeted Pivniak's witticism was interrupted by a sudden question:

"And what would you do with Benish?"

Pivniak rose to the bait eagerly:

"Why, you silly fool. Everyone knows that Benish has slapped his own face!"

A hush ran through the crowd. Benish heard someone whisper to Pivniak that he was nearby. He felt people staring at him, but when he looked up they were afraid to meet his eyes. His heart pounded so rapidly that it ached, and it seemed to be engulfed in a seething hot fluid. Pivniak's jocular voice sounded strange and unreal as he continued, unruffled:

"It wouldn't hurt him to hear it. By this time he's even poorer than Shloyme the Lip."

A very loud ringing was in his ears. His heart began to pound harder and faster and the fluid in which it seethed became hotter than ever. He saw no one but his tormenter, the tall stooped joker to whom he felt drawn like a magnet, and whom he finally approached with a proud and resolute reply:

"Take that!"

His hand came down angrily against Pivniak's cheek, and he tasted the intoxicating pleasure of revenge.

"Now go and haul *me* up before the county judge!"

By way of reply he heard a wild, enraged scream.

It was not clear to him, however, whether the scream was his own or whether it came from the tall stooping man who was clutching his face with both hands. Someone grabbed him from behind and pinned back his arms. He struggled to free himself, still savoring the vengeance of his short and final challenge:

"Now go and haul *me* up before the county judge. . . ."

Some good friends dropped by a few days later to warn Benish that he had better leave the depot. Pivniak's twenty-five-year-old son had just been discharged from the army. Tall and husky, wearing a short jacket and high boots, he was hanging around the depot, on the lookout for Benish. The fellow had the healthy face of a gentile, powerful shoulders and strong hands. His brain was shrunken and flabby from lack of use, and if told to beat a man up he would probably kill him. Was there any choice? He had to leave.

Actually, his head had begun to hurt, and the joints of his arms and legs were aching, but was there any choice? He would go to bed early and leave the next morning on the six o'clock train.

During the night he awoke from a long troubled sleep and felt an awful chill running through his body. He stuck one shivering foot out on the cold floor, and reached for his warm, heavy robe, which he flung over his blanket. But his body trembled and his teeth chattered even under the warm coverings. He shut his eyes and dozed lightly, mindful of the six o'clock train that he would soon have to board.

Suddenly, there he was aboard the train. The lamps were still burning in the sleeping car. Bare feet dangled from the upper berths. When he tried to settle into a dim corner of the car, familiar faces were already there awaiting him, smiling and asking:

"Where are you bound for, Reb Benish?"

The question was unbearably painful, yet he had to smile and say that he was going home to his father's . . . for Passover.

His friends did not seem to understand. With the smile still on his face, he explained that he was bringing his father a gift, the gift of a well-established, married son. His father was a sleepy burgher, a tall lean man who had lost all his money and possessions except for a dilapidated, rotting house and a prominent seat in the synagogue of his outlying shtetl. He was proably living off hand-outs and private charity from the well-to-do who still remembered his father-in-law's wealth. His mother was a clever woman with stooping shoulders who could never quite forget the good old days of her youth. She would wipe away hot tears with the edge of her apron, and transfix him every now and then with a red-eyed expression of self-pity: "Dear God . . . to have lived to see this day . . . ."

The nice young people of the town would all turn out to see him, and his friends to whom he had once boasted that he would be a very rich man some day, and the sorrowing relatives of his first wife. . . .

The beloved shtetl where he was going to spend Passover was the home of everything that mattered. Why couldn't these traveling companions of his leave him alone and quit their sly and nagging questions:

"Where to? Where to, Reb Benish?"

Back in his little room in the misshapen farmhouse it was very hot. The pale rays of a dull and chilly morning fell softly into the room. When he opened his eyes he was puzzled: he was apparently still in the same place.

A noisy cricket was chirping somewhere inside a crack of the well-stoked woodstove, deliriously happy in the warmth. The room was dark, and it was dark on the other side of the square little window, where the old apple tree stood trembling with its sad naked branches.

He remembered Pivniak's powerful son who was lying in wait for him at the depot, and feeling suddenly weak, closed his eyes. His limbs ached, his head was heavy and hot, and he wanted badly to sleep.

But some visitors had dropped by; well-meaning grain dealers had taken pity on him and had come to bring him comfort: "Why the fuss? It's only a small matter."

It seemed that the slap he had dealt Pivniak was not so important, except as a source of amusement to Avromchik and the other dealers. At Avromchik's house they sat around speculating:

"He must be almost penniless by now."

It was obvious that anyone else in his place would be living happily at the depot with his money intact and beyond the range of Pivniak's sneering insults. A shudder ran through all the feverish limbs of his body, and he woke up.

His dark little room was empty except for a strong healthy fellow who stood beside his bed holding a very cool hand over his burning forehead. When he looked up from under his heavy sleepy lids he saw a familiar rosy face with an amiable smile.

"Is that the way it is?" the smile was asking. He recalled that Itsik-Borukh had just such a smile and his own expression answered: "That's the way it is."

The thin girl with the bobbed hair stood beside Itsik looking very frightened. She asked Itsik softly whether it might not be wise to send for his wife.

Itsik smiled but made no answer. Slowly Benish closed his eyes again and fell back asleep.

When he awoke, the lamp in his room was already burning. The local doctor was examining him with cold, prodding fingers and breathing cold air into his flushed face.

"Pneumonia or typhus," the doctor pronounced with a sigh. "Who knows?"

Neither he nor Itsik nor the thin girl with the bobbed hair was frightened by the pronouncement. Volodye's yellowish watery eyes did show surprise for a moment, but soon relaxed into a smile.

CHAPTER 9

The days were warm again. Birds danced and twittered along the gnarled boughs of the sun-spattered apple tree, hopping and swinging from every damp little branch. Through the open window the landlord could be seen walking bareheaded around the garden, examining each sapling to see if it had been damaged by the winter frosts. His two huge dogs, shaggy and well-fed beasts, followed patiently at his heels. From time to time they broke into play, pretending to fight and nip one another. Noticing a strange pig at the edge of the garden, they suddenly made for him, lunging over the black clumps of damp earth. As soon as he saw the dogs, the frightened pig forgot where the entrance was in the fence, and set off in the wrong direction. The dogs grabbed him by the ears, and he began squealing loudly. Meanwhile the farmer, who had been talking to himself, stopped shamefaced when he noticed Benish standing by the open window.

Benish dressed slowly and ventured out for the first time since his illness. It was remarkably warm outside. The skies were languid and blue, and the sun showed off its charms with coquettish delight. He stood with his hands in his pockets, looking at the world.

A narrow footpath wound its way among half-dried clods of earth and disappeared in some ditch or other near the station. Should he go there or not? He touched his sunken cheeks and looked down at his thin, weakened hands; then he took out his wallet and with clutched, trembling fingers put it back again.

"This is some sad state of affairs," he sighed.

He moved haltingly, like a baby learning to walk, and concentrated on his feet which were leaving tracks in the soft ground. Everywhere it was calm and still. The sun shone serenely, pouring down its loving warmth over all the scattered cottages.

The houses dozing in the soft sunlight heard in their sleep the faraway blows of the blacksmith as he hammered out a slow and sorrowful tale: the story of a beaten man, a miserable, unfortunate creature who earned his livelihood through sweat and toil.

Just as he was nearing the depot, Avromchik Kaufman caught up with him, gave him a playful poke and shouted:

"What about a small loan, Benish, eh?"

By the time Benish could crease his sunken cheeks in a weak smile, Avromchik was rushing off in the company of a frightened agent to whom he was complaining, half-jokingly, half in earnest:

"You silly ass, couldn't you tell that to the police on your own?"

Benish went on smiling, and his thin weak hand remained outstretched in the direction of the receding pair.

Then he saw two familiar agents coming toward him from the depot. Without stopping or even acknowledging his presence they cast one look at his pale and sickly face and began to discuss him in their own idiom as soon as they were behind his back.

"Well, what do you say!"

"What is there to say?"

"Through thick and thin, eh?"

"You said it!"

As he walked on with feeble little steps, his thin smile gave way to a bitter expression of unworthiness and failure. Something puzzled him, but he couldn't fix his mind on what it was. His surroundings were normal enough: everything wore an expression of languid calm and luxuriated in the radiance of the huge western sun. The day trains had already departed. Little birds hopped around the station grounds, springing from one spot to another and stopping occasionally to peck under their wings.

Four young grain dealers were sitting on a bench catching the warmth of the setting sun and gossiping about tradesmen and pretty young wives. He was noticed by one of the young men, who smiled meaningfully at the others and immediately bowed his head. At this signal the others looked at him and appraised him with a knowing smile. He lowered his head and moved a few steps forward to the big square windows of the second-class waiting room. Several out-of-town merchants were sitting inside around a table playing cards with Pivniak, Shloymke Perl, and the florid agent with the curling mustache. They looked relaxed, like people who, having just enjoyed a good sleep, have awakened with a yawn and a bright idea: why not a round of cards?

But suddenly Pivniak pointed to the window. They all turned in his direction and smiled knowingly. He turned away from the window and started home with the same halting and feeble steps that had brought him to the depot.

Later he lay in bed, fretting that the illness had cost him his last few pennies, and that at Avromchik's house people were probably taking their tea on the veranda, warming themselves by the last rays of the sun.

Volodye, with the golden buttons and watery eyes, dropped in to see him and sat for a long time. He reported that Itsik had gone back to his studies in the city, that the thin girl with the bobbed hair was planning to follow him, and that Avromchik's wife was so pretty and charming that he of the freckles and watery, good-natured eyes, was attracted to her.

Suddenly something occured to Volodye that made him jump to his feet excitedly and begin a heated monologue in which the name of Avromchik's wife figured prominently, coupled with the name of that strapping agent with the curling mustache and the silly handsome face.

"What persistence!" Volodye marvelled. "He really set his mind to the task."

"Is that so?" asked Benish. As he sat thinking of this man who had applied himself so successfully, and was now strutting around the station grounds with an occasional yawn and a mien of self-assurance, Volodye gave him a nudge and winked broadly:

"And what about you, Benish? Come on now, own up."

Benish recalled how often he had spoken to her of himself and of his ugly, sickly wife, and felt a dull pang of shame and regret.

Still later the room was dark and very quiet. A clean moon shone from the skyblue heights through the open window. The sculptured tips of the gilded trees looked up at the moon in respectful homage, waiting for it to reveal its secret of eternal gloom and sadness. But the moon remained engrossed in heavenly matters.

Somewhere nearby a passerby was being attacked by a pack of dogs. They set upon him fiercely, yelping and barking in fury, as though he were the villain for whom they had been lying in wait these many long years. Then the passerby was heard shouting and chasing off the dogs, one of whom received a resounding blow that drove him away with a pitiful moan. And then it was quiet once more. In a dark corner of the room Volodye's face still seemed to be winking and grinning:

"What about you, Benish? Come on now, own up."

Outside, there was a scratching sound against the wall. Steps were heard coming toward the window and a head, shrouded in a black shawl, was thrust inside. He leapt to his feet and saw Avromchik's wife. In the same moment, garbled thoughts concerning her and the agent rushed through his mind and threw him into confusion. She was asking him something in her soft and pleasant voice, but he was so confused he did not hear her.

"Wait," he said, groping for something on the table, "I'll light the lamp."

But he couldn't find it on the table and the room remained in darkness. The silence clinging to the walls was broken by her sad, subdued voice:

"It's such a lovely night, so warm and peaceful."

In a soft, hesitant voice, she began to tell him about a life that was lost, and about a vague dream that had long beguiled her without ever coming true.

Everything was quiet and attentive. The moon moved a little closer, casting a pale yellow sheen over her bowed head, and he listened with half an ear to what the woman in the shawl was saying. Her village, she began, was very far away, on the slope of a mountain. At that very moment the moon was probably out, and the frogs were poking their heads out from under the lily pads to croak at the moon. The water made a rushing sound as it turned the millwheel in the valley, and boys played with the fresh flour dust, tossing it high into the air with a hearty shout. . . .

All at once she laughed aloud and then fell silent. The atmosphere grew heavy and oppressive. A human figure slipped away from a corner of the room and vanished. From out in the garden came the sounds of a dog chasing an excited cat that scrambled up the closest available tree.

Someone sighed deeply. Benish stirred as from a sleep and started to say something, but then waved it off: it was of no importance.

But she had begun to talk about a subject that held for him a morbid fascination. She spoke about his illness, and of his wife who had come from town to be with him: she was there for two days and then took sick herself. She was on her way somewhere and suddenly fell down in a dead faint.

Later they walked together along the narrow moonlit path leading to the depot. They walked with their eyes on the ground in front of them.

Damp green rooftops shone in the moonlight. Somewhere a lost bird was shrieking, and reddish green lamps, visible from some three *viorsts* away, sent greetings from people who were not yet asleep.

"Do you understand?" she lamented with a sigh, "Everyone played me false, and I foolishly believed them. Later, I was the one who lied and they foolishly believed me. You see how it is: I too made a very bad bargain. I loved one man and married another. But what difference does it make now? I'm the subject of gossip here."

On the path ahead they saw approaching them a city grain dealer who had just come down to the depot. They stopped when he came abreast of them. The dealer laconically removed the spectacles from his nose, wiped the lenses, and said laughingly that by sheer coincidence he was on his way to see them, her and Avromchik that is. There was no one at the depot and he was looking for a game of cards. Then he replaced his spectacles, looked Benish over from head to foot and apparently satisfied that he was not someone to be reckoned with, said to her simply: come along.

And she walked away with the out-of-town dealer without even a parting glance in his direction.

When they had disappeared from sight, he sighed and walked back to his lodgings. Volodye came running to meet him, panting and eager to know: wasn't that her beside the window?

Upon his admission that it was, Volodye winked and gave him another nudge:

"What about you, Benish? Own up now!"

CHAPTER 10

He paced his room for days on end without saying a word, thinking of the good fortune of others and of his own misery. But everything was behind him now, and it was useless even to think of it. He stayed away from the station not because he was ashamed, but because he begrudged them the satisfaction of seeing his haggard face and of feeling sorry for him.

Standing unnoticed at the depot one evening, he had heard them speaking about him:

"Who, Benish? He's talking to himself by now."

One of the dealers found it funny, but another interrupted with the assurance that it was perfectly true:

"Do you think I'm inventing it?"

They concluded that possibly he was not fully in his right mind, and Pivniak boasted of the lawsuit that would soon be brought against him on account of the slap:

"You'll see. I'll have him buried nine cubits under ground." He turned and moved away, trying to forget about Pivniak.

The case was finally brought to trial. It coincided with the eve of Shavuot and provided the dealers with a lively topic of gossip.

At the outskirts of the village that held the district offices of the Tsar, stood the bright, freshly whitewashed house of the district judge, nestling in a verdant garden heavy with the aroma of early summer. The blossoming trees, like new brides, shielded the green earth from the bright new sun that was sprinkling light through the branches. It was eleven in the morning. Benish stood unnoticed near some bushes, watching one carriage after another deposit the dealers who were to bear witness. He tried to ignore them by concentrating on something else.

Avromchik noticed him standing there alone. He came over to mutter a few hasty words which Benish, however, failed to understand, and then he disappeared. For the grain dealers the event was a festive occasion, but they were concerned about the time: couldn't things go a little faster? After all, tonight was a holiday. Back in town, the front doors of their homes stood open, the fish was being chopped on the chopping boards, and children were decorating the tidied rooms with green Stars of David.

But the local justice, an evil-tempered retired general, would not be hurried; he examined every witness thoroughly, scolding each of them in turn. The hearing dragged on until evening. The witnesses, who were afraid that this nasty military man would banish them from the depot, gave garbled testimonies or answers that were not to the point. Some simply refused to testify:

"We don't know . . . we didn't actually see it ourselves . . . we only heard about it afterwards."

The judge lost his temper with them and with Pivniak who had initiated the action; he warned that he would throw them all into prison. But in the end, it was only Benish, the haggard and discouraged young man with the terribly pale face and dry lips, who was sentenced to two weeks in the county jail.

Relieved that the trial was finally over, the dealers and brokers scrambled into their carriages, and told the drivers to hurry up. The coachmen whipped their horses to make up for lost time, swearing under their breath:

"It's too late for the bath, as I am a Jew! Giddyup!"

The sun began to go down.

Benish was left alone, biting his fingernails. He had no desire to return either to his wife or to the depot and would willingly have stayed there forever, ruminating and biting his nails beside the judge's freshly-whitewashed cottage.

He decided that he might as well begin serving his sentence.

A bare half hour later he was on his way to town, walking between two peasants who had been hired to guard him. The sky was clear and blue overhead, green fields like gigantic wings lay on either side of the road and the evening air smelled of newly-mown grass. One of the peasants blew his nose rudely and told him to step it up:

"Hey there, faster, it's almost night."

He didn't hear, so absorbed was he by the sight of a solitary farmer still out in the field with his horse and wagon. His lips moved involuntarily and he whispered softly:

"Five hundred rubles . . . ."

He served his sentence locked up in a square little hut near the house of the chief of police. He was weak and dejected, like a mourner, and his thoughts kept turning to a certain Yisep Yageshpolski, a respectable young man and even something of an intellectual, who had once had several thousand rubles, an attractive wife, two pretty daughters, and a princely life. One day his affairs took a bad turn, and people stopped greeting him in the street. Why should they greet him? Had they never seen a pauper before?

So Yisep took a trip to the city, registered in the finest hotel, and retired to his room for the night. In the morning they found him hanging from a rope. But at least the fellow had left an attractive widow and two pretty daughters to mourn him. Who would ever mourn for Benish, especially as he was already thought to be slightly mad?

The real question was not that, but whether Yisep had made the right decision. His head was too numb and his heart too sore for him to think the matter through, but even in the midst of his misery he felt sure that Avromchik, wherever he was, was light-hearted and gay.

Every evening he watched from his square little window as the decked-out city girls promenaded to the outskirts of town. He saw their rosy smiling faces, but his own eyes were bloodshot and his lips were parched and pale.

He grew thinner from day to day. Occasionally he coughed tentatively to test the sound of his chest. He had always been so well looked after, but what would happen to him now were he suddenly to take sick or waste away. . . .

The evening came when he was released from the cramped, dirty room and told he was free to go. A plan of action had formed in his mind. He waited until it was dark, then hired a buggy to drive him to the depot.

His mind was so exhausted that it refused to serve him, and by the time the buggy reached the first valley outside town, the whole plan had begun to disintegrate. He tried vainly to reconstruct it and couldn't. Confused thoughts tumbled around in his head. As soon as he arrived, he would collect his belongings. He would leave. But he couldn't remember where he was going or why and so he watched the moon as it rose from behind the opposite hill.

The narrow, empty road on which he rode was already bathed in magical yellow light. The road twisted in both directions, going uphill and down and onward to that point on the horizon where the full quicksilver moon hung over the dark depot.

The driver whipped the horses harshly. They flicked away the whipmarks with their tails and began galloping harder; the buggy trailed its shadow on the ground and a small cloud of damp yellow dust rose in the air. The dark yellow world was in repose. His head sank slowly to his chest and he momentarily forgot his suffering.

But as they drew closer to the station, he heard the sounds of a drum and the tootings of a horn: he sat up in fright. The music was coming from around the reservoir. It poured out in all directions and then faded off in the distance. He looked closely at Avromchik's house, which was more brightly lit up than ever, and suddenly remembered that Avromchik's sister was to have gotten married at just about this time. All at once he felt himself growing pale. His heart began to pound with a dreadful realization: they would be passing Avromchik's house. His wife and mother-in-law were probably at the wedding. . . . Pivniak and his gang would catch sight of him and surround his buggy with cries of "Hurrah! Hurrah!"

To avoid being seen, he dismissed the driver and buggy, cut across the tracks to his left, and slowly made his way to the tiny garden alongside the depot. There he sat down on a bench in deep shadow, with his head on his chest, as though asleep.

The gilded tips of the poplar branches were perfectly still, and not a leaf stirred. The only sounds came from beyond the long shadows of the trees, where the salesgirl at the bookstand was laughing her distinctive laugh, evidently amused by the story that the lanky student was telling her.

The station bell began to toll.

Ten minutes before the ten-thirty train, the families of the bride and groom appeared in the garden. They walked slowly in pairs down the long sandy footpath, and their snowy white silk clothes rustled as they moved. Avromchik's wife passed almost in front of him, complaining to a tall elderly woman. He was not a bad husband, she was saying, he did as he was told. But at night he snored in his sleep and drooled.

Benish was suddenly reminded of Shloymke Perl who had started out, after all, without so much as a cent to his name.

He walked slowly to the station and waited in a corner. Avromchik, dressed up in a black coat, black trousers, and a white cravat, was talking to one of the relatives. He went over and motioned him aside:

"The Lozovker still has a fair supply of beans left. It might be a good idea to take a ride over tomorrow."

And since Avromchik calmly, and without the least surprise, began to discuss the Lozovker's beans, Benish took courage and urged him on: things would certainly go well, he suggested, because he and the Lozovker were on excellent terms. Avromchik scratched himself behind the ear and showed his commercial acumen. Benish, he replied, would undoubtedly agree that they had better cut Pivniak in as their broker; otherwise he would be sure to wreck the deal.

And on the following day Benish, Avromchik, and Pivniak set out together for Lozovke.

At first they were all quiet, listening to the buggy swaying from side to side as it strained up a hill and Shloyme the Lip clicked his tongue at the horses. Then Pivniak livened up and said for no apparent reason:

"Ay, Avromchik, what a wife you've got!"

A comfortable smile spread across Avromchik's thick and amiable face. He sat back in the buggy and pointed to Benish:

"He can vouch for that, can't you Benish?"

But Pivniak objected. You couldn't know a woman until you'd. . . .

His conclusion was not in very good taste. Benish preferred not to hear the rest of the conversation and concentrated instead on a letter he would shortly send to his wife:

"To my dear wife, Frumke, may you be in good health; since I intend to come home for the Sabbath, would you kindly. . . ."

On the hilltop that now lay behind them, the somnolent red station house stood, staring frozenly into the deep unknown.

ROMANCE OF
A HORSE THIEF

BY JOSEPH OPATOSHU

INTRODUCTION TO ROMANCE OF A HORSE THIEF

THE INTRODUCTION of the underworld into literature, as by
the University Wits of sixteenth-century London, or the French
naturalists in the late nineteenth century, generally accompanies a
claim to greater honesty and a rejection of stilted fictional modes. In
presenting the underside of society, an author proclaims the noble
intention of baring certain crucial matters of fact that his precursors
conscientiously ignored. Other claims to honesty follow: the more
obvious presence of violence and sexuality in the lives of the characters is contrasted favorably with the repression and sublimation that
are the norms of ordinary middle-class life; and the simplistic moral
code of the underworld, cynical about such trappings of civilization
as law, love, and charity, exposes any imperfect attempt at decency
as so much hypocrisy and sham. Portrayals of the underworld thus
readily become indictments of respectability.

Joseph Opatoshu's Romance of a Horse Thief is one of several
underworld works in Yiddish which appeared at the beginning of
the century, signifying a departure from the clearly respectable
concerns of earlier writing. Opatoshu is a less sensational writer
than, for example, Sholom Asch, whose 1906 drama, God of Vengeance, is set in a brothel, and whose attack on false gentility is
entrusted to a pair of lesbians. He eschews the stylistic shock tactics
of I. M. Weissenberg and the heavy eroticism of Zalman Schneour

in favor of a vigorous yet gentle prose, thick with detail, affectionate in tone. In Opatoshu's account, the substantial normalcy of the horse thief's household is emphasized; the author has selected underworld characters as heroes only in order to admit them to their rightful place in the Jewish social fabric.

Shloyme is a professional thief, but otherwise there is little in his life to suggest the criminal type: a devout Jew, and in his aspirations a proper one, he wants good marriages for his daughters, a good seat in the synagogue for himself, and a God-fearing son who will recite grace after meals. Zanvl, the story's youthful protagonist, is more "honest": a thief, he declares, doesn't need to pray. Yet he too is attracted to law-abiding ease, and his love for Rachel, the daughter of a well-to-do householder, reinforces his dreams of propriety. He is at the familiar crossroads of youth, but with the roadsigns reversed, having to choose between his father's way and the alluring high road to uprightness. In Zanvl the raw energy of the earth-bound, illiterate renegade is sharply contrasted with the safer mores of the shtetl. His impulsive nature yields him up to the advances of women who are distasteful to him, and he follows any call to adventure, whatever the risk. His few efforts at systematic planning or thought end in sleep or else in frustrated rage. Unable to tame himself, he forfeits his chance at self-advancement, and ends where he began.

As if in the spirit of Zanvl, Opatoshu's prose is direct and unreflective. The story is told straight through from beginning to end with no time deviations; characters are revealed in their actions and thoughts without irony or analysis. The two lovers, Zanvl and Rachel, are drawn to one another like figures in a ballad, and they remain together until the social distinctions they represent and embody force them apart. The "villain," Moyshe the horse dealer, a former thief turned successful middleman, personifies the "decent folk" who profit from the crimes of others without sullying their own reputations. It is for him that Shloyme reserves his final hatred, for the man who sleeps in warm comfort while he must drag his aging bones through a long night on a dangerous job. A similar judgment is later pronounced on Rachel, who lacks the courage to follow her heart, succumbing instead to the benefits of becoming a rabbi's wife, with a permanent seat at the head table.

Romance of a Horse Thief was written in 1912, five years after Opatoshu had settled permanently in New York, and for all its

tough immediacy, it is also part of a mainstream of nostalgia-litera-
ture dedicated to preserving the rapidly disappearing world of the
East European shtetl. Earlier writers, particularly the classical trio
of Mendele Mocher Sforim, Sholom Aleichem, and I. L. Peretz,
had done well by the devout, mild-mannered, "milkhik" Jews, to
apply the traditional distinction between a milk- and meat-typology;
Opatoshu is one of the more prolific and enthusiastic portrayers of
the gamier, "fleyshik" shtetl types. In Romance of a Horse Thief he
has captured both their glowing vitality and the pathos of their
predicament. Crafty and capable in their encounters with border
guards and peasants of the outside world, they are yet strangely
vulnerable within their own, the abused rather than abusers, robust
in body, but scarred by the insecurity that is the outsider's fate.

ROMANCE OF A HORSE THIEF
BY JOSEPH OPATOSHU

CHAPTER 1

SATURDAY AFTERNOON. Twin beams of light, like two silvery pillars, fell into the room through the open window, and quivered in the air. Between them, on the floor, sprawled a heavy white cat with a white patch on her nose, presumably asleep, her chin nestling in outstretched paws. A fly flew by. The cat lunged forward, caught the fly, swallowed it, then resumed her position and went back to sleep.

Shloyme the Rustler, a tall, gaunt Jew with a sparse beard, lay on a featherbed near the door. Beads of sweat, like peas, stood on his broad forehead, hung for a moment, then trickled sideways in long skinny threads of water over his cheeks.

Shloyme's daughter, Chane, a girl in her early twenties, was combing her hair in front of the mirror. She took a few steps backward, holding up her starched skirt, then extended her foot flirtatiously, as if about to dance.

"Haven't you had enough primping?" asked Sarah, her younger sister, who was just walking out the door. "Berke will like you just the way you are."

"Here's salt in your eye!" Chane called after her. She flounced around the room several times and then followed her out. Shloyme's wife Tirzeh sat near the open window in her red slip with a colored night cap on her shaven head,* grating a turnip and listening with a smile to the stories the men were telling. Several elderly horse dealers in vests and black cloth caps with small peaks, sat on the bench outside, just beneath the window.

"Do I know Elye Vilner?" exclaimed one of them, a red-haired man with a freckled face, "And how! I worked for him for over two years. Went with him to all the fairs, and shared his grub. That man could put away a whole side of veal at one sitting, as I am a Jew. I spent ten months in jail because of him . . . on account of the mare. . . ."

The horse dealers were amused.

"You're laughing, but I feel sorry for him. Believe me, he's not a bad sort."

"It's quite a story," Tirzeh chimed in, helping herself to a spoonful of scrapings.

"The police, you know, have been combing the Radzenov Forest for him for over ten years. If Stakh hadn't fallen in love with Elye's mistress and turned him in to the police, they would never have caught him. There's something strange about him though; the fellow had almost nothing to do with Jews, and besides he was always fooling around with his mistress. Yet in all these years I never heard of him attacking a Jew; he only went for rich landowners and priests. . . ."

"You'll see," someone muttered, "they're going to teach that fellow a thing or two!"

"Like hell," answered another, "you don't know Elye. He can break in through the chimney, put a whole household to sleep, crack the safe and leave a note saying that Elye had come and gone! It's not the first time Elye's been tried. Today he's sentenced and tomorrow he's back with his gang in the Radzenov Woods. Don't worry about him!"

The redhead cleared his throat. "When I remember how Elye stabbed that goy, my hair stands on end. Listen: it's been . . . how many years now? I've lived here for ten years, in the village for two, in the service for three, so all told it must have happened—"

"Fifteen years ago!" cried several voices at once.

"Fifteen years already. . . . Well, where was I? . . . The Ri-

*Like all pious married Jewish women, Tirzeh shaves her head, and otherwise adheres to religious law.

maker lord had a chestnut mare with white hooves that was worth about five hundred rubles. The mare caught Elye's fancy and he dragged me to see it night after night. But we couldn't lift her. I thought Elye would go nuts. At the end of the harvest he says to me: Listen, today the locals are celebrating. The farm hands have been guzzling all day and should be out cold by now. Come on, today we'll grab the mare. Anyway, we took along Kostek, the caretaker's son. I stayed behind at the fence and they went into the stable, brought out a few bundles of straw, spread them out over the yard and led out the horse. All of a sudden a colt came on the scene—she must have missed her mother—and began to neigh. Elye told us to take her down to the ditch and leave her there. So Kostek took the colt down to the ditch. We waited. Suddenly the colt began to neigh so loud the blood froze in my veins. Elye climbed down into the ditch—there was Kostek slitting the colt's throat with a dull knife! I tell you, I was scared! Elye was pale as chalk. He spat in the boy's face, said 'Son-of-a-bitch,' and walked away.

"Elye kept his mouth shut all the way back. He clenched his fists and walked with his hat pulled down over his eyes. When we got to the Olshina River, Elye stopped and looked Kostek in the eye.

"'Son-of-a-bitch, why did 'ya slaughter the colt?'

"Kostek got flustered and tried to say something, but Elye belted him one in the jaw. Kostek slipped a knife from his boot. Elye threw himself on the boy, grabbed the knife and stabbed him through and through, panting: 'So you'll slaughter a colt, will you. . . .'"

The redhead fell silent. The men lowered their heads.

"Those were the good old days," sighed a graying Jew with a bulbous nose and a thinning mustache—apparently a snuff taker—as he passed around his birchbark pouch.

Suddenly the door flew open and a tall, broad-shouldered fellow with blue, childish eyes burst in. He pulled off his cap and threw it on the table, and a mop of flaxen hair tumbled out over his sweaty forehead.

"Ma, I'm dying to eat! I haven't had a bite since morning."

"Who asked you to run around all day?" said Tirzeh.

"C'mon, Ma, we'll discuss it later. Right now I want to eat."

Shloyme shuddered in his bed. His mouth felt awful and he spat.

"Tirzeh, Tirzeh, I'm dying for a drink!"

Tirzeh handed him a bowl of prune juice. Shloyme drank it down, licked his lips, and stretched with a hearty yawn.

"Well, Zanvl," Shloyme turned to his son who was already sitting over a bowl of boiled chicken and *khala*, chewing evenly, "How's Elye doing?"

"What d'ya think? They brought him down in chains! Pa, you should have seen the crowd. The whole town stood around watching."

"Believe me, he won't serve his term." Shloyme drew nearer his son. "Listen, I'll let you in on something."

"What?"

"A *lamia's* been sneaking around with our horses."

"What!" asked Zanvl in amazement, "a *lamia?*"

"That's right. She's just about tired them out. Every morning for the past few days I've noticed the horses covered with sweat. I figured they were sick. As soon as you left this morning, I got up and went into the stable—the sweat was pouring off them and colored hairs were tangled in their manes. I saw that something was up. When I told old Dukhne about it, he says to me: 'Bah, poppycock, you're to blame, a *lamia's* in your house.' Anyway, Zanvl, don't let Ma know, and you sleep in the stable tonight. If you want to, take along my phylacteries."

"Hell," said Zanvl, "that goblin won't get out of my hands alive!"

CHAPTER 2

Tirzeh cleared the table, swept the floor, chased off the flies with a towel, and covered the window with a sheet before going out. Shloyme put on his red jacket and went out to feed the horses. Zanvl was left alone in the house. He stretched out his long legs in their polished boots and leaned his head back against the chair, thinking about Elye. . . . Elye's figure looms before him as if chiseled in stone—the high forehead and thick, long, drooping mustache. Elye is walking in chains, soldiers with drawn swords on either side; his step is steady, not a muscle moves on his face, only his eyes search the crowd. Suddenly he catches sight of a young wench with bluish-green eyes and a long, thick flaxen braid. Elye places his shackled hands around his mistress's neck. Bursting into tears, the girl kisses his hands and whispers something to him. . . .

Zanvl shook his head and muttered "Son-of-a-bitch" for no apparent reason. He began pacing the room, hands in his pockets. Then he stretched out on the bed, with his hands under his head, and spat.

At that very moment, he mused, his Rachel with the black eyes and black, knee-length hair was probably sitting with her old father in their straw hut in the middle of the field. All week long Rachel was on her own. She took care of the farm, supervised the peasant girls and shipped off the vegetables to the market in Prussia where her father sold them. But on Saturdays, when he returned home, father and daughter spent the night together in their hut.

Zanvl avoided the farm on Saturday. Rachel had warned him that her father would be upset to see her in male company. Only in the middle of the week, late at night, did Zanvl make his way stealthily along the back roads to the farm, where Rachel awaited him. There he lay at her feet like a loyal puppy, looking up into her black eyes, and listened to her stories, stroking her dress so lightly that she never felt his touch.

Zanvl never told anyone about Rachel and no one knew of their friendship. Now, as he lay alone, his heart ached for her. He decided to give up the life of a thief, as of tomorrow. He would avoid his old friends and soon the whole town would know that Zanvl had become an honest Jew. Then he would approach Rachel's father with a hearty—"Reb Nosn!"—and the old man would welcome him with open arms and a slap on the back.

"Yes, my son, I know everything. . . . Have a seat."

But Zanvl remembered how down in the mouth he felt whenever he met Reb Nosn on a Sabbath morning. Reb Nosn *did* seem to know everything, and to have suspicions about him: that rascal, that horse thief has the nerve to court my daughter. . . .

Rachel never asked him how he earned his living. She must have known he was a horse thief, he comforted himself, but she didn't want to cause him pain. At other times it seemed to him that if Rachel did know the truth, she wouldn't be speaking to him. He had therefore decided to tell her everything. Yet whenever he met her, his resolution faltered and he was reduced to servility.

Actually only a few weeks had passed since he met Rachel for the first time. On the eve of Shavuot, walking home along the highway from a neighboring village, he heard a shout as he approached the edge of town. Two farmhands were running across the field carrying heavy sacks, chased by a barefoot girl who shouted at them to stop. Zanvl blocked their path. The boys dropped the sacks and ran. He brought the sacks over to where she stood, wide-eyed in fear and gratitude. She thanked him with a glance that took his breath away. From then on he couldn't keep away from the farm. He began seeing Rachel more and more often. . . .

Zanvl got out of bed and began to pace the room making plans: the Polish church was said to contain a golden Madonna with diamond eyes that was worth a few hundred thousand. He would break in and steal the holy statue. The money would buy him some long-tailed Cossack horses and the weapons he needed. Then he would round up a band of trusty men and hole up in the Radzenov Forest. They would build a hideout among the oaks, near the Zholdevke River, so that in case of danger they could swim across to Prussia; they would do as they pleased. Every week they'd saddle the Cossack horses, take their rifles and loot the neighboring estates, or ambush a group of merchants travelling to Plotsk or Warsaw. . . . Soon the whole region would lie in fear of them. But they wouldn't harm the poor, and in time, every dispute would be brought to them for arbitration. He, Zanvl, would be king; his pale Rachel with the beautiful black eyes and long black hair would be his wife, his queen!

CHAPTER 3

Shloyme walked into the stable, rolled up his sleeves and poured some fodder for the horses. They neighed, digging into the trough, and joyfully kicked up their hind legs.

"Out of the way, glutton!" Shloyme shouted, slapping a white horse between its haunches. It jumped aside, and Shloyme went on to the next. "Other horses work themselves to the bone for a bit of pasture. Mine do nothing. I end up supporting you, like a father-in-law. All right, what are you getting all heated up about? Did I beat you? You'll get it all right, in the kisser, my plump beauty! And

you?" Shloyme turned to the mare, grabbing her by the long tail.
"Just you wait. Tomorrow, God willing, I'll take you to the count's
estate and choose the finest stallion for you. But remember," he
added, slapping the mare on the forehead, "see that the colt is no
worse than its father! The goblin's been knocking you out, eh? She'll
get hers in the end, believe me. She won't come out of Zanvl's
hands alive!"

Shloyme sliced some carrots for the white horse and patted its
smooth neck and muzzle. "Here, gorge yourself!" The horse ate out
of Shloyme's hand. It rubbed affectionately against Shloyme's neck
and cheeks with lips like moist rags, and neighed into its master's
face.

"A horse is a horse." Shloyme wiped his splattered face with his
jacket, patted the colt on its back and left the stable. He stretched
out under the apple tree by the window. "The sun's setting already,"
he thought, watching the light blaze against his windows. He looked
toward the stream that flowed through the green fields into the
distant Vistula.

Young wagon drivers, skinners, and a few local boys lolled on
the bank of the stream. Some lay on their stomachs, others face up,
singing songs from the liturgy and looking up at the flaming sky.
Their fettered horses grazed around them. Huge dust clouds rose
on the other side of the stream as the livestock plodded homeward.

Several servant girls walked by with colored ribbons braided in
their hair. The young men grew livelier, and sang louder, winking at
the girls as they passed. Then they began shoving each other around
and snickering. On the grass nearby, some boys were playing bat-
tledore.

Shloyme lay back, tugging at his sparse beard, and enjoying the
scene. A honking flock of wild geese flew by, so low that their wide,
outstretched wings seemed to touch the ground. The geese, in
triangular formation, finally disappeared over the wide fields.

"Tonight it'll rain for sure," he thought, yawning. He noticed
Berke stand up, brush off his jacket, twirl his mustache and start
toward him, nervously buttoning and unbuttoning his jacket.

"Good Shabbos, Reb Shloyme. What do you say to this heat
wave?"

"Sure is broiling," Shloyme replied. "And how are you, Berke?
Sit down."

A smile flickered in Berke's eyes. He took out a white handkerchief and spread it under him as he sat down.

"You know, Reb Shloyme, there's something I want to talk to you about," he said nervously.

"It just so happens that I *don't* know," answered Shloyme in a sing-song, "but if you like, go ahead and tell me!"

"I've wanted to speak to you several times," Berke began again, unsure of where to fix his eyes. "You know how it is . . . running around for days on end . . . I wanted to ask you . . . you know. . . ."

"What? Speak up!" Shloyme burst out laughing. Berke blushed, blinking his eyes and cracking his knuckles.

"Reb Shloyme, there's no use beating around the bush. You know, I'm only a simple man, a wagon driver by profession. I'll say it simply: I like your daughter, Chane, an awful lot. If you want me for a son-in-law, make me a harness, buy me a few mares and I'll be a match for anyone. I'll drive up to the ramp, load up a wagonful of goods and roll into town. I'm no rotten apple. You know very well, Reb Shloyme, that I'm an enterprising fellow. I've worked enough for other people, it's time to make Shabbos for myself!"

Berke fell silent and smiled, wiping the sweat from his brow: "I flubbed it," he thought to himself, "but at least it's over and done with."

Shloyme stolidly heard Berke out to the end. He found the offer to his liking. "Berke," he said, slapping the boy on the back, "you're all right. Come over tonight with your father and we'll talk about it."

Berke got up with a radiant face; arms akimbo and legs spread, he looked like an opened pair of tongs. He mumbled his thanks and left.

"With God's help, we might find a match for Sarah as well. We'd be able to marry them both off on the same day." Shloyme noticed a star. He stood up, very pleased with himself, and made his way into the house: it was time for evening prayers.

Berke turned down a side street and began to breathe easier. He lit up a cigarette, feeling as if a heavy weight had been lifted from his heart. For almost a month, Chane had been urging him to talk things over with her father, but every time Berke approached with his well-rehearsed speech, his tongue got twisted, as if in spite, and he started babbling about all kinds of other matters. Later, he would stomp around for hours seething and cursing himself roundly. Who knows how long this might have lasted had not Chane finally lost patience with him?

Now he felt fresh, almost younger. The whole dreadful

business for which he had prepared for weeks turned out to be quite simple—mere child's play.

By the time he reached the market place, a few of the grocery shops were opening. The women shopkeepers, still half in their Sabbath attire, sat back comfortably watching the people strolling along the sidewalk. A group of girls walked by haughtily, followed by some boys in starched collars, cracking jokes. The girls nudged one another and giggled.

From Plotsk Street a gang of young boys with wooden swords suddenly swarmed into the market place. They stationed themselves in the middle of the market and awaited the enemy—the boys from Warsaw Street. From one of the open windows, a lively, hasidic melody was heard, marking the end of the Sabbath.

Berke looked dotingly at everything around him; he was now the happiest person on earth. He wanted all the passersby to know that he was to be Chane's bridegroom, Shloyme's son-in-law, Zanvl's brother-in-law! Zanvl, the toughest guy in town. He would be treated with respect at the loading platform; no one would dare start up with him. Berke felt his chest swell with pride; he had a great urge to dance through the market place. In joyous abandon, he grabbed one of the little boys with a wooden sword, pulled his cap down over his eyes and raised him into the air. The child became frightened and began yelling and kicking. The other boys danced around him gleefully shouting. Berke let go of the boy with a pinch on the cheek and continued on his way.

Passing through the park, he noticed three beggars with packs on their backs sitting on a bench. "Let them know that I'm going to be Chane's bridegroom," he thought. He went over to the beggars, handed them a few coins and said with a laugh:

"Here, pray for my blessed Chane!"

The beggars exchanged glances and smiled.

"*Variat Zhid,*" they said in Polish, "Crazy Jew."

Everything in Shloyme's house had a festive air about it. The floor was sprinkled with yellow sand. The round table in the center of the room was covered with a white tablecloth. Shloyme in his skullcap lay on the bed smoking a thick cigar and enjoying the sight of the rising smoke rings. Zanvl was at the window, teaching his black dog Morva how to beg. The dog stood on his hind legs wagging his tail and looking at his master with obvious devotion. Zanvl grabbed Morva by the head and pressed him to his face. The dog cuddled up to Zanvl and slapped the floor with his tail, licking him and squealing with joy.

Chane, decked out in a pink blouse, sat at the table trying vainly to embroider. At the slightest noise, she stopped and felt her color rising and her heart beating faster: Berke was expected momentarily. Tirzeh and Sarah were in the kitchen making pancakes.

"Zanvl," Shloyme turned to his son, "What do you say to the match? He seems like a decent fellow, and a good breadwinner, eh?"

Zanvl saw Chane blush and bend over her work so as to avoid anyone's eye.

"He's fine," replied Zanvl, "but why not ask Chane herself? Maybe she doesn't want him?"

Shloyme burst out laughing. "Not want him? Believe me, she's known him longer than you have. All right, just for the fun of it— Chane, are you pleased with the match?"

Chane's flush deepened. "Leave me alone!" she cried angrily. "Mother, tell him to leave me alone."

"Come on, Zanvl, stop that horseplay," Tirzeh shouted from the kitchen. "What do you want from her? You think she's one of those girl friends of yours who hangs around the edge of town all night? Believe me, Berke's got himself a gem. Any mother would feel blessed with such a quiet child."

"Still waters run deep!" shouted Sarah from the kitchen.

"But who was caught with the barber's son in the cemetery?" Chane teased in a sing-song.

"Ha, ha," retorted Sarah coming in from the kitchen with her face flushed, hands on her hips. "Take a look at Miss Modesty! Can't even count to two. Just ask her—"

"Enough, enough!" roared Shloyme. "Shut your mouth, all of you."

Steps were heard outside, followed by the sound of someone blowing his nose.

"The in-laws are here!" shouted Zanvl, pulling in his head from the window.

Chane's face kept getting redder and redder. She dropped her work on the table and looked around fearfully. At the sound of the footsteps, the dog ran barking to the door. Chane, at a loss, grabbed the dog by the ears and led him away through the kitchen.

The door opened to admit Moyshe "Head," a tall, skinny man with a goatee and a head too small for his large body: it was barely visible over the high shoulders, and were it not for the pair of large black eyes, might have escaped notice altogether. Berke was right behind him, eyes lowered, hands in his pockets, and the brim of his cap turned up.

"Good week! A good week!"

"Welcome. A pleasure to see you," said Shloyme and Tirzeh in unison. "Please sit down."

Moyshe sat down with a sigh, and wiped his perspiring forehead with a red handkerchief. Feeling somewhat out of his element, Berke took hold of a chair, and pretended to examine it closely; but then he remained standing and twirled his mustache.

"And you, Zanvl," began Moyshe, "You've grown into a man, haven't you! How are you doing?"

"Getting along," said Zanvl with a smile.

"And where is the bride-to-be?" asked Moyshe.

"The bride was bashful and ran away," replied Shloyme with a laugh.

"That's all right," said Moyshe. "A Jewish girl ought to be shy. I didn't see my own wife, may she rest in peace, until the ceremony. Did it do me any harm? On the contrary, I'd wish such harmony as we had on all Jewish children."

Tirzeh served whiskey, tea with lemon, and the pancakes. After downing a few glasses, everyone relaxed and livened up.

"The bride-to-be still hasn't come?" asked Moyshe cheerfully, helping himself to another whiskey.

"Believe me, Reb Moyshe, your Berke has made no mistake. Even the pious Reb Shmaye would be proud to have such a daughter," volunteered Tirzeh.

"Who needs Shmaye?" said Shloyme with irritation. "Shloyme's daughter is just as high class as Shmaye's."

"Of course, of course," mumbled Moyshe in reply, taking a stiff pinch of snuff. He grimaced, as if in preparation for a sneeze, but try as he might, it wouldn't come.

"Well Shloyme," said Moyshe, "it's getting late. Let's get down to business."

"Why not?" replied Shloyme.

"What about the dowry?"

"Father, I thought we agreed you wouldn't mix in," interrupted Berke. "Reb Shloyme will do me no harm!"

"If you don't want one, you don't need one," laughed Moyshe. "If you can do without it, it's certainly all right with me!"

"I've always said that Berke's a fine fellow," said Shloyme with a smile. "Berke, this foolishness is not for you. You're standing on hot coals and your heart's throbbing for Chane. Go find her. The two of us will manage without you. Don't I know? I was a groom once, too. Tirzeh, you aren't listening. Admit it, you pined for me, didn't you? Ha, ha, ha!"

"Go on, you old fool," said Tirzeh smiling.

Berke threw a grateful glance at Shloyme and eased his way out of the house.

Late that night, Shloyme and Zanvl escorted their future in-laws home. On returning, Shloyme entered the house and Zanvl went directly to the stable to watch for the *lamia.*

The stable was quiet. The horses slept with drooping ears, their bellies heaving up and down like balloons. A sooty lantern cast a dim light.

Zanvl was drowsy, and dropped down on a bundle of straw. He thought of Moyshe, his future in-law, a dark mass of body with a tiny head, like a bird with spread wings that had landed on a tall, branchless tree. He stretched out on the straw and suddenly saw himself as the groom, just returning from the engagement. . . . He could see Rachel sleeping, her hair disheveled. . . . There was Elye Vilner with his long mustache and there, too, was his mistress, his mistress. . . .

In the middle of the night the door opened and a woman came in wearing only a night shirt and colored ribbons around her neck; her hair was wild and disheveled. She mounted a horse and galloped away, her white shirt billowing up like a carousel, and the ribbons whipping like snakes around her throat. With the speed of a magician, she wove the ribbons into the horse's mane and braided its tail, singing in a shrill peasant's voice the sacred melodies that accompany religious processions.

Zanvl shuddered with fear. He saw the horse gallop and rear, its mouth foaming. As he watched, the wench turned back and winked at him with a smile. Her eyes pierced him through and through, and froze the blood in his veins. He wanted to shout, but couldn't. He wanted to reach out—his hand was petrified.

She dismounted and came toward him. "This is the end for me," thought Zanvl, "the girl's got me in her clutches." He felt her beside him. In a cold sweat, he grabbed a wooden peg and thrust it into the *lamia*'s shirt. . . .

There was nobody in the stable but Zanvl, lying on a bundle of straw. "The things a witch can do!" thought Zanvl, drenched in sweat. "She put me to sleep. Who could have known!"

CHAPTER 4

Zanvl was sitting beside Rachel, in the hut.

"Why do you look so glum?," she was asking, "what's the matter? I'm afraid of you."

Zanvl blushed and broke into a smile: "It's nothing, Rachtshe."

"You should be ashamed of yourself, coming to me so depressed! I hate you!" Saying so, she threw herself at him and folded her arms around his neck.

Zanvl embraced her. Like a fish, Rachel wriggled and squirmed in Zanvl's arms and curled up on his chest.

"I read a wonderful story today," she remarked a little later, looking at Zanvl in the small wall mirror. "Is it ever beautiful!"

"Well, let's hear it," he said.

"I don't feel like it! I'm not going to tell you anything, anything at all, do you hear!" Rachel turned around, tossed half her hair over her face and watched for Zanvl's reaction.

"You'll tell me all right," he said and burst out laughing.

"Not on your life," replied Rachel with the caprice of a little girl. "You know what? Let's get angry with each other!"

Zanvl was aroused by her teasing. He jumped up, grabbed Rachel in his arms and began rocking her furiously back and forth, whispering: "Will you tell, will you. . . ."

"I'll tell, I will! Zanvl dear, let go!" she screamed. Zanvl loosened his grip.

"You're wild," said Rachel, sitting down on a bundle of straw, and patting the place next to her. "Sit down." She drew Zanvl's head down on her lap and began telling him a story about a lost prince who rode through many forests looking for his beloved. Hearing a female voice in the distance, the prince spurred on his horse and drew nearer.

"'Lovely damsel, why are you crying?' asked the prince.

"'How can I stem my tears,' she replied, 'seeing that I've lost my intended?'

"'Do not cry, my lovely damsel. I am your bridegroom. Come with me!' And he wrapped his white cloak around her and lifted her up onto the black horse and disappeared with her into the forest. . . .'"

Rachel fell silent. Zanvl was troubled. He felt his insides rising, pulsing into his throat, choking him.

"Rachel doesn't know that I'm a thief," he thought. "I must tell her right away." He clenched his fists and stood up.

"Rachel!" he called out with a choked voice. "Do you know that I'm a thief, a horse thief?"

"You're so strong!" exclaimed Rachel pressing fearfully against him. "They say that you can finish off a three-year-old ox with one blow between the horns. You're no thief. I can tell a thief right away, by his cold, piercing eyes. And you have such good eyes. . . . Take me into your arms again," she pleaded, "Rock me . . . that's the way. Harder, harder!"

Zanvl forgot his intention. He walked around the room cradling Rachel in his arms. She snuggled up as close as she could, trying to join him, body and soul.

Late at night Zanvl escorted Rachel home. He wanted to tell her about his plans, but remained silent, unable to find the words.

"Why don't you ever tell me anything?" asked Rachel in mock anger.

"Believe me, Rachel, I'd tell you everything. When I'm by myself, with my own thoughts, everything comes out so nicely, just like in your stories. But as soon as I try to tell you about it, my tongue gets stuck in my mouth."

Rachel squeezed his hand and smiled.

"Tomorrow," began Zanvl, "I'm doing a job that should bring me several hundred rubles."

"Like what?"

"Listen. Since the outbreak of the war with Japan, the border has been closed. 'Ivan' has stopped the traffic of horses into Prussia, probably afraid that he won't have enough for himself.* Yesterday Moyshe the Horse Dealer came to me with an offer to smuggle a party of fifty horses across the border."

"Aren't you afraid? You could be shot."

"Who thinks of getting shot? They don't shoot. And if things do get going, you shoot right back!"

"Aren't you worried about Rachel?"

Zanvl grew confused, wanted to say something, blushed, and kissed her instead. Rachel walked happily along, stroking Zanvl's hand. At the edge of town they parted, and walked off in different directions so that no one would see them together.

CHAPTER 5

Tirzeh rose early the following morning, cooked some schav, beat in several eggs, boiled a pot of potatoes, and put the food on the table to cool. As soon as she sat down, she remembered that Shloyme would soon be back from prayers and that it was almost time to wake Zanvl. "The boy runs around night after night—devil only knows where."

Tirzeh looked over at Zanvl who was sleeping near the door, his mop of hair tumbling over his forehead. "I've raised quite a fellow, thank God! He could smash in a wall with his bare fists. Anyone else would rejoice with such a son, but all I can do is worry. Even today, God forbid, he might be caught." She sighed. "It's no easy matter smuggling fifty horses across the border. I told that fine father of his that one horse dealer in the family was enough! The boy should have been taught a trade. But the look and the curses he gave me were enough to curdle a mother's milk!"

Tirzeh blew her nose into her apron, without interrupting her flow of thought: "Never had much joy from my children. Of twelve only three remain. Zanvl was always wild. Children never wanted to

*The Russo-Japanese war lasted from late January, 1904 until September, 1905. "Ivan" is the colloquial personification of Russia.

play with him—he'd beat them up . . . even clobbered the Rebbe!
The neighbors said all along that no good would come of him. The
child was born with a caul on his head and a wild scream! Who ever
heard of such a thing? And Sarah—doesn't she run me to the
ground? Always bumming around . . . every day there's some new
scandal posted about her on the synagogue wall. We probably
should have married her off before Chane, even though she's
younger. Dear God, I only hope Chane brings us some
joy . . . she seems to be getting a decent fellow. . . ."

Zanvl turned over, opened his eyes, and stretched with a wide
yawn:

"Must be late!"

He jumped down, washed, put on his polished boots, combed
his hair Polish style, and broke into a dance, hands on hips, shouting:

"*Matko, Podavay*—Ma, gimme something!"

"You're worse than a goy," Tirzeh complained. "When a goy
gets up, the first thing he says is his Pater Noster. And you—"

"Not a word, mother," he laughed, catching the barefoot Tirzeh in his arms, and dancing with her despite her struggles.

"Let go of me, you bum! Poison's what I'll give you!"

Zanvl burst out laughing. He poured himself a glass of whiskey,
tossed it off and then sat down to his bowl of schav and potatoes.

Shloyme came in, with his prayershawl-bag under his arm. He
was about to say something, but Tirzeh cut him short: "A fine job
you've done on this son of yours, who's supposed to ease your way
into heaven! I wish it on my enemies' heads! Gets up like an animal,
doesn't say one word of prayer but wolfs down potatoes and schav.
Shloyme, you're getting what you deserve!"

Shloyme's lips tightened and he turned pale.

"Shut up, you old busybody! Who asked you?"

Zanvl went on happily chewing: "A thief doesn't have to pray."

Shloyme paced the room without answering. Tirzeh, he felt,
was right, but admitting it was out of the question. He loved Zanvl
dearly and forgave him much. "When he gets older," Shloyme told
himself, "he'll change. I wasn't any better myself at his age. At least
Zanvl's strong and brave—good qualities in a horse thief: they
command respect from the other thieves." Shloyme knew that ever
since Zanvl had entered his "business," people looked at him with
new respect.

"Saw Moyshe the Horse Dealer today," said Shloyme, breaking the silence.

"So?"

"He'll be here soon. From the drift of his talk I think he wants to bargain us down a few rubles. Claims he can get it cheaper."

"Cheaper? The devil take him! A penny less, Dad, and I don't budge from here. That sly bastard! I'll get him yet."

"All right, all right. Stop shouting, he's here," Shloyme said quickly, going to open the door. A tall, thick-set Jew in a loose overcoat came in.

"Good morning."

"Good year, Reb Moyshe," Shloyme replied, offering him a chair. "Have a seat."

Moyshe let himself down slowly, with a groan. He took some cigars out of his pocket, and passed them around. "Well, Zanvl," he began with a cough, "are you ready to go tonight?"

"If we come to an agreement, I'm ready at any time."

"What do you mean? I thought your father and I had settled it already."

"What's the use of beating around the bush, Reb Moyshe? Until I see two hundred rubles on the table, I don't budge. You claim that you can get it cheaper? Go right ahead. I won't mind a bit."

"Bah, Zanvl, you've a little too much pepper in you. You must be doing a flourishing business if you can throw away a hundred and fifty rubles like that. Listen, you've got to use your head. The whole thing will take less than an hour, and a hundred and fifty rubles for an hour's work seems pretty fair. Rothschild himself wouldn't turn it down. Come on, Zanvl, don't make a fool of yourself. Now if I were sure that the horses would get through, another fifty rubles wouldn't matter. But what do I do, God forbid, if the horses are seized? Will you stand partner on the loss, eh? You're not answering. That's no way to do business, Zanvl!"

Zanvl sulked and said nothing. He knew that Moyshe could talk him into anything, the old fox! Nearly all Moyshe's horses were brought in by him, and Moyshe got them for a song. Now he wanted to cut down the price by another fifty rubles. Nothing doing!

Zanvl stood up. "Reb Moyshe, you're wasting your breath. I won't take less than two hundred rubles."

Moyshe looked straight into Zanvl's eyes and smiled.

"Eh, Zanvl, you're getting much too excited. Shloyme and I will settle it between us. Bring in the whiskey."

Tirzeh brought some whiskey and a snack. With a groan Moyshe pulled out a thick wallet, counted out two hundred rubles and handed them to Shloyme.

They drank *l'khayim*, prayed the Lord to grant them success, and parted.

CHAPTER 6

In the evening Zanvl strode calmly into the courtyard of Moyshe the Horse Dealer, tapping his riding crop against his polished boots.

The horses were already in the forest outside town, but his own chestnut stallion stood saddled in the middle of the yard wagging its long tail. Its muzzle was covered with white foam. Every so often the horse threw back its proud head and stamped its hoofs, causing lumps of earth to fly in all directions.

Zanvl went up to the horse and began to pat its gleaming neck. The horse, recognizing him, broke into a welcoming whinny.

A blond girl sat at the open window, with a book in one hand and the other lightly rubbing the leaves of a myrtle plant that stood in the window. It was Moyshe's youngest daughter. Catching sight of Zanvl, she lifted her eyes from the book. Zanvl noticed it and struck a pose: like an actor he stared her right in the eye. The girl blushed, lay down her book and left the window with a ringing laugh.

"Big shot," thought Zanvl, "Moyshe's daughter. She and her swelled-head father aren't worth the nail on Rachel's little finger."

Soon Moyshe called him in for a glass of good wine. Zanvl paced stiffly over the plush carpets, found himself an armchair, crossed his legs and lit up a cigar. He was very pleased with Moyshe's fawning, ingratiating hospitality.

Eventually Zanvl took his leave. As he mounted his horse and rode out through the back gate, he forgot for a moment about the task before him. He had promised Rachel that he would ride along the highway near the gardens, so that she might see him in his glory. Like the storybook prince, he would lift her onto his horse, draw her close, and whisk her off. . . .

Once on the open road, Zanvl spurred the horse on. The animal strained forward and flew down the road as light as a bird. Rachel stood near the highway, waiting. She shuddered as she caught sight of the beautiful horse galloping down the road with its rider straight as a ramrod in the saddle. Zanvl rode up to Rachel. The horse began turning round her in circles. She took hold of the bit.

"Zanvl, how handsome you are on the horse! If I weren't ashamed of being caught, I'd climb right up there with you. Jump down, I'll give you a kiss," she said, dropping her eyes.

Zanvl blushed and jumped down to embrace her.

The horse stood still, pricked up its ears, and widened its clever eyes to observe the couple.

"Are you sure you won't be caught, Zanvl? If you are, what will happen to me? Will I ever see you again?"

"No one will catch me! Don't be afraid, dear Rachel. We'll meet again tomorrow."

"Then hold me once more. Just like that. Tighter!"

When Zanvl was once more up in the saddle, he gave Rachel a final loving, childish smile, and squeezed her hand.

She patted the horse and told it to ride very swiftly.

Zanvl bent down and gave his horse a slight prod. Instantly the horse stretched, lunged forward and clouds of dust sprang up over the road.

For a long time Rachel stood lost in thought, until Zanvl was out of sight.

CHAPTER 7

As soon as Zanvl approached the wood, he caught sight of his father with two young helpers. Quickly he dismounted and began tying up the horses single file, the tail of one to the bit of the next. Then he said goodbye to his father, and left the woods slowly, taking narrow bypaths, the two youths right behind him.

During the ride Zanvl tried to fix his thoughts on the border, but the image of Rachel kept intruding. What if they shot him tonight, after all, he suddenly worried. With a broad smile, he pulled a small flask of whiskey from his boot and took several gulps to drive away the fear.

Before very long they reached the edge of the stream. "Stop!" called Zanvl softly, raising his hand. They all stood still.

"We'll wait here until it gets good and dark. Here, fellows, take the whiskey and rub it over the animals' muzzles to keep them from neighing. But do it quietly. Not a sound, understand?"

The horses soon grew calmer, as if they too sensed the danger. They crowded together with lowered heads and stood as if chained. Zanvl looked at them, pressed together, their heads hanging drowsily, and a strange feeling of pity overcame him.

Everything was quiet. An occasional breeze brought the wet, keen smell of juniper and ripe plums. The stream flowed calmly along, its small violet ripples tumbling and swallowing one another up. Zanvl lay on his stomach, watching the dark blue mountains grow out of the water and into the sky. A red belt of light cut the mountains in two, leaving them suspended between the elements.

Zanvl felt a force surge through his limbs, making him livelier and wilder. He imagined the dark violet ripples calling to him and he longed to throw off his clothes and leap into the water.

"Hey fellows, let's take a swim!" he said, turning to the other two. They raised their heads, looked at each other and shrugged as if to say, "Some guys will go *looking* for trouble."

Zanvl spat contemptuously into the water. "Sissies!" he muttered and began swifly to undress.

The still water suddenly broke with Zanvl's dive. He swam in a circle a few times and came out. "Fools, you don't know a good thing when you see it," he said. He grabbed hold of a thick branch and began swinging it back and forth.

It grew darker and darker. The horses stood motionless, as if chiseled out of stone. It took a dousing of cold water to rouse them back to life. The party moved on quietly. There was only the rhythmic beating of the horses' hoofs and an occasional neigh. A red light appeared in the distance, illuminating the long chain that dangled from a high block of wood, painted white with black stripes, that marked the border.

Zanvl turned off into a side-path and slowed down. He kept patting his stallion and treated him now and then to a lump of sugar.

There was a sound of footsteps. They halted and listened. All was silent again, and they moved on. Zanvl looked around. Another fifty paces and they would be in Prussia. They turned into a small sandy path and began driving the horses through prickly gooseberry bushes.

Two soldiers were approaching from a distance. For an instant Zanvl shivered, but he pulled himself together and ordered the boys to whip the horses with all their might. The horses whinnied in fright. The soldiers raised their rifles and took aim. The boys jumped off and ran back into the bushes.

Zanvl was furious. Shouting, "Cowardly dogs! A plague on you!" he rode toward the soldiers who stopped him and began untying the horses. Zanvl argued and tried to bribe them, but to no avail. A cold sweat covered his body. He gritted his teeth and dug his spurs into his stallion as hard as he could. The horse leaped forward and with its forelegs knocked down one of the soldiers. It sped away like an arrow with the other horses in pursuit. The second soldier began shooting in confusion, killing several of the animals, but Zanvl had already reached the other side of the border and gleefully thumbed his nose.

Two Germans were waiting for him on the other side. One of them led the horses away and the second invited Zanvl to join him in a mug of beer.

Near the tavern Zanvl noticed clusters of people sitting on the grass. He knew them as professional smugglers of second-hand clothes. They were waiting for the one o'clock train from Berlin, carrying the old-clothes dealers. That very night they would unpack the goods, each of the smugglers donning several suits of clothes before crossing the border back into Poland.

A group of elderly Jews in long loose coats sat nearby, enjoying a quiet talk. They envied the tavern keeper, whose establishment, situated on the highway, was busy day and night. They themselves were Hasidim of good family, but poor; they had tried all trades, even teaching, and had failed at them all. Now they made a meager living crossing between Poland and Prussia, and back again, wearing several jackets each and several pairs of pants.

A cluster of pious Jewish women wearing wigs were gossiping indignantly about the Jewish girls sitting a little further away with a group of Gentile boys and girls. Laughter rang out from where the young people were sitting. The boys held a girl down on the grass, wagering she had nothing on under her dress in order to leave as much room as possible for smuggled clothes. The girl lay there yelling until an old Jewess, unable to restrain herself, came over and began railing at them. They let the girl go. An impudent young fellow jumped up, hugged the old woman and tried to kiss her. She screamed, while everybody roared with laughter.

A German sauntered by smoking a thick cigar. He stopped, spat "Dirty Jews!" and continued on.

In the tavern, Zanvl downed several mugs of beer, smoked a cigar, and took his leave. The merchants with their bundles of clothes had already arrived and spread out their merchandise in the middle of a field. The smugglers threw off their clothes and stood there in undershirts and drawers, the women blouseless in their petticoats—all of them pushing, straining to get to the merchants, with the stronger ones grabbing most of the clothes. The women fought with the girls and the girls tore the wigs from the women's heads. Meanwhile, a half-naked Gentile boy came over and carefully untied the string of a girl's petticoat. When the girl reached out to get hold of a jacket, she found herself standing in a pair of short linen drawers. The young ruffians formed a circle and began dancing around her, refusing to let her out.

A friendly guard came by with his gun on his shoulder, joking with the Jews and giving them advice. And when the time came, a buxom girl took the guard's arm and went off with him into the woods.

Zanvl stood at a distance watching the scene. With a spit of disgust, he shouted "Stinkers!" and vanished into a side street.

He was approached by a group of smugglers with packs on their backs.

"Hey, Zanvl," called a red-haired man, "what are you doing here?"

"I had a date with a German," he said quietly, walking on.

"Tell it to your grandma, Zanvl. We know what you were up to," interjected a small, broad-shouldered fellow.

"Louse! Who asked you? Is it any of your business?"

"That's right." The red-head turned to the little fellow. "Always poking your nose into everything. If he belted you, do you think I'd lift a finger? The hell I would! You'll put your foot in it one of these days. And you, Zanvl, why get so excited? Let the dog bark. Maybe you'd like to take along a package of silks?"

"Sure!" said Zanvl. "How much do I get?"

"A ten-spot, the usual."

"No deal, brother. Fifteen."

The red-head thought it over and agreed.

The smugglers put down their packs, while the red-head went off, returning after a few minutes with a large bundle of silks. Zanvl put the straps over his shoulders, lifted the bundle lightly on his back and set out. When they reached the border, they split into two groups, the red-head in the lead. They took off their boots, rolled up their trouser legs and waited. The red-head went into the woods to check things out. Soon he returned with some soldiers, signaled with his hand, and the group easily crossed the border. They walked through the woods in single file. No one said a word; at the slightest sound they slid into the tall grain with their bundles, lay there until it was again quiet, and then moved on.

Zanvl was tired. The day's activities had exhausted him and all his limbs ached. Several times he tried thinking of Rachel, but he couldn't collect his thoughts.

At about three in the morning they reached the last village just outside town. They dropped their bundles and sat down to rest in a meadow. Suddenly there came the sound of hoofbeats. They grabbed their bundles and scattered in all directions. Zanvl ran without his cap. He was exhausted through and through. Shots rang through the air.

"They're chasing us!" Zanvl thought, coming to a standstill. He saw before him the ancient graveyard, and scaled the fence, jumping down lightly as a cat on the other side. Calmly, quietly, he began to walk among the tombstones. Beside a tall mound he put down his bundle for a pillow, flung himself on the ground and fell asleep. . . .

CHAPTER 8

Ever since meeting Rachel, Zanvl had begun to avoid his old friends and even stayed away from the tavern for weeks on end. In his free time, Zanvl's greatest pleasure was walking Morva along the riverbank where he would stretch out in the tall grass, with the dog beside him, to do some thinking. If he was in especially good spirits, he would tumble through the grass, with Morva pawing and licking him and wagging his tail furiously.

Nevertheless, from time to time Zanvl was seized by a great longing for his friends and for the tavern. He felt a tightening in his muscles, and a pounding in his chest, and at such moments he would pull his cap down over his eyes and set out for the familiar haunt.

The day after Zanvl returned from Prussia, he badly wanted to see his friends, and share his exploits with them. Early in the afternoon he set out for the tavern.

Across the entire length of the room, along the wall, stretched a counter with kegs of whiskey and beer barrels, and glasses, copper measuring cups, and mugs set out on a long copper tray. The ceiling was supported by a heavy square beam on which were engraved the names of various thieves and the dates of their exploits. Behind the counter a tall, heavy woman named Brayne the Cossack sat picking her nose. Young men were eating at some of the tables. In a corner, three fellows were drinking, one of them with a young girl on his lap who was smoking a cigarette. The girl's name was Manke. The inn smelled of roast meat.

"Look who's here!" yelled Brayne. "My, my, what a fine fellow you are. Too much of a snob to come to the tavern!"

Zanvl was greeted by cries of welcome and thronged from all sides. He sat down gaily with the gang at a large table.

"Fifteen bottles of lager!" he called. "How have you been, all of you! Honest to God, I missed you guys."

"Now that you've become such a nobleman, we never see you any more. What do you do all day long?" This came from Gradul, a tall, pock-marked fellow with two scars on his left cheek.

"Beats me," replied Zanvl. "I don't even know myself how I manage to kill so much time."

"That's the truth, brother," said Gradul with a wink at the others. "Our buddy here had better not get too tangled up with broads. That's a fool's business. If you like a woman, marry her; if not, take her and leave her. Believe me, Zanvl—Manke can't hear me—" he interjected with a lewd wink, "you can live with her for a year without marrying."

The fellows choked with laughter. Manke was incensed.

"You can drop dead, you pock-marked beast. I'll never speak to you again!"

"But what's all this about, anyway?" Zanvl asked Gradul.

"I'll tell you," said Moyshele, a giant of a fellow. "The other day, 'Calfer' came by and said that you had been up to something. Late at night he drove out with a wagon to pick up some corn from Nosn the Gardener. On the way he stopped dead in his tracks —there you were walking through the field with a girl in your arms, and rocking her to sleep as if she were a child! He nearly passed out laughing, but for fear of you, he left."

Zanvl paled and then gave a smile.

"Is she pretty?" asked Manke approaching him. "Prettier than me? Zanvl, remember, once I was yours. You used to buy me patent leather shoes. Remember? . . ."

For reply, Zanvl embraced Manke and set her down on his lap. With that, the fellows opened the bottles, took a swig and began exchanging stories. Meanwhile Gradul crept up behind Manke and poured beer down her back. She shivered and feigned anger, threatening to tell his wife.

"What, since when are you married? I don't believe it," said Zanvl in amazement.

"What else, buddy? A dog's life gets you down. Should I spend my days begging Manke for a kiss? Today you buy her a pair of shoes, later a corset, and when the chips are down she'll give you the bum's rush. Who needs it? My wife, lemme tell you, is a real find. She's from Warsaw, she's small and dark, like a mouse, and when she starts kissing—I've had it! And you should see the way she cooks. What else do I need?"

"Looks like a happy guy, doesn't he?" said Manke turning to Zanvl. "But he gives me a pack of trouble just the same."

The men grinned. Gradul emptied his mug in one gulp and slapped Zanvl on the back.

"Come on over, Zanvl. My woman wants to meet you."

"Where did you find her?"

"Where? I was at the Praga Fair, met a girl I liked, we got married, and that was it!"

Zanvl ordered another ten bottles. A skinny fellow took out a harmonica, folded back the peak of his cap, and began playing a waltz. Manke stood up, and holding the hem of her short skirt in her hand, tapped out the rhythm lightly. A peasant girl and boy soon emerged from the corner and started dancing. The boy was half drunk, his eyes glazed and his hair disheveled. He held the girl very tightly, lifted her into the air and grunted loudly as they danced.

Manke pulled Zanvl up by the hands and drew him into the waltz. He danced for a while, but then changed his mind, paced the length of the room a few times and sat down. The harmonica player struck up a mazurka.

Manke took hold of Gradul. They began to dance faster and faster. Her light dress billowed like a carousel. When it came time for her to stomp her foot and bang her heel, she turned her leg in such a way that the dress flew up and her legs looked out temptingly from beneath her striped stockings. The fellows gaped.

The harmonica player stopped. He wiped off his sweat, took a sip from his mug and began playing a song that was then in vogue from Goldfaden's musical comedy *Shmendrik*. Everyone joined in:

> *Hotsmakh cannot see.*
> *Where can his children be?*

Manke returned to Zanvl, sat down on his lap and joined in the singing. Her face was aflame; her nostrils twitched like a young colt's. Zanvl embraced her tightly. The singing grew louder. The drunken peasant boy lying nearby shrieked raucously. It sounded like the scraping of dull knives against iron pots. Manke leaned her head on Zanvl's chest.

"Zanvl, come to me tonight. Will you? Remember how you used to say that you loved me? Go on, you're a good-for-nothing! You have someone else already. Tell me, Zanvl, which one of us is prettier? Is it Manke?"

Zanvl felt himself going pale. He lifted Manke by the hands and sat her down in an empty chair. He imagined Rachel standing in a corner, watching his behavior with a pale and tearful face. He shuddered, gave Gradul a slap on the back and went out into the street.

For a long time he walked around in silence, vaguely depressed. Now his friends knew that he had a girl. He was especially angry for having held Manke on his lap the whole time. If only he could be with Morva now, and stretch out under the apple tree with his eyes closed, to do some thinking.

"What's eating you?" asked Gradul, who had caught up with him.

"I dunno . . . I've got this awful taste in my mouth and my head's killing me. . . ."

"Zanvl, you're worse than a dame. Big deal, so you finished off five bottles! Look at me, I don't feel a thing. . . . Listen, I've been thinking about Manke. You know, the broad's getting more beautiful every day. And she's wild about you."

"What the devil, are you crazy? You just got married, and you're back to Manke already."

"Zanvl, you're an idiot. A wife's a wife! She's mine forever. But Manke is something else. Don't worry, I'll have enough left over for my woman. I'm a healthy fellow, thank God."

Zanvl did not answer. He felt his insides churning.

"I live right here," Gradul announced pointing to a small cottage. He opened the door wide and let Zanvl in.

"Beyle, this is my friend Zanvl I've told you about."

Beyle was a short, dark-complexioned woman in a flowered dressing gown, with a long braid hanging down like a young girl's. She gave Zanvl a blushing smile and extended a small, warm hand.

"Well, Zanvl, how do you like my wife?" said Gradul, taking hold of Beyle from behind and turning her around to face Zanvl, who grinned childishly, not knowing how to answer.

"Say, Beyle, let's have a bite to eat. Something good, in honor of our guest."

"Yes, of course. Zanvl, excuse me, I'll be right back." She said this with a smile and hurried into the next room.

"C'mon Zanvl, tell me the truth. Do you like her? She's a find, isn't she?"

"Eat dirt! With a wife like that, why fool around with Manke? Shame on you, big shot."

"Don't shout. She'll hear you." His pock-marked face beamed.

Soon Beyle entered dressed in a black, light skirt, and a white silk blouse with black stripes. She carried a tray with fruit, wine, and preserves.

"Take a look at her, all dolled up! She'd never do it for her own husband, but at the sight of a stranger, she gets all decked out."

Beyle looked at Zanvl with a smile.

"Take something, Zanvl. Feel at home," said Gradul joyfully.

Beyle sat with her legs crossed and told stories about Warsaw. How smoothly she spoke, how fine! Zanvl couldn't take his eyes off her. Her voice was so pleasant, and when she smiled, he noticed that a small tooth was missing up front; this seemed to make her even more attractive. She spoke with the "r" and the broad vowels of the Warsaw dialect, and smiled fetchingly—Zanvl was entranced.

Gradul stretched out on the couch and listened to his wife. If

only she proved suitable, he thought, she could become the "mother" of all the thieves and then his troubles would be over. In his joy,
he hummed a tune and so doing, fell asleep. His foot rose into the
air like a pillar and he began to snore. Beyle and Zanvl burst out
laughing.

Several times, as Zanvl rose to go, Beyle detained him. When
he finally said good-night, she held his hand for a long time, gave
him a captivating smile and insisted on a definite date for his return.

Once outside, Zanvl breathed easier. He thought: yes, indeed,
she's a good woman. Soon a vague confusion set in and he sighed,
as if a heavy load had suddenly been placed on his heart.

"Ice cream!" bawled a tall Russian in a blue shirt, right under
Zanvl's ear. He carried his barrel of wares on his head.

"How the devil did that Russkie get over here?" muttered Zanvl
angrily. Just then he caught sight of Moyshe the Horse Dealer
dragging himself along the street, puffing like a stuffed goose.

"Look at him sweat! He can barely drag his ass!" said Zanvl to
himself. "If only I could catch that guy in a back street, I'd grab him
by the ears, bash my knee into that potbelly of his and thin him
down a little."

"Hey, wake up!" shouted Shloyme, seeing his son in the middle
of the street talking to himself.

Zanvl looked around, and smiled at his father. "Damn it all, the
guys got hold of me. You know how it is, we washed down a
couple."

"Then go lie down for a while. If anyone saw you now, he'd
think you were off your rocker."

Zanvl went into the house and announced that he wanted to be
awakened around eight o'clock. He grabbed a pillow and blanket,
and, taking Morva along for company, stretched out under the
apple tree. He fell asleep immediately. The dog lay down beside
him, stuck out its tongue, and dozed.

CHAPTER 9

For Rachel, the day of her rendezvous with Zanvl seemed to last a
year. All day her movements were livelier; she did everything quickly, as if to speed up the hours. On the farm she ran around in a state

of excitement and drove the girls in their work. Several times she withdrew into the hut, lay down, tossed about, and then emerged again. She let the girls off an hour earlier than usual.

When she got home, Rachel took down the brass basin and filled it with cold water. Washing herself with a bar of scented soap, she took pleasure in the crackling sound of the lather as it wriggled through her open fingers. The white suds scattered and heaps of rainbow-bubbles appeared. She studied her fresh white skin in the mirror and then began to massage it with soap and cold water. As she rubbed, she felt her skin become fresher and tighter, like a violin string.

When evening came Rachel put on a light calico skirt, a polka dotted blouse, and a red beaded necklace. She stood before the mirror for a while humming to herself, then hurried off to the farm. On the way she gathered bluish-white cornflowers and wove them into a wreath. To pass the time, she strolled between the farm and neighboring woods, thinking about what she would say to Zanvl. When he failed to appear on time, she grew impatient. Knowing the way he would come, she set out to meet him with the wreath of cornflowers on her head, looking in all directions. She saw a shadow and then a tall, looming figure. Rachel called out happily and ran forward. The figure continued on for several paces, turned away and disappeared.

An hour passed. Rachel grew more anxious. She ran into the hut and burst into tears.

"He'll never come," she argued with herself, "and if he does show up, I'll tell him to leave! What does a horse thief know about love, anyway? While I'm lying here, tearing my heart to pieces in anticipation, he's probably prowling around in some stable lifting horses. It serves me right!

"But maybe he was shot yesterday?" she suddenly thought. "He had to take a party of horses across the border and the border's guarded by so many soldiers! He must have been shot. Otherwise he would have come." She threw herself face down on the grass and began to sob.

Thick dust clouds rose before her eyes. Through the dust appeared Zanvl riding a black horse, at the head of his gang. Soldiers suddenly approached. Shots rang out. Zanvl fell from the horse and lay in a pool of blood. The horses galloped over him but the air echoed with his cry: Rachel, Rachel! My Rachtshe. . . .

CHAPTER 10

Even in his sleep Zanvl knew he was late, and he tried unsuccessfully to awake. At last he jumped up with a shout, as if scorched, and looked around. It was already quite dark, but the droves of stars in the purple sky broke through the darkness and illuminated everything round about. Zanvl looked at his watch.

"Damn, I'm an hour and a half late! I thought I told the old man to wake me up. Who knows if she'll still be there? Now she'll think—'that's what you get for going with a thief.'"

Teeth on edge, Zanvl threw off his jacket and made for the well at the edge of the courtyard. He pumped a bucket of water, drank, and washed. Then he set out for the farm.

He ran almost the whole way. His mind was blank, he felt only the beating of his heart. When he reached the meeting place, no one was there; he felt as if one of his limbs had been severed. He stopped and looked around. Someone seemed to be sitting near the hill. Nervously, he drew closer—it was nothing but a log. He sat down on it with clenched fists and tried to think calmly, but he could only come up with curses for the old man. He picked up a heavy branch and began snapping it into bits.

Suddenly he caught sight of Morva. Zanvl vented his anger on the dog, grabbing him by the ears and shaking hard. Morva doubled up on the ground and stared up at his master in bewilderment. The dog's silent plea aroused Zanvl's pity; he stretched out beside Morva on the grass, and lay there for several minutes. But the thought of Rachel brought him back to his feet and he began pacing through the field. When he reached the hut, Zanvl looked in and gave a start—someone was lying face down on the ground.

"Rachel!"

She turned over quickly, then turned back again at the sight of him. In confusion, Zanvl knelt down beside her.

"Rachel, are you angry? Don't be angry. Honestly, it wasn't my fault. I told them to wake me up an hour early and they didn't wake me up at all! Don't you believe me? Rachel, please!"

She turned to look at him, half angrily.

"And what about me? Why did I get there ahead of time?"

Zanvl dropped his eyes, like a little boy caught fibbing.

"Yes, I know why," she said more emphatically. "It's because you don't even think about me. All you care about is your horses or who knows what else. Ever since this morning I thought only about you, waiting for night to come. When you didn't show up, you can't imagine what went through my mind. Good God! Maybe you were killed, or—"

Zanvl's heart felt lighter. He wanted to blurt out everything, about Manke, about Beyle . . . but as soon as he met Rachel's dark eyes, he became tongue-tied.

Sensing his discomfort, she moved to his side and raised a finger at him like a mother.

"Do you promise me that—"

"Take my word," Zanvl interrupted, "I'm not to blame. They didn't wake me up. Rachel, believe me, I'll never fall asleep again!"

Rachel burst out laughing. She sat down in Zanvl's lap and took hold of his chin. "I thought you wouldn't come, that I'd never sit with you like this again. So tell me, how did you lead the horses across? You can't imagine how handsome you were, sitting on the black stallion. All you needed was a white cloak. Do you love me at all, Zanvl, do you?"

Zanvl was drunk with joy. He told her how he crossed the border. She cuddled up on his lap like a kitten, listening attentively. She took the wreath of flowers from her head and put it on his, then clung even closer. A huge, thick forest loomed before her eyes. She was sitting under an old oak tree, her hair down, weaving a wreath. A lost Prince of the Forest appeared before her on a black horse. He bowed to her three times and asked for the wreath. She placed the wreath on the Prince's blond head. He wrapped her in his white cloak and rode off with her deep into the forest. . . .

Late that night, Rachel got up, stretched, and went out, still in a daze. All at once she shrieked, and stood stock-still in fright. There was Morva straining toward her and barking.

"You bloody hound!" yelled Zanvl, pulling the dog by the ears. "He's mine," he explained to Rachel. "Don't be frightened."

Rachel looked at the black, shaggy dog with new affection. She and Zanvl set out silently for town, hand in hand.

"Rachel, you know, my sister's getting married soon."

"Really? To what's-his-name? The wagon-driver?"

"Yes, to Berke."

"Zanvl, would you like me to come to the wedding?" she stopped and looked him straight in the eye.

"*Would* I? . . . but I dunno . . . what'll people say?"

"If *I* don't care, why should you, silly? Listen, Zanvl. Before the wedding, have your sister come and invite me. Father will let me go. I'll make myself a gown the likes of which no one in all of Poland has ever worn. You'll see what your Rachel looks like in a long, white silk dress. And I'll put a white rose in my hair—I'll be lovely! But remember, at the wedding you must pretend you don't know me. Why don't you say something? Go on, I hate you!"

Zanvl pulled her into his arms and covered her face with kisses.

CHAPTER 11

For several days, Reb Shloyme's door swung to and fro with the passage of people. Each time the door opened, Shloyme had to open his purse, but he could not complain. After all, marrying off one's firstborn child was no mean feat. When would he have another such occasion? Dressed in his Sabbath caftan, he sat at home for days on end, seeing that all was properly done.

In the middle of the room Chane was busy putting her trousseau into a large wicker basket. She shook out a skirt with an embroidered petticoat, and lost herself in a moment of reverie before folding it up and continuing with her packing.

Tirzeh and Sarah were in the kitchen, blouseless, counting the pastries that the baker had just brought. From time to time, Tirzeh went out to Shloyme, covering her bosom with her apron, to ask why the fish hadn't yet been delivered. "Don't worry, Tirzeh! We'll have fish all right—fresh and lively ones! I just sent five boys down to the river."

Tirzeh poked Shloyme with her elbow and pointed to Chane who stood with a flushed face, holding up her blue silk dress.

"How long has it been since I stood that way," said Tirzeh with a sigh. "Shloyme, just for fun, do you remember what kind of wedding dress I wore?"

"Ask me a tougher one than that," he replied with a smile.

The door opened and in came Israel the Teacher, a spectacled, skinny little man, in a coat that was cut short—but not too short. He straightened his protruding rubber collar with one hand while with the other he took off his hat and wiped the sweat from his brow.

"Welcome," said Shloyme extending a hand and offering his guest a chair.

"Thank you," replied the teacher, smiling. "So my little student Chane is getting married. How time flies!"

Chane served him whiskey with honey cake. Israel drank a toast to Shloyme and to Chane's well-being, and his thin nose reddened. Then he took pen and ink from his breast pocket while Chane dictated the names to whom wedding invitations were to be sent.

Shloyme watched Israel's pen fly across the envelopes, turning and quivering, forming beautiful letters. He wondered why such a learned man as Israel was so poorly off, going from house to house tutoring children for a ruble a month.

When Israel grew tired of writing, he wiped the pen with a piece of paper, helped himself to another whiskey and began telling Shloyme the latest news. He was an expert on all the world leaders, knew the exact strength of each, and his descriptions of a war sent a shudder through the heart.

Shloyme listened openmouthed. As usual, he tried to steer the discussion to the Turkish war. He knew beforehand what Israel would say, but no matter, he loved to hear the teacher talk.

Throughout the conversation, Chane sat with eyes lowered. When he was her teacher, Israel had often hugged her and kissed her. Once, as he held her on his lap, his wife had come in with one of their children, and from that day forward Chane took no more lessons from him. As a result, she had never learned more than her prayers.

The sexton, accompanied by several "inviters," arrived to pick up the invitations. When they left, Shloyme went with them. Israel immediately grew livelier, joking with Chane and asking her questions that made her blush scarlet in shame. His work finished, he took a ruble note and downed another whiskey. Chane packed some honey cake for his children and invited him to the wedding.

"Of course, of course, what do you think?" he smiled, and went into the kitchen to share a joke with the women. Tirzeh and Sarah doubled up in laughter.

Outside Zanvl and some of the neighborhood boys were building a wooden platform where all the guests would eat. The makeshift structure covered the entire yard.

CHAPTER 12

On a festively-bedded sofa sat the bride in her blue silk wedding gown. She wore a crown of myrtles, to which was attached a wide, white veil that fell lightly over her shoulders and down to her waist.

The sounds of a waltz filled the hall. The girls paired off with each other and danced gracefully, their brightly colored gowns rustling with the movement of their bodies. The boys watched hungrily from the musicians' stall.

Mendel the Contractor's daughter, in whose house the bride was staying, had invited her girl friends from boarding school. Now she called them to join her on the balcony to take in the sight of "simple folk" enjoying a wedding. The hall became more and more crowded with women of all ages. Tirzeh and her relatives-to-be walked around the hall carrying trays of sweets which they offered to the guests.

Suddenly Beyle, Gradul's wife, appeared, in a green silk gown with buttons down the side and two shimmering rows of forget-me-nots. Her arms were almost bare, covered only by some black silk tulle. Around her shoulders and neck was a sky-blue scarf that writhed like a snake. She wore long, white silk gloves. Her black hair was parted in the middle and her two thick braids were piled in coils on either side.

Beyle caused a stir as she made her way across the hall, her well-shaped legs offering a secret provocation to the watching men. She embraced the bride as if unmindful that everyone was staring at her; then she began to twirl a golden chain from which a small bottle of perfume was suspended.

"She must be from Warsaw," the women chattered.

Beyle caught sight of Zanvl and smiled, beckoning to him with her finger. Zanvl hesitated to enter the hall, but before he could decide one way or the other, the small, dark-complexioned temptress came bustling up to him.

"Mazl tov, Zanvl," she said, stretching out a small gloved hand.

Blushing, Zanvl shook her hand and thanked her.

"Why don't we see you, Zanvl? You're not a man of your word. I thought you promised to visit and you haven't shown up!"

Unable to think of an excuse, Zanvl began to stutter and turn redder still. Beyle seemed to enjoy his discomfort.

"I'll forgive you this time, but from now on you be a good boy, do you hear?" Saying this, she leaned toward him roguishly and poked him with her knee. Zanvl felt the blood rising to his face. "And now, Zanvl, throw in some money and we'll dance."

"But the women . . . they'll—" he stammered.

"Big deal! I'll tell them I'm one of your aunts, all right?" Beyle laughed and her black eyes sparkled.

Zanvl threw the musicians some money, took Beyle by the arm and made his way through the couples. Some of the older women looked askance, but it was a wedding, after all! Everyone watched Beyle soar, float lightly as a bird, barely touching the floor. Zanvl held her lightly, and with his head bent over he felt himself becoming drunk on the perfume of her bosom, floating in a magical dance in which Beyle's silk dress seemed to be hissing like a horde of snakes. Beyle shouted across to the musicians: a polka!

Everyone stopped dancing. Beyle stood at one end, Zanvl at the other. Beyle lifted her train with her right hand. She hummed along with the music, practicing the step, until finally, she raised her leg, brushed aside her short white petticoat, and moved toward Zanvl, raising her shoulders seductively, her dark eyes sparkling. They embraced. Zanvl felt her tightening her hold and heard her ask: "Why didn't you come to me?"

The dance ended. Zanvl wiped his perspiring brow and began heading back to the musicians when he noticed Rachel.

She had watched as he danced with the beautiful woman, and her heart froze: Zanvl seemed infatuated with her. Never for a moment did his eyes stray from her; he held his lips so close to her dark hair he might have kissed it. How beautiful she was and how well she danced! Rachel was overcome with sadness and regret; she looked for an excuse to leave the hall.

For a moment, on meeting Zanvl's eyes, she felt somewhat

better, but a second later she dropped her eyes again, more miserable than before. Zanvl walked into another room and sat down. He wanted to go up to Rachel and plead his innocence. He would not have entered the dance hall at all but for his desire to see her in her white ball gown. . . .

"What's the matter, Zanvl? Here, have some of this." Next to him stood Beyle with a tray of sweets in her hand. She laughed and nudged him with her shoe. He took a piece of chocolate. Beyle sat down next to him with her hand on his leg and began to say something.

Across the room Rachel stood watching them, in her white floor length gown with her long braids hanging down. Zanvl turned pale as chalk.

"What is it? Is something wrong?" asked Beyle. She turned her head and noticed Rachel.

Rachel froze on meeting Beyle's eyes. "He's laughing at me, he's pointing out the girl who's in love with him," she thought as tears formed in her eyes. Rachel walked out on the balcony, wiped her eyes, and prayed for a rapid end to the evening.

"Who is that girl?" asked Beyle.

"A friend of my sister's," came Zanvl's blushing reply.

"Why is she staring at us? Is she jealous?"

Zanvl did not answer. He lowered his eyes and began biting his nails. Beyle got up to return to the dancing. Zanvl remained seated, a buzzing in his ears. Several times he stood up, buttoned his jacket, and prepared to go over to Rachel, but his feet would not move from the spot.

Meanwhile, Rachel sat down in a corner, so as not to be seen, and waited impatiently for the ceremony to begin. She felt that if she had to sit there much longer, she would burst into tears. Suddenly she noticed sixteen girls dancing a "Lancer." Eight stood on one side as the "Gentlemen" and eight on the other side facing them as the "Ladies." With arms raised, they swam past one another, formed a circle, turning and bending their bodies gracefully, then parted and continued dancing.

Rachel felt as if everyone were looking at her, pointing at her. She tried to avoid their eyes, but almost in spite of herself her eyes met Beyle's frivolous glance, then recoiled as if scorched by a flame.

"What's the matter, Rachel, why so glum?" asked Sarah, her face flushed from the dancing.

Rachel was on the verge of tears. She shook her head, bit her
lower lip and replied with a feigned smile: "I have a bit of a
headache, but it doesn't matter. If you like, I'll throw in for a
dance." So saying, she jumped up, threw a coin to the musicians,
and took Sarah soaring through the hall. She sensed the elegant
lady staring at her. In the heat of the dance Rachel dropped her
pride and asked Sarah about Beyle. "Was she a friend of Zanvl's,
from Warsaw?"

Suddenly it grew quiet. Then the musicians struck up the
traditional wedding tune and from all sides people shouted: "To the
khupe! To the ceremony!"

When Zanvl finally stood up, the hall was empty. He quickly
made his way into the street and started pushing through the crowd
that filled the street from the market place to the synagogue courtyard.

Manke came up to him, in the company of a red-haired boy.

"Mazl tov, Zanvl," she said. "A fine fellow you are, ignoring
your old friends. Your sister's getting married and you don't even
invite me."

"Don't be silly, Manke. I'm thankful *I* was invited. If I don't
invite you to my own wedding, then you'll have cause for
complaint," he smiled.

CHAPTER 13

The platform that Zanvl had constructed was illumined by lanterns
from the wagon drivers' synagogue. Two tables stretched across its
entire length: one for the men and one for the women. Outside, a
group of boys stood around, admiring Shloyme the Rustler's lavish
celebration.

Zanvl sat among the guests, drinking for all he was worth. He
felt everything going to his head; in a moment his brain would pop
like a cork.

"Zanvl, come help me bring in another keg of whiskey. There's
none left."

"What the devil!" flashed through Zanvl's mind and he followed
Beyle out. Instead of going into the house, they went behind the
apple tree.

"Zanvl, where's the whiskey?" she asked, looking at him with wanton eyes.

"Shut up!" he muttered and embraced her forcefully.

"Zanvl, please don't! My husband's coming!"

Zanvl released her at once, looked around, then growled: "Get going, then, to your husband!"

Beyle left in a huff and Zanvl stretched out under the tree. There was a bitter taste in his mouth; he felt only disgust for the woman. Rachel's face swam before his eyes, but only for a fleeting moment. To soothe his throbbing temples, he went over to the well, pumped a bucket of water and dunked his head.

Lively melodies and wild laughter resounded from the platform, but it only served to annoy him. As if on stilts, he turned around and walked through the quiet streets where an occasional night watchman sat dozing, cudgel in hand.

Zanvl came upon Rachel's house involuntarily. The house stood in the middle of a small clump of trees, encircled by a high wooden fence. For a moment he stopped in front of the fence to clear his thoughts. Through the silence, he seemed to hear soft crying and then sobs.

Without stopping to consider, Zanvl cleared the fence and in a few steps reached the cottage. The window was open and by the moon's light he saw Rachel, in a white nightshirt lying on the bed. In an instant, Zanvl caught hold of the window ledge and climbed into her room. Then he stood there in confusion.

Rachel trembled slightly, opened her eyes, and closed them again. Suddenly, as if remembering something, her eyes shot open and she gave a loud scream. Zanvl turned pale, and tried to calm her.

"Get out! That's just what a thief would do! How dare you steal into a girl's room at night. Get out of here, this minute!"

Zanvl was thunderstruck. Speechless, he scrambled back through the window, but caught his foot and shattered a pane of glass. Frightened and angry, he spat, and pulled his cap over his eyes. With a curse, he jumped over the fence, then climbed back again imagining she had called his name. But there was no one in sight, and so he turned once more and went on his way.

He thought his head would split apart. His ears rang with the words: "That's just what a thief would do . . . a thief!"

". . . They're all like that. When Moyshe the Horse Dealer

meets me in public, he pretends not to know me. But when he needs me, he kisses my ass. Damn! I'll tear his guts out. Now Rachel has me down for a thief, but when she wanted me, I was a prince. I'll never go to her again! No, sir! Gradul was right: you can't get too mixed up with a girl. . . ."

Suddenly Zanvl felt cold raindrops on his face and stopped in his tracks. The sky was covered with a heavy, dark cloud that thickened and sank ever lower over the town.

Out of nowhere a homeless dog appeared with its tail between its legs and began to rub against Zanvl. He gave the dog a vicious kick. The animal yelped piteously and limped away, its wails echoing strangely in the dark night and filling Zanvl with a terrible sadness.

A white, serpent-like flash sliced through the cloud, leaving the night even darker in its wake. Then a huge crash reverberated and the rain poured down.

Zanvl stood still, his head tilted back and his mouth open. The rain slapped and beat against his face. The heaviness within him dissolved; it was as if a cold compress had been placed on his burning brain. Soon the rain subsided and the cloud split apart, admitting a clear, newly washed moon.

Zanvl shivered with cold. He was soaked to the skin. He lifted his jacket collar, pulled down his cap and continued through the streets to a small cottage at the edge of town, where Manke lived. He hesitated for a while, then spat and disappeared into the dark house.

CHAPTER 14

He spent most of the next day asleep in Manke's bed. Several times she tried to wake him and get him to eat something. He would roll over like a bear after hibernation, lift his shaggy head to growl, slurp down a ladle of water, and curl up to think. He was looking for a way to humiliate Rachel, something she would remember forever. He concentrated on every new idea, improving and embellishing it until he was certain of its power to cause her grief and bring her begging his forgiveness. She would come to him very pale, with eyes

lowered, and stand silently near the door, while he would pretend
not to know her. He would walk around the room talking to his
friends and take no notice of her, until she raised her tearful, dark
eyes and came to him, quivering with fright.

Zanvl felt his heart beating stronger. His strained forehead
relaxed, he opened one eye a crack and a strange insect flew out,
swirling upward; then came a second that chased and swallowed the
first, and then a third—Zanvl felt he was losing something. He
strained his mind, making a great effort to retrieve whatever it was,
but all at once something burst and he woke with a violent shudder.
Opening his eyes wide, he realized he was in Manke's bed and that
Rachel had chased him out like a dog. He clenched his fists in anger
and gave a loud bellow.

"Go back to sleep, if you can call that sleep! Do you want
anything, Zanvl?" Manke asked.

"A drink."

"How can a person pour so much into himself? You haven't
even taken a bite to eat all day."

Instead of answering, Zanvl drank half a ladle of water at a
gulp, stretched out with his face to the ceiling and yawned. He
wanted to leave town immediately, saddle a horse and make off right
now into the wide world. . . . If he stayed in town, he would do
something terrible;—the horrors he envisaged made his blood curdle.

Where to go? That was no problem: it was two days before the
Loyvitsh fair. He decided to get up, go over to Gradul's, and leave
that very night for Loyvitsh. There he would certainly forget about
everything.

Zanvl began composing a letter to Rachel. The words came
easily and the letters seemed to grow large and black before his eyes.
Rachel appeared before him, her thin lips pressed together in agitation; she held his letter and the tears trickled from her eyes.

Suddenly Zanvl remembered that he could not write. In his
great disappointment he spat at the ceiling.

"Manke, you know how to write, don't you?"

"I used to. Why all of a sudden?"

"Write a letter for me."

"To whom?"

"You'll see later. Sit down and write."

Manke found a small sheet of paper, an old dusty inkwell, and a pen, and sat down to her task. Zanvl got out of bed and sat barefoot near the table.

"Well, who's the letter for?" asked Manke dipping the pen. "I mean, who's it addressed to?"

"No address!"

"What do you mean, no address? What idiot writes a letter without an address? There has to be one!"

Zanvl grew angry. "The peasant and the Pope—to each his own. If I tell you there's no address, then there's no address!"

"All right, Zanvl, no address. I should worry! But you don't have to shout. Well, what next?"

Zanvl's mind now became confused. The well-phrased letter that he had just finished in his head suddenly dissolved. In an effort to remember, he rubbed his large hand over his forehead. It was no use—his head was empty!

"Well?" asked Manke with a smile.

"Wait a minute, Manke. Believe me, the letter's at the tip of my tongue. You've got to understand, I like a letter to be written smoothly, it should read like a prayer. Here it is! Now write: 'I never believed that what happened between us yesterday would ever happen.'"

Here Zanvl stopped and watched Manke pressing down the pen with her thin fingers. She wrote slowly, but every so often she missed the line and the letters seemed oddly misshapen. Zanvl imagined that instead of writing, she was actually drawing birds. He noticed Manke's face becoming more earnest and flushed, and each time she formed a letter, she would trace it simultaneously with her tongue, first on one cheek, then on the other. Enjoying her tongue-writing, Zanvl burst out laughing.

"What's so funny?"

"You write better with your tongue than you do with the pen."

"If you don't like it, find yourself another scribe," Manke laughed good-naturedly. "All right, what's next?"

Zanvl pondered, but try as he might, he could not come up with anything else. Each new thought he found impossible to articulate. Finally he lost patience and tore up the sheet. "To hell with it! I'm not doing any more. If I can't write myself, then it's no use at all!"

"What's the matter with you today? Are you going into mourning? Who are you writing to, anyway?"

Zanvl did not answer. He walked up and down the room in his bare feet, then hurried to get dressed.

"Where are you going?"

"To Gradul's."

"Will you be there long?"

"I dunno," came his curt parting reply.

CHAPTER 15

Zanvl found no one in at Gradul's house. Then Beyle's voice came from the kitchen: "Who's there?"

The question remained unanswered as Zanvl went up to the curtain, opened it, and peeked in. Beyle, barefoot and blouseless, with her short striped slip tucked in between her legs, stood washing in a small tin basin. Her small body bent through various motions as her long braid swung easily behind. Zanvl could not tear his eyes from her slim brown legs; her every movement aroused him. He coughed.

Beyle stopped washing and turned around. Seeing Zanvl, she quickly raised her hands in embarrassment to cover her bosom. With a hearty laugh Zanvl went back into the living room. Soon Beyle entered, wearing a white polka dotted dressing gown, her braid thrown over to the front and a pair of woven slippers on her feet.

"Honestly, I thought it was Gradul," she said smiling. "Who would have guessed that you would come by today? Please, have a seat. I hope you'll excuse me," she said lifting her leg to indicate her attire.

His gaze intent upon her, Zanvl felt himself catching fire.

"A fine person you are," Beyle continued, taking Zanvl by the hand. "Why did you chase me away yesterday, eh? You ought to be ashamed of yourself. Later, when I came back out, you were gone. Where did you disappear to?"

By now Zanvl stood face to face with Beyle, feeling her hand warming, burning, lighting a fire within him. Suddenly he embraced her and lifted her up. He felt her moving, quivering in his arms; he felt the loose flaps of her gown flying open as they enfolded him and he noticed the white bow of her undershirt. He tightened his embrace, pressing his lips to hers. Then he let go in embarrassment. He walked over to the window and began chasing a fly buzzing on the hot pane. Looking out, he asked: "Where's your Gradul, anyway?"

"He's gone over to the smithy's," she said. "You know, he's planning to go to the Loyvitsh fair. Here he comes now."

Gradul came in wearing brass knuckles. "No good, buddy boy," he said bending back his cap and scratching his head, "You're having too good a time with Beyle."

Zanvl turned red and smiled sheepishly. Beyle sat down, tucked her dressing gown between her legs, then crossed them and said in a teasing tone:

"Why not? He's a handsome fellow, isn't he?"

"You know why I'm here?" Zanvl interrupted her. "I'm planning to go to Loyvitsh."

"Then let's go together!" exclaimed Gradul. "I'm bored with staying home. I can't remember the last time I did any work and sitting around eating up our cash supply is not going to make me any richer. Even a gold mine lets out!"

"Who else is going?" asked Zanvl.

"I dunno. I was supposed to go with Moyshele Bik. Now we'll be a threesome. I'm glad you're coming along. If I'd had a partner like you last year I'd have made a fortune."

"When do you want to go?" Zanvl cut him short.

"Today!"

"Great! I'm going right home to get my things together."

CHAPTER 16

From all over Poland merchants and peasants thronged to Loyvitsh, bringing their cattle, horses, and swine. The narrow streets were impassable, the roads leading to town packed full with carriages. From a distance it looked as if the city were under siege by foreign hordes who had descended upon it with all their goods and possessions, barring the roads and storming the city with loud cries.

Zanvl and his companions went to the fair grounds early in the morning, wandered around, taking everything in, and reached the horse market late in the afternoon. It looked like a military camp breaking up: wagons and carriages lined the sides of the market while the horses stood unharnessed between their shafts to allow the merchants to inspect them. In the middle of the market were a number of thoroughbreds and a runway on which their speed was being tested. A merchant would inspect a horse by looking into its mouth and squeezing its neck till it sneezed. Then a hired boy would take it for a short trial run.

Zanvl strode through the market, looking everything over, feeling perfectly at ease among the horses. A young man came toward him with a basket of tin roosters, holding one in his mouth and blowing on it like a whistle. Zanvl bought one and for a while he walked about, crowing loudly. But he soon tired of this and threw the toy away.

A cross-eyed fellow in a cap with a split visor came ambling through the market, hands in his pockets, looking for someone.

"Well, I'll be damned! Look who's here! What are ya doing here, Zanvl?"

Zanvl gave a joyous cry and threw his arms around Kishke. "I thought you were doing time behind 'the gates of mercy'!"

Kishke did not answer. He looked Zanvl's companions up and down, spat curtly, and taking Zanvl by the arm, led him aside.

"D'ya wanna be in on a sure thing?" he asked.

"I'll say!"

"Well, listen," said Kishke in a low voice. "Just a little ways off there's a peasant with five lovely colts. If everything goes right, the loot will be in our pockets by ten tonight."

Zanvl called Gradul and Moyshele and they began to work out a plan.

Beside a cart stood a young peasant tearing chunks from a loaf of bread under his arm and stuffing them into his mouth. Behind him were five beautiful horses. Zanvl brushed against the peasant as if by accident and stepped on his foot with all his might. The peasant grabbed Zanvl with both hands and shoved him away. Zanvl spat on his open palms, clenched his fists and hurled himself at the fellow. One blow and the peasant lay stretched out. He tried to get up, but Zanvl smashed him between the eyes and he rolled over.

Soon a crowd of peasants and Jews gathered from all sides.

Cries rang through the air: "Kill the Jew! The blaspheming dog, kill him!"

Meanwhile Gradul and Kishke had untied the horses and led three of them unobtrusively away. The others Moyshele guarded until after the fight, and when the peasants were on the point of making peace, he sent them galloping off. As soon as the peasants began to chase the runaways, Moyshele and Zanvl beat a retreat.

CHAPTER 17

Late that night Zanvl sat in a tavern drinking in the company of the horse merchants.

"Hey guys, let's go on over to the Victoria!" cried Gradul and let out a piercing whistle. Half-drunk voices hailed his suggestion and the men went outside.

"But listen guys, don't lose your heads," Kishke warned. "Tomorrow afternoon there's a new job waiting for us."

They hailed a carriage and piled in. The driver eyed them suspiciously, but then whipped the horses on through back streets.

They barged into the Victoria. Behind a counter stood a blonde of about nineteen, carefully coiffed and in a low decollete. She was talking to a heavyset gentleman in wide, striped trousers and a white pique vest from which a gold chain was suspended. In response to Zanvl's hungry stare the blonde smiled and stared back, then flushed, and dropped her eyes. Picking up the banknotes Zanvl had dropped on the counter, she called out, "Ignatz, take the guests into the salon!"

A man in tails emerged from an alcove, bowed to the guests and led them upstairs to a green-carpeted salon, lined with green plush couches. The walls were hung with pictures of women in seductive poses. An elderly, bald man sat in a corner playing piano for the young men and girls drinking at marble tables around the room. Hostesses paraded around in short, transparent silk dresses that showed off their shapely bodies. Two girls danced, swaying voluptuously, their bodies tantalizing the customers.

Zanvl and his friends looked around, recognizing some familiar faces, then sat down at a corner table where they ordered several bottles of champagne. Girls converged on them from all sides.

Zanvl sized up each of them but found none to his liking. His mind was still on the blonde who kept crossing the room, making overtures at him with her eyes. One after the other, each of his friends chose a girl and disappeared into the side rooms, leaving Zanvl all alone at the table. Some of the girls, the blonde in the middle, stood whispering nearby.

"Just take a look at that jerk," said one, with a pug nose. "Sits down like a hen on its eggs, and sends everyone else away. The guy's loaded too—he's paying for his friends!"

"He's probably a country yokel," decided one of the older girls with a laugh.

"That's what you think!" the blonde broke in. "He's nobody's fool. The trouble is, you're all a bunch of dogs. I'll show you. If I go over, he'll follow me like a lamb."

"We'll see about that," the girls retorted.

Zanvl overheard the conversation, and regretted having come; he began devising a way of humiliating the blonde.

"Pani X, why are you sitting here all alone and so sad?" said the blonde, sitting down next to him.

Zanvl wanted to tell her that it was of none of her business, but on confronting her dimples, he stammered, "I dunno. . . ."

"Nonsense," she said, putting her hand on his knee. "Choose yourself a pretty girl and have a good time. Your buddies are sure enjoying themselves. And if the Victoria can't help you, then even a doctor won't be of use!" She burst out laughing.

"Beyle's tricks!" shot through Zanvl's mind. Now all he could think of was embracing the girl. Turning to her with a smile, he said: "And what if I were to choose you?"

The blonde smiled back, then turned serious: "What d'you need a married woman for? Aren't there enough girls around? You want my old man to sue for divorce?" she ended in a hearty laugh.

Zanvl remained silent, as if slapped in the face. Then he felt her take him by the hand.

"Listen, Pani X, stay here for the time being and if at all possible—" She cut the sentence short with a seductive laugh, tossed her head and left the room.

Zanvl downed bottle after bottle. He was interrupted now and again by the drunken Gradul who came to embrace Zanvl and tried to pull him into his room. As he drank, Zanvl felt his limbs grow heavier as if weighted down with lead. Late at night the waiter came over to him and led him up to the third floor, to a small square room with pink carpets smelling of perfume and feminine odors. A table lamp with a pink shade cast a sensual light over everything. Dominating the room was a large canopied bed with pink silk curtains.

Zanvl stood wide-eyed, in a trance. He noticed a white hand beckoning to him through the air. On a plush Ottoman rug lay the blonde, wearing a pink silk nightgown and silver embroidered slippers. Zanvl felt himself dissolve.

She stretched out her shapely hand and her fingers, sparkling in a sea of greenish red flames, motioned him down on a tiny footstool next to the bed. Zanvl sank down obediently and breathed easier.

"Are you pleased?" Her lips parted on a sparkle of white teeth.

Zanvl took her hand and covered it with kisses.

"Believe me," she said softly, "I liked you the very moment I saw you. After all, I came upstairs to look at you more than once. Who are you?"

At first Zanvl was taken aback by her question, but a moment later he replied: "The leader of the Radzenov Robbers."

Her blue eyes opened wider like a frightened deer. "Are you a robber too?"

"I am their king."

"And you live in the woods?"

"Of course! In a huge underground cave."

"Aren't you cold there?"

"When it gets cold, you chop down trees, make fires, and warm up."

"Really?" She thought for a while, playing with her silky braid. Somehow she seemed so childlike. "Would you want me for your girl?" she asked playfully.

"Of course . . ." he said, laughing.

"Why are you laughing?"

Zanvl was staring at her delicate hand on the pink silk tulle; its transparent whiteness and the network of silky blue threads enchanted him utterly.

At daybreak he awoke, tired. He stretched and looked around. She sat in a rocking chair wearing a green silk dressing gown, her cheek snuggled up against a puppy's white fur.

"It's still early. What's your hurry?" She went over to him carrying the puppy in her arms.

Zanvl's bleary eyes looked at her with a strange earnestness.

"What, are you angry?" She smiled and pretended to toss the dog at Zanvl. The puppy squealed and jumped down.

"What makes you say that?" He took hold of her hand, but suddenly his head began to throb. The dog was leaping all over him, barking loudly. She quickly grabbed the puppy by the ears and took it out of the room.

Left alone, Zanvl felt himself gradually cooling off, until he was almost freezing. In an effort to rid himself of the lingering sensation of her body, he began rubbing his hands together. He wanted to smash the bed, tear the curtains. But soon she returned, locking the door behind her and when Zanvl saw her delicate white feet, he forgot everything.

Zanvl left the Victoria, promising to return that night. By the time he reached his inn he was exhausted. His companions were asleep in their clothes. Zanvl threw a sheet over his head, curled up, sighed once or twice and fell fast asleep.

He was awakened around noon.

"Get up!" Gradul shouted pulling him by the leg. "Kishke's waiting for us."

Zanvl opened a pair of bloodshot eyes; his body felt on fire. He pulled his foot away and muttered: "I'm not going."

"Whad'ya mean, you're not going?" asked Gradul in amazement.

Zanvl did not reply.

"Well?" Gradul shook him again.

"Drop dead!" Zanvl shouted angrily and turned over.

"Who needs you?" Gradul shouted back, walking to the door.

Zanvl was alone. His every limb felt about to crack. Several times he tried changing position, but his limbs failed him. His head dropped back onto the pillow and he lay like a lump of clay. The previous night passed before him like a dream; he could still feel her impassioned kisses on his lips, kisses he could almost touch with his fingers. Suddenly he felt his strength come surging back.

Whenever the thought of Rachel passed through his mind, he grimaced, as if swallowing a bitter pill, and forced his thoughts back to the blonde. He'd bring her home with him, promenade her through the streets. Everyone would stop and stare at Zanvl's beautiful, elegant girl, more lovely than a duchess! And when he met Rachel, she would stare in disbelief, while he, with perfect nonchalance, would pass her by, conversing with his lady.

In the evening he woke with a start, and then lay quietly, looking around him. The fire was back in his limbs. His feet ached as though leeches had sucked out all his blood. Filled with disgust, he felt that if the blonde were there, he would strangle her; she had deceived him, sucked his blood and marrow. He felt suddenly as weak as a child and a terrible fear engulfed him.

"Who knows if she hasn't got it! If she hasn't done me in?!" He buried his head in the pillow. Now he would return home sick with the most horrible disease of all, and with almost no way of being cured. Wasn't "Dew and Rain" once a hero whose exploits were known far and wide? But when he got the clap and started falling to pieces, all his friends abandoned him: wild eyes, a red, rotting nose, face covered with red splotches, and a body that walked as if on stilts.

Zanvl shivered. He clenched his fists and imagined himself at home. Everyone knew of his illness, and avoided him. He was forced to sleep in the poorhouse, growing weaker day by day until he could no longer go out into the street. And all because of Rachel, that scrawny pious girl!

Suddenly, hearing shouts from under the window, Zanvl jumped out of bed and began to get dressed. Moyshele was talking loudly to the hotel owner. A moment later the door burst open and two horse dealers helped Moyshele Bik carry in a bloody body and lay it on the bed. Zanvl recognized Gradul by his clothes; his features were almost obliterated from the beating he had received. He lay there moaning, his eyes two black and blue lumps and blood dripping from his mouth and head.

"What happened?" shouted Zanvl.

Moyshele sat down on the edge of the bed and stretched his legs. "Snores all day long and now he's yelling."

Zanvl didn't answer.

"You'll argue later," one of the horse merchants interrupted. "Right now run for a doctor; the fellow may lose all his blood. And you'd better not stick around too long. The cops are after him!"

"Bik, not a word, do you hear me!" Zanvl ordered Moyshele. "Go get a doctor right away."

Moyshele left at once.

"How did it happen?" Zanvl asked the Jews.

"Very simple. He tried to lift a couple of horses, but they caught him, and if not for us, they'd have killed him too."

Zanvl took a bowl of water and began wiping the blood off Gradul's face. Zanvl felt personally responsible; he decided to take Gradul home that very day.

CHAPTER 18

"Believe me, Rachel," Nosn said to his daughter, "people think Baruch is too good for us. Let's not fool ourselves—Baruch is still the best match in town; he has rabbinical ordination, he's getting ready for his final examination, and pretty soon, God willing, after the wedding, I'll lay out a few hundred rubles and Baruch will get a position and become a Rabbi. What could be better?" With this, Nosn fell silent, took a pinch of tobacco and looked at his daughter.

Rachel did not answer. She turned pale and lowered her eyes.

"What do you say, daughter?" said the old man, clearing his throat.

Rachel's eyes filled with tears. "Do what you want!" She burst out crying and rushed into another room.

"A child, she's probably shy. Let her cry a bit, it doesn't matter," thought Nosn as he lay down on the sofa.

Rachel went into her room and began to pace back and forth: something was happening, people were doing things, planning things, planning for her happiness. She quickened her pace in the tiny room, her mind racing from one scheme to another to rid herself of the match. Suddenly she hit upon an idea and stopped, wrinkled her brow and stared at the floor, trying to work it through . . . but the idea vanished. She kicked her foot angrily and continued pacing. When her feet began to tire, she stretched out on the covered sofa and decided to tell her father, that very evening, that she refused the match, that her whole life with Baruch would be miserable, that . . . she herself didn't know why. . . . The image of Baruch appeared before her, much uglier than he really was. His nose, it seemed, was longer and thinner, growing down into his mouth, his pale, young face somehow so old and decrepit, and the ridge that separated his nose from his forehead kept moving, as if someone were sitting there pecking away at it . . . he looked like the skeleton of a herring.

Rachel felt herself grow cold. She pressed both fists against her temples and decided that even if her life depended on it, she would not marry Baruch. But in the back of her mind she knew that she would never tell her father of her love for Zanvl the horse thief, that all these thoughts were merely a diversion, that she was fooling herself. All at once she felt as weak and helpless as a child. Her hatred of Baruch suddenly disappeared. If Baruch were to become Rabbi after the wedding, then she would be the Rabbi's wife and all the women would look up to her. Everyone would consider it a privilege to be in her company and hear her opinion. She would be invited to every celebration in town, have the seat of honor, be served the best foods.

Rachel tried to pursue this train of thought, but just then the town Rebbetsin appeared before her eyes with her silk headdress and long diamond earrings. Before the wedding, they would seat her in a large chair, let out her locks and the Rebbetsin would cut them off. Rachel clutched her two long braids, examined and kissed them as if she were parting from them forever. She thought suddenly of old Kreyndl, the *Khala* and *tsholnt** baker; one Friday afternoon, when Rachel came in to her shop, she found old Kreyndl standing behind a partition brushing out the hair of a young woman and then cutting it off with a razor. The young woman looked like a shorn cat.

Once more Rachel was overcome by hatred for all of them, even her father. They were all plotting to make her miserable. No one understood her, or even wished to. . . . In her anger, she forgot her quarrel with Zanvl: he would rescue her, whisk her off from under the canopy. She had to see him right away.

Greatly perturbed, she left the house and hurried to Shloyme's. She saw a light in the window and entered without thinking.

Tsholnt is a Sabbath stew, placed in a low oven on Friday before sundown (since no stove can be lit on the Sabbath). In most Jewish towns, special ovens were available for this purpose.

"Well, look who's here, a guest," said Tirzeh and wiped a bench clean with her apron.

Rachel blushed. In confusion, she screwed up her eyes as if trying to remember something. "Thank you, Tirzeh. Don't trouble yourself. I just wanted to remind you to pick up the carrots.'

"What carrots?"

"Don't you know? I'm amazed!" Rachel exclaimed, her face completely flushed. "Last week your Zanvl ordered a whole bushel of carrots for the horses and he hasn't come to pick them up. It keeps raining and they might spoil. . . ."

"Did he pay you for them?"

"Of course!"

"Believe me, Rachel, that boy will be the end of me. You see, he buys carrots and doesn't say a word. He's been gone almost a week at the Loyvitsh fair and who's to know that he bought carrots! Thank you for coming, Rachel. On my word, I'll send the old man for them tomorrow. What did I want to tell you? Oh yes," Tirzeh went on with her work. "Rachel, you let us down. You didn't even stay for the wedding meal and my Zanvl looked all over for you."

Rachel stared at Tirzeh. It seemed to her that the old woman knew everything, that she was smiling because she knew Zanvl had never bought any carrots, and that she, Rachel, in her longing for him, had made up the whole story as a pretext to see him.

CHAPTER 19

On returning from the fair that evening, Zanvl was informed that Rachel was to marry Baruch Gitels. Restless, unable to sit still, he headed for Gradul's. A wind broke loose from somewhere and began to bluster, lifting whole clods of earth, twisting through the street with a whistling sound. Zanvl quickened his pace, then stopped short—Nosn and Rachel were walking toward him.

The wind whistled louder, lifting a piece of tin from a roof, ripping off Nosn's cloth hat and spinning it through the street. The old man and his daughter stopped for a moment, helpless, exchanged glances, then set out after the hat.

With a single bound, Zanvl grabbed the hat and respectfully brought it over to Nosn.

"Thank you very much for your trouble, Zanvl. This is some wind!" said the old man donning the hat.

Zanvl wanted to say something, but when he looked at Rachel, and saw her startled fear, he could produce nothing but a silly smile. Only after Nosn and Rachel had passed and were some distance away did Zanvl run after them in excitement. "Hurry home, Reb Nosn! It's going to pour any minute now!" he blurted out, turning red.

"God grant it," Nosn replied, "the potatoes need rain as a baby needs milk."

Zanvl saw Rachel smile and his spirits livened. He followed them. In the distance huge boulders seemed to be cracking and rolling toward them, crashing with the sound of countless drums. Then the rain came down in torrents.

Zanvl took shelter in the house opposite Nosn's, shivering nervously as he caught sight of Rachel standing in the doorway. He walked toward her. Rachel grew frightened and retreated into the house, but soon reappeared.

They stood in silence for a few minutes, eyeing each other with a serious expression. Zanvl was the first to lower his gaze.

"Rachel, I must see you. I have to talk to you. Be at the farm tomorrow at eight. Will you?"

"I will, " she replied and without another word, disappeared into the house.

The sound of her steps and the squeak of the door echoed for a long time in Zanvl's ears. He felt the ground under his feet swaying, floating away entirely, leaving him suspended in the air. He finally sat down in exhaustion, on the doorstep, buried his head in his large hands and squeezed his eyes shut. A grinding sound, like a saw cutting through an old oak, came from between his teeth.

He couldn't pick up and leave, just like that. If he had Rachel there right now, he'd grab her by the throat. He wouldn't let himself be pushed around. Who did she think she was, anyway? Doesn't a thief have a heart too? And why that story about the carrots? When did he ever buy carrots from her? She was probably lying in bed now, laughing up her sleeve to be rid of him. He'd show her he wasn't so easily duped!

Zanvl ran halfway up the street in search of a rock to smash her window but none of the stones he found was to his liking. Soon he was back, grumbling to himself. He stared through the window but saw nothing.

A night watchman with a heavy stick stood at a distance watching Zanvl suspiciously. Slowly, he approached. Zanvl was so preoccupied that he heard nothing until the watchman grabbed him roughly by the arm shouting: "Come with me, my little night bird!" Zanvl came to and turned around.

Holding Zanvl securely with both hands the night watchman let out a loud whistle. With superhuman strength, Zanvl fell upon his captor, wrestled him to the ground and kicked him in the chest. Then he fled through the fence into Nosn's orchard.

Soon whistles could be heard from all sides and the heavy steps of the town watchmen trampled the stillness of the night. Frantically, Zanvl looked for a hideout. At the far end of the garden there was a potato pit covered by a large rock. Zanvl pushed the rock aside, crawled in and closed it up again. He lay down in a pool of water and waited fearfully.

The search party entered the garden. Zanvl heard Nosn's voice and knew any minute he would be caught and dragged out and beaten while Rachel stood by watching. He drew brass knuckles from his pocket and slipped them on.

Quiet. Zanvl lay still for a long time. Then he crawled out, soaked to the skin, and made his way through side streets to Gradul's. He found the house lit up. Gradul lay in a large wooden bed. His face seemed covered with ash, and a cackling sound came from his chest. Beyle sat tearfully at the table.

"What's new? Has the doctor come?" Zanvl asked quietly.

"He's come," she said with a sigh.

"Well, what did he say?"

"Who needs a doctor?" the invalid said with a rasping voice and coughed up a blood clot the size of a copper ten-piece. "Listen, Zanvl, only God can help me. It's no good, brother. My strength's giving out. . . . Promise me that tomorrow morning you'll bring the warden of the Talmud Torah a five-spot, so they'll recite Psalms on my behalf."

Zanvl stood scratching his head, as if he were fully responsible for Gradul's accident. Then Beyle began to sob and Zanvl, unable to listen, went into the bedroom and undressed on Gradul's bed. He imagined that he was still being chased, that soon he would be caught, dragged from bed and led away in chains. Suddenly a huge man with one eye in his forehead came at him through the window. The man kept coming until he filled the entire room, every nook and cranny, and his eye flamed with phosphorous rays. Then he grasped his large, flabby stomach, burst out laughing and winked his one eye.

"Fool! Rachel has thrown you over! Thrown you over!"

In anguish, Zanvl spurred his foaming horse, drew his long, curved sword and a vicious battle ensued between him and the one-eyed man. With each slash of his saber, Zanvl cut the man in two, but two men appeared in his place and soon the whole room was full of one-eyed men and all of them clutched their flabby stomachs and laughed, their eyes shooting phosphorous rays. In fury, Zanvl dismounted, grabbed one man by the throat and poked out his eye. Then there was a thunderous crash—and everything disappeared.

Zanvl awoke in a cold sweat. He opened his eyes: the room was in darkness and outside it was still pouring. Beyle sat on her bed. She held the pillow to her face and wept quietly. Zanvl got up from bed. He couldn't stand to hear her cry.

"Beyle?"

"Zanvl, you're not asleep?"

"No," he answered. "Beyle, what good is it to cry? Believe me, Gradul will recover. You'll see. . . ."

"Oh, Zanvl," she sobbed and sat up, "no one knows how terrible I feel. We've been married for half a year—and the doctor says there's no hope. . . ." And once more she burst into tears.

Zanvl regretted having come here. He blocked his ears with his fingers and buried his head in the pillow. Eventually, Beyle quieted down and began to reminisce about how she met Gradul, how he fell in love with her, carried her around in his arms, and what was she lacking then?

Zanvl felt his exhaustion disappear. Beyle's stories revitalized him; he twisted and turned under the blanket. He no longer heard what she was saying. He imagined instead that he was Gradul, carrying little Beyle in his arms, with her burning eyes and her long hair.

From the brothel opposite Gradul's window came a moaning, like a choked weeping. Zanvl listened carefully: it seemed to be a woman crying. The crying grew louder and nearer. Apparently, someone was beating one of the whores. And the rain poured down in torrents on the window.

The crying unnerved Zanvl. Then he noticed Beyle in a long white shirt, getting out of bed and going over to the window. He waited in expectation, his eyes opened wide. Beyle looked out the window; seeing no one, she shruged her shoulders and turned back. As she passed his bed Zanvl tugged lightly at her shirt.

Beyle caressed his face gently with her soft hand. Zanvl felt her irregular breathing, and seized her like a maddened lion.

CHAPTER 20

Zanvl awoke with a start. Beyle lay next to him, her feet wrapped in her white shirt, her black hair spread over the pillow and the little finger of her right hand in her mouth. Sounds of wheezing and groaning from the other room made Zanvl shiver. He got out of bed, dressed hurriedly and started toward the invalid, but stopped short at the doorway. It seemed to him that Gradul had seen everything . . . through the wall. . . . Now he was reproaching him—was that the way to treat a sick friend? A cold sweat broke out on Zanvl's forehead. Then he smiled: "Ah, what nonsense! He's lying there sick as a dog."

Hesitantly, he entered the room. Gradul was asleep. His nose seemed longer and more pointed, his eyes more sunken, as if they had been hammered in and closed. Occasionally, when a rattle sounded from his throat, his eyelids would open very slightly, and reveal a pair of glaring chicken's eyes. Zanvl was taken aback. He spat and left quietly.

The streets were empty, except for Reb Yankev, Zanvel's former teacher, who sat in front of a small house, wearing only his trousers and his tasseled undergarment. He was holding a goose between his legs, forcing open its beak and pouring in spoonfuls of millet. The goose stared glassy-eyed, choked, then swallowed.

"Good morning, Rebbe," Zanvl said smiling.

The old man looked up. "Good morning to you. How are you, Zanvl?"

"Very good, and you, Rebbe? I see you're still raising geese."

"Of course, child. In my old age, all the teaching positions have gone away—the Litvaks, may their name be blotted out, overran us, and stole my livelihood. But I'm not ready to lay my teeth on the shelf yet, so I raise geese. It isn't easy."

All that Zanvl could gather from the old man's prattling was that he was having a hard time. "Rebbe, here's something to buy snuff." Zanvl handed him a ruble note and continued on to the Talmud Torah.

The warden, a heavy man with a broad, black beard and a satin vest, listened to Zanvl with a smile.

"No, I cannot send the children to recite Psalms."

"Why not?" asked Zanvl in surprise.

"Because . . . well . . . turning pious all of a sudden when the knife's at your throat . . . I can't!"

"Why can't you?" Zanvl blurted out angrily. "I'm willing to pay. Here's five rubles and if it's not enough, tell me!"

The warden stared first at him, then at the bank note and cleared his throat. "Believe me, Zanvl, I'm not trying to start anything. Gradul has been a thief for ages, and now you want me to send the children to recite Psalms for him? You tell me. What kind of business is that?"

Zanvl turned pale as chalk. He had an urge to slug the warden and leave. "Sure he's a thief. I'm a thief too, you hear me? But we're Jews. I'm telling you again: send the children to recite Psalms. Are you gonna send them, or not?"

The warden stared fearfully at Zanvl, then at the money, and blew his nose into his red handkerchief. "Well, what can I do? I'll send them."

Zanvl took another five ruble note from his pocket and threw it down on the table. "You see, when I'm treated like a human being, I can act like one too."

At lunch time Zanvl walked whistling down the street. Old Franek was plodding along with his large drum to take up his place in the market. He set the drum down in the middle of the square, rested for a while then began drumming for all he was worth.

People poured in from all sides and soon the market place was packed. The old man looked them over, then called out in the voice of a veteran army commander: "A pig with a black spot was lost. Anyone who finds him is requested to bring him to the city hall. Last night there was an attempted robbery at Nosn the Gardener's. Everyone be on guard!" His announcements done, the old man gave three beats on the drum and turned to go, followed by the catcalls of children.

Zanvl stood by and smiled. He was pleased by the whole affair. He let out a whistle and set out into town in a carefree mood.

Evening. Zanvl awaited Rachel at the farm. He chainsmoked in agitation and searched the night for a sign of her approach. All of a sudden he felt played out; he felt that Zanvl was no longer himself, that a girl with black eyes had bewitched him. Worst of all, why was she still making fun of him? She could have said she had no intention of coming and that she no longer wished to be seen with a thief. That way he would know for sure and could stop thinking about her once and for all. But to lead him on—to promise and not come—damn! He wouldn't let himself be stepped on. He'd go right over and make such a scene she'd see stars!

He hurried into town to Nosn's place. The house was brightly lit, and the blinds were lowered. Zanvl peeped in and saw Rachel dressed up, sitting at a table talking to Baruch. Zanvl was determined: if he didn't disrupt them now, he was nothing but a lily-liver. They'd find out that Zanvl wasn't dead yet. As for that jelly fish, he'd break a rib of his tonight, just for fun!

Blurting out an obscenity, he picked up a stone from across the street and hurled it through the window. He heard a scream and the sound of breaking glass. Hiding under the wooden steps of the house across the way, Zanvl saw everyone come outside, look around, and talk for a while. Then all was quiet.

This was the last straw. He was nothing but a coward. Anyone else in his position would never have allowed his girl to be taken. Look at him, hiding under the steps the whole night through, in agony! Zanvl heaved upward against the stairs with all his might, felt the frame give, and with a sudden moan the whole step turned over. Zanvl shook himself free; he felt as if a heavy load had been lifted from him. But where to go? If he went back to Gradul's, he'd have a repeat performance of last night.

Dispirited, he made for home. Then he stopped and smiled. He found a rag, wet it, smeared it with soot, and returned to Nosn's house.

Late at night Baruch came out. Zanvl grabbed him and gagged

him with the rag. Baruch struggled and shouted. Rachel came running out. Seeing her, Zanvl let go of Baruch and ran away.

CHAPTER 21

In the tavern at a large table, Zanvl sat drinking with a few of the fellows. Ever since Gradul died and Beyle had confided to him that she was pregnant, Zanvl had been in a constant state of turmoil. He felt responsible and began to avoid her. He was restless at home, and uncomfortable everywhere else, so he sat in the tavern getting drunk.

Like a lump of wood, his head framed by his large hands, he stared into his half-empty beer mug. His blue eyes were clouded, and their expression seemed dull, simple-minded. Church bells, large and small, swam before his eyes, ringing continuously; his mind heaved and danced as if on springs.

Moyshele Bik crawled out from under a table, bareheaded, his hair disheveled. Standing in the middle of the tavern, he yawned, cleared his throat, and began spitting across the room. Then he went up to Manke, who was asleep on a bench, wrapped in a warm winter shawl with her hand for a pillow, and put his arms around her. Manke opened her sleepy eyes and pleaded:

"Moyshele, leave me alone. Let me sleep."

Moyshele adjusted the shawl, gave her a pinch, and struck up a conversation at Zanvl's table.

At the sound of Nosn the Gardener's name, Zanvl sobered up. Without lifting his head, he listened attentively to what they were saying.

"And when is she getting married?" asked a redhead with a harelip.

"Next week, on the Sabbath before Hannukah," answered Moyshele.

"Then let's go arrange it with Martshin," said the redhead.

"There's nothing to arrange," replied Moyshele mischievously.

"Last year me and Zanvl hardly missed one bride. The day the bride's taken to the ritual bath, we'll go to Martshin and give him a bottle of forty proof. His wife will let us up to where the kettle is. But there, guys, you gotta be careful—one false move and you land in a kettle of boiling water!"

"Will it be worth it?" asked the redhead licking his chops.

"Wait and see how you'll enjoy it," said Moyshele with a laugh, winking and pointing at Zanvl. "She used to be *his;* they fooled around together for nights on end."

Zanvl paled. He grabbed the mug and threw the beer in Moyshele's face.

"Tell me I'm lying!" Moyshele went up to him with clenched fists.

Manke, no longer asleep, jumped between them, and tried to pull Moyshele away.

"He's only joking. Right away you explode."

Moyshele tried to get free of her grip. "Lemme go! Who's joking? Who does he think he is? Who's afraid of him, anyway? I said something bad about his highness. I said that he went around with Nosn's daughter. Was that a lie?"

Zanvl sprang up, pushed Manke aside, and threw himself at Moyshele. Soon they were both on the floor, struggling like two shaggy dogs. They grabbed at each other's eyes and hair. Victorious, Zanvl jumped up, spat into Moyshele's bloodied face, and left.

It was dark and cold. He paced up and down the street, fists clenched, muttering: "This is the last straw. I can't live like this any more!" He raised the collar of his fur jacket, stuffed his hands into the breast pockets and tried to think. Each new thought was pushed aside by a thousand others, incidents and long-forgotten particulars that now arose to confuse him. "And what does Gradul want of me?"

He saw before him a thick forest—and himself sitting on a large tree stump. Large bonfires blazed, whole sides of lamb were roasting, kegs of whiskey, barrels of beer. His gang was stretched out on the grass, eating, drinking, laughing. The Cossack horses with their long tails, grazed nearby. Beyle and Rachel were sitting next to him. Suddenly a trumpet sounded from afar. They mounted their horses in a flash, grabbed their rifles and prepared to fire. Bands of people appeared, riding tall white horses with black spots on their bellies. In front, on a black horse, rode a man who was bones without flesh. He rode bareback, head down, carrying a long spear. Zanvl shuddered. Then the man of bones dismounted, burst into a wild laugh and waved to Zanvl and his men.

"Hey, you stalwart fellow, come over here! We have to settle something!"

Zanvl shook his head, dismounted, and began wrestling with the corpse. He felt the skeleton boring a hole through his chest with his bony chin. Zanvl's blows struck air. A frenzied laughter echoed through the woods. . . .

Zanvl wiped the sweat from his forehead and plodded onward. As he walked he shuddered, for fear of meeting Gradul. He knew that Gradul had not been in his grave for long, that he was prowling the city scaring people. Why, his own mother had nearly died of fright: one morning she went out to draw a bucket of water, looked around and was over her waist in snow—and the well was gone . . . then suddenly a goat in shrouds jumped out of the ground and laughed.

Zanvl felt cold shivers go through his body. All at once Beyle came to mind. He knew she was expecting any day, that she lay crying for days on end, and his heart ached. "I'm just a no-good son-of-a-bitch. Got mixed up with Nosn's daughter. She'll leave the wedding wrapped in white linen before I'm through with her. As I am a Jew! I'll move in with Beyle. I'll show them all!"

He stopped. An expanse of silver white fields stretched before him, the whiteness blinding against the dark, violet leaden sky. Zanvl imagined the snow fields were rising, growing higher and higher, leveling off at the tops of the trees in the forest. He relaxed, feeling comfortable in these deeps. He shouted jovially: "All those broads can go to hell!" and jumped into the snow meadow, stretching out to his full length. He lay this way for several minutes, staring into the cold, violet sky. Then he got up, looked at the imprint his body had made on the snow and burst out laughing.

A metallic echo resounded. He stretched out his hands and began beating his chest loudly like a drum. Then he looked around and remembered he had promised his father to stop by at Shidlovke to find out what was happening there. He pulled his cap down over his ears, stuffed his hands in his pockets, and set out on his way.

"Stealing horses," he thought, "is no job for a real thief. Any guy with guts can do it. At night, when no one's in the stables, you just pry off a board and lead the horse out. It's no big deal. But stealing into a house when people are asleep, breaking open the safe and taking a pile of money—there's a job for you! Horses are the old man's business."

Zanvl noticed a woman at the crossroads. When he came closer he recognized Crazy Bashe. She was wearing a kaftan stuffed with feathers, and a straw hat with flowers, and was singing quietly.

"Bashe, what are you doing here?"

She opened her mouth, showing two rows of pearly teeth, and laughed idiotically. "I'm looking for my groom," she answered with a smothered laugh. "He wrote me he would come in a carriage with four horses, and here I am going to meet him."

Zanvl laughed and slapped her on the back. Bashe broke into a fit of wild laughter.

"Who stuffed your caftan with feathers?" asked Zanvl.

"What d'ya mean? My fiance sent me the caftan from Danzig." She unbuttoned the coat and took out a photograph that had been cut out of a book. "Look here, this is my fiance! Isn't he handsome? Ha, ha. . . ."

Crazy Bashe was naked under the caftan. Zanvl turned in horror and walked away. But after several steps he heard her singing again and, pulling his cap down low over his ears, looked back. Bashe was gazing at him and laughing. He shook as if in a fever.

"Bashe, show me your fiance again!"

"He's a handsome one, isn't he?" she said, unbuttoning the coat.

White warm flesh. Once again he was overcome with disgust, spat determinedly, and walked away. The crazy woman pursued him.

"My fiance! My fiance. . . ."

Zanvl gritted his teeth; his blood was seething. He turned around, aimed a punch at Bashe's heart, and she collapsed in the snow like a stone.

He ran quickly. Behind him he heard hysterical weeping, a howl that made his blood run cold.

"My fiance! My fiance!" The wild cry resounded through the white open fields.

CHAPTER 22

Night. Shloyme the Rustler took a loaded revolver from a chest of drawers, put several pairs of boots in his bag, and glanced at the large clock on the wall.

"Hm, twelve . . . another hour to go."

In bed, under a large down quilt, lay Tirzeh, snoring tumultuously.

"Blowing that old horn of hers!" Shloyme grunted and spat. He looked at his daughter Sarah, who lay on her couch with her right eye open. "At her age other girls are mothers already," he sighed.

Shloyme blamed himself for Sarah's spinsterhood. He might have had a half-dozen grandchildren by this time.

"We've seen better times, when we came by our rubles easier than we do now. Matchmakers were always knocking at our door. The young men were crazy about Sarah. And now?"

The gander that slept under the stove suddenly awoke, stretched on its thin legs, and began beating its wings against the cage. The bird snatched some oat grains with its beak, stuck its head into a bowl of water, stretched its neck, rolled its eyes and swallowed.

"Yes," thought Shloyme, "if it please God that this business turns out sucessful, then first of all a dowry for Sarah. It'll be a burden lifted from my mind. And after all, why should she wait any longer?"

Shloyme opened his tobacco pouch and rolled himself a cigarette. Then he opened the door of the upright stove, drew out a glowing coal, and lit up. The dark walls veiled in shadows filled him with melancholy. Outside the wind whistled. He shivered, and leaned back against the warm stove. His son Zanvl was now on the way. If everything turned out all right, they would cut through the woods, quietly lead out the two mares, walk them to the hill and—away to Moyshe the Horse Dealer. This little job would bring in over two hundred rubles. The thought of the money raised Shloyme's spirits.

"And on my word of honor, if with God's help I get the rubles, the first thing I'll do is marry off Sarah."

A smile lit up his face and tears came into his grey eyes. He sat down, reached into his boot for the flat bottle of whiskey and took a couple of swigs, then went to the cupboard and stayed his hunger with a piece of cheese.

Out on the street the long whistle of the nightwatchman sounded, followed by the howling of a homeless dog. Shloyme gazed at the frost creeping over the windowpane. He picked up several peat bricks and shoved them into the fire, then stood back against the stove: "And suppose we get caught?" His thin old body trembled. Not long ago he was caught with an officer's nags. He could still feel the sticks beating his body, cutting his skin, drawing the blood. They beat him so badly he had to lie in bed a whole month. From that time on, Shloyme had begun thinking of another trade. Every time some new little job came his way, he vowed it would be the last.

"A dog's life. I've lived over fifty years and what have I got to show for it? Nothing but fear all the time. Money? For the birds!"

Shloyme took hold of his sparse beard and held it straight out from his chin. He noticed several grey hairs: a summons—they were calling him to the other world.

Shloyme recalled how once on a Sabbath afternoon he sat in the old study house listening to a Lithuanian preacher describe the other world—paradise and hell. Soon after dying comes the Angel of Death, knocks three times at your grave, and asks your name. If the dead man is righteous, he answers immediately; a sinner forgets and is lost.

Shloyme imagined himself dead. The Angel of Death, a tall, bony Jew with thick eyebrows—just like Simkhe the Undertaker —was asking him his name. And he—he has forgotten. . . .

Shloyme felt his heart sink. He pressed heavily against the stove and scratched his head. Suddenly he felt a fierce hatred for Moyshe the Horse Dealer. Thirty years ago they were both stealing horses together, and now—Shloyme was the thief and Moyshe the dealer, the respected Jew, warden of the old study house. Just last year he had presented a Torah scroll to the synagogue. He gave his daughters dowries of two thousand rubles and still supported his sons-in-law, while Shloyme spent sleepless nights, working to make Moyshe even richer.

Shloyme could envision Moyshe sleeping in his Viennese bed with the carved headpiece, his long, broad beard spread luxuriantly over his pudgy breast. The quilt rose up and down: he must be dreaming he was elected mayor. And he, Shloyme, a thin old man, sat here in the small hours of the night getting ready to steal a couple of horses for which he would get half and Moyshe half. And who knows but that he'd be caught?

Shloyme sighed dully and looked at the clock. "Time to be off." He put on a warm shirt, tied a green belt around him, and stuck in a pair of woollen mittens, pulled on his long boots, turned down the lamp, and left.

On the outskirts of the city, near the woods, Shloyme lifted the bag from his shoulders and waited. He craned his long thin neck and listened like a hungry old wolf to the silence. Then he put two fingers to his mouth and whistled. From the other side of the woods came an answering whistle.

"A clever boy!" Shloyme thought. "If only he weren't so wild, and listened to his father—I'd be fixed for my old age, all right."

Zanvl emerged from the woods and called: "Come on, Dad, it's late."

Shloyme grabbed his bag and hurried over. "How are the horses getting along?" he asked.

"They're all right. They're asleep in the stable."

Shloyme and Zanvl strode on determinedly. Neither spoke. They looked like two wolves stealing out of the forest onto the broad highway. The old man kept feeling at his breast to make sure the revolver was there, mumbling to himself: "Bay horse. Roan. Chestnut. Stallion. Damn. Moyshe the Horse Dealer. . . ."

Every now and then he took Zanvl by the arm: "Somebody's coming!"

Zanvl halted, pricked up his ears, and stared around him. No one. He smiled—the old man was getting shaky—and strode onward.

Shloyme felt a sharp chill run through his bones. He thought of Tirzeh lying under the warm quilt, snoring. "A dog's life. About time I retired from this fine business."

A dog barked. "Damn the dogs!" Shloyme muttered. "A vile death on them! Why the devil did God ever create them?"

Scattered houses appeared on the hillside. Zanvl took the bag with the shoes and walked into the village. A black shaggy dog jumped at him, barking loudly. Zanvl drew back, but the dog came after him. He leaped at the dog, grabbed him by the throat and began to choke him. The dog didn't struggle long; it rolled its eyes glassily, stuck out its long pointed tongue, and fell lifeless at Zanvl's feet.

Zanvl stood up and looked at the dog stretched on the ground, the long red tongue hanging from its mouth. He spat sharply and looked around: the old man had disappeared.

At the bottom of the hill stood Shloyme, his teeth chattering with terror. The sight of Zanvl choking the dog had been too much for him, and he had run to the bottom of the hill.

Zanvl took hold of the bag. With the swiftness of a young gypsy he lifted the barn door off the hinges. Warm animal steam beat at his face. He drew out the bottle of whiskey, wiped some on the muzzles of the horses, and placed boots on their feet. Then he led them softly out of the stable.

At the foot of the hill Shloyme removed the boots and replaced them in his shoulder bag. They mounted the horses and rode off into the gray night.

BEHIND A MASK

S. ANSKY

INTRODUCTION TO BEHIND A MASK

In THE first chapter of his Memoirs, Ansky* recounts the adventures of his seventeenth year, the year 1881, when he left his birthplace, Vitebsk, to become a private tutor in a neighboring shtetl, "with the purpose of spreading the ideas of the Haskalah among local youths and of opening their eyes." His undertaking was characteristic of the period: a young man, inspired by the ideals of the Jewish Enlightenment to which he has only recently been exposed, tries to share his new rational, skeptical approach to knowledge with the students he undertakes to tutor, and thereby to subvert the cultural conservatism of their home and community. Meanwhile the shtetl, accustomed to pitting itself against external enemies, but threatened beyond sanity by this enemy from within, does its best, which is its worst, to expel the heretic from its midst. †

The Memoirs cover the same ground as Ansky's fictional treatment of the subject in Behind a Mask, which includes some of the same incidents and even some of the same phraseology, although its

---

*Shloyme-Zanvl Rapoport assumed the pseudonym of Ansky, son of Anna, when he became a Russian, later a Yiddish, writer. An English translation of this part of Ansky's Memoirs is to be found in The Golden Tradition, ed. Lucy Dawidowicz, pp. 306–311.

†For a very similar account, see Abraham Cahan's autobiography, The Education of Abraham Cahan (Jewish Publication Society, 1970), early chapters.

tone is noticeably different. The Memoirs take the progressive idealism of the boy at face value. Like the youth he was, the mature
Ansky expresses outrage at the vicious fanaticism of the orthodox
townspeople who burned "guilty" books at a private auto-da-fé and
who held the Maskilim responsible for the anti-Semitic pogroms
instigated by the Tsar. The story, on the other hand, is more
even-handed in its characterization of the struggle. Traditional Jews
and rebellious enlighteners figure here as antagonists in a fierce
cultural battle, in which the claims of one side are put forth no more
persuasively than the convictions of the other, and the focus is on
the hardening, darkening atmosphere rather than on the stated
causes of the clash. In his Memoirs, Ansky is content to describe the
encounter between the Haskalah and the solidified East European
Jewish tradition as a conflict of world views; in Behind a Mask, he
concentrates on the strategy, on the cat-and-mouse games in which
deception becomes an end in itself, and on the mounting tensions
that could, and in this story do, lead to madness.

The subject of Behind a Mask is the stuff of Jewish life, but the
literary spirit is that of Russian mysticism. As in The Dybbuk,
Ansky's world-renowned drama, characters seem possessed by a
driving force that propels them beyond self-interest or any "reasonable" calculation of means and ends. The atmosphere throughout is
morbid and mysterious, the fascination with subterfuge and secrecy
all the more striking because the ostensible subject is the spreading
clarity of enlightenment and rationality. In the plot itself, the young
Maskilim of V__ do seem to come out ahead of the thin-lipped
preservationists of Bobiltseve, but thematically, the pretenses of the
Haskalah are decisively exposed by the wholly irrational, subcon-
scious, and self-destructive instincts of its leading proponent,
Krantz. If the man of light succeeds in his venture, it is only because
he is so thoroughly possessed by the powers of darkness.

Ansky himself was a dedicated socialist, and for several years
served as secretary to Pyotr Lavrov, the great Russian Populist
theoretician who held that "socialism was a movement of ideas
deriving much of its authority from ethical imperatives."* Like
Lavrov, Ansky seems to have felt that the ideals of socialism could
best be disseminated by rational persuasion. At the same time,
Ansky's interest in "the people" was that of an inspired ethnogra-

*Avraham Yarmolinsky, Road to Revolution (Collier, 1962), p. 198.

pher and folklorist, trying to peel away all the later "rational" accretions in an effort to reconstruct the fundamental myths of Jewish society. In much of his writing he appears as a scholar and critic, but in his poems, dramas, and stories, he gives himself over to the "lower depths," transferring to sophisticated literature those conflicts that seemed to him most deeply submerged in the folk consciousness.

In Behind a Mask, Ansky deals with the major intellectual crisis of European Jewry in the nineteenth century, and he does so as a mythifier rather than as an historian or sociologist. Ansky's dramatic sense is given free rein. The narrative, gripping and suspenseful, has no more nuance or subtelty of characterization than the usual murder mystery or folk tale, but focuses sharply on the two polarized warring forces. The drama of the Haskalah, in this singular exposition, is part of the age-old conflict of generations, in which sons will always outwit and overpower their fathers, winning their mastery and losing their innocence in the process.

CHAPTER 1

Anton KOVADLE'S ramshackle house in the gentile section of
V ——— was considered the center of the town's heretical activity.
Known to the pious as "The Nest of Abomination," it had achieved
almost legendary fame. Whenever elderly Jews had to walk past the
house, they hitched up their coats, turned aside, and quickened
their pace, sometimes even spitting as they went by. The women
walked past slowly, shaking their heads mournfully and muttering
softly. But if a high-pitched argument was heard from inside, or a
chorus of male voices harmonizing a sad, sentimental ballad, the
frightened women scurried across the street.

Kovadle's house first acquired its notorious reputation when a
certain young extern, a fiery exponent of the radical ideas of the
Haskalah, became a lodger in one of its modest rooms, attracting
soon after his arrival a small circle of young Maskilim like himself,
most of them ex-yeshiva students. The student was not there for
very long, but the room passed to a like-minded young man, and
then to another, so that little by little it became the headquarters of
all the local Maskilim. Lodgers changed frequently; sometimes
there were several, at other times none, but the room was kept in
the group's domain. As for Kovadle, the landlord, he was a Russified
Lett, a childless widower who loved his bottle and loved to

philosophize as he drank. Once he got used to the boys, he accepted as a matter of course the constant noise they made and the transitory nature of their stay. He never quite knew which of the young men was his lodger. Only one name, Borukh, remained fixed in his mind, and by that name he addressed whoever happened to be living in the house, or all of them together. He kept no record of the rent, but when short of money he would enter the room, stand at the door with a stern expression on his face, and call out in a terrifying voice to no one of them in particular:

"Borukh! Who d'you think you are, not paying me my rent?! Let's have a ruble right this minute, or I'll take your whole gang and. . . ."

He would conclude with an expressive gesture or an even more expressive threat. The "gang," unintimidated, usually tried to patch things over with promises. If he was adamant, the bargaining began, and if they finally agreed on half a ruble the money was collected on the spot. Kovadle would then leave contentedly.

Kovadle enjoyed frightening his tenants, especially when he was drunk. He would stop at their door and twirl his moustache with a murderous look in his eye. "Just you wait, Borukh!" he would threaten in his most menacing voice, "I'm going to tell your rabbi that you eat pork! That'll be the end of you!"

He was sure he had them all frightened to death.

At his work in the foundry he discussed "his boys" with great affection:

"What a jolly bunch! They never stop talking and shouting; they sing as if they'd just downed a pailful. But the truth is, they don't drink anything except tea. Maybe their liver is made different and they can get drunk on a glass of tea!"

CHAPTER 2

When Joseph Krantz became Kovadle's lodger, the room already had one permanent occupant, a young man named Braines, about twenty-four years old, very skinny, with a blond goatee and weak, myopic eyes. His shoulders were hunched, and he spoke little, but his face sometimes registered a slow, world-weary smile. Ill-suited by temperament to the frivolous merrymaking of the group, he nonetheless tried to show an interest in all that interested them, taking active part in their pranks and disputes. His smile was clouded by the sadness in his eyes, and his forced laughter was frequently interrupted by a hacking cough. Actually, Braines was interested only in his textbooks. He was preparing to take examinations at the local college and was completely engrossed in his studies. Twice before, in different cities, he had taken the same exams and failed. His self-confidence had been badly shaken, and he was on the lookout for an "easy school."

As soon as Krantz moved in, Braines immediately deferred to him, letting the newcomer take over the iron cot, the most respectable bed in the room, though it lacked a mattress and had only a sofa cushion for a pillow. It turned out that Braines had never used the bed in the first place, but slept on the settee, knees curled up under his chin.

Braines' voluntary surrender of seniority was due primarily to his deep respect for his new roommate. Krantz was three years younger than he, but could already boast a "heroic past." His father was a distinguished rabbi and he had been raised in strictly orthodox surroundings. Yet somehow, by the age of fifteen, Krantz had already become a fiery heretic, seized with the passion of the Enlightenment. One day in the synagogue, in the presence of his father and other worthies, he publicly referred to the prophet Moses in a derogatory manner. The congregants were outraged. His father fainted on the spot. People hurled themselves at the "heretic," and he barely managed to escape the synagogue alive. He never returned home again. About two weeks later, several students were caught reading forbidden books and driven out of the yeshiva. Krantz tore into the place and slapped the rabbi, an old and revered teacher. He broke off all relations with his parents, apprenticed himself to a Russian locksmith, donned a red shirt, and in his new garb strolled through the streets in the company of his Christian fellow workers. He used every conceivable means to outrage the older generation, and exhibited a fanatical, passionate hatred for everything that smacked of religion and orthodoxy. The older generation he held responsible for all the evil and ignorance in the world. Small wonder he soon became popular among the Maskilim not only of his own town but of the entire region.

CHAPTER 3

Soon afterward the room acquired its third occupant. His name was Shekhtl, he was only seventeen, and he came from Mohilev where he had studied in the yeshiva until expelled on suspicion of heresy. A slight, friendly boy with lively eyes and curly hair, he was not studying with any particular goal in mind and gave no thought to his future, but just gobbled up as many of the new Hebrew books as he could lay his hands on. Each new volume made him wildly enthusiastic: new vistas had opened before him, the deepest chasms of thought had been plumbed. Besides reading, he was always bursting with fantastic plans for the improvement of mankind. Once he came up with a foolproof way for turning all Jews into freethinkers: the police need only decree that every Sabbath, before the reading of the Torah, a representative of the "new ideas" give a lecture in each synagogue. What good Jew would leave before the reading of the Law or the conclusion of services? The congregation would be compelled to hear out the Maskil's lecture, and having heard, would be converted. Another plan was for ridding the world of poverty: the poor, he said, should be treated as yeshiva students; if every wealthy or comfortable Jew agreed to support one or more of the indigent, no paupers would remain. Once Shekhtl even proposed that the mountains be leveled and the valleys filled in— then all the world would be flat and beautiful. These fantasies annoyed his friends, but they were so naive and childlike that no one could stay angry with him. Once in a while Krantz even took sufficient interest to engage Shekhtl in a discussion of his ideas; in order not to insult his roommates, Braines would toss in an occasional remark, but he kept one eye on his textbook, and the smile on his lips remained ironic and pitying.

It goes without saying that Kovadle's tenants lived in a commune; that is, they shared in the common hunger. None of them had a steady means of support. Once in a while a low-paying tutoring job came along, or an odd bit of work. A few rubles a month came in from the collection taken up by students of the local college, but it simply wasn't enough. For a long period their diet was limited to bread and tea, and there were times when they even did without that. Their clothes were threadbare, their shoes were in tatters, and their underwear hadn't been changed in months. But they handled their poverty like true philosophers, always with a merry quip, making light of their hunger, and laughing at the way their toes had begun to protrude from their torn shoes. They even flaunted their poverty, as though it were a sign of high idealism.

Eventually, however, the steady hunger began to make itself felt, and their personalities underwent a change. Frustration and bitterness overcame them, and they grew steadily more depressed. They scarcely did any work, but wasted their days in an endless search for a few pennies to buy some bread. Stretched out across the cot or settee, they traded stale jokes and dull witticisms, livening up only briefly when one of their more prosperous comrades brought a little money or some food. At such moments a meal was served up "with tea and cigarettes," and the requisite songs and disputes. Debating or singing, they preferred to lie stretched out at full length. According to them, this was the more aristocratic pose, but in fact they lacked the strength to sit upright.

The most successful at coping with poverty was Braines, who had gone hungry as a child. His mother was a cook, and his sister worked in a hat factory. He worried more for them than for himself. Krantz, on the other hand, with his carefree frivolity, could not endure the destitute life they were leading, especially since it promised to drag on for years. Shekhtl too was beginning to tire. As long as he had remained in the Mohilev yeshiva he had received a few rubles every month from his parents, and he had been well provided with eating days at the homes of several local families. Since his arrival in V ——, his parents had stopped sending him money. Vague rumors had reached them about the goings-on in the Mohilev yeshiva, and they had insisted that their son come home. Shekhtl wrote his parents that he had been accepted into the yeshiva at V ——, thereby hoping to allay their fears and to win their renewed support; but in the meantime he went hungry. During his five or six months in Kovadle's room, he grew gaunt, and lost his former cheerfulness. Sprawled across the cot, he sometimes chanted Biblical passages in a tearful strain:

"Ay, who shall give us flesh to eat, ay, ay, ay . . . in vain do we remember the fish that we ate in the land of Egypt, and the cucumbers and melons, and the radishes and onions, and the garlic . . . and now is our spirit faint, for we have nothing. . . ."

His fantasies now began to take a new turn. Instead of broad plans for religious and social reform or geological transformation, his mind turned to the simple dream of finding a wallet stuffed with money or an easy way of making a bar of silver: if you took ten thousand silver coins and filed a little off each of them. . . . The only trouble was, he didn't know where to find the ten thousand silver coins.

CHAPTER 4

Late one night, when everyone was asleep, Shekhtl suddenly woke Krantz with a shout: "Get up! I have a brand new idea!"

Krantz started, and opened his eyes; when he discovered the cause, he flew into a rage: "Go to hell! Leave me alone with your ideas! I want to sleep!"

"You'll have plenty of time to sleep. Just listen to this inspiration I've had. You'll hit the roof when you hear. It's a gem! If it works, we're all saved!"

Accustomed though he was to Shekhtl's harebrained schemes, Krantz was intrigued in spite of himself. Maybe this inspiration was worth something—maybe it really could save them. But he didn't want to lose the edge of his anger too quickly, so he said roughly: "Get lost while you can, otherwise I'll give you such a beating you'll forget every idea you ever had!"

"Fine. Go right ahead!" said Shekhtl agreeably, "go ahead and beat me up. But first you have to hear me out. When you hear what I have to say you'll want to kiss me."

Remembering that Braines was also in the room, Krantz pointed to the settee: "Tell *him* your plans. Let *him* shower you with kisses. Just leave me alone."

"Fine, I'll tell him," Shekhtl agreed, "but you'll have to listen too. Do you want to hear?" he asked Braines.

Braines, lying on the setee, covered by an overcoat, poked out his head like a turtle, then his long bare neck, and said attentively: "Why not? If the plan is as good as you say, let's hear it."

"You see," Shekhtl persisted, "you're not going to get to sleep anyhow; you might as well pay attention."

Krantz gave in and pulled himself into a sitting position. "All right, go ahead. But don't beat around the bush. Get to the point."

"It's very simple," said Shekhtl firmly, "you have to go to Bobiltseve, assume the proper disguise, and get to work."

"Go where? Where in hell is Bobiltseve? What are you babbling about?" shouted Krantz in exasperation.

"Wait!" Shekhtl calmed him, "Who's to blame if you're ignorant, and your memory is like a sieve? I've told you about Bobiltseve dozens of times. It's my home town—that great center of Jewish life, that metropolis! Who hasn't heard of Bobiltseve? Once there was a famous holy man called the "Jew of Bobiltseve!" You've got to go there and become a tutor."

"Wait! Wait!" he cried, before Krantz had a chance to interrupt, "You can get teaching jobs in the best families at fifteen or twenty rubles a month, maybe more. The whole town will be taking lessons from you. I can't understand why this didn't occur to me before."

"Is that the whole plan?" asked Krantz in genuine dismay.

"Give me a chance to finish!" Shekhtl insisted. "What a strange guy you are, you won't even let anyone speak. . . . Do you have any idea what can be done there if the thing is undertaken seriously! You can lead all the boys in town off the straight and narrow, and I do mean all! The whole town can be fired with the golden rays of the Enlightenment!" he concluded with a flourish.

The project began to interest Krantz, and he promised to give it serious thought. This in turn made an impression on Braines, who crawled off the settee and went over to sit on the edge of the cot.

"Yes," he agreed softly, "it is an interesting plan."

"You see, I was right," Shekhtl crowed, "but you still haven't heard all of it. Listen to this. If you go to Bobiltseve, behind a mask, a really solid disguise, you'll have no trouble convincing my parents that I'm enrolled in the yeshiva, that I'm pious as a pickle, that I spend my days and nights in study and prayer, and that in just a year I'll be ordained a rabbi. If you do that, they'll start sending me money again. You get it?"

"An exquisite plan, as I live and breathe!" Krantz exclaimed.

"Exquisite," echoed Braines.

"But will you be able to carry it off? It needs a genius."

"Don't worry. If I decide to do it, I'll manage it. I have a knack for that sort of thing," answered Krantz, brimming with confidence.

"Taking my mother to the cleaners won't be easy. She's a smart old lady. At first you'd think she was a mouse, that she could hardly count up to two; but she's really very sharp, believe me. You'll have to stay on your toes."

"Don't worry. I'll find a way of getting around her."

They discussed the matter far into the night, but the final decision was postponed until morning.

CHAPTER 5

It wasn't easy for Krantz to decide to leave V——. He was reluctant to abandon his friends and his settled routine, and he was afraid of going to some isolated backwater where the older generation was still fully in power. He was even more frightened at the thought of becoming a teacher and having to do systematic, responsible work. But on the other hand, the artful cloak-and-dagger skills that the plan required appealed to him. He would have to don a mask of piety, infiltrate the enemy camp, and work behind the arch-foe's back, sowing by the handful the seeds of Enlightenment. There was also the prospect of comfort and good food. And he would be doing Shekhtl a favor. After due consideration, Krantz decided to head for Bobiltseve.

The group set about equipping him for the journey. The first problem was travel expenses: Bobiltseve was quite a distance away, a full day and night by train. Fortunately, a new recruit turned up, a boy who had just left home with a brand new coat which was sold the very same day. Then there was the costume: like an actor preparing to step onstage, Krantz studied every detail of his wardrobe. The jacket should be long, but not too long; a kerchief at the neck, but only in black; the cap neither velvet nor satin, but of plain cloth; the trousers, worn over the boots. And of course the phylacteries and prayerbook.

At the same time, Shekhtl briefed Krantz on the town. He

described its leading citizens, especially those who might be dangerous; he explained how each one of them ought to be handled, and from whom he could expect to get work. The most fascinating information concerned the secret cell of enlightened radicals, a well-organized group of some eight or ten youths who met under the leadership of Khayim-Wolf, the butcher's son, a young man who was already married. Khayim-Wolf was considered one of the most pious young men in town. Shekhtl spoke of him with great admiration, and kept repeating: "When *he* puts on a mask, it's a real mask all right!" He made Krantz swear at least ten times to keep the name of Khayim-Wolf a secret. The cell had its own library, but no one except Khayim-Wolf knew where the books were kept. Potential members were admitted only after a difficult series of tests. The cell even had its own password. For four or five years it had been doing its work slowly and methodically; thanks to the strong leadership of Khayim-Wolf, it was still intact, and not one of the local worthies even suspected its existence. Shekhtl gave Krantz the password and the name of a contact with whom he could set up a meeting.

Together they also worked out a detailed plan for deceiving Shekhtl's parents. Krantz was to meet them accidentally; they were to learn only by coincidence that Krantz was acquainted with their son. After that he was to fill them with stories of Shekhtl's prodigious scholarship, his dedication to learning, and so on.

Listening to Shekhtl's descriptions and careful advice, Krantz was struck by his practical bent, and his keen insights into human psychology. How did this jibe with those wild fantasies and outlandish projects? When Krantz asked him about it, Shekhtl burst out laughing: "Silly fool! You can't confuse the two. When you're flying, you're up in the clouds, and when you're walking, you keep both feet on the ground. As it says in the good book, 'The heavens are the heavens of the Lord, and the earth was given to the sons of man.'"

CHAPTER 6

Krantz's trip to Bobiltseve took five days. As might be expected, he traveled without a ticket, by hopping a freight. Part of the distance he covered on foot, and the final stretch in the back of a wagon, where he made the acquaintance of a young man from Bobiltseve, a storekeeper, who began to ask about the purpose of his trip but then immediately supplied his own answer: "Why are you going to Bobil-tseve? If you like, I'll tell you why. I can tell just by looking at your nose. You're going to try to get a job with Riebelman."

From Shekhtl's briefing, Krantz knew that there was a wealthy man in Bobiltseve named Riebelman who owned a sawmill. He decided to use his fellow-passenger's shrewd insight as the ostensible reason for his journey, although he knew as well as the storekeeper that no jobs at the mill were available; this way, though, it would appear that he was being forced to take up teaching as a substitute livelihood.

"Perhaps you're right, and perhaps you're wrong," Krantz replied coolly, "I've heard that it's very hard to get a job there."

"It's not just hard, it's impossible! You've come here for nothing!"

"What are you saying!" Krantz cried fearfully, "then what will I do?"

"What will you do? You won't do anything. You'll go back to where you came from."

"But I can't go back, I can't," said Krantz with mounting anxiety, "I must find some job or other. Do you understand? I have to!"

"No one can help you," droned his companion, rubbing salt into Krantz's wounds. "Now if you had some coin of the realm, say a few hundred rubles, I could send a nice little bit of business your way, the chance of a lifetime. There's a landowner who's getting rid of a load of oats for next to nothing."

"If I had the money, I wouldn't need your advice," Krantz interrupted. "Let's see if you're really so smart. Tell me what I can do without money. . . ."

"Without money you're in trouble," he answered firmly. "Do you know how to make punch? Lemonade?"

"No, I don't."

"Ink?"

"No. But I can write in ink."

"Can you draw up petitions to the authorities?"

"No. . . ."

"Ha! So what are you good for?" But then relenting somewhat he added, "Is your handwriting good?"

"Beautiful. Like a painting."

"Well then, you could become a teacher."

Krantz, who had been waiting for this suggestion, hesitated a moment, and sighed:

"It's a bitter way to earn a living. . . ."

"And where will you find a sweeter?"

"It's so common. . . ."

"And where will you find something more refined?"

"Well then, tell me, are there at least pupils, I mean ones who will pay?"

"And how! As many as you want! The teachers in this town were rolling in money."

"So where are they now?"

"The devil take them! Who knows? One led a respectable girl down the primrose path and then took off. Another was a heretic of the new kind who smoked on Sabbath, and spoke against God and religion, so he was sent packing. A third got married and gave up teaching. . . ."

"No! That's no job for me." Krantz was indignant. "My family would be humiliated if I stooped so low."

"Don't worry," the young man consoled him, "If you're from a good family, and if you're good with a pen, you won't have any trouble finding a match in Bobiltseve, with a dowry of several hundred rubles. That's the best business of all nowadays. . . ."

CHAPTER 7

In a while Krantz turned the conversation to lodgings, and asked where he might find a room. His companion reeled off about a dozen unfamiliar names; he also mentioned Krayne, Ephraim's wife, who had a small room to rent. Krayne was the name of Shekhtl's mother, but in order to make perfectly certain of her identity Krantz asked, "What does Ephraim do?"

"He's a *cheder*-teacher."

"What kind of a man is he?"

"He's just an ordinary man, that's all, neither too smart nor too stupid. A simple, honest man. But his wife, Krayne, is a real Cossack! She runs a little shop and at home she runs the show."

"So you'd advise me to stay at their place? Maybe you could point out where she lives."

"Any child in town could tell you that. When we pass it, the driver will stop and you can get off."

The wagon drove into town, and after passing several narrow streets, stopped in front of a small, run-down cottage. This, said Krantz's traveling companion, was Ephraim's house.

Krantz climbed down, paid the driver, and took up his parcel. In the doorway stood an elderly woman, rather stout, with an energetic face and calm, clever eyes. She had come out to see why the wagon had stopped.

"Krayne! This young man needs a room. Do you have one to rent him?" inquired his companion on Krantz's behalf.

Krayne studied the newcomer slowly, from head to toe.

"I'll see. . . ." Still looking him over, she invited him into the house.

The room they entered was dim and low-ceilinged, with signs of poverty and disorder everywhere. There were books, however, in plenty, all over the cupboards, dressers, tables, and windowsills.

"Sit down. Where are you from?" asked Krayne.

"I'm from V___."

"From V___?" she repeated in surprise. "Is that your home?"

"Yes."

Krayne lapsed into silence, but without once taking her eyes off the newcomer. Krantz understood that she was probably eager to ask about her son, but for the moment she restrained herself.

"Why have you come to Bobiltseve? On business?"

"Yes . . . I was hoping to find a job. At Riebelman's sawmill if I'm lucky."

Krayne opened the door into the other room:

"Have a look. That's the room. A whole family used to live here."

The room was tiny, almost without light. It was separated from the main room of the house by a thin partition that did not even extend all the way to the ceiling. Nevertheless, Krantz immediately decided to take it so as to establish close contact with Shekhtl's parents. Once he had settled the financial arrangements for his friend, he would move on to other quarters. He and Krayne agreed on six rubles a month for room and board. Krantz was a little surprised that Krayne was prepared to rent the room without even consulting her husband; apparently he had no say whatever in household matters.

"You'd probably like something to eat," Krayne ventured,

"we've already had our lunch, but I'll prepare something for you."

She placed some bread and butter, a couple of eggs and a glass of buttermilk on the table. Krantz washed up in the traditional manner. She sat down opposite him at the table, but for a long time remained silent. Then abruptly she asked:

"Tell me, is there a big yeshiva in V___?"

"And how! One of the biggest in Lithuania!" Krantz spoke without taking his lips from the glass of buttermilk.

"Are there many students?"

"About a hundred, I think . . . maybe more."

She paused for a few more seconds, and then said offhandedly:

"I have a son there, in that yeshiva."

"In V___?" asked Krantz in surprise.

"Why are you so amazed?"

"It's very far from here. Aren't there any yeshivas closer by?"

Krayne dropped her head and said in a pained voice:

"It just happened that way . . . you've just come here from V ——— yourself, in spite of its being so far away. . . ." She smiled weakly with this last comment, and then probed further: "Do you know any of the yeshiva students there?"

"I know almost all their faces, and I'm friendly with a few. I used to attend the daily lecture there myself. "

"My son went, to V___ only recently, about half a year ago."

"What's his name?"

"Hillel . . . probably 'the Bobiltsever,' after this town."

"Hillel? 'The Bobiltsever'?" repeated Krantz, as if trying vainly to recall, and then firmly deciding that he could not: "No. There's no one at the yeshiva by that name."

Krayne blanched, and her face took on a very anxious expression; the bitter truth was about to emerge—her son was not at the yeshiva. Watching the woman, Krantz felt the elation of an actor who knows that his performance has captivated his audience.

"Maybe you haven't noticed him," Krayne tried to calm herself. "He's not a very tall boy . . . dark, nice-looking, and very gentle. . . ."

"Not very tall? . . . dark and nice-looking . . ." Krantz rehearsed the description as if racking his memory. "Who could that be now? The Yonevitser . . . the Lyozner . . . the Mohilever. . . ."

"Yes! Perhaps the Mohilever!" Krayne grasped at this straw.

"He used to be at the yeshiva in Mohilev."

"Does he have curly hair?"

"Yes! Yes!"

"When he speaks, does he sometimes blink his eyes very quickly?"

"Well! That's him!" Krayne determined. She was completely reassured, and even rose from the table as though to show the matter was settled. "In other words, he's at the yeshiva and you know him."

"Of course! The Mohilever! I know him very well. I used to see him at the synagogue almost every day. . . . What a shame I didn't know he was from here. I would have brought you a letter from him."

"Well, how is he doing there? How is he managing at the yeshiva?" Krayne began to probe, finding it difficult to phrase the questions properly.

"I don't know exactly how he's doing. . . . He eats days like most of the boys, but I don't know if he has a house for every day of the week. Actually, his clothes are not in very good condition, but of course that's nothing unusual. As far as his studies go, it's hard for me to say because he's way ahead of me. He's considered one of the star pupils at the yeshiva. . . . The rabbi thinks the world of him."

Krantz, speaking with deep humility, seemed to be carrying off his role successfully. Krayne's eyes shone with joy. She walked over to the open window and called to a little girl who was playing near the house:

"Hannah! Run over to the *cheder* and tell Ephraim to come home for a while. Tell him we have news of Hillel."

CHAPTER 8

The man who came in was a thin, little old Jew with a sparse gray beard and round bulging eyes. His moustache was stained yellow from snuff and his whole face was the color of earth. Beard and earlocks were disheveled, as though the hairs were about to run off in different directions. His coat fell to his heels, and the fringes of his soiled undergarment hung below his knees. His expression was absent-minded, as if he were still engrossed in whatever he had just been doing in the cheder.

"Well? Regards from Hillel?" he muttered dreamily, looking all around him. When he caught sight of Krantz, he shook his hand quickly and sped through all the formalities:

"*Sholom aleichem!* Where are you from? How is Hillel doing over there?"

"Why do you pounce on him, before you even know anything?" interrupted Krayne with ill-concealed annoyance. "Sit down and talk to him like a human being. . . ."

At her reproach Ephraim came to. He tucked his coat up and seated himself at the table. Krayne briefly explained who their visitor was, the purpose of his coming, and the news he had brought of their son. As an aside, she mentioned having rented him the room.

Too impatient to wait until she had finished, Ephraim suddenly asked:

"What's he studying now? Which section of Talmud?"

Krantz casually replied with the first chapter that came to mind: "*Erubin.*"

"What do you mean, *Erubin?* Didn't he write that he was studying *Zeraim?*" cried Ephraim almost fearfully.

"The head of the yeshiva lectures on *Zeraim* at a separate class for some of the better students. Your son is considered one of the brightest lights of the yeshiva. He has an exceptional mind. . . ."

"Are you telling me? Don't I know it, eh? If that boy weren't so lazy, he would have been ordained long ago."

"I think that he's working seriously toward it now."

"Is that right? Working seriously?" repeated Ephraim, his eyes boring into Krantz. All at once he turned on his wife with a bitter outcry:

"And she tries to drag him home! Drag him home by the hair! Once a tyrant, always a tyrant!"

To Krantz's amazement, Krayne did not try to stop her husband. Instead, she faltered, and found little to say in her own defense:

"You don't know what you're talking about. . . ." Then, as if gathering strength for a confession, she began to speak in a much softer, intimate tone: "I'll tell you how things stand. I didn't believe that my son was really at the V— yeshiva."

Krantz showed surprise, but said nothing.

"Have you ever heard anything like it?" laughed Ephraim. "She didn't believe it! Go talk to a woman! A woman is afraid of everything and believes no one."

"Let me finish!" his wife interrupted. "You must understand what happened. In the yeshiva at Mohilev there was a whole . . . I don't know what you'd call it. . . . Students were caught with 'books' and expelled on the spot. And at the very same time my boy suddenly moved to V__. So you see, I was sure that . . . I'm only a mother, after all. . . ."

"Why didn't you write to the director of the yeshiva at V__?" Krantz was so certain of his success that he took the most direct and perilous course of action.

"That's true. . . . Somehow it never occurred to me."

"Now have you finally stopped worrying?" challenged Ephraim, pointing toward her with his beard.

"Yes. I've stopped worrying. You can go back to *cheder*!"

"But that still isn't enough. You have to do something about it . . . you know what I mean!" he persisted.

"I know, I know! Go on!" Krayne shooed him away. When he had gone, Krayne explained that it was a long time since she had sent her son any money. The very next day, God willing, she would send him a few rubles.

In the evening, when Ephraim returned from *cheder*, they resumed their conversation about Hillel, the yeshiva, and the details of life in V ——. Having exhausted these subjects, his hosts began to show an interest in Krantz, who spoke freely of himself and his past. His father had been a very wealthy man and Krantz had been tutored in everything there was to know. But without warning, his father went bankrupt one day and then suddenly died. Krantz was left with a widowed mother and two grown sisters to support. Somehow, it didn't really matter how, he had to provide for them. When he heard about Riebelman who was rich and involved in so many businesses, it seemed like the ideal place to apply for a position, and hence he had come to Bobiltseve.

The story stirred Ephraim's and Krayne's sympathies. They even promised to put in a word with Riebelman through an acquaintance of theirs, warning, however, that the effort would almost certainly be in vain. Riebelman was already known to have a surfeit of employees.

"On the way here, the young man sharing my wagon tried to persuade me to become a tutor, to teach children to read and write

Russian. He said I could easily grow rich. . . . What do you think of that?" he concluded with a chuckle.

"That's Borukh Leyzer-Ber," explained Krayne to her husband. "He's got crazy ideas."

"Maybe he's right. Teaching might pay very well," Krantz said earnestly, but with obvious reluctance. "On the other hand, what sort of work is it for a decent boy of good family? Why should I go crawling in the mud before I've been tripped? To tell you the truth, I don't think I'm really suited for it. I may know ten times as much about reading and writing as the greatest teacher, but nowadays that's not what people are looking for. They want a teacher to be a freethinker, and I don't know what else besides. That's not for me!"

His hosts expressed their sympathy. Letting a few moments pass, he then added in a strained voice, as if to himself:

"But what shall I do, with a sick mother and two sisters to support? I can't let them be thrown out into the street."

The question hung in the air, the answer seeming only too self-evident.

Before retiring, Krayne came to Krantz with a request: could he write out an address for her? She handed him a crumpled letter and said:

"This is where Hillel lives. Tomorrow I'll give you five rubles and ask you to address the envelope so that I can send him the money."

Krantz glanced at the letter. The return address was given as: Kovadle's house, c/o Joseph Krantz, for Shekhtl.

"This is the wrong address," he said, erasing his own name and putting down the name of Braines in its stead. (Money could not be sent directly to Shekhtl because he lacked a proper residence permit.)

"What luck!" Krayne exclaimed happily. "If not for you, the money would certainly have been lost!"

CHAPTER 9

That night, Krantz lay awake for a long time in a state of high excitement, like an actor after a particularly brilliant performance.

Going over in his mind the many incidents and conversations of the day, he buried his head in the pillow and giggled madly. Had anyone told him that in fact he had spent the day cheating and lying with more malice and treachery than a thief, Krantz would simply have been incredulous, so intoxicated was he by the artistry of his performance.

The next morning he accompanied Ephraim to the synagogue, deliberately making his first public appearance in the guise of a pious Jew. On the way, he asked detailed questions about what Ephraim was teaching his young pupils, lacing his conversation with enough references to show that he himself was no ignoramus. Several townspeople stopped to ask Ephraim about his companion. He introduced Krantz as a young man from V ——, a friend of Hillel's, who had come to town on a matter of business.

There remained before Krantz the prospect of making contact with the underground cell of Maskilim. In giving him the password, Shekhtl had told him to approach a certain young man by the name of Leivick, of whom he had provided so perfect a description that Krantz recognized him immediately upon entering the synagogue.

Toward the end of the services, Krantz strolled past Leivick's seat, intoning the indicated verse from the Psalms: "But it was thou, a man mine equal, my companion and my familiar friend. We took sweet counsel together, in the house of God we walked with the throng."

Leivick, without turning his head, nodded acknowledgement, and Krantz went back to his seat beside Ephraim. He waited for a signal, a note, a stealthy message whispered in a corner. But the contact was quite straightforward. After services Leivick came up to Ephraim and, indicating the newcomer, asked who he was.

"This is a young man from V ——, a friend of Hillel's in the yeshiva," Ephraim answered.

Leivick greeted him, asked about V —— and about Hillel, and ended by inviting Krantz over to his place for afternoon tea. When he left, Ephraim said:

"That's Reb Shmerl the lumber-dealer's son. A fine young man. Studies day and night. A friend of Hillel's. You should go over for tea if he invited you; his father might be able to put in a word for you with Riebelman."

Krantz was reminded that he still had to play out that particular farce, and right after services he set out for Riebelman's office. The waiting room was full. Several hours passed before he was given an interview with the owner. Bathed in humility, as if he were begging alms, he pleaded for a position. But Riebelman did not even let him finish before waving him from the room:

"Leave me alone! I have no positions! I don't have any, and I won't have any, so go home and stop bothering me!"

Krantz did not press the matter.

In the afternoon he went to call on Leivick. The secret free-thinker met him at the door and led him upstairs to his bedroom, shutting the door behind them. It was a large room, with books scattered everywhere.

Leivick was a young man of about twenty, with a drawn, angular face and only the barest trace of a beard. His eyes were dark and piercing, like those of a mouse. There was something dry in his expression, a severity beyond his years, as though he had spent his youth without once having smiled. Even his voice was dry, expressionless, and a little rasping.

Leivick studied his visitor carefully, and asked, almost as a reproach:

"What is Hillel doing in V—? Is he at the yeshiva?"

"No. He has thrown off that pretense altogether."

"Pity," Leivick cut him off. "He should have stayed at the yeshiva. There would have been time enough to jump the fence. . . . Well, and what did you come here for? Lessons?"

"Yes. I'd like to talk to you about it."

Krantz told him his plans and of his deception of Shekhtl's parents. Leivick listened impassively.

"You haven't begun too badly, but where do you go from here? To tell the truth, I don't have much faith in tutoring. . . ."

Krantz was startled: "What do you mean? Why?"

"We've had a few tutors who did more harm than good. They came here, caused a commotion, raised everyone's dander, and left with nothing to show for their stay. . . ."

Krantz was more and more surprised by this attitude, and could only answer lamely that they were probably the wrong kind of people for the job.

"That's not the point," Leivick interrupted, "I just don't trust the big-city Maskilim. They love scandal. They want to show off their powers and their wit, to put something over on the pious, but they don't know how to work in the dark, with a steady energy. What's worse, they love to write long, sarcastic letters about everything that ought to be kept secret, and their letters have a habit of falling into the hands of the rabbi or the head of the yeshiva. And they feel a constant need to stuff their pockets with radical pamphlets. . . ."

The scathing irony of this speech cut Krantz to the quick. He got up and said drily:

"You may be right. But I expected something different from our conversation. If you think that tutors can do nothing but harm, then we have nothing more to discuss."

"Now wait a minute," said Leivick impatiently. "You're angry for no good reason. I didn't mean to insult you. I just wanted you to know my opinion. Go ahead. Tell me what you hope to accomplish as a tutor."

"How can you ask? I don't understand you."

"Very simple. A good friend, someone he knows, can more easily open a boy's eyes and expose him to new ideas than a tutor can. The fact that a tutor teaches a couple of boys and girls to read and write doesn't impress me one bit. It's like this: if someone sees the light, he can learn everything there is to know even without a mentor. Take me, for example. In two years, while pretending to sit over the Talmud, I've covered the whole curriculum for the eight grades of high school and college. But if someone is still blind, then knowing how to read and write won't make any difference."

This was a new idea to Krantz, and he found it difficult to disagree.

"I'm not telling you this in order to convince you to give up your plan," Leivick added. "I don't know you, after all, so how can I know what kind of a job you'd do? You're off to a good start, and if it continues as smoothly as before, you'll be able to help us in our work. . . ."

Coming after the previous attack, these words offered Krantz some slight encouragement. "You'll see how well I work!" he assured his host.

"Naturally I'll help you as much as I can. You'll find as many students as you want. Go to see Nakhman the dry-goods grocer. We'll see to it that he takes you on for his children—he has a son and a daughter—and others will follow his example. But I'll say it again: work quietly, and without fuss. Bear in mind that when you lead someone off the straight and narrow, it's best if he doesn't even notice the bend in the road."

In coming to call on Leivick, Krantz had been expecting to

meet a provincial, someone who would defer to his visitor from the city, listen to him avidly and follow his advice. Instead he found an independent young man, more mature and better educated than he, who treated him like a disciple. Krantz found himself looking up to Leivick. But he was still eager to meet the other members of the cell, particularly its leader, the butcher's son.

"How do I get in touch with Khayim-Wolf?" he asked of Leivick.

"Who? Who's Khayim-Wolf?"

"What do you mean? Isn't he the leader of your group? Hillel told me that. . . ."

Leivick fixed Krantz with a puzzled stare. "Khayim-Wolf, the butcher's son? Has Hillel gone out of his mind? Was he making fun of you? Khayim-Wolf is one of the greatest fanatics in town. You'd better avoid him like fire."

His tone was so earnest that for a moment Krantz was sure Hillel must have made a mistake. But then he quickly realized that Leivick was simply suspicious. "Don't you trust me?" he asked with injured pride.

Leivick looked at him in bewilderment. "You're the one who doesn't trust *me* if you don't believe what I tell you. But go ahead, if you like, try to approach Khayim-Wolf. What a story that will make! Listen . . . Hillel was hardly even a member of the group, and he never knew what was going on. What he told you isn't worth a tinker's dam."

By the time he left, Krantz felt humiliated, badly fallen in his own self-esteem. He vowed to take his work so seriously and get so much done that Leivick and his bunch would come and beg him to join them.

CHAPTER 10

It didn't take Krantz long to get settled. Shekhtl's parents, out of pity for the supposed condition of his mother and sisters, encouraged him to take up tutoring, and before long his lessons brought him a full twelve rubles a month. He soon found a pretext for moving out, and took up new lodgings at the home of a teamster at the edge of town, thereby freeing himself from Krayne's careful surveillance. But he continued eating his meals at Krayne's, so that his board might insure the five rubles a month she was sending to her son.

At first it was rather difficult for Krantz to maintain a steady workload, and even more difficult to maintain a rigorous outward piety. But little by little he grew into the part. He singled out some of his most promising students and slowly began to undermine their faith.

Two months went by, and the shtetl grew accustomed to his presence. But the main task he had set for himself did not get off the ground. His conversation with Leivick, and his awareness that a radical cell was operating without his participation, had clipped the wings of his enthusiasm, and eventually undermined his will to work. He was also growing very bored with the monotonous life of the town, the absence of any congenial society or entertainment. He missed the noisy cameraderie of Kovadle's house; even eating in abundance, as he now did, seemed a vulgar habit which could only coarsen the spirit. Heaviest of all was the burden of his disguise, which he could not safely put aside even in the privacy of his room. The daily prayers in the synagogue, the pious bearing, the conversations on matters of observance, were briefly interesting as a test of his artistic skill, but it was hard to walk in these chains for months on end, and after a while it seemed to lack purpose.

Gradually, imperceptibly, Krantz began loosening the bonds, allowing himself greater freedom. In his room he took to sitting bareheaded. When smoking on the Sabbath, he did not always take the necessary measures to avoid detection. Several times he realized too late that he had left Krayne's table without saying the proper blessings. Once, in conversation with a traditional Jew, he inadvertently let fall a skeptical remark. Another time, when the enthusiasm of a Hasid got on his nerves, he permitted himself a scoffing reference to the holy Rebbe. None of this was lost on the townspeople, who now began to watch him closely. Behind his back rumors began to spread about "those freethinkers" and "Berlin Jews." News of his former life—not wholly accurate, but remarkably like the truth—circulated widely. Leivick warned him several times that a storm was gathering over his head, and that he must be more cautious. But by then it was too late; inevitably, the storm broke. On a Sabbath morning, as a very tardy Krantz hurried to the synagogue, he was stopped in a quiet lane by an unfamiliar young man who said nervously: "Don't go to the synagogue. They're out for your blood. Last night, through a crack in the shutters, you were seen smoking."

Krantz returned to his room to await further developments. Luckily for him, the incident came to nothing. Krantz's landlord, a simple teamster who believed that his tenant was a pious young man, unaccountably swore that he had been sitting with Krantz after supper until late into the night. When it was pointed out to the landlord that Krantz might have smoked later, as he was going to bed, the landlord flew into a rage, threatened to crack the skull of anyone who dared to make such suggestions, and tried to drag the rabbi to his home to prove that there were no cracks in his shutters wide enough to see through. The teamster's protestations convinced no one, but peace was temporarily restored.

Thereafter, the attitude of Shekhtl's parents to their guest noticeably changed. Ephraim, who had formerly prattled freely on matters of learning or told endless tales of his Rebbe, now kept a sullen silence. He avoided Krantz's eye, limiting himself to occasional muttered remarks about the weather or household matters, and these only to preserve the amenities. Krayne now hardly ever mentioned her son. Often Krantz would feel her suspicious, probing stare on his face, and he was convinced that both husband and wife had lost faith in him completely.

Before leaving V__, Krantz had been warned by Shekhtl not to rely on the local postman. Since the warning was later repeated by Leivick, Krantz took to handling his mail directly through the post office. One day, he was asked to deliver a card addressed to Shekhtl's parents. The card had on it only several lines of writing—the conventional salutation, and the following message: "Your query came as a surprise. There is no Hillen ben Ephraim at the yeshiva, nor has anyone by that name ever been registered here. You would do well to find out if some misfortune, God forbid, may not have befallen your son." The signature was illegible, but just above it was the title: "Director of the Yeshiva at V ——." Clearly, Shekhtl's parents had sent an inquiry about their son—just as Krantz had once suggested they do. He would have had a jolly time of it had the card ever reached its destination . . . which, of course, it never did.

CHAPTER 11

One day, not long after the furor over smoking, Krayne approached Krantz with a request:

"I'd like some advice. It's been almost two years since Hillel went off on his own. We invited him home for the holidays, but he said that his studies were too important to be interrupted. I know that he's right, but I'm only a mother, and I'd like to see him. So I've decided to go to V ——. It's hard for me to undertake such a long journey, and it'll cost me a pretty penny, but somehow I'll find the strength. What do you think? Is it a good idea? Do you think I should go?"

Krantz realized that he was being tested. For a moment he was shaken, but quickly regaining his composure he answered coldly that it had nothing whatever to do with him:

"Why shouldn't you go if you can manage it? See for yourself what his life there is like. As a matter of fact," he added with what he hoped was utter nonchalance, "if you do go, I'd ask you to bring back a small parcel of my clothes. . . ."

Apparently he had carried his assumed indifference a little too far. A smile crept over Krayne's face, and ignoring his last remark she said as if in mockery:

"Thank you so very much for your kind advice. I will indeed go to V ——. How does the saying go. . . . your own eyes are the trustiest witnesses. A stranger can be deceived, but a mother's eye sees everything."

"Quite right! You ought to go!" Krantz exclaimed, barely able to keep his fury in check.

Though still uncertain whether or not Krayne would undertake the arduous trip, Krantz wrote to Shekhtl and Braines the very same day warning them of the impending danger, and advising that they take all the necessary precautions to prevent Krayne from learning the truth.

Two days later, Krayne set out for V —— without even bidding him good-bye.

Krantz realized he was on very shaky ground, and awaited her return with less than perfect composure. It was hard to believe that once in V— she would fail to discover the truth about her son.

A few days later, Leivick, who received mail for Krantz at his own address, sent over his brother with a letter from Braines containing the following ominous words:

"As soon as you receive this letter, gather up your few belongings and get you gone from Bobiltseve. We have failed miserably, and the fearsome witch is now on her way home breathing fire and eager to wreak her vengeance on thee."

There followed a detailed account of what had transpired between Krayne and her son. Immediately upon receipt of Krantz's letter, Braines and Shekhtl had gone to work, removing everything of an "un-Jewish" nature, and filling the bookshelves with dozens of Talmudic volumes and other religious books. Their friends were told not to show their faces for several days. Shekhtl and Braines borrowed long coats, tassled undergarments, and skullcaps, and wore them during those hours of the day when Krayne could be expected to arrive by train. And in fact, when Krayne did come upon them they were poring over the texts, swaying back and forth and chanting aloud. But it was no use. As soon as she had arrived in V —— and located the Gentile section, Krayne set out to find her son. Not far from Kovadle's house, she stopped at a little Jewish shop to make inquiries. When the shopkeeper's wife heard Krayne mention Kovadle's house, and the dark young man with the curly hair, she slapped her hands together and launched into a tale of horror: the inhabitants fed on swine, smoked on the Sabbath, acted like out-and-out Gentiles.

"Tear your son away from that house of iniquity and drag him home by force! Otherwise he is lost forever!"

The woman then went on to tell about the ringleader of the group, a rabbi's son who was now gone off somewhere to become a tutor. So accurately did she describe the vile heretic that Krayne instantly recognized her boarder.

She burst into Kovadle's house with a wild lamenting shriek, grabbed hold of Shekhtl by the lapels, and began tugging at him and screaming: "Murderer! Home with you!" Her eyes were so wild that Braines, as he himself wrote, shook like a leaf. Shekhtl tore free from his mother's grasp and fled into hiding. For two days Krayne turned the city inside out looking for him; she went to the rabbi, to the director of the yeshiva, to the leading citizens, wailing and begging for help. Ten times at least she burst into Shekhtl's room, and finding only Braines, cursed him roundly, threatened to call in the police, and finally threw herself at his feet, pleading with him to yield up her son. She pushed a ten-ruble note into his hand for "the gang" if only they would "give her back her child." After two more days of scouring the city in vain, she left for home.

Krantz's first reaction was panic. But soon the prospect of the impending battle filled him with a surge of energy: let it come! Krantz would not flee the battlefield. He would throw off his mask entirely and launch an open attack on the town. Leivick and his group might disapprove, but Krantz could no longer bother himself over those sleepy spirits.

The letter from Braines arrived Friday morning, while Krantz was still in bed. He was certain that Krayne would arrive in time for the Sabbath, and determined to take his dinner there, as usual: he would meet the enemy head-on.

He sat down to a glass of tea and began to map out his strategy.

§⟨◊⟩§

CHAPTER 12

Footsteps sounded in the passageway. Slowly, the door to Krantz's room opened and Krayne's voice was heard from the hall:

"Is it all right to come in ?"

"Come right in!" Krantz shouted, louder than was necessary. He was startled by her sudden appearance. That Krayne would come to him was something he hadn't anticipated.

She came in slowly, closed the door behind her, took several steps forward, and gave a friendly nod: "Good morning."

Her face was pale and drawn, but expressionless, as always. A demure, good-natured smile was on her lips. Only the gray eyes admitted something secretive and quizzical. It would have been impossible to guess from her appearance the purpose of her visit.

Krantz quickly saw that Krayne was determined to play cat and mouse with him and was looking to catch him off guard. He too played dumb, and replied with a friendly smile:

"Ah! Welcome! Back so soon?"

"As you can see. . . ."

"Have a seat!"

"Thank you." She seated herself on the edge of the chair.

"Will you have a glass of tea?"

"Thank you, but I've just had one. . . ."

Even as she spoke, Krantz noticed that her lips were parched and she had to keep moistening them with the tip of her tongue.

"Well, I've traveled far, and seen a lot . . . visited with my son Hillel, may he live and be well," she launched into her account calmly, in a contented singsong. "I'm satisfied, thanks be to His Holy Name, completely satisfied!"

"There you are! What did I tell you?" responded Krantz, with no less satisfaction.

"Yes, you were quite right," she agreed, "but what can you do with a foolish woman? She always imagines the worst . . . a mother after all."

There was a brief pause, after which she resumed in a lively tone:

"I don't regret having made the trip. So much to see. So many people. I met Hillel's friends. By the way, what's the name of the boy he shares a room with? The tall one, with the goatee? He seemed like a very fine boy. You must know him."

"Yes, I know him. His name is Braines. He really is a nice chap."

He stole a sidelong glance at Krayne. The calm voice, the polite smile and bashful reticence made her seem like a panther stalking its prey. He braced himself for her pounce; but Krayne was in no hurry.

"I met some of my son's other friends. I heard a lot of fine things about you as well. . . ."

Her voice was caught by a momentary spasm, but she soon regained control.

"I didn't know that you were so well descended, the son of a rabbi. . . . And I had no idea how much help you've been to my son. . . ."

Suddenly she erupted from her seat, red in the face, her eyes glaring in savage hatred. She banged her fist down on the table and cried:

"Apostate! Sit down this very moment and write to my son, whom you've murdered, to come home at once! Do you hear me, you blasphemer of Israel? This very instant! Otherwise you won't get out of this place alive. I'll light a funeral pyre under you! I know everything, everything! Sit down and write!"

She threw on the table a sheet of paper and an envelope which Krantz had failed to notice in her hand. What Krantz might have done had the ambush been sprung unexpectedly, it would be difficult to guess; but prepared as he was, he simply rose to his feet and said deliberately:

"I will write no letters to your son!"

"You'll write! You'll change your tune!" Krayne shouted with savage conviction. "If not, I'll stir up the whole town against you! They'll tear you to shreds! Jews will take my part for the blood you've shed."

"You won't do it," Krantz retorted with a calm smile.

"Why not? Why won't I do it?" she cried in bewilderment.

Krantz advanced on her and spoke in a menacing voice:

"Listen to me, Krayne! If you dare to say one word against me to anyone, I'll write to Hillel at once and order him to be baptized! Do you hear me? Baptized! You can be sure that if I give the command, Hillel will obey it. You know very well that I'm the highest-ranking member of the group, and a leader is obeyed! I'll say no more. You can do as you please."

Krayne blanched and staggered. Dizzy, she held on to the chair to steady herself. For a while she stood motionless, biting her lips and muttering. Then a suppliant smile, a mixture of entreaty and hatred, appeared on her face. At length she gathered up enough strength to say in a trembling voice:

"There's no need to get angry with me. . . . You must understand that it wasn't I who shouted at you, but the pain crying out from inside me. Of course, I won't mention a word about you to anyone—what would I stand to gain? Why drag my own good name through the mud? Well, if you don't want to write him, you don't have to. It happens, sometimes, that a son may die. . . ."

"Now that's the way to talk!" Krantz exploded triumphantly.

Stifling a deep sigh, Krayne added a final plea:

"I must ask that this remain between the two of us. The old man must never find out. It would be unbearable for him."

Before leaving, she paused at the door to ask: "Are you coming for supper?"

"Of course I'll come. Why not?"

When Krayne had gone, Krantz paced his room excitedly, rubbing his hands together in satisfaction. He had not anticipated so decisive and glorious a victory. The idea of threatening her with Hillel's conversion was a last-minute brainstorm, inspired by Krayne's scream of "Apostate!" As he remembered his exact words, that if he ordered Hillel to be baptized the command would be promptly obeyed, he burst into a fit of laughter. He was only sorry that he had not made Krayne swear to go on sending Hillel the five rubles each month.

In the evening Krantz went over for the Sabbath meal. In speaking of Hillel, Krayne used the same tone she had earlier assumed with Krantz. But several times she stopped short, as if forgetting her train of thought, and stared blankly ahead of her. Ephraim sat dejectedly, without a word. He sensed that something was wrong, that something was being withheld from him, but unable to get at the truth he simply looked at Krayne and Krantz in despair.

Several days later, Krantz stopped taking his meals at their house and made ready to leave Bobiltseve. It seemed that Krayne had kept her lips sealed, as she had promised, but the atmosphere had grown so heavy around him he could hardly breathe, and there was nothing to be accomplished by staying.

CHAPTER 13

About a week after Krantz stopped eating at Krayne's, he happened to be passing the house and noticed her sitting in the window. When she saw him, she motioned him over.

Krayne was greatly altered. Her drawn face had lost its stolidity, and was now more agile and expressive. There was a new expression, a kind of rapturous passion, in her eyes. As Krantz drew nearer she greeted him with a smile of savage pleasure, as if preparing to spring at him—either to embrace him or to sink her teeth into his throat. She began prattling very rapidly, as if sharing a merry confidence that would have to remain a secret between the two of them:

"Listen, outcast. It's just your luck that you stopped coming to eat at my home. I was prepared to poison you like a mad dog! With rat poison!"

She gave a soft little chuckle.

It was so unexpected and awkward that Krantz could not keep from laughing:

"You would have been deported to Siberia," he protested.

"I? Because of you? Who would have informed on me? What Jew would have taken your part? They would have buried you like carrion, behind the fence—and that would have been the end of you!" And she gave another pleased litttle chuckle.

But suddenly her head shot up and the eyes that she fixed on Krantz were wide open in stark, indescribable terror. Her gaze so astonished him that he sprang back and almost fled. For the rest of the day he was haunted by the horror of her eyes, with their heaven-piercing agony. . . .

The next morning there were rumors that Krayne had gone mad.

OF BYGONE DAYS

MENDELE MOCHER SFORIM

INTRODUCTION TO OF BYGONE DAYS

OF BYGONE DAYS (Shloyme Reb Chayim's) *is the fictional autobiography of Sholom Jacob Abramovitch, better known by his persona-pseudonym of Mendele Mocher Sforim, Mendele the Bookpeddler. Though Mendele once warned that his autobiography was to be sought in all his works, this is the only self-styled story of his life, and it offers what is perhaps the most detailed study of a shtetl in all of Jewish literature.*

The author's approach to autobiography differs sharply from that of his European contemporaries who were baring their lives to the very bone in an effort to achieve absolute personal honesty. Contemporary Hebrew literature was also rich in dramatic exposi- tions of the anguished, lonely quest of the modern artist and the modern Jew. But when Mendele in his introduction accounts for his reluctance to embark on biography, he discounts the validity of the first-person approach. The individual, he maintains, cannot be arbitrarily differentiated from the collective; the only valid form of biography is ethnography.

Mendele's characteristic literary trait is his interruption of the narrative flow for the sake of an argumentative aside on, for exam- ple, the varieties of pauperism, or for a scrupulous depiction of a wayside inn, or a Jewish cow, or a woodland storm. Of Bygone Days is composed of a series of such portraits and arguments, but with an almost total suspension of narrative line. Time has virtually come to a stop in this work, and only space remains. Mendele's portrait records every corner and character in the shtetl, every nuance of attitude and mood. With the passion of an anthropologist he notes the inflections as well as the topics of conversation, the character and the extent of family life, the sources of harmony and the causes of friction within the community as a whole.

The most highly personal section is the introduction, where the author's two literary personae meet for the first time. The bookpeddler, an amiable wanderer with a folkish, home-spun wisdom, comes to call on the literary man, Abramovitch, at the height of the latter's fame. As might be expected, the bookpeddler is the more winning figure, while the literary man, in a painful scene, reveals how remote he has grown from some of his fellow Jews, and from his own past. The ensuing autobiography is undertaken as a kind of penance, as though by returning to the past Abramovitch can atone for the social and personal estrangement of the present. This is by far the "softest" of Mendele's works: although it is informed, as is all his writing, by a keen sense of the injustice of class discrimination and the repressive strangulation of Jewish small-town life, of his early satiric anger only sadness now remains. An old man, Mendele writes elegiacally of a world he had once engaged in mortal combat.

The conclusion of the work circles back to the opening chapter, in which the father's death has already occurred, and the family has entered into decline. The body of the work is thus provided with a double setting, the hero's boyhood contrasted to a later and bleaker period when his mother has become a miller's wife, and to the much later and in some ways even bleaker period of the writer's maturity. The double setting serves to emphasize the radiance of childhood, which sparkles in the memory like a jewel. We begin at the end, sharing the author's perspective. As though turning the pages of an album, Mendele reveals scene after scene of a world which has vanished—how utterly, he himself never knew.

Written in two languages and in many stages, this work raises problems of redaction and classification that demand bibliographical explanation at the outset. * The introduction was first published in Hebrew, in 1894, as a separate work called Of Bygone Days. The

---

*An annotated, variorum edition of Shloyme Reb Chayim's in Yiddish can be found in his Collected Works, eds. A. Gurshteyn, M. Viner, M. Litvakoff and I. Nusinov (Moscow, 1936), Vol. VI.

first eleven chapters of the fictional autobiography were published in Yiddish, in 1899, as Shloyme Reb Chayim's, and the complete work, ending with the death of the father, and including the introduction, was published in the Jubilee Edition of Mendele's Yiddish works in 1911. In the parallel edition of his Hebrew works it appears in the same form. A so-called Part II of Shloyme Reb Chayim's began to appear serially in 1913 and 1914, but was not printed in book form until after Mendele's death in 1917. Since Part II is not formally or thematically related to the earlier work, the two sections are best considered separate; here only the first is presented.

OF BYGONE DAYS BY MENDELE MOCHER SFORIM

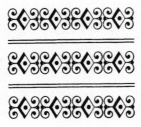

AUTHOR'S PREFACE

MENDELE the bookpeddler says:* Whenever a Jew comes to a journey's end, he feels as if his hips are breaking, his back aching, and his knees shaking from being crushed and squeezed into one seat with seven other people. From the moment he enters the carriage the Jew abandons any claim to his own limbs, and his feet become a doorsill for everyone to tread upon. But even worse than usual were the aches and pains that racked every bone in my body—may you never suffer such pains—when I arrived at the distant metropolis of N__,† after wanderings and adventures and many hardships. At that moment, every bone in my body felt the aptness of the interpretation our ancient sages applied to the words of Scripture: "I have forgotten comfort (Lam. 3:17)." Our sages explained that the "comfort" whose loss made the destruction of Jerusalem so bitter for the prophet as to occasion this outburst was none other than the bathhouse, by which they meant quite literally

---

*Mendele the bookpeddler says: a parodistic use of the Talmudic formula for introducing an argument, e.g., "Rabbi Tarphon says. . . ." The author begins most of his fiction with this phrase.

†N ——: generally thought to refer to Odessa where the author was living at the time he wrote this preface.

an actual bathhouse and all its accessories, with its broad benches, long beams on which to hang trousers and stockings and miscellaneous items of a man's clothing, with an expert doctor sitting in the corner, a lighted candle before him, shaving and bleeding our fellow Jews in the approved fashion. I could really have used that "comfort" just then, but alas!—it's not to be found in this city any more than the other advantages of which the little towns of our region boast. It is this deficiency which makes the cities unlivable, and for our poor shtetl Jews, unthinkable.

As soon as I realized that I wouldn't be able to remedy my discomfort in the customary way, I did what every Jew does when there's no other way out—I closed my mind to my pains, and turned my attention to other things: after saying the evening prayers, I left the hotel to go about my business and meet with some fellow book dealers and friends.

An unseasonable wind blew in suddenly from the North, bringing black clouds with it and darkening the sky; people panicked and began rushing about in confusion. These days the climate has gotten out of order; the wind is unpredictable and erratic, like the value of shares in the stock market, and like this whole modern generation. By the end of summer, the normal pattern of the weather had changed with the sudden appearance of clouds and cold and wind. The sun darkened and almost seemed to go black, the whole world fell desolate, engulfed in an ominous gloom. Goats hopped about the gardens, trampling and eating whatever was left there; the pigs came like an apocalyptic plague, rummaging and gnawing, digging up plants by the roots with their teeth and making a wreck of man's labors. The trees lost the finery that had been spring's gift to them, and stood destitute and empty-handed,* swaying and trembling, creaking and groaning, beating their bald tops with their boughs; no one would have believed that once they had bloomed and grown fruit for people to eat. Animals burrowed into the earth for shelter, flies hid in chinks in the wall, and people abandoned their homes and headed for distant seas. The land went into mourning, and everyone became melancholy and apprehen-

*In the Yiddish version, the text reads, the trees stood empty-handed, "vi melamdim on bletlakh," like teachers without their leaves, punning on the final word which had as well the slang meaning of work permits. The untranslatable simile makes evident the implications of the entire passage, which describes the insecurity and "storminess" of the early 1890's.

sive: very soon the great lord winter would come, and lay the land waste.

Now the High Holidays were over, Sukkot was past and winter had come, but with no storms and gales; not cruel and ill-tempered as one had anticipated, but rather kind and conciliatory, gracing the land and its inhabitants with a warm smile. People breathed more easily, and life had an unusual taste, sweet as honey, but with a dash of vinegar too. The flies reappeared, buzzing madly about and doing drunken Cossack dances on the windowpane; mosquitoes too swarmed out of their hiding places, carousing and making a regular carnival in the streets; an acacia tree took it into its head to put forth a flower—congratulations!—while elsewhere in the garden, a bud appeared. And man, as usual, deluded himself into thinking that miracles were happening, and he got his hopes up. Paupers were happy and beggars rejoiced; there was yet hope of sunshine, and —with God's help—a pleasant sun would soon warm them. But just at that moment winter revealed itself in all its terrible might, storming, raging, and shaking with fury, making the wind blow and the rain pour over the world and its inhabitants, with snow and frost like breadcrumbs, and thick mud.

The wind was raging with no letup and stabbing my body with needle-sharp bits of ice. I lowered my head and held tight to my caftan so the skirts wouldn't blow into my face, and walked alone at night, all hunched over, toward the home of Shloyme ben Chayim,* my good friend of many years.

This man Shloyme once lived in Glupsk,† and its inhabitants used to provide him with a good living. Not that they would give him any money, God forbid! They didn't take a penny out of their pockets for his support, for your Glupskite loves his coin as he loves

---

*Shloyme ben Chayim: The actual name of the author, Sholom Yakov Abramovitch. Shloyme, the autobiographical person, is the central figure of the novel, first in his adult role as a renowned author, then in the bulk of the work, as a child. The facts of the story are largely autobiographical.

†Glupsk: From the Slavic term *gloopsk*, fool. This fools'-town reappears under the same name in many of the author's works. A medium-sized, largely Jewish town, the model for Glupsk is Berdichev, where the author resided from 1858 until 1869 when he was forced to leave because of pressure from the respectable citizenry. The immediate cause of his expulsion was the publication of his bitterly satiric drama, *Di takse* (The Meat Tax, or the Band of Town Benefactors), in which he exposed the hypocrisy, greed, and cunning of the leading members of the community. (On the meat tax, see note on page 285.)

his life, and you couldn't get him to give it up by any expedient short of tearing out his sidelocks. The coin is his first principle. It gives him respect and stature, makes a man of him; it makes him arrogant, stubborn, pushy, and a leader of the community. But as Shloyme was a writer, the Glupskites provided the material for his stories; in other words, he would observe his neighbors and study their behavior, in the same way scientists study the nature of living creatures, and after he had observed the Glupskites and uncovered their inner life, their goings and comings and all the behavioral characteristics of their particular species, he would describe them as they actually were, and tell fabulous stories about them, both entertaining and edifying. These stories, which were read throughout the Jewish world, brought in hard cash, and provided his family with ample support.

On the face of it, the inhabitants of Glupsk ought to have had no cause to complain about Reb Shloyme's activities, since his profits were made at no cost to them; but even so, they chose to take offense, and made trouble for him for reasons that have never been clear to me. By rights, the Jewish court ought to have compelled them to tolerate his activity, which entailed no loss to them; the force of Jewish law should have been used to shut their mouths, to tie them up like animals and set them before the author so that he might sketch them, with or without their consent, for his own benefit and for the benefit of others. But he abandoned his legal rights and dropped the whole issue. Why? First of all, out of pity for dumb animals, because it's wrong to torment any creature, even mosquitos and fleas. Second, because he himself got tired of this business of constantly dealing with Glupskites; after all, even honey will make you sick if you eat too much of it. Third, everything, as we know, is finite; could the Glupsk fountain flow with stories forever?

Reb Shloyme realized that this source had begun to stagnate and stink, and to swarm with all sorts of inferior creatures. At the same time, he heard that a new species had just appeared among us, to all appearances identical with the Glupskites, but chameleon-like, characterized by a pretentious manner of speaking and queer habits. The public was avid to find out all about them, but as no pen had yet attempted to do them justice, and as they were still virgin territory, awaiting an author, Shloyme abandoned his Glupskites. Whether this strange new breed and Shloyme got along, and how long he stayed among them, and what return he got for the work he did among them with his pen and ink, I don't know. Perhaps he got tired of them too, perhaps he decided that he would rather make his living by skinning carcasses than by dealing with creatures of their kind. All I know is that now he lives in N —— where he maintains a school for Jewish children.*

After a difficult walk through the rain, and a lot of groping about in the darkness, I found a door, and with God's help entered the house, very cautiously. It goes without saying that I entered politely by the side door, through the kitchen, as Jewish etiquette requires. Your Jew normally enters a house on tip-toe, hunched over meekly, not making a sound, only to materialize as if out of nowhere before the man of the house, like a hungry bear lying in ambush to seize his prey before he has a chance to run and hide. This Jewish custom commemorates the poverty and pauperism of the exile, going back to time immemorial. When the beggars among us got to be so numerous that more people had their hands out to take than to give, they had to learn to employ all the stratagems used by hunters in stalking their prey, especially the indirect, stealthy approach, which leaves the miserly householder no chance to get away. This way of entering is practised among us down to the present day as our ancestral legacy.

I stood very quietly in the hall for a while, straightening my caftan and sidelocks, taking off my hat and putting on my skullcap, as custom requires, while my eyes took in the room before me. People were sitting around a long table covered with a white cloth. An old man sat at the head, with three men on his left, and a matron with several young girls at the right. On a little side-table stood a boiling samovar giving off clouds of ash-gray steam, to which the light of the chandelier imparted a warm red glow as the steam rose toward the ceiling. Light and warmth and a snug, homey atmosphere pervaded the house, as people drank tea and chatted together in an affectionate, friendly way.

When I had collected myself in the hall, I entered and stood in the doorway, but without speaking.

"Who's there? Who is it?" the old man called, without moving from his place.

"Nothing special . . . a Jew is here . . . good evening!" I answered softly, still standing in my place.

---

*The author was director of the "Talmud Torah" school in Odessa between 1881 and the year of his death, 1917.

"What's he saying over there?" the old man asked in surprise, now getting up from his place and coming over to me.

"What's he saying? . . . Nothing at all . . . I said 'Good evening.'"

"'Good evening'—it certainly is a fine evening. But what does Reb Jew want, what can I do for him?"

"What do I want? I don't want anything. I just thought that once I was in town, I might as well pay respects to my old friend. How are you, Reb Shloyme? It's been years since we've seen each other—so long that we've both gotten old in the meantime. You've gotten gray, but even so you haven't changed much. I recognized you right away by that high forehead and nearsighted squint, those sparkling eyes and those lips whose smile is humorous and angry at the same time; by that same old fervor, and those gesticulations when you speak, just as when you were young. You're a child-man, with all due respect! And me? Don't you recognize me?" I concluded with an affectionate smile, drawing myself to my full height and grasping my beard.

"Wait a minute, just give me a minute," Shloyme said, regarding me closely. "Now I've got it: Reb Mendele . . . my dear old friend, Reb Mendele the bookpeddler! Welcome! Why did you tiptoe through a dark alley to the back of the house and stand like a beggar at the door?"

"Does a person have to make a fanfare with bells and cymbals, 'Hear ye! Hear ye! So-and-so is making a public appearance?!' In fact, pardon me for tracking mud into your house and dirtying the floor."

"Forget it. For us Jews, mud is a memorial to the time of the Exodus,"* Reb Shloyme answered. Then, taking my arm affectionately, he presented me to his family, and introduced the three guests. "These are Hebrew writers, my dear and faithful friends."

"Hebrew writers and faithful friends!" I marveled to myself. With a mental picture of cats tied up in a sack, biting, scratching, and tearing each other's fur, I twisted up my nose in disbelief.†

* The reference is to the clay that the Jews used for building during their Egyptian slavery.

†The author's home in Odessa was a center of literary and intellectual life. Among the friends who gathered at his table during the early 1890's were the historian Shimon Dubnow, the writers I. Ravnitski and Yakov Ben-Ami, and the theorist of Jewish nationalism, Ahad Ha'am (Asher Ginzberg). The author was also involved in a number of literary controversies (particularly with the writer I. Linetski) as this passage implies.

My host seated me at the table, and a glass of tea was placed in front of me. The conversation was no longer as spirited as it had been, and in a few minutes' time all fell silent, as people often do when a newcomer enters their circle. Behind this silence you can hear the muted growling of the evil-tempered dog that lurks in our hearts, a growl which implies suspicion, hatred, rivalry, and an unspoken hint: "'Fly, my beloved'—to the Devil, or to the four winds, but just leave me alone."

Only cows greet each other in true generosity and sincerity. When one cow stands at the trough and another comes along and sticks in her head, the first doesn't try to stop her; the two eat at the same time, contentedly filling their bellies together. It isn't at all surprising that cows behave in this way: the cow's an animal, after all, a crude and lowly creature with no judgment or intelligence. Humans are different: they encounter each other in the typically human way, displaying the shrewdness and cunning that was granted them at Creation. This silence is hard on the newcomer; it deprives him of control of his limbs, so that his hands and feet move about unconsciously and to no purpose, and everywhere his eyes encounter strange, inhospitable faces. The nose is full as a gutter, so confused it doesn't know where to turn; the heart is empty and oppressed; and the soul struggles and twitches, unhappy as a bird in a cage.

Reb Shloyme deserves credit for tactfully helping me out of my confusion. He reopened the conversation with the guests, and thus broke the ice, so that in a short time they were all talking at once. Everyone knows that authors are naturally gossipy and more talkative than women; the minute they open their mouths they overflow like a river, pouring out nine-tenths of all the words in the world. I too opened my mouth to show that I could talk endlessly with the best of them. They liked me for that, and we became friends instantly, as Jews will.

"Let's go back to what we were speaking about before," said Reb Shloyme, trying to get them back on the track. "We can bare our souls to Reb Mendele; no one understands this problem better than he. In fact, let's put it to him and hear his opinion too."

"What was the conversation about? What was your argument?" I asked calmly.

"What are writers always quarreling about?—books and other writers," Reb Shloyme answered. "Instruct us, Reb Mendele, our teacher: what is writing, and what is its purpose? That's the gist of what we were arguing about before."

"What did these sages have to say about it?" I deferred to the company.

"It is a divine spirit in man," was the authoritative opinion of one of the group, and another concurred.

"I dissent," said the third. "Writing is an acquired skill; anyone with normal human intelligence can write if he learns how."

"Writing," I contributed when my turn came around, in the hope of giving them all a laugh, "writing is lunacy, a kind of weakness and folly of the ego, like the compulsion of some people to step to the pulpit and treat the congregation to a sample of their gargling."

"Reb Mendele is being cynical," said Reb Shloyme, striking his nose with his forefinger as if to intimidate me, his eyes twinkling. "Now I myself don't want to get involved in the first part of the question that my colleagues are debating, namely, what is writing. But I would like to say what I think about the second part: what is its purpose? Man's intellect is the source of all his thoughts, but these thoughts do not become intelligible and mature except through the agency of speech, which fleshes them out and gives them their proper form. Accordingly, the whole superiority of man lies in his speech. Now, because speech, like an artist, gives corporeal form to the thoughts of the mind, it requires special equipment to assure that the product will be flawless and of high quality. Writing, which is nothing more or less than written speech, is this special equipment. One who writes minds his language well, selecting the words that suit his intention and arranging them carefully, threading and combining them methodically with the intention of bringing about a harmonious union of form and content, like the union of body and soul in all substances, with no element lacking and none superfluous. It follows that through written speech, oral speech achieves perfection, thought is clarified, and the cause of reason is served."

"That has no bearing on us," one of the group criticized. "Have a look at our contemporary literature and you will find nothing but empty words: sententious moralizing, advice and casuistry, opinion stated as fact, fairy-tales and overstatements, extravagant praise and exaggerated criticism, exactly like the talk that goes on in the council of idlers behind the stove in the study house, showing small-mindedness and intellectual sterility. Not only is it barren, not only does it beget no viable thought or original idea, but it isn't even conscious of its own disability; hence even the most miserable scribbler puts on airs, makes himself out to be one of the seven wise counselors, and never stops using pretentious phrases in the first person, like, 'In my considered opinion,' 'It is my feeling that,' 'I would counsel. . . .' They are the elite: the people's conscience, resource-men, counselors, strategists, and legislators. Each one would like nothing better than a Mount Sinai of his very own, where he might teach his people laws and ordinances, where he might hand down ten thousand commandments whose first and last words are 'I.'"

"Eh, Eh, Eh!" I protested, forcefully rejecting the critic's speech. Deep down I knew that he was right, but even so I stubbornly—and vainly—strove to uphold the honor of our insulted intellectuals, long may they live.

"Our writers themselves make no specific contribution to any science or to any of the problems of the day," another criticized. "They merely comment, from the outside, on this or that subject, their whole purpose being to lecture and harangue others, to demonstrate how worthwhile it would be to have this, that, or the other subject treated. But when it comes to the particular problem they are dealing with, they never take into consideration what earlier writers have said, so as to make their own treatment of the subject cohesive from the ground up. Each writer is the Adam of his age, inventing the alphabet all over again. Our people have no memory of past experience, and even events of our own times disappear into oblivion like a dream. Many things have happened in our lifetime that have not been recorded in any book only because of the foolish belief held by many people that nobody but the historians of the next generation can properly ascertain the true facts and form a correct and balanced picture. But by that time, many of the events of our age will have been forgotten. When a historian finally does arise among us and sets out to rebuild the house of Israel out of the shivered stones of memory, he will end up with more chinks than walls, his building will be no more solid than a spider's web—unless we honestly believe that Jewish historians are prophets, granted visions of past events in dreams or in their imagination, able to create whatever they want, *ex nihilo:* only give them the eye of a needle, they will fashion the elephant to pass through it. . . . The future scholar of merely ordinary human capacities, however, who will have to labor long and hard to write the chronicle of our times, will hold this generation's writers responsible. He will blame them for not having drawn the inspiration for their books from the lives of our people and for neglecting to transmit to the next generation enough material to work with, filling their essays and stories instead with banalities and pure figments of the imagination. And the writers who will bear the fullest share of the responsibility," he added, fixing his glance and pointing at Reb Shloyme, "will be those who know our people well, who are conversant with their way of life, whether high or low, and are too lazy to set it all down in detail."

"Gentlemen, you're frightening Reb Mendele with your vehemence!" said Reb Shloyme with a smile, when he saw me getting agitated and grimacing in astonishment. "There's nothing to worry about, Reb Mendele, no one means anyone any harm. When authors hold forth, they become enveloped in a blazing fire, not, God forbid, a consuming, destructive one, but the fire of their blood and spirit; for every word of a scholar, even his small talk, is like a glowing coal. I know you well enough, my friends, to be certain that your hearts are not as severe as your words, and that you didn't mean what you said to apply to all the writers—God forbid!—but only to certain ones. I even know why you are more severe than usual today: at this very moment while we sit here talking, a storm rages outside, which explains why your spirits have become stormy too. I feel it as much as you do; the thunder and lighting are making me jittery. It is not an auspicious time, my friends. I am also aware that our friend here means to include me among those who he says will someday be held accountable for neglecting to make a record of conditions in our times. The justification for my negligence is something like what happened, according to the traditional legend, to the coffin of Muhammad, which is suspended in the air between two magnets, and which therefore. . . ."

Reb Shloyme was interrupted by a cold draft that suddenly blew into the room from outside, almost extinguishing the candles, and a commotion of raised voices among the women of the house coming

from the corridor. Immediately after the tea was finished, Reb
Shloyme's wife and daughters, feeling that they were superfluous in
the company of men who had serious things to discuss, had gotten
up and left the room. There can be no doubt that wives of scholars
have a portion in the world to come, for they certainly get no
pleasure from their husbands in this one. Scholars differ from
uncultured people in a number of ways: the average man spends a
lot of time talking with his wife, even more with the wives of others;
but a scholar doesn't talk even with his own wife. When the ordinary
person goes out walking with his wife, he paces slowly at her side
and follows her in and out of doors; a scholar strides ahead of his
wife and goes in and out of doors ahead of her. The uncultured man
hands his wife her coat and waits on her, while a scholar's wife
dresses and waits on him. When the average man invites the boys
over for a game of cards, his wife joins them and they play all night
long; when a scholar's colleagues pay a call, his wife pours the tea
and waits on them, and as soon as she has finished her work she
leaves. That was what had happened with Reb Shloyme's wife and
daughters. We were so involved in discussing our affairs that we
didn't know whether they were still there or had gone, until their
voices, the furious draft, and the sound of slamming doors in the
hall startled us as if from a deep sleep. After a moment, one of the
daughters came in and whispered to her father, "Father, some boy
is here . . . he wants to stay overnight in the school."

"What, some boy off the street, and he wants to stay overnight!"
Reb Shloyme shouted in surprise and anger. "It can't be as simple as
that, there's something going on here. So much cheating and theft
in the city because of the rackets. . . . Let him in!"

A poor, downcast-looking boy of about seventeen appeared
shyly at the door. His torn and patched caftan was soaked through
with rain, and he stood trembling and staring at the ground.

"Where are you coming from, boy, and what do you want here
in the middle of the night?" Reb Shloyme asked angrily.

"A place to stay the night," the boy stuttered. "I'm a stranger
here."

"Is my school some kind of hotel?" Reb Shloyme asked sarcastically. "Where did you get such an idea? I know those tricks—on
your way!"

The boy left just as he had entered, silently, submissively, not saying a word, just looking at us with his eyes—dear God! How much hurt and suffering, sorrow and pain and supplication were revealed in that look! . . .

Reb Shloyme sat silent and depressed after the wretched boy left, with an absent look on his face. His expression was so changed that I hardly recognized him; before me sat a depressed and broken old man, his face creased and wrinkled with age. The rest of us too became dispirited, and began belching, yawning, and sneezing in turn, and no one spoke a word. Outside, the storm was getting worse, rattling the windows and blowing in the cracks, using the chimney for a *shofar*, and trying to sneak into the house. We got up cheerlessly, and left for home on our separate ways.

Next evening we all met again at Reb Shloyme's house, and were told that he had a headache and hadn't been out all day; but his wife went in to tell him that we had come, and he invited us into his room right away. The room wasn't very large, but it was cozy and neat, and to judge by the walls, furniture, and book cases, clearly the regular habitat of a scholar. Reb Shloyme was sitting at his desk deep in thought, with his eyes closed; in front of him was a piece of paper covered with writing, much of it scratched out, and a pen still moist with ink. At first he didn't notice us, but then he came to and gave us a warm welcome.

A Jew is obliged by his religion to visit the sick, and we did our duty on that occasion in the customary manner. The Jewish custom is to make fun of the patient in a gentle way and to belittle his illness, to hint that it's all in the patient's mind, and thereby to lessen his worry and pain. It is usual to scold him, and for this, everyone has his own technique. One person may say, "Such a clever Jew, a grown man with wife and children, how could you go in for such stupidity, to lie down in bed and be sick—ridiculous!" Another says, "Talk yourself out of your pain, take your mind off your sickness—it doesn't become you. Think of your teen-age girls, get well so you can soon dance, God willing, at their weddings." Yet another may call upon his own bowels to testify: his constipation and hemorrhoids gave him excruciating pain, but it turned out to be nothing, and he's alive and well, thank God!

While the others were going on in this way, showing off their expertise and worldliness by naming and swearing by all kinds of weird remedies, I made my smile do service for speech and sighed, "Eh, Reb Shloyme," just to do my duty by Jewish custom. At times like that, and whenever condolences or good wishes are called for, I am altogether inept, as is well-known.

Reb Shloyme got up and from a box took out a little bundle, which he unwrapped and placed before us: "Look at what's inside, gentlemen."

"Just buttons," we all said. "Buttons made of white bone. What about them?"

"These are the buttons of the one caftan I had to cover myself with when I wandered from my home in Lithuania as a boy, about forty years ago," Reb Shloyme said, shaking his head.

"But what do the buttons have to do with your indisposition? What made you think of them now?" we wondered.

"They have everything to do with each other, they're very closely connected. I wish I hadn't forgotten about them yesterday," Reb Shloyme sighed bitterly. He sat down on his chair again, and, closing his eyes, fell silent, sunk deeply into his thoughts. Then he fixed his gaze on us and launched into the following speech:

"I confess to you, gentlemen, that because of my inordinately bilious temper I committed a grave sin yesterday. A poor and lonely boy, far from home, came last night and asked if he could spend the night in my school. He was naked and hungry, and it was dark and stormy outside, with a cutting rain. I threw him out. No, gentlemen, he did not come with intention to defraud; he really was a stranger and a wanderer, and not only that, but a Lithuanian yeshiva-boy. I realized everything as soon as he left, when I thought about the serious way he stood and the way he was dressed and the very nature of his request. No one from around here would ever come with such a request. It would only occur to a wanderer from some corner of Lithuania, where the synagogue and the study-house and the yeshiva serve as hostels for poor boys. I myself made use of them more than once for this purpose when I was a boy. Last night I couldn't close my eyes because of the torments of hell I suffered and because of the terrifying, awful visions I was shown. This wretched boy's image and my own image when I was still a boy, dressed just like him, hovered before me all night and racked my spirit with terrible torments. In fear and trembling that poor boy stood before me. He didn't say a word, only his eyes told his heart's sorrow, and his face pleaded: 'Take pity on a suffering and hungry soul, protect the homeless and the naked, let me stay overnight in some corner!' He stood there with a broken heart, waiting for help—but instead of help he got a scolding: 'Out of here! Get out!' He left in silent humiliation, bowed over as if anticipating a beating.

"This apparition vanished, and another appeared in my own image, reminding me: 'Recall, Reb Shloyme! Thus you too came, like a migrant bird, to some little village, in a ragged caftan with white bone-buttons, begging for a place in the study-house to rest your head. And now that you're a somebody, are you so arrogant as to have forgotten all this? Now that you have come—thanks to God's help—into comfortable circumstances, have you become too proud to remember the feelings of the humble stranger, which were your own feelings not so very long ago? If for some reason you weren't able to take him in yourself, at least you might have opened your hand, and given him the price of a hotel room. And at the very least, if you couldn't give from your pocket, you shouldn't have refused a charitable word of encouragement; but as if it weren't enough to send him away empty-handed, you even scolded him on his way out the door.' My brothers, may you never suffer torments like the ones my sins have brought upon me yesterday and today."

"Nevertheless, you oughtn't take it so seriously," I consoled Reb Shloyme, "Things like this happen every day among us, and no one thinks about them twice. What about those big businessmen, famous bankers, gentlemen of substance, who exploit their servants unmercifully—who are they? By and large, they're servants who have risen from their humble station and who now put on airs. As boys, they worked in shops and inns and hostels, and heard their masters curse them and the mother that bore them a hundred times a day. That's been the way of the world since the day of creation: everyone forgets. Whoever has the whip in hand uses it, and never stops to think that his own back was beaten just yesterday, and with the same weapon. A fat belly and a fat wallet protect you from memory, your own and others'; for money, people are ready to overlook anything."

"Your so-called condolences don't help me very much," replied Reb Shloyme. "The fact that evil is widespread doesn't make it the less evil. To whitewash a sin by saying that it's a common human failing is like saying, for example, that the inability to hear or speak or see properly is not a defect, because there are so many deaf, dumb, and blind people in the world. It would necessarily follow from that reasoning that the instinct for good and the instinct for evil are chimeras with no basis in reality. No, Reb Mendele, no glib consolations, please. I know my sin, I can feel in my heart that I've done wrong."

"This incident is God's punishment for neglecting to write your autobiography as a permanent record," said one of the group. "You've never listened, no matter how many times we've urged you."

"This boy has come like a messenger from God to prod you into thinking of the past," said another, coming to the support of the first speaker. "Now you have been awakened and, like it or not, you've brought to mind those old buttons of long ago. You need only recall the rest of our peoples' customs in past ages, lest they sink into oblivion."

"How did you know what has been on my mind?" Reb Shloyme said, his face blazing. "As I was tossing and turning last night, terrified by nightmares, when the house was quiet and the storm was raging outside, I had a moment of inspiration—and realized in a flash that the incident with the boy was a sign from on high, commanding me to write. There are events in a man's life that can compel even a diehard rationalist to believe in the existence of a mysterious force by which all events come to pass at a time and under circumstances that have been stipulated in advance. The path preordained for me seems to be a stormy one. My life is a turbulent ocean, my days and years are raging waves, and my soul is the storm-battered ship; even my first conscious realization of my self began with a storm.—It was springtime. Suddenly it got dark, and in the garden path, amid the fresh foliage, a young boy ran barefoot and half-naked, with nothing but a linen shirt on his body and a cap on his head. Now he hurried and now he stood still. His eyes took in everything, and his ears were cocked like a rabbit's. That boy was myself. That was the day when my eyes were opened and I was revealed to myself as I really am.

"I was alone there; no living creature was with me, only the sky above and the earth below, and a fence on either side. All of a sudden there was thunder, a crashing sound from the sky, a noise rolling to the ends of the earth and exploding into many mighty sounds, while fiery serpents and angels of fire flitted about in the sky. I imagined this to be the thundering of God's chariot, the Lord of Hosts who rides the clouds, who cracks the whip and splits the tongues of fire. Dust and straw and chaff flew up from the ground, whirling around in the face of the storm like a wheel. Soon the rain poured down, a warm and pleasant rain, a reviving rain. Big drops drummed down on the garden plants; the radishes and onions and garlics bent their heads like little children in their mothers' laps, and enjoyed a delightful bath. Outdoors, streams of water poured from a hundred different directions and flowed together, onward and onward, with a cheerful rushing sound. And then, lo! The wheel of His chariot appeared, the Chariot of God, a great and terrible wheel in the celestial heights, only half of it visible; it looked like a bow in the midst of the clouds, a beautiful splash of color. There was a gleam of light in the west as the sun came out from behind a canopy of clouds like a bridegroom, looking toward the earth and making it smile, winking at the clouds to cause them to blush. . . .

"That was the moment I first came to know myself, God, and His world. All these things were revealed to me in thunder and lightning, and human intelligence came to me in the storm. That great vision is engraved on my heart and I can never forget it. In my heart—the heart of a naive child—I comprehended the vision before me, and I understood the language of nature round about. I knew the speech of the plants and the garden vegetables, the song of the running waters, and the frog's croak, as he lay up to his neck in the fetid marsh, staring upward with great eyes—all this I understood well and answered in the same voice, croaking with joy.'When I came to the yard of my house the calf came out of the barn and stretched his limbs, dropped his head while raising his tail, and lowed; the hen too came out of the corner with her chicks and pecked about in the dung, clucking all the while, and with them was the rooster strutting proudly about, crowing; I also saw the cat coming down the roof, slinking along the wall and springing with a meow—I knew what they were saying and what they all wanted and I answered each in his own language, lowing and meowing and clucking aloud. What I couldn't understand was the slap my father gave me on the cheek; nor could I figure out why my mother should shout at me when she saw me coming in the door all soaked from the rain. What they wanted then, and what my teachers and other grown-ups wanted afterwards, was hard to understand. . . ."

Reb Shloyme rested his head on the arm of the chair and was silent for a little while. From the contorted expression on his face and the twitching of his eyelids it was clear that he was upset, and we knew why. The path of his life had been full of thorns and trip-stones, a bitter struggle to the tops of cliffs and a plunge to deep abysses. Now that the bundle of his old troubles had been opened, and a finger was poking at wounds that had never quite healed, he could not help but feel great pain. When he had regained his control, he continued:

"I want to finish what I was saying yesterday when I was interrupted. For some time now my pen has been trapped motionless between two contradictory opinions, like Muhammad's coffin which is said to be suspended between two magnets. While the one strives to attract it toward the past, the other tries to attract it toward what is happening now in our own time. These two forces are bickering within me like two shopkeepers that jump on the same customer and deprecate each other's merchandise. One says: 'God save us from the new merchandise and the baubles that are now fashionable among Jews! Nothing that you see here is genuine. It's all a fraud: silver-plated clay, an empty shell; mascara, rouge, and jewels on the outside, filth, dirt, and muck on the inside. Nothing is authentic, nothing has any character of its own; everything is crude, like those dolls that seem to open their lips, beat a drum, blow a horn, sound a cymbal, and squeak, but only thanks to the key that wound up their spring. Forget them: here you have fine antiques, every one the work of our ancestors, and each with its own authentic value. . . .' The other one shouts: 'Come to me! Look at my merchandise—what do you want with outmoded things from an age that is dead and gone? Do you think you're some kind of medium who can raise the dead? That's exactly why we are in so much trouble now: Jews are oblivious to the present; they attend only to the past. They can't see where they're going because they face backward, so they stumble and fall. Whatever they do, at home, in their synagogues, in their writing, they are as though dead, dead while alive, and expecting to live after death. A living Jew is worth nothing, but when he dies he gets a fine reputation, and a fine tombstone. The dead are all pure and righteous, munificent and sage; a mere radish or onion turns into a cedar of Lebanon and a sardine becomes a whale as soon as he reaches the cemetery. But after all, imperfect though the present is, much as it needs improvement, it is still real life, the core of our existence; any man who eats and drinks and has the same needs as his fellow creatures, is responsible for their improvement and development, and this means work-ing with and for all the people of his time.'

"Wait a moment," said Reb Shloyme, seeing that we were trying to interrupt him. "I know, you want to argue as follows: 'Neither of these opinions alone is satisfactory, because they are polar opposites. Every contemplated course of action presents logi-cally opposite possibilities, but a sensible, well-rounded person tries to reach a middle ground on which he may realize the benefits of both.' But the ability to do this is found only in a man of unusual wisdom or in his opposite, in a simpleton who will try his hand at anything and, like a day-laborer, accept whatever work comes his way in the marketplace. What does he care whether he works in bricks and straw or rummages about in the garbage? Moth-eaten clothes and worm-eaten books and a box of dung and a cow's stall are all the same to him as long as he has work and gets paid for it. But I am somewhere between the extremes: I'm the type that doesn't jump on whatever work is offered, but the work he does accept becomes a life-long trade. Besides—I admit it—I'm naturally lazy. I'm much more inclined to stop and think than to get up and do; and as soon as anything at all comes in the way of my work, I put it aside gladly. Therefore, whenever my mind is divided between two opinions that are both grabbing at my pen, each one claiming exclusive right of ownership, I decide the case according to the legal principle: 'Let judgment be reserved until Elijah comes.'

"But now he . . . this boy has come in the storm and returned me to the past. My mind is now completely in the world of my youth. I have returned to it an old, bitter man, worn by hard experience, my heart wounded by the arrows of life's battles. Imagi-nation, like the witch of Endor, has conjured up pictures and images and faces and many odd and old things from days gone by. They arise and glare angrily at me, knowing full well my motive for returning to them and what they are wanted for: they know that I am coming to set them up on display for the public to gawk at. My world, alas, is very small. The pomegranate doesn't blossom there, nor does the rose bloom; you don't hear great shouts of joy there, nor do you navigate rivers of milk and honey. The people are simple Jews with beards and sidelocks and long caftans, emaciated, withered, and poor, stooped, sickly, and downtrodden, timorous and fearful, and altogether unenlightened. I hate to disturb those dry bones, gentlemen, to trouble those shades now sleeping in the dust, to ask them to step to the front of the stage when I can't even guarantee they will be received with applause. Many of our people today are self-conscious about their noses, which stand forth and announce: 'These are the seed of Jacob!' If it were in their power, they would happily exchange them for different ones. Now, out of the clear blue sky, the literary wind will deliver up some old-fashioned Jews, authentic to the last detail, with 613 antiquated features that have lost all meaning, as though purposely to expose them to public ridicule.

"No, friends, it's no light-hearted matter; I'm telling you exactly what was bothering me earlier, the problems that had me brooding when you came in. And even if I wanted to, what could I possibly say about our life in those days? None of us ever did anything to set the world on fire. Dukes, governors, generals, and soldiers we were not; we had no romantic attachments with lovely princesses; we didn't fight duels, nor did we even serve as witnesses, watching other men spill their blood; we didn't dance the quadrille at balls; we didn't hunt wild animals in the fields and forests; we didn't make voyages of discovery to the ends of the earth; we carried on with no actresses or prima donnas; we didn't celebrate in a lavish way. In short, we were completely lacking in all those colorful details that grace a story and whet the reader's appetite. In place of these we had the *cheder*, the *cheder*-teacher, and the *cheder*-teacher's assistant; marriage brokers, grooms, and brides; housewives and children; abandoned women, widows with orphans and widows without orphans;* people ruined by fire and bankruptcy, and paupers of every description; beggars who make the rounds on the eve of Sabbath and holidays, new-moons, Mondays and Thursdays and any day at all; idlers and officers of the community; poverty, penury, and indigence, and queer and degrading ways of making a living. This was our life, if you call it a life—ugly, devoid of pleasure and satisfaction, with not a single ray of light to pierce the continual darkness; a life like tasteless food cooked without benefit of salt or pepper."

"You're wrong," we objected. "It may be true that Jewish life lacks spice, as you said, but it has its own unique flavor. There is a certain kind of cheese with worms in it, that gourmets are always

---

*The childless widow sometimes constituted a special problem. She was obliged to marry her dead husband's surviving unmarried brother, unless a special ceremony of *khalitsah*, or refusal, was performed. Like abandoned wives, such widows were unable to marry if the brother, by reason of absence or stubbornness, refused to refuse.

looking for though it costs a fortune. The bitterness in our life that you speak of is its most important ingredient; it appeals to the connoisseur far more than mere sweetness, which can sometimes be nauseating. Only children really have an appetite for honey-cakes. Even though the life of the Jewish people seems repulsive from the outside, it is pleasant enough within. There is a mighty spirit, a divine spirit, blowing through it constantly, like a storm wind, purifying it of dirt and rot. The thunder and lightning that occasionally overtake the Jews purge them and renew their vigor. Israel is a Diogenes among the nations, its head in the heavens, absorbed in esoteric contemplation of the almighty God, while its corporeal self inhabits a barrel only two feet in diameter. Under a pile of dirt in the *cheder* and in the yeshiva and study-house the fire of Torah blazes, radiating light and warmth to our people; all our children, of whatever age, study, and know their way around books. . . . It is altogether fitting and proper that such a life be set down in a permanent record."

"What you say," Reb Shloyme answered, "may be true of the life of the people as a whole, but what's so special about my life? What has ever happened to me, that makes my life deserve the distinction of being recorded? What has happened to me has happened to thousands of our people; it's a familiar story. Is there any other people in the world among whom the life of every individual, from the moment he comes into the world until his last breath, goes on and on according to a single pattern as it does among us? The way they are reared and educated, the words of their prayers, the tunes of their hymns and liturgical poems are all identical; even their food and drink are the same. Who has ever heard of a people who at a given hour, say, Friday night, all over the globe are all eating fish, noodle pudding, and vegetable stew; and on Saturday morning, radishes, jellied cow's foot, liver with onions and eggs, and dried out *kasha* with a marrow bone in it; on a certain day, *kreplakh*, on another day *hamantashen*, on another day twisted yellow *khala* with saffron.* At the very moment when someone in Berdichev is

---

*Cheese-stuffed *kreplakh*, or dumplings, were eaten on Shavuot, the Feast of Weeks. *Hamantashen* are three-cornered pastries, filled with poppy seed or plum preserves, named for Haman, the villainous counsellor of the story of Esther. They were eaten on Purim, which commemorates the defeat of Haman in his attempt to destroy Persian Jewry. The special twisted saffron *khala* was baked for the New Year, Rosh Hashana.

The author assumes these customs to be "universal" in the Jewish world. In fact, although Jews do eat special foods on each of the holidays, there is considerable regional variation in food customs.

singing "He who sanctifies" on the Sabbath Eve, or shouting "He lives forever" on Rosh Hashana, the same tune and the same voice reverberate in Argentina at the other end of the world. We are an ant-hill, in which the individual has no existence apart from the community. In books on natural history, scientists devote a separate chapter to the genus of ants as a whole, but not to the individual ant."

"What you're saying is only superficially correct," the group replied. "The life of the Jews seems to have a single pattern like that of ants, but in fact there is a great variation among them. Each ant is required by its nature to do its job like the rest of the members of its species, and it cannot deviate a hair's breadth from the group. This is not true of human beings. A single characteristic shared by every member of the race turns up in individuals in seventy different varieties; though every man displays the same quality, each does so in his own peculiar way, which is not identical with that of his neighbor. Every man has his own individual character which finds expression in his speech, his smile, his wink, his gait, and his manner of eating and drinking, though God has granted the entire human race the ability to do all these things. A man's writing style is even more individual: no two prophets speak alike, and no two writers have the same style. Your defenses and excuses are futile, Reb Shloyme. It is your duty to write your autobiography."

"It is my duty only to myself, not to the public," Reb Shloyme said, trying to rescue his position. "I now concede only that I ought to write my memoirs for myself, and put them in the box together with these buttons so that both can serve, like the fringes of the prayer shawl, to remind me of the past and so keep me from sin."

"No, Reb Shloyme," we cried together. "You can't get away with just writing your memoirs—you have to print them as well!"

"When you begin a reckoning, you have to finish it," conceded Reb Shloyme, with a soft smile on his lips. "Once you mention printing, why don't you add up the other thirty-nine labors of a Jewish writer: to write; to collect subscriptions and letters of recommendation;* to print and proofread; to train and teach the typesetter; to compile a huge table of errata, with as many entries as there are words in the book; to go peddling from house to house,

---

*The letters of recommendation, or *haskomes*, were generally printed as introductions to the book.

humbling oneself to every dolt; to think up arguments against the stingy and tight-fisted; to beg and bow and scrape in fear and trembling for a penny, for the sake of God and the Torah and the union of the Holy Tongue and the People Israel; to give away innumerable volumes to 'friends' and book dealers on credit; and after all these tribulations, to sell the leftover copies like old rags at forty pounds for a penny. No, my friends, I'm no good at that work."

"Have you forgotten that the world has a Mendele the bookpeddler and that God didn't create him to go idle?" I announced, speaking as an authority, with pride. "Furthermore, with all due respect, you haven't finished the list of labors. You've forgotten the exchange, that is, the transmigration that Jewish books undergo. I exchange one author's book for a copy of *Devotions of Sarah Bas Tovim*, which gets exchanged for *Tisha b'Av Lamentations*, which gets exchanged for a brass candlestick, which gets exchanged for a *shofar*, which gets exchanged for a High Holiday prayerbook, which gets exchanged for a wolf's tooth, which gets exchanged for a *Kol Bo*, which gets exchanged for a ritual garment, and so it goes from one form to another, getting more and more tattered, mildewed, and worn, until it turns into rags.* Then there are other works that lie there like a stone because of the authors' sins (God save us from their fate) and the best one could do with them would be to turn them into cuspidors, except that it's forbidden to spit on Hebrew writing. Go to it, Reb Shloyme! Write, and I undertake to do whatever has to be done when the writing's finished. The whole thing is clearly ordained by heaven, because you notice that I too have come to you in a storm."

Reb Shloyme said nothing, but gave me his hand as if promising: "Your wish is my command."

Reb Shloyme was good enough to fulfill his promise, and the next year he honored me with a manuscript of his writings. And now I

---

*The *Devotions of Sarah Bas Tovim* are a collection of *tkhines*, or Yiddish prayers, which were very popular among Jewish women. The *Lamentations* are recited on the ninth day of the Hebrew month of Av, Tisha b'Av, the mid-summer fast day commemorating the destruction of the first temple at the hands of the Babylonians in the sixth century B.C.E., and of the second temple at the hands of the Romans, in 70 C.E. *Kol Bo*, literally, "everything is within," a complete compilation of customs and laws. The ritual garment here referred to is the *talis kotn*, the fringed undergarment worn by observant Jewish males. Mendele is giving a list of the stock-in-trade of the typical bookpeddler.

bring them before the public, in consecutive chapters, in the order in which he wrote them.

CHAPTER 1

Not far from the town of Kapulie* there is a little village surrounded by woods. Through these woods flows a beautiful river, and by that river stands a mill, which has given the village its name of Mlinitse.† On one bank of the river three tiny, low peasants' huts peek out from among the shrubbery and trees, while across from them on the opposite bank by the woods, there stands a solitary house, with wooden boards for walls, little windows and an ancient sloping roof. There, together with his wife and children, lives Chone the miller, in whose family the tenancy of the mill has been passed down for generations. Mlinitse is an isolated, hidden nest, far from civilization. No public highway passes through it, only narrow paths threading their way through the woods, up mountains and down valleys, to other settlements and villages of the district. Though visitors are few, and the place hasn't the hustle and bustle of cities and towns, the woods fairly hum with activity and there are crowds and swarms of living creatures in the ponds and fields. You can hear the chatter of animals: in summer, their whistling and cooing, cackling and croaking and chirping, and in winter, the barking and howling of hungry wolves, or even the faint, distant roar of a bear that has strayed in from the far north. And over this cacophony, you hear the constant roar of the river as its waters fall over the wheels of the mill with a thundering, grinding crash.

*In the Yiddish version the shtetl is represented by the letter K, signifying Kapulie, the author's native town in the Province of Minsk, Lithuania. In the Hebrew version, the town is called Dalfona, or Paupersville. The author probably withheld the actual name of his town, in the style of those years, to maintain a certain discretion and distance, which time and circumstance have now assured. Since the chronicle is so steeped in specificity, we have preferred the actual name, Kapulie, of the shtetl here described.

†Mlinitse, from the Slavic term *mlin*, for mill.

It was Passover, the festival of spring. The last day of Passover was a warm, pleasant holiday. As the sun came out it scattered the morning clouds and peered from the blue sky with a radiant face. All of God's creatures, great and small, were awakening from their long winter's sleep, and cheerfully setting about their duties. Fresh spring flowers shot their heads up among the tender shoots of grass and stole an affectionate look at the outside world. Willows hurriedly threw on a green cloak and leaned their heads forward to catch their reflection in the stormy river water. Flocks of birds that had migrated to warmer lands were returning from exile. Wild geese swam and flapped out of sight among the reeds, and wild ducks flew through the cane with noisy cries. Swallows soared among the trees, busily building new nests and repairing old ones. Welcome back! A pair of old friends, the storks, were also there, Madame Stork standing on one leg, craning her neck to get a look at her old nest in the treetop, and her handsome, long-legged companion strutting about in the pond and casting glances at a marsh where a crowd of frogs croaked in unison. Suddenly he thrust with his beak, then *peck! peck!*—devoured his prey. Awakening and revival were everywhere: creeping, leaping, running, singing, buzzing; it was spring, and the world was on holiday!

Chone's whole family was outdoors. Chone had come out after his holiday nap to sit on the bench outside the house; his caftan undone, he was relaxing and taking in God's world, yawning from time to time. His grown sons were standing nearby, looking earnest as they spoke about a bridge that had been washed away in the neighboring town; about the trip to town scheduled for the next day to stock up on necessities for the local nobleman and for themselves; about their venerable mare, now thirty years old, with filmy eyes, who was stretched out on the grass, rolling from side to side to stretch her aching bones; and about other important household affairs. The younger children were running about preoccupied. Some stood by the millhouse on the bridge staring at the water that looked like a single stream of glass as it flowed through the sluices, then fell violently with a great roar and exploded below into thousands of droplets sparkling like diamonds in the sunlight. Other children were setting out pots to catch the sap dripping from slashes in the trunks of the cedar trees. Everyone was on holiday, and everyone had his own way of enjoying it! Tsutsik the dog, with his fat belly, short legs, and dirty white coat covered with black spots, was happy too; he too was aware that it was a special day, for he had collected enough bones under the table to make a holiday meal of his own. He was wagging his tail in honor of the holiday and scampering madly about, barking good naturedly in a dog-like song of joy.

In a clearing behind the house, Chone's wife, a good-looking woman, sat on the log of a great fallen pine tree, together with her daughter, a girl of about twenty-five, while opposite them, reclining under the bushes, were two of her children, a fifteen-year-old beauty with blond curls, and a boy of twelve. But while everyone in front of the house was happy, genuinely caught up in the holiday mood, those sitting here were distraught and glum, like mourners reciting lamentations on Tisha b'Av. Both mother and daughter seemed to be deeply distressed, burdened with things to say to one another, but each waited for the other to begin.

"Leah," the mother blurted out, when the silence had become oppressive, "the holidays are nearly over, and then what?"

"Then we're back again with the same old troubles. One way or the other, mother—tomorrow I'll go home."

"And what harm would be done if you stayed another two or three days?" the mother begged.

"I can't, mother, I can't!" the girl answered, brushing off the suggestion with a gesture.

"She can't!" the mother said, with tears in her eyes. "She can't stand being here with her mother!"

"But you see that I did come to you, mother!"

"You did, and I'm grateful, but . . . a mother's heart knows when her daughter is unhappy. All during your stay you were sitting on pins and needles; not a word, but your eyes spoke for you: every glance, a stab of rebuke, every look, a dagger to my heart. Woe, woe is me!"

"Mother!"

"Woe! What else was I to do? Things were so bad when your father died that there was nothing left for me but to die of starvation. And then what would have become of these children?"

"And now what will become of them?" Leah said, sighing deeply.

"Now? Edel is old enough to marry, and Dovidl. . . ."

"Dovidl is a bone in the throat, a burden to everyone here. Edel old enough to marry—what an awful thing to have to hear! . . . Edel, precious, what's wrong?" Leah said abruptly to her little sister, whose face suddenly twisted and paled. "Is it that pain in the chest again?"

"It's nothing, Leah, it came and went, just a stitch."

"Go, child," the mother said, pityingly. "Go lie down in the house. And you, Dovidl, go and cover her with my shawl."

The children got up unwillingly and went.

"Look what's happened to them!" Leah said with a sigh, shaking her head. "Edel old enough to marry—old enough for misery unending: a wretched bride she'll be. A tender and delicate rose that bloomed and withered!"

"Leah, I can't stand it any more! My heart is full of wounds and you're pouring salt on them. What did I do wrong? What could I have done? Be kind, be kind to me, Leah!"

"Enough, mother! Let's go find Shloyme. Where has he gone to? Where does he hide all the time?"

"You think I know? When he first came here, at the beginning of winter, he kept an exact schedule every day: first thing in the morning he would study Talmud by himself, then later on he would teach the other children; how proud I was, watching him. Now all of a sudden he's a different person. No more Talmud. He sits by himself all day, and all he does is write. Do you think I have any idea what he's writing all the time? Since the weather got warm and the grass began to grow he's taken to going off alone in the woods. You know what? There's only one solution—to marry him off. But I don't think he'll have any luck in that department."

"How do you know, mother?"

"It's painful even to talk about. The broker suggested three prospects, one after the other. When I went to look them over, what did I find? One was blind in one eye, one had a flattened nose, and the third had a limp. That seems to be his fate . . . but if we don't marry him off, then what? He won't hear of going back to the yeshiva. I say to him: 'Go back, son!' and he says, 'Stop pestering me about your yeshiva and all the other "practical" careers for Jewish boys! I've had enough of that, eating charity meals at strangers' tables, groveling, wearing out my pants on yeshiva benches—why should I go back? There are enough rags in the Jewish world without me! . . .' Do you hear how he talks, a boy seventeen years old? Have you ever heard such talk? I'm talking to him about the yeshiva and he's talking to me about rags. . . . Look, Leah, here he comes, and he's alone. Please, Leah! You can talk to him, you're his sister after all."

A good-looking boy with a broad forehead and curly hair emerged from the woods. He was absorbed in reading as he walked, unaware of what was going on around him.

"Shloyme, why so preoccupied?" Leah said, blocking his path.

"Leah!" Shloyme exclaimed, throwing a glance at his sister, then returning to his book.

"Someone would think you're no longer among us, but up there among the heavenly spheres," Leah teased, covering the book with her hand. "Please, tell me what you've seen there."

"There, nothing is like here," Shloyme said, looking up at his sister's face. "Here everything is awful. . . ."

"The holiday's over! Tomorrow I'm leaving," Leah said, with tears in her eyes. "Let's say what there is to say now. Come, Shloyme!"

The mother went into the house, on the pretext of looking in on the children, while brother and sister walked and talked together. Their talk was not a happy one.

Meanwhile, dusk fell. Little by little, the buzzing and humming and other outdoor noises subsided. One after another the stars, those little candles in the sky, began to twinkle. Wood and field fell silent, and everything came to rest. A warm spring breeze caressed them all, rocking them to sleep with a mother's tenderness. The nightingale sang a lullaby, the frogs croaked their old bed-time stories, and God's creatures fell asleep. Even the river slept under a canopy of trees and reeds, wrapped in a blanket of mist and haze, its slumber disturbed only by one impudent fish that leapt twice in the air, giving the river a loud slap in the face.

But Chone's family was not asleep. They were all busy bidding the Passover farewell. Giving a proper send-off to this holiday, with all its pots and dishes and special equipment, is a melancholy task for a Jew. My, my, what a charming jar for keeping licorice-water; what a lovely decanter for raisin-wine; just look at the dishes of metal and china, the pitchers and the cups. This little glass, just an ordinary glass any other night, on Passover night is a sacred goblet, lovely and sparkling. If it could speak, it would remind the owner of his ancestors who used it before him, and it would bring greetings from grandfathers and grandmothers to their grandchildren. . . .

It's always hard for a Jew to make the transition from holiday to weekday, but leaving Passover behind is especially hard. When Passover is over, the freedom of the freed-man is also over, and he becomes a slave once again.

Early the next day, a wagon left Mlinitse, drawn by the old mare who had been stretching herself on the grass the day before. On top of the wagon sat Leah, ensconced on the baggage platform, with a big cushion under her; one of Chone's sons sat in the driver's seat with a whip in his hand, but only to keep up appearances and not, God forbid, to lift it disrespectfully against that venerable lady, nearly twice his age, who had served his grandfather, may he rest in peace. This old creature lumbered along sedately, with a peculiar stoop-and-hop gait all her own. Tsutsik, the dog, like a true comrade, never deserted her. Sometimes he would stand in her way and get entangled in her legs, then he would jump up and hang on to her neck and bark into her ears, and finally he would lift his tail, put on a burst of speed, run to a point far ahead and wait for her there, with his tongue hanging out from the exertion. After bounding along for a few hours the wagon entered the main street of Kapulie and drove straight into the marketplace.

CHAPTER 2

Among the ring of houses encircling the marketplace, the town's finest spot, there is one house identical in appearance to all the others except that it is white-washed on the outside. The lives and manners of the people of small towns are all the same, and even the construction of their houses scarcely varies from one to the next, any more than do the lives of animals and birds and the way they build their nests. It will suffice to describe here in detail one of the houses of Kapulie, as an example, so that future generations may know what kind of dwellings our ancestors inhabited, the houses in which they lived out their lives together with their children of all ages, as well as their married daughters and their families.

When you open the door you step directly from the marketplace into an ample living room, which is the apartment proper. In the wall facing the entrance you see a door which opens onto a dark hallway with no windows. This is the storage room for wood and other necessities; on occasion it also serves as a stable, when the winter is very cold, or when one of the animals is pregnant, and cannot safely pass the night in the street as usual. To the left of the back door of the living room, next to the wall, stands a large oven for cooking and baking. Beneath the oven is a chicken-coop, where the hens cluck and lay their eggs, where they sleep at night, and where they awaken early in the morning to prance about the house and jump up on the tables and benches and beds or wherever they like. Next to the oven is a long, high stove made of green tiles which warms the house in winter, flanked by two benches, known as the meat-bench and the dairy-bench.* The stove and oven, together with a wooden partition containing a double door, extend the whole length of the house, dividing it into two. One half is the spacious living room already mentioned, while the other half is subdivided into a number of cubicles which serve as bedrooms for the married members of the family and for guests. From the living room ceiling, opposite the oven, hangs a ceramic bell-shaped object with two rings attached at opposite points on its rim. From these rings, an iron pan hangs by a chain, and on the pan dry sticks are kindled to illuminate the house at night, except on the Sabbath eve, when tallow-candles are set in candlesticks on the table and in a six-branched brass candelabrum hanging from the ceiling.

The candelabrum is the household sun, giving light and warmth and pleasure to everyone. The family passes winter evenings around it, engaged in various tasks or just talking. The women of the house, and sometimes a neighbor or two, sit together on the meat or dairy bench plucking feathers and indulging in gossip of both the innocent and the not-so-innocent kind. On Saturday nights the table is moved close to this lamp and the entire family sit around eating boiled potatoes to their hearts' content and listening to someone read aloud from *The Greatness of Joseph* or *The Book of the righteous.*† On the nights of Chanukah the children play *dreydl*‡ at the table, while the grown-ups play cards

---

*Since dairy and meat products and the dishes in which these are prepared are always kept separate in Jewish homes which conform to the laws of *kashrut*, the two benches were also designated according to the foods that would be placed or prepared upon them.

†*The Greatness of Joseph:* a popular drama, one of the many versions of the Joseph story, this one in Yiddish, by Eliezer Paver, 1801. *The Book of the Righteous* was another immensely popular work, dating from about the second half of the twelfth century, Spain, and translated into Yiddish from the original Hebrew. The anonymous book retells the major Biblical legends, from the creation of the world till the Exodus, in a heroic-epic manner, interweaving post-Biblical legends with Biblical materials.

‡On Chanukah, the eight-day winter holiday commemorating the victory of the Maccabees over the Syrians in the second century B.C.E., games of chance are common; children play with a small lead spinning top, the *dreydl*.

and eat potato pancakes. And whenever the fatty skin of a goose is being fried, the household is up the whole night telling stories and eating cracklings.

Let it be known to posterity that our forebears didn't waste money on household furniture. Our grandfather's house contained the following furnishings: several long, flat wooden benches along the walls; a long red table with four legs, with a black and white checkerboard painted in the middle. A wooden cabinet with three sides fitted snugly in a corner, reaching to the ceiling, and through its glass doors peered silver goblets, *kiddush*-cups, a filigree spice-box for *havdala*, a Chanukah candelabrum, a box for the *etrog*,* a snail's shell (good for curing certain disorders); a tray with cups of white glass for preserves or candy; and a dozen small gold-plated spoons that had been given to our grandfather when he delivered his wedding sermon. High on the wall hung a mirror that was impossible to look into unless you stood on a bench; and after all that trouble, the reflection that you saw was an unusual one indeed—your face would be green and your jaws swollen as if you had toothache. The mirror was there only as a decoration, not for primping, God forbid; and yet, if you did take the trouble to climb up on the bench, the effort wasn't completely wasted, because then you could see the pictures which hung on either side of the mirror: one, the portrait of a Jew, evidently a once-famous scholar, in his prayershawl and phylacteries; the other an equestrian portrait, half eaten away by flies, of an army officer. There was also a *mizrakh*, an embroidered landscape to mark the east wall of the house, elaborately decorated with fabulous and exotic beasts.

May our posterity also note that our grandfather's house was suited for a variety of functions. Besides serving as a kitchen, a bedroom, and even a synagogue, on occasion it also served as a tavern. For the few local Gentiles there was whiskey and bagels; but on market days, when the people from the surrounding villages came to town, there were rare delicacies like boiled eggs and pickled herring. And on the Gentile New Year's Eve, the whole room was filled with young folks, boys and girls sitting together, cracking nuts, flirting, laughing, and chattering, pushing and shoving each other, and having a boisterous time, as is the custom, until finally someone

---

*The *kiddush*-cup is a special cup for the prayer over wine on Sabbath and holidays. Spices are used in the *havdala* service marking the conclusion of the Sabbath. The *etrog*, which resembles a lemon, is the special fruit associated with the Festival of Booths, Sukkot.

poured a jug of water over them and threw them out of the house, this too according to custom. And if our grandfather's house made a good theater, it goes without saying that it was also fit to serve as a military parade ground. There was no better place for teaching soldiers their drill on a winter's night—the house was warm and well-lit, and the eye had no trouble locating the cheek and guiding the hand to the spot where a slap was destined to fall.

Very similar in plan to the house just described was the white-washed one that stood among the ring of houses facing the market-place, and that belonged to Reb Chayim, one of Kapulie's most distinguished householders.

To be a substantial householder in Kapulie, a man had only to have a room and a cow and any source of income whatsoever; but no amount of wealth was in itself sufficient to make a man loved and respected. There was a time in Lithuania—it may not be so any longer—when the scholar was more respected than the rich man. An uncultured boor is an uncultured boor, no matter how much money he has, as the proverb says: you can't make a fur hat out of a pig's tail. It's true that a boor always speaks up first and lets everybody know his opinions, but that's only because of his innate arrogance. People have no choice but to hear him out in silence, but deep down inside they despise and resent him. The only way to win real respect in Lithuania is to be a scholar and a pious man: a man's wallet can't win him honor. This is true everywhere in Lithuania, but especially in Kapulie, which has always been a place of Torah, where every citizen studies. The study-house is full of scholars: hoary sages and child prodigies, yeshiva boys and recluses who have abandoned their wives and wandered here to study Torah, eat "days"* and live a life of suffering. Every afternoon, between the late afternoon and evening prayers, the town's artisans and poor gather around the tables in the study-house at each of which someone conducts a lesson on a holy book: the Bible, Midrash, *Fountain of Jacob*, or *The Heart's Duties*.† Every Sabbath and holiday afternoon a preacher stands at the pulpit by the Holy Ark wrapped in his

---

*Eating days refers to the custom whereby yeshiva boys were fed by various local families on designated days of the week. It was not uncommon for the students, especially in some of the poorer yeshiva-towns, to have less than a full complement of "days."

†Midrash: post-Biblical exegetic literature. *The Fountain of Jacob*, by Rabbi Jacob ben Shlomo Khaviv, is a collection of Talmudic legends and teachings. *The Heart's Duties* is an ethical treatise written by Rabbi Bakhya ben Joseph ibn Paquda in eleventh-century Spain.

prayer shawl and harangues the people, spicing his talk with proverbs and flowery Biblical phrases, verses of the prophets, and quotations from the ancient sages, kindling a love for the divine in the Jewish heart. It speaks very well for a man's character and learning if he manages to achieve general respect in such a town.

Reb Chayim was a man with these qualities. While still in his prime, at an age when most gentile men are only beginning to think about marriage, Reb Chayim had already become a grandfather, and Sarah, his wife, a grandmother. By a simple retroactive computation, from his seventh son to his firstborn, who was still eating at his father's table though he had a wife and children of his own, it may be deduced that Reb Chayim married when he was still a boy. As Sarah always used to enjoy telling it, she was only a little girl and her husband a little boy when they were rushed to the marriage-canopy in the period of the Panic (may we never live to know its like!). What was this Panic? When was it?—The answer is that for a Jew it hardly matters; there's no difference between one panic and another. Who could draw up a list of all the panics? Who could even remember them all? It could be that Sarah was talking about the panic that occurred when the government decreed that all Jewish children were to be subject to military service.* At that time the Jews cleverly hurried their little children to the marriage-canopy because they reasoned: "Since you're old enough for martial life, my boy, you must certainly be old enough for marital life."

Reb Chayim divided his time between making a living, studying Torah, and taking part in community affairs. For many years he farmed the meat tax† in his town and served as government

---

*The ukase of Tsar Nicholas I, issued on August 26, 1827, ordered Jewish youths from the ages of twelve to eighteen conscripted for military service. At eighteen they were to be assigned to the regular army for twenty-five years, the normal term of military service. The duty of enlisting these recruits was imposed on the *kahal*, the Jewish community council. There are horrifying accounts of the sufferings of these children, and of the degradation of the communities forced to select them. See Louis Greenberg, *The Jews in Russia* (New Haven, Yale University Press, 1944) I, 48–52; Simon Dubnow, *History of the Jews in Russia and Poland* (Philadelphia, Jewish Publication Society, 1918) II, 18ff.

†The meat tax, a heavy impost on kosher meat, was levied by government authorities but was collected by the Jewish communities themselves. The tax was usually farmed out to the highest bidder, with the obvious concomitant dangers of abuse. The meat-tax collectors were a permanent target of Haskalah criticism, but the author, probably because of his father's example, portrayed the main holder of the license as a man abused both by the demands of the job and by the unfair criticism of his fellow burghers.

rabbi* without receiving a salary. He would voluntarily tutor the young scholars in Talmud and Codes every day. People were continually in and out of his house. Nothing was done in the town without his say-so. He arbitrated every dispute. Whatever difficulty the community faced, he was consulted, and they benefited from his counsel. But why fill an ocean with words when a single example will suffice. . . .

CHAPTER 3

It was a Saturday night in winter, after *havdala*. The family was sitting around a table by the warm stove, beneath the light of the brazier that hung from the ceiling. One of the women from next door was there too, full as a drum with gossip. The women were plucking feathers and listening to the story of the pious Joseph and his brothers, which one of the boys was reading to them in Yiddish. They thrilled to the heroic deeds of Judah—this lion among the ancestors of the twelve tribes who made the whole land of Egypt tremble at his roar. The cat was curled up in a corner by the warm stove, licking his paw and perking his ears, evidently also enjoying himself. Supper was in the oven, and a pot of potatoes had been put up to boil for a pre-dinner snack. Reb Chayim was walking up and down the room, still in his Sabbath clothes, singing "Elijah the Prophet"+ with deep feeling. No sooner had he finished the words: "May he come to us soon," than the sound of footsteps was heard at the door: a group of distinguished citizens had come to wish "a good week."

"A good year," Reb Chayim replied.

The intelligent reader does not need to be told that distinguished citizens defer to each other upon entering, each one saying

---

*Government rabbis, or crown rabbis, acted as intermediaries between the central authority and the community, discharging such civil functions as the keeping of official records. They were distinguished from the ecclesiastical rabbis who remained in charge of purely religious matters.

+ The song, "Elijah the Prophet" is sung at the close of the Sabbath; Elijah is invoked as the herald of the Messiah and the messianic age.

to the other: "You first," and keeping the door open so long, even in winter, that the householders are fortunate not to die of cold. Similar rules of etiquette are observed in seating; there is much motioning, begging of pardon, scraping of benches, pushing and bumping, before everyone finally takes his place. Sarah, the lady of the house, welcomed the guests with a brew made of boiled herbs— for which tea is but a poor substitute—and bits of rock-candy compared to which our modern sugar is a poor second-best. All sat in polite silence, blowing hard at the brew, sipping tiny sips and resting between swallows. One dignitary lit his pipe—a procelain bowl, bent like a *shofar*, with a silver cover on top and a tube extending from the bottom; putting the end of the tube into his mouth, he went "pima-pim-pim" and made smoke. Two of the visitors gave out a little sigh, and pulled at their noses and beards; then they began to talk about this and that, moving from one subject to another until hitting on the one that moved them all to eloquence:

"Ach, ach, cha!" they all sighed. "The Clothing Decree is an awful thing—Jews having to dress like Gentiles and wear a cap with a fur brim. How queer! How ugly! And why? Why, O God, why? What good does it do 'them'? What will 'they' gain if the Jews wear German clothes? Can anyone make anything of it?"

"They say there's a serious reason behind the decree," says the pipe-smoker, twisting his lips, drawing in smoke and blowing it out through his mouth in rings. "Who do you think started the whole business?—Montefiore."*

"Reb Ber! What are you talking about?"

"You hear me. And what if I tell you that I heard it from no less reliable a source than Reb Baruch son of Reb Hillel? Reb Baruch has just come from the fairs and he heard with his own ears. . . ."

"I heard something similar," one of the guests broke in, a vivacious and high-strung Jew who accompanied his every word with a gesture. "Wait a minute, gentlemen, wait a minute while I try to remember what I heard."

"Please Reb Yosl, don't confuse the story," his friends begged, "listen and let Reb Ber talk."

Reb Ber began again, calmly weighing his words, and enunciat-

*The noted Jewish philanthropist, Moses Montefiore (1784-1885), came to Russia in 1846 to intercede with the Tsar in behalf of the suffering Jews. This visit was the source of innumerable legends, stories, and songs.

ing clearly, "They're saying out there in the world—that is to say, among the people at the fairs—they're all saying: When Montefiore saw how terrible the situation was he gave it some thought and then came to the king with this proposal: 'Your Majesty! Sell me your Jews and I'll pay you so and so many millions for them. . . .'"

"A hundred thousand I heard, a hundred thousand million!" Reb Yosl again interrupted Reb Ber, not out of concern for precision as much as to let his peers know that he too had an idea of what was going on in the world and was no worse informed than anyone else.

"What difference does it make?" Reb Ber returned to his story, making a face in Reb Yosl's direction. " 'I'll give you so-and-so many millions,' Montefiore said. 'You're welcome to them' the king replied. The long and short of it was that the two sides came to an agreement and concluded the deal formally and Montefiore gave a down payment. . . ."

"God forbid! A hundred thousand million he would have paid immediately in cash!" Reb Yosl shouted and gesticulated as if quibbling over a page of Talmud.

"Pipe down, Reb Yosl, quiet, with all due respect!" his colleagues angrily silenced him and begged his pardon in one breath.

"The long and short of it," Reb Ber returned to his story without paying any mind to Reb Yosl, "he, that is, Montefiore, gives a down payment and he obligates himself to pay off the balance within a certain time upon receipt of the goods, that is the Jews. And so the sale is made official and each side goes home satisfied. After breakfast the king goes for his daily meeting with the Parliament, pleased as punch. 'Your Majesty!' the minister asks, 'why are you so proud of yourself? What are all the smiles for?'— 'This is what happened,' the king answers, his face beaming. 'I struck a good bargain today. I sold my Jews for such-and-such a figure.' —'Your Majesty!' says the minister, wringing his hands in horror and shock. 'What have you done? What a terrible mistake!' As he talks, the minister makes an exact computation from the royal ledgers and proves, black on white, that the revenues that this merchandise, the Jews, brings in over a period of so many years are much greater than the amount being realized through the sale. 'So what should I do now?' says the king, his face purple with confusion. 'The royal decree is irrevocable. You use your brains and figure a way out of this bad business. After all, you're a minister, you have the mind for it.'—'Your Majesty!' says the minister, after thinking it over for a while. 'I've got it! Here's my idea. Enact a decree ordering the Jews in every province in your kingdom to wear German clothing, but do it now and don't procrastinate.'—'Are you making fun of me?' the king says in a fury. 'What has the one thing got to do with the other? I'm talking to you about Jews and you're talking to me about clothing which has got nothing to do with the subject.'—'It has everything to do with it!' says the minister with a squint and a gesture. 'I speak to you in the manner of a shrewd politician, in hints; I don't have to spell it out for you to understand. As soon as the Jews, now listen carefully, as soon as the Jews change their clothes, the whole thing will automatically be dropped . . . and why? Because you were dealing with him—with that merchant—in Jews, and now when you decree . . . do you see the point of the decree? . . . A shrewd man needs no more than a hint. Think about it and you'll see.'—'Oy!' says the king, jumping up with joy, 'Such good advice! For that you deserve a gold medal! . . .' Listen now to the end of the story, gentlemen," said Reb Ber, scraping out his pipe with an iron nail and blowing down the stem, "exactly on the appointed day, he, that is Montefiore, comes to the king. . . ."

"That's not how it was, it was a little different. He didn't come in person, he sent a representative ahead to announce. . . ." Reb Yosl couldn't contain himself and impetuously interrupted Reb Ber again at this moment when everyone was on tenterhooks to hear the end of the story.

"Shut up, please! Be considerate, Reb Yosl, control yourself. Muzzle your mouth for a minute," his friends pleaded in chorus.

"He comes," Reb Ber goes on, distinctly repeating the word "comes," so as to irritate Reb Yosl, and smiling with pleasure, "the great man comes just as I've told you, on the appointed day, he comes in person and says, 'Your Majesty! Here's the balance of the purchase price, so now let me have my merchandise as we arranged —the Jews . . .'—'They're all yours!' said the king. 'But if your honor doesn't mind, go yourself to all the provinces of my kingdom and take whatever Jews you find, your merchandise, in the name of the God of Israel.' Montefiore didn't protest too much and went his way. He came to a town, and looked for a Jew, but there was none. He went to a second town, to a third, a fourth, and there was none. The long and short of it was that even in Berdichev there weren't any Jews. Not a single Jew could be recognized in the street by the usual signs—the Jews were all dressed in German clothes, they were all Germans! . . ."

"Astonishing!" the guests exclaimed, everyone expressing his surprise and screwing up his face in his own way. "There must be something to it." Tumult and commotion.

"Not everything that people say has something to it," said Reb Chayim, and from his smile it was evident that he thought the rumor stuff and nonsense.

"Whether the story is true or not, the decree is certainly real," they all said, sighing and groaning. "The caftan is no big problem: an extra stitch here and an extra button there won't hurt, and it will still be a caftan if it has a slit in the back. But the hat, what about the hat? Dear Lord! How can we exchange the hat of the scholars, the glory of our heads, for a cap with a fur brim! Think of something, Reb Chayim!"

"I was just thinking," Reb Chayim answered after rubbing his forehead in silence for a few minutes, "I was just thinking how effective the actions of our ancient sages were, in devising the right responses to meet every need. For example, the Torah forbids carrying out-of-doors on the Sabbath, so they stretched a string from the top of one post to another, and carried what they had to. You can't lend money for interest, so the sages devised a means of allowing themselves to borrow to their hearts' content.* There are many other examples . . . I have an idea, gentlemen! Do you know what a 'two-eared' hat is?"

"What a question!" all the guests exclaimed, staring at Reb Chayim. "Who doesn't know what a 'two-eared' hat is? A plain weekday cap, with two ear pieces of mole-fur, padded with flax, sticking up on each side and one strip of fur a few inches wide stretched from one ear-piece to the other sewn tightly to the top over the forehead."

---

*The author is addressing various examples of legal fictions: according to Biblical Sabbath law, carrying is forbidden except within the confines of a private domain. (The courtyard is considered part of the house, no matter how many houses face onto it.) By stretching a string from post to post around their entire quarter, Jews "enclosed" it, and thereby made carrying permissible. This device was called an eruv. Similarly, the charging of interest is strictly forbidden in the Bible. But when the Jews moved into a non-agricultural environment this law had to be modified. The heter iska, to which Reb Chayim is referring, is a transaction permit defining a loan as a form of partnership between the lender and the borrower.

"And where is it written in the Torah," Reb Chayim said with a gentle smile, "that this strip has to be stitched top and bottom to the front of the hat? Why can't it be sewn to the hat by its bottom edge only so it can be bent easily? Then it's up to the wearer: if he prefers, the strip can be upright and his hat is a perfectly acceptable Jewish hat; or if he prefers, he can flip it down so that it becomes a kind of a visor and everyone is satisfied. What complaint could there be against a Jew who wore such a hat?"

"'Where there's Torah there's common sense' as the proverb rightly says. May God give you a long and happy life, Reb Chayim!" said the distinguished citizens, beaming with pleasure.

This hat with its flip-down brim came to be accepted throughout the entire Jewish diaspora, and good Jews still wear it. It now goes by the name of the "Napoleon" hat. We should be aware that it originated in Kapulie; in the book which will record the history of fashion, from the fig leaf of Adam and Eve to modern times, it will be attributed to Reb Chayim who was its inventor. It is possible that Napoleon wore such a hat, but Reb Chayim had no dealings with the Frenchman and consequently cannot be accused of plagiarism.

Reb Chayim's opinion was also sought for cures. Kapulie had no proper doctor but there was an expert barber-surgeon who knew how to bleed, apply leeches, and cup. If a Jew fell sick this barber arrived with all his equipment, beat him on the thighs, arms, and head, let large quantities of blood, wished him a complete recovery, and went his way. If his ministrations failed to help and the patient got worse, the family would come weeping and pleading to Reb Chayim to have a look at him. And Reb Chayim went to look—what else could he do? It wasn't because he had ever actually studied medicine that he was considered an expert in such things, but because he had had plenty of experience. Reb Chayim had been sickly and weak from boyhood. Beside the constipation and hemorrhoids that he had inherited from his parents, he never lacked for other illnesses such as stabbing pains in the lower back, angina, headaches, and weakness of the limbs, which nowadays is called "nerves." He consulted famous doctors concerning these ailments whenever one happened to be in town, though usually he made light of them—"an ache, nothing, it will go away." But once he became so sick that a famous specialist was brought in, just as he was on the point of death; he was cured as if by a miracle. He had been sick so often in his lifetime that he felt himself to be an expert on disease, an opinion shared by the other people of his town. And when you think about it, why should medicine be different from law? In a certain town near Kapulie there is a man named Reb Aaron who is not a Torah scholar, and who has never in his life studied in Gentile schools, and yet he has come to be considered by his fellow townspeople an expert in the law. If anyone has business troubles, God forbid, he goes and explains his problem to Reb Aaron. How did he acquire his reputation? Reb Aaron was imprisoned a number of times on suspicion of theft, robbery, embezzlement, slander, perjury, and similar crimes. In this way he came to have dealings with officials, and stood before judges and officers. The experience thus acquired taught him legal devices of all kinds, including what to write and what to say at the right moment in any situation.

Reb Chayim was only sought out for those who were seriously ill, patients who could not be moved. For those who merely had aches and pains and weren't bedridden, there were other experts in Kapulie, each a specialist in his own field. For eye trouble, there was Reb Fishel. He had a kind of eye-salve, a secret recipe handed down in the family, which he would give away, a few drops per patient, as a pious act. For thinness, Petrucha, an old gentile woman, prescribed some herbs and an elixir to drink. For lethargy and epilepsy there was Miyash the Tatar. Spells against the evil eye and toothache, the pouring of molten wax and the rolling of eggs on an invalid's belly—these were the specialty of Gitl, the women's prayer-leader, compared with whom all the gypsies and miracle-workers in the world were no better than a garlic-peel. For malaria of all kinds, Lipe Ruvens the teacher was very effective. He was also a fine man, and quite an unusual personality. . . .

CHAPTER 4

Lipe Ruvens was a gifted man, one of those individuals endowed at birth with a quick mind, clever hands, and a good heart, and who lack nothing in this world but luck. Just as they are leaving God's storehouse of souls, the angel in charge of conception flings them like a grain of wheat into some dark corner where they are sure to lack the wherewithal to sprout and grow. Some of these people, longing for light and freedom, stumble repeatedly until their spirit gives out, their high hopes fail them, and in despair they take to the bottle and disgrace themselves. Others wage eternal battle with adversity, but because they are poor they never have the time to master any one craft. They grab whatever job comes their way, and as a result their careers are raw and unfinished, like the products of nature itself; they come to be known as men with a talent for everything but success.

Lipe Ruvens was a thin, near-sighted man with a pale face, soft-spoken and good-natured, kindly to his fellowman and well-liked in return. His character, his orderly way of life, even his neat house and clean furniture gave indication that he had in him a bit of the artist's flair. He was good at drawing, and he knew how to carve wood, engrave stone, and etch copper. He did these things not for pay, but for the sheer pleasure and because he was driven by a compulsion to master a craft. The townspeople naturally took advantage of his abilities: he was honored with the task of decorating the Holy Ark; of drawing the mizrakh with its buds and blossoms and fantastic beasts; of engraving tombstones; and of etching signet-rings. Young girls pestered him for designs they could embroider on silk khala covers for the Sabbath and on phylactery-bags for their fiances. And since he was a man of many talents, and since he was so good-natured, was there any reason housewives shouldn't take advantage of him too? At their request, he wrote out various charms on almonds or plates; when diluted with water the ink was then given the patient to drink—and it helped to cure! In addition to all these skills, Lipe Ruvens was also a teacher.

It was Reb Chayim who had made him a teacher.

Reb Chayim's son Shloyme, a boy of seven, showed signs of sensitivity, intelligence, ability, and sharpness of wit. Under Moshe Shleyen, the elementary teacher, he had learned to read Hebrew quickly and accurately, and had begun to study the Bible, beginning, as is usual, with Leviticus, and covering as much ground in one year as children his age normally do in two or three. Reb Chayim's household, and even strangers who dropped in to visit, were drawn to Shloymele for his liveliness, his clever answers to the trick questions adults like to stump schoolboys with, and especially for his talent at mimicry. At a glance he could take in someone's personal mannerism, whether it be a twitch or a special turn of phrase, and copy it so exactly that his audience split its sides laughing. He was particularly fond of imitating Gitl, the women's prayer-leader, kissing the *mezuza* as she entered the house, her jacket half on and half off, twisting her lips to say, "God help us!", then lowering her back like a cat until one shoulder sloped upward and the other down, with her chin resting in the palm of her hand and one finger on her cheek, frowning and snorting as she lifted her eyes toward heaven and said ceremoniously: "Praise and honor to the Almighty (blessed be He and blessed be His Name) who saves and redeems and sustains His people Israel in mercy and kind-ness. . . ." Gitl liked to spice her speech with snatches of Biblical quotations and rabbinic proverbs and tales from the pious books. Even his mother joined in the laughter at Shloymele's antics, but at the same time she would threaten him with her finger. "You just wait and see, my fine fellow! I'll tell your father. You'll find out what a boy gets for mimicking his elders. Dear God, what will become of this boy? May my enemies suffer the plagues of Egypt if I have any idea what he's all about. . . ."

But the father well understood his son. He knew that, taught the correct subjects in the correct order and by a good teacher, the boy might some day be a great scholar in Israel. The Jews of those days, especially the Jews of little villages like Kapulie, did not include among "the correct subjects" such worldly studies as science and foreign languages. If a person had "filled his stomach with bread and meat," i.e., Talmud and law-codes, and had studied a little Bible, with grammar for dessert—that was all he needed: he was a learned man, perfect in every respect; other subjects were considered frivolous and superfluous. Was there a father in those days who taught his son any more of the Bible than the first chapter of the weekly portion? Fathers kept their sons from studying the Bible as from something that smacked of freethinking. Of the 150 explanations that have been offered for this astonishing state of affairs, not one does the Jews credit. But that's how it was, and still is among some of our people to our great shame. Rabbis were never well versed in the Bible, but nowadays they don't even recognize a Biblical quotation. Even so, one mustn't harbor suspicions about their scholarship. There must be a good explanation for their igno-rance which the ordinary mind isn't able to comprehend; perhaps it *is* possible to be an extraordinary Torah-scholar and Talmudic lawyer without knowing the verses of the Bible. . . .

Reb Chayim, in any event, wished to break with the time-honored curriculum by having his son taught the entire Bible with its Aramaic translation, in consecutive order, from the first word of Genesis to the last word of Chronicles. Reb Chayim himself was very well versed in the Bible, and this gave him an elegant epistolary style. His ornate phrases were sweeter than honey to the taste of his friends, who much admired his eloquence. Reb Chayim's only problem was to find a teacher: which of the local instructors was right for his purpose? He searched and searched until finally he hit upon Lipe Ruvens, who became a teacher at his request. Reb Chayim permitted him to accept a few other pupils in addition to Shloymele so that he and his wife and little daughter would have just enough to live on, in the style to which all Jewish teachers are accustomed. . . .

Master and pupil were admirably suited to each other; the match couldn't have been more perfect. The master taught conscientiously and the pupil studied diligently. During the lesson, while the master sat teaching, his hands busied themselves at drawing, or engraving a signet-ring, but this never resulted in a loss of time; quite the contrary, it affected Lipe Ruvens as a glass of schnapps affects a laborer, exhilarating him, giving him confidence, mellowing his attitude toward his fellow man, and loosening his tongue. He became talkative, explaining every detail of the lesson with absolute clarity, his eyes blazing with the light of the Torah. His pupil was caught up in the enthusiasm, and thrilled by his teacher's explanations, took in every word. Study was not the drudgery it is in most cases, when the master tries to force-feed the pupil by shouting, scolding, and beating, and the pupil must resort to lies and pretend he is absorbing his lessons when he is not. It was never that way with Lipe Ruvens. He taught so calmly and quietly that the lesson was rather like a conversation between two dear friends, where each one hangs on the other's words, and understands what is in his heart: a conversation that gives pleasure to both participants, and which both would like to extend, hour after hour.*

Shloymele grew into a fine boy, like a flower under sensitive care. Although his mind was maturing from day to day, he still acted like the child he was. When studying, he was completely absorbed, hard at work to understand everything. But the moment he put down the book and walked outside, he went wild with boyish pranks

*One of the author's first published pieces was a Hebrew essay on education reform, very much in the spirit of this description.

and turned into a regular devil. The soul of man is generally less uniform than we suppose, but the degree of heterogeneity varies from person to person. Shloymele's soul exhibited a high degree of confusion: he could be obstinate, hard as nails, but also soft as putty, easily led by the nose; irritable and sweet-tempered; bitter as gall and sweet as sugar; serious and frivolous; pensive and lighthearted. Shloymele had a passionate temperament that could be kindled by the slightest spark. The fiery speeches and divine visions of the prophets enflamed his imagination and gave him much to ponder:

> *I saw the Lord sitting on a throne high and exalted,*
> *the hem of his robe filling the Temple.*
> *Fiery angels stood above him*
> *Each with six wings . . .*
> *Each called to the other saying:*
> *"Holy, holy, holy, is the Lord of Hosts."*
> *The foundations of the threshhold shook*
> *and the Temple was filled with smoke.*
> *Then I said: "Woe to me, for I am lost,*
> *For a man of unclean lips am I*
> *and in the midst of a people of unclean lips do I dwell."*

These words of Isaiah's prophecy captured the boy's imagination. He began to draw mental pictures of God surrounded by ministering angels with wings, and to wonder about all kinds of mysteries that were pecking away at his brain, demanding an explanation. He didn't feel comfortable asking questions about these matters, as they didn't pertain to the subject of his lessons. Once he did try to put the problems before his teacher, his face burning as he spoke. But Lipe Ruvens merely shook his head with a little smile as if to say: go on, now. Sometimes he asked bearded elders about the things that were bothering him, but he always got the same angry answer: "Hold your tongue! Your business is to obey the rules as they appear in the books, to study, and to pray; if you don't, God will punish you in the next world with whips of leather and whips of fire." Shloymele was terrified of these whips, not for the pain so much as for the humiliation. He thought of God as a powerful nobleman with a bad temper and a thirst for revenge, wielding His strap at the slightest sign of misdemeanor. Whenever he accidentally skipped a word in his prayers, or forgot to say Amen, or drank water without saying the blessing, or uncovered his head to scratch, he instantly became terrified and thought to himself: "Woe is me, I am lost!"

It goes without saying that around the time of the High Holidays, when even the fish in the sea tremble before God's judgment, Shloymele was numb with fear of the Lord. The entire ritual—getting up early for *Selikhot*,* hurrying to the synagogue and the cemetery, the wailing and the weeping, the sad melodies of the prayers, the face of his mother looking as if she were about to be stretched on the block to receive forty lashes—all these things ruined the holiday so completely for him that he even lost his appetite for the fish and stew and apple in honey and other New Year treats.

But bad and good always go hand in hand in this world, and even the High Holidays were not a time of unmitigated dread. There was, for instance, the presence of the "villagers" from the surrounding countryside who came to town with their families for the holiday. Their arrival put everybody in good spirits, relieving some of the tedium of daily life like the flavor of pepper and onions with honey.

Our sense of responsibility to the history of Israel demands that we explain this subject in greater detail. Not to do so would be to leave this book without some important pages, and who knows? —perhaps forever to deprive future generations of their understanding of this matter.

CHAPTER 5

The month of Tishre is the month of Jewish holidays. The first two days are Rosh Hashana and the tenth of the month is Yom Kippur. Together they are called the Days of Awe, or the Days of Judgment, and with the week in between they are also called the Ten Days of Repentance. These are terribly busy days in heaven, days of bustle and commotion. As the prayerbook describes it, on these days the

---

* *Selikhot* are the penitential prayers recited daily from the Sunday before Rosh Hashana through Yom Kippur.

heavens quake as God takes His place on His holy throne. The angels go about in terror, muttering: "Today is Judgment Day." All the world's inhabitants pass before Him like so many little sheep, and He weighs their deeds, counting and figuring, until finally He writes down each one's sentence: who is to live and who is to die (and by what manner of death); who will be allowed to remain where he is and who will be forced to wander to the four corners of the earth (and whether by land or by sea).

On earth there is no less commotion than there is in heaven. As early as a month in advance the *shofar* is blown in the synagogues, sounding the alarm: "Wake up, ye sleepers! Examine your deeds and repent! Remember your creator, you who have allowed a frivolous life to distract you from contemplating Truth, you who have whiled away a whole year with trivialities. Give some thought to your souls, turn over a new leaf, and change your bad habits." All Jews everywhere begin thinking over their deeds of the past year, using all kinds of devices to curry God's favor: they come to the synagogue at night to recite *Selikhot*, they exercise the virtues of repentance, prayer, and charity, and they count on the merit of their ancestors to intercede before the throne of God the Highest.

These are the days when the innkeepers and villagers from round about come to the nearby towns with their families and belongings to stand before the heavenly court with the rest of their people and to beg Him who listens to the prayers of Israel for a good year and for release from evil, on behalf of themselves and on behalf of all mankind.

At that time of year Kapulie becomes a different town. Ordinarily deserted, its streets empty, and its life as quiet as still water in a pond, it comes alive a few days before the High Holidays with newcomers who flock in from the countryside, bringing women and children in wagons piled high with bedding, bundles, bags full of food, and hobbled chickens. Householders, mischievous boys, and hoary elders all turn out to greet the arriving villagers, each one seeking out the family that is to stay with him for the holidays. Everyone talks at once, and the chatter can be heard from one end of the town to the other, a medley of sounds and voices. The hosts have many questions: Why so late? Why this? Why that? And the guests have many stories about the miracles and wonders that befell them on the way: the axle of a wagon broke, a horse fell down, a bridge was washed away, a hobbled chicken broke loose, a pregnant woman suddenly decided to have her baby; in short, every one has good reason to thank God he's still alive. The country dogs, who had not really been invited, but simply tagged along after their masters from the villages, pick fights with the town dogs who resent the intruders. The town dogs and country dogs can't stand the sight of one another. As long as they are together in town there is continual barking and yelping, fighting and bickering. Street urchins also mix in, sicking the dogs on one another, throwing stones, and contributing to the general commotion. Mothers stand in the doorways scolding and cursing their boys. Jewish passersby grab up the hems of their caftans in terror and run for their lives.

In short, the shtetl has come alive again, like a little pond at the beginning of spring, which fills up to the brim and overflows with the sound of rushing water.

At the height of the confusion, a jam-packed wagon came into town, carrying the entire household of Chone the miller. The old mare, who had had to stop many times along the way, put on a burst of energy as she approached the town, and pranced into the market-place with her neck high, in pride and pomp. In honor of Kapulie and all those in the wagon, she raised her tail, perked up her ears, lifted her hoofs, and trotted vivaciously to the thunderous accompaniment of the wagon wheels. Tsutsik the dog ran ahead, heralding their arrival. But though preoccupied with this important responsibility, he remembered to be cautious in his encounters with the town dogs, lest he get into trouble. First they sized him up, sniffing at him with their noses as if to say, *"Sholom Aleichem!"* He returned the greeting, but in a perfunctory way, just to be polite; the formalities over, he ran ahead again, the old mare following in a great public display. Finally they reached Reb Chayim's house, where Chone the miller had spent the holidays for many years, together with his wife and sons and daughters and sons-in-law—a good-sized group (may they be spared the evil eye).

Their arrival opened up a whole new world of activities for Shloymele. He had plenty of curiosity and lots of time, thank God, so he was quite busy. Right after the mare came to a halt and Chone's family alighted, Shloymele and a few of the other boys climbed up onto the wagon, while two others hung from the back between the wheels. The boys in the wagon grabbed the reins and tried to get the mare to move by cracking the whip and beating her with a strap, whistling, shouting, and calling out all together:

"Hiyya! Hiyya!" The poor thing took a few lumbering steps, groaned, and stood still. They examined her ratty tail, each one plucking out a few hairs, and then started in on Tsutsik, talking to him in dog language and making him dance on his hind legs.

Shloymele was also interested in the family of Chone the miller, who seemed to him rather queer. The girls wore new shoes and stockings of coarse material, and new clothes in garish colors with huge red flowers; they stood there, finger in mouth, staring with their big calf's eyes. The boys too, in brand new clothes—shirt, pants, fringed undergarment, skullcap, and smock—stared bashfully at the ground, picking their noses; they didn't answer when spoken to, or even when shouted at; but an odd giggle might suddenly erupt into the palm of the hand followed by a nose-wipe with the sleeve. Furthermore, the country-folk had a clumsy way of speaking and eating: instead of talking they mumbled, and instead of eating they gobbled. Their very faces and flesh were somehow rustic, different from those of townspeople.

Chone himself was not exactly a barbarian; nevertheless, as Shloymele immediately sensed, there was no comparison between him and Reb Chayim, or between his own mother and Chone's wife, Toibe-Sosye. Toibe-Sosye was a fat, fleshy woman, with arms and face tanned by the sun. She had a good, solid way of walking, that let you know when she was putting a foot forward; her voice as it emerged from between a pair of thick lips, fairly pierced the ear. She was good-hearted but simple. When lighting the candles on Friday night she would weep piously, and in the women's section, wail at the first sound of the prayer-leader's voice, though she understood not a word. By contrast, Shloymele's mother Sarah was frail and slight, with small, white hands crisscrossed with tiny purple veins, and the pale face and thin lips of a pious woman. She seemed to be pure spirit, to float rather than walk. She was a learned woman, who knew all kinds of prayers, prayers of the Land of Israel and prayers of Sarah Bas Tovim; she was well-versed in the laws of *khala*, menstruation, and candle lighting, which are the particular province of women, and she read such books as *Tsena Urena, The Shining Candelabrum,** and the like. It was she who showed the

*The *Tsena Urena*, first issued by Jacob ben Isaac Ashkenazi around 1600, is probably the most popular Yiddish book ever printed. Intended for women, it is a lively arrangement of Biblical and Talmudic stories which includes some emotive moralizing and practical wisdom. *The Shining Candelabrum*, by Isaac Aboab, translated into Yiddish by Moshe Frankfurt in 1722, is a compendium of Talmudic and Midrashic sayings, a rather serious volume of moralistic literature.

women how to pray: what hymns to say, when to rise, when to stand
on tip-toe in the *kedusha*-prayer. In the women's gallery of the
synagogue she kept a lemon and other pungent remedies to revive
herself or the other women whenever they felt faint.

And in fact, it was hardly possible to keep from fainting when
Sarah read. She would read with great emotion, her melody melting
the soul and pulling at the heart strings. When she wept, everyone
wept with her; her tears would have melted a stone. . . .

Before Yom Kippur, it was customary for each woman to make
one candle for the synagogue, known as the Candle of the Dead,
and another candle to light at home, known as the Candle of the
Living. Sarah would stand very solemnly, surrounded by the neighborhood women. She cut many threads for each wick to make it
thick and strong, one thread for each of Israel's patriarchs and
matriarchs, and as she cut each thread she read the accompanying
text with tears in her eyes:

"Lord of the World, merciful God. May these candles which we
are about to make in honor of your great Name and in honor of the
pure, holy souls, arouse the holy patriarchs and matriarchs to pray
for us from their graves so that no evil, trouble, or suffering befall
us, and may our candle and our husbands' candle and our children's
candle not be extinguished before their time, God forbid.

"This thread I am laying down in the name of our father
Abraham. Just as you saved him from the fiery furnace, so may you
purify us from our sins and may our soul return to you as innocent
as when it entered our body.

"This thread I am laying down in the name of our mother
Sarah. May God remember in our favor what she suffered when her
dear son Isaac was taken from her and was bound on the altar. May
she intercede for us before You that our children not be stolen from
us, that they not be led away from us like sheep."

Here, the women would burst out weeping, for those were the
days when little children were snatched from their beds at night and
turned over to the army to live far from home among the Gentiles,
and to endure terrible sufferings. Some died before their time;
others were scattered to the four winds or killed in battle; the
remainder assimilated among the Gentiles, never again to return to
their own people. The women wept until the wick was drenched
with their tears.

"This thread I am laying down in the name of our father Isaac.
May you mercifully grant us the ability to give our children a proper

upbringing, to hire for our sons a teacher who will enlighten their eyes and teach them Torah.

"This thread I am laying down in the name of our father Jacob, whom you saved from all his enemies and from Esau. So may you save us, through his merit, from all who want to destroy us and denounce us; do not let them slander us with blood accusations* and besmirch our name. . . .

"This thread I am laying down in the name of Solomon, who built the holy Temple. At its dedication he prayed to You to accept also the prayers of the non-Jew, the stranger from another nation, who comes to the Temple to worship You. Through his merit, may the gates of heaven be open to my prayer, and may I be remembered, together with my husband and my children and all men, for good in the coming year. Amen."

If anyone can find it in his heart to laugh at this prayer, or mock it, let him do so. But then let *him* point to souls as pure as these, let *him* duplicate these tender feelings, these burning tears, this love of Torah and wisdom, this regard for one's fellow man and all mankind.

Better yet, let him listen carefully to the prayers of these Jewish women, and discover what the "Jewish heart" is all about. Let him listen . . . and hold his peace forever.

CHAPTER 6

Two years from the time he began to study the Bible, Shloymele had experienced so much and seen so many wonderful things that in some respects he was already an old man, a Methuselah. He had been in Mesopotamia and Canaan and Egypt and Persia and Media and Susa and all the other provinces from India to Ethiopia; he had travelled in wildernesses and deserts, and had seen and heard untold wonders. But not because any catastrophe had befallen Reb Chayim, forcing him to uproot himself and his family and wander

*The blood libels hurled against Jews accused them of killing Christian children in order to use their blood in the baking of *matza*. These libels, coinciding with Eastertime, sometimes touched off widespread pogroms.

abroad; no fire, epidemic, or riot had occurred to make the towns-people flee into exile, as Jews are used to doing. God forbid! Nothing had changed or gone wrong. The shtetl was the same as ever, its inhabitants the same, and Reb Chayim also. Each man was in his accustomed place, and Shloymele hadn't set one foot outside of town. How then did he manage to travel so far, to see and hear so much? Among Jews it is quite common for a child to spend his life in one place but with no idea of what goes on around him, with no conception of how to enjoy a normal human existence; instead, such a child transports himself and his thoughts to another world, another age. There it is possible for a man to grant the past a priority over the present, to overlook things that are in front of his nose, and to occupy himself with things that existed long ago, and that are accessible only to memory and imagination.

Shloymele was still a child, unacquainted with his surroundings and the other human beings with whom he shared them; but his imagination bore him to distant realms: to the land of Sichon, king of the Amorites, to the land of Og, king of Bashan, and to the land of Nebuchadnezzar, king of Babylonia.* The people of his world spoke Hebrew and Aramaic; they lived in tents, rode mules and camels, drank water from leather bags, went barefoot, and wore rings in their noses. Shloymele knew nothing of the pine tree, the birch, or the oak. What had he to do with grains and potatoes, which he ate every day in the form of buckwheat soup and bread? In his mind's eye he pictured only vineyards and date trees, fig trees, pomegranates, olive trees, gopher and carob trees. Of animals, he knew the rainbow-colored Tachash of Moses' time, with the single horn in its forehead; the wild ox which feeds each day on the grass of a thousand mountains; the antelope which is said to be the size of Mount Tabor and which was so huge at the time of the flood that only its nose could fit into the ark. Of reptiles, Shloymele knew only the shamir-worm which was created at dusk on the first Friday of creation and was used to split stones for the Temple.

Among birds, he knew of the wild cock that guarded the shamir-worm; the Bar Yochna, whose egg fell once and broke, flooding sixty cities and felling three hundred cedar trees. He had

---

*Sichon, king of the Amorites, and Og, king of Bashan, were defeated by the Israelites during the conquest of Canaan. Nebuchadnezzar was king of Babylon at the time of the conquest of Jerusalem, 597 B.C.E.

also heard of the Ziz-sadai, the great bird whose wings can darken the disc of the sun. In short, Shloymele may have been born here, but he passed his life somewhere over there . . . here he was a stranger, but there he was at home. He came to his parents' house only for a brief moment, as a guest to an inn: there he ate and slept, but bright and early in the morning he was on his way again. . . . His life, like the lives of thousands of other Shloymeles, was one continuous memorialization, commemorating the lives of our ancestors; this is how our ancestors lived in their time, this is what they used to do, in those days, in times gone by.

But to exist in memory of the past, to stand in the middle of history circling back to the same spot again and again, refusing to budge forward an inch—this is not living, but dreaming. Our ancestors who sat by the rivers of Babylon thinking of nothing but their lost homeland noticed this in themselves only later, on returning from their exile, when they described their earlier situation in the Psalm: "When God restored the fortunes of Zion," meaning, when we were restored to Zion, "we were like dreamers," we saw that life in Babylon had been unreal and unsubstantial.

And since life was a dream, small wonder that chimeras and superstitions assumed a real existence, and that demons and evil spirits and animals in human form and other kinds of fabulous beasts were believed to hover everywhere. Had it not been for Shloymele's confidence in the protective powers of ritual fringes, the mezuza, and the "Hear O Israel," prayer, he would have died in childhood from the terror that these creatures instilled in him.

At irregular intervals, a certain Jew with long sidelocks, a wild beard, and a blind eye, put in an appearance in Kapulie. He dropped in without warning, as if from the sky, with a wild look and a dark scowl, his head slightly stooped. His arrival always caused a stir and made the whole town buzz. "He's here, Rabbi Eliya the miracle-worker is here!" People never tired of telling stories about Rabbi Eliya's miracles, his charms and amulets. In one town he was said to have exorcised the soul of a dead man that had entered a living person's body. In another place he had had dealings with "them," the demons, who thereafter trembled in fear of him. This was the reason given for his partial blindness: whenever Rabbi Eliya called up the demons he scattered a bagful of poppy seeds and, by the force of a magical formula, ordered them to gather the seeds and replace them in the bag, because if demons are allowed to go idle for even a moment they inevitably cause damage. Once, when he forgot to set them to gathering poppy seeds, they ganged up on him and pecked out his eye.

When Shloymele saw this Rabbi Eliya about whom such terrifying stories circulated, his blood curdled. To be sure, he had never actually been physically present when Rabbi Eliya was handling evil spirits, but Rabbi Eliya's unseeing eye was evidence of the story's truth; otherwise, how did he become blind? Once he even managed to observe Rabbi Eliya in action.

On winter nights, Shloymele and his friends came home from *cheder* at about nine o'clock, carrying paper lanterns to light their way. They made a happy racket as they went, singing and whistling and trumpeting into the hollow of their fists. But as soon as they approached the huge, cold synagogue, where the dead are said to pray at night, they lost their tongues and hurried by in terror, grasping at their ritual fringes for protection and crying a silent "Hear, O Israel." Having escaped the danger, with God's help, the children continued on their way, their courage restored, and their mouths opened in renewed song.

On one particularly cold winter night, coming home from *cheder* and running into the house with his usual clatter, Shloymele was abruptly silenced by sour looks and gestures for silence, so that his "good evening" stuck like a bone in his throat. The light in the room was dim, his mother and father were absent, the children sat alone in the corners looking miserable. What should he do? Moving silently on tiptoe he clambered unnoticed up to the top of the oven to warm himself a little from the cold. From the tiny cubicle on the other side of the oven that served as living quarters for his older brother and his wife, a strong light shone in his eyes. He stretched out full-length and caught a stealthy glimpse of the room. What he saw there made him freeze with horror. Around his sister-in-law's bed hung a curtain set from top to bottom with packets of pins that sparkled in the candlelight. The bench that ordinarily stood by the oven had been removed, and in its place was a pit in the ground like an open grave. Some wild-looking person was grasping a black rooster and making frightening grimaces, striking the rooster on its head and emitting sounds that did not correspond to any human language: "eyabeya stitoyo, agrefti, merum, shmariel." He rolled his eyes in all directions, puffing, and mumbling: "matsafats, metsofots, matsifats, motsofots, metsefets, metsefots, metsofets, metsifets," kicking and striking as if scuffling with someone, and with every "matsafats" beating the rooster on the head with such force that the poor creature nearly squawked itself to death. From behind the curtain came human screams and groans that would tear your heart out. Then the stranger really began to throw himself around furiously; he drew his breath in deeply and forced out his voice so that it seemed to be coming from the pit of his stomach: "tilmecho chayshe uvsusbik psalmigyo." While uttering these charms, he grasped the rooster by the throat and whirled it about his head the way you do with the *kapore*-rooster* the day before Yom Kippur; then he strangled the bird, threw it into the pit, covered it with dirt—and the bench was returned to its place. No sooner was the hole filled than a terrible scream came from behind the curtain and with it, a weak little cry. *"Mazl tov!"* cried Shloymele's mother and a second woman, as they stuck their heads out from between the curtains. "It's a boy, may he have long life!"

"Mazl tov!" replied the wizard, panting. "I've had a good little fight with 'them' today. But from now on, this woman will have no more miscarriages, and the 'snatcher' will never give her any more trouble."

Shloymele didn't know what a "snatcher" was, or what he had witnessed. But a few days later, he overhead the conversation of some grownups about the demon Lilith, called the "snatcher" because of her habit of stealing children from women in labor. They also spoke very solemnly of a hair-raising incident recorded in a certain book:

"In the little town of Galink, near Khelem, lived a certain Reb Gavriel. When Reb Gavriel's wife gave birth to a healthy little boy, he sent for the Rabbi of Khelem, Rabbi Eliya the miracle-worker, to circumcise the child. This happened on a Thursday in the month of Sivan. Rabbi Eliya set out that very day, and when he came to the outskirts of the city toward evening, he saw more than 100,000 wizards and witches gathered there, each one spewing flames, and the whole group surrounded by fire as they stood there playing with the newborn infant. As soon as he saw what was going on he called to his servant: 'Quickly, give me some water from my pitcher!' Before washing his hands he recited a charm, invoking the secret

*The kapore-fowl is the sacrificial scapegoat to which one's guilt is transferred on the day before Yom Kippur. The bird is held above the head and the formula "This bird is a sacrifice in my stead" is repeated three times.

name of God; then he took seven knives and seven little boards and two Sabbath loaves and seven shoes; in each shoe he stuck a knife; then he took off his own shoes, washed his hands in water twice, stuck up his right thumb, and said: 'By the power of God's holy names (here he uttered some of the magic names of God) I annul the witchcraft of these creatures so that they will have no power to harm the child.' By means of the holy name, Rabbi Eliya killed all the wizards, and then took the child home to his mother and father. As soon as he entered the house he uttered the sacred name *Shamshiya*, and everyone present realized that the child who lay on the bed by his mother was nothing but straw and rope—a phantom, an illusion (God protect us!), with only the appearance of a human child. Rabbi Eliya took the child that he saved from the 'husks' of evil, the real child, and returned him to his mother."*

From that moment on, Shloymele's mind was in a turmoil, and nothing in the world seemed to him to be other than an illusion. Nothing was real, nothing what it seemed to be. At any given moment the evil spirit might enter this person or that, or perhaps they were long since possessed. They only seemed to be human, but in fact their soul was straw; perhaps he too was only a rag doll, straw and rope.

CHAPTER 7

A masterful teller of terrifying tales was Yachne-Sosye, also known as Lebtsiche, after her husband. Of the ten measures of gab used by God in creating the human race, women took nine, and of these nine Yachne-Sosye got the lion's share. God seems to have created Yachne-Sosye for no other purpose than to serve as a model of the ideal woman, the embodiment of female qualities in their purest form—an extraordinary talker, a heroic gossip. Through her awesome stories, she became a powerful influence on Shloymele's development.

*The author's own footnote here indicates that this story was taken from the book *Toldot Adam* (The Chronicles of Adam) by Eliya Baalshem, Eliya the miracle worker.

This Lebtsiche lived in Reb Chayim's neighborhood, and was always dropping in to borrow a pot or a pan from his wife Sarah; nearly every morning she would come to get a hot coal from Sarah's oven. Matches were not as widely available then as they are now; instead, all kinds of different fire-making techniques were needed. Lebtsiche would scoop a hissing coal into her own pan and blow on it while pouring out whole bagsful of gossip. Once a week there was sure to be a fight between Yachne-Sosye and Sarah, usually on market day over some bargain or other, but these battles never lasted beyond the day. First thing in the morning, Lebtsiche would be there with her pan, as bubbly as ever, blowing into her coals and talking up a storm.

On long winter nights, Lebtsiche often came to sit with Sarah over some task, usually a stocking, and to consult with her on whether it was time to begin the heel or how many more rows to knit. But she never let her work interfere with her gossip. She would tell incredible stories of things that had really happened to others, to herself, and to her grandfather (may he rest in peace), and swear up and down to the truth of everything she said. From one story she passed straightway to another, so that sometimes the two merged in confusion. No matter what was being discussed, she had a story to tell. Were they speaking of typhus, for example, Yachne-Sosye had the following to say:

"Typhus, you say? Listen to what happened. Pesach Klotz, the innkeeper, a red-faced, healthy villager, a real peasant-type, was sitting one day over a bowl of sour milk, gulping it down like a pig—what do you expect from such a peasant? As he sat there, working on that bowl with everything he had, a stranger came into the inn. You want to know who the stranger was? Wait a minute and you'll find out. The stranger stood watching Klotz as he ate, never taking his eyes off him. Then, just as Pesach lifted a spoonful to his mouth, the stranger gave him a good hard slap on the hand, so that the spoon fell into the bowl. 'You see that little black speck floating around in the bowl?' the stranger asked. 'That isn't just a speck. You're lucky I was able to get that spoon out of your hand before you had a chance to swallow it. It's typhus! Now watch what I'm going to do! He took a calf's bladder, poured the sour milk into it, closed it, and hung it over the oven. Pesach realized that the stranger was one of the unholy company. He thanked him very nicely, and the very next market day he went to the synagogue in the city and had himself called to the Torah to recite the prayer of Thanksgiving. You want to know what happened to the bladder? Dear God, may our enemies come to the same end! It dried up like a stick and the slightest breeze made it shake as if it had typhus."

After Shloymele heard this story, he could never again eat sour milk; in fact, he lost his appetite for other foods as well, because every little black speck in the plate made him shudder in fear of the dread typhus.

One winter night, Lebtsiche and Sarah were sitting by the warm stove contentedly plucking feathers. The cat was lying on the bench with its hind legs tucked underneath, flicking its tail, and staring out with greenish eyes. A small fire burned in the ceiling-brazier and the boys took turns stoking it with dry sticks, keeping the house warm and well-lit.

"What did you say about your cow, Sarah?" Lebtsiche interrupted Sarah's talk, "You complain she doesn't give enough milk? It's the witches who steal her milk. I'll give you a piece of good advice: boil your strainer; there's no better trick. When I was still a little girl the same thing happened to my grandfather, in the same year as the incident with the force-fed gander, may he intercede for us in heaven—my grandfather, I mean. Such a thing has never happened before or since. He was so heavy he couldn't be moved from his place, that's how fat he was—a hundred pounds or more—the gander, I mean. He should have been good for several jars of fat and plenty of cracklings. But when he was being taken home from the butcher's, slaughtered and all, he suddenly got up on his feet, gave a loud crow, flew away, and disappeared from sight! That was no gander—it was a human soul transformed into a gander. . . . *Tfui*, what am I talking about?—I'm mixing milk with meat, telling two stories at once! I wanted to tell you about milk: my grandfather's cow suddenly stopped giving milk. I was a little girl then—dried-up teats, an emaciated body, an empty stomach, skin and bones, that was all there was to the cow. My grandmother Tema, may she rest in peace, got angry with the cow and said, 'I refuse to feed her! Let her eat dirt, that disobedient, rebellious cow!' Neither would give in: my grandmother wouldn't give the cow any food, and the cow wouldn't give her any milk. If it hadn't been for old Petrucha, who knows how it would have ended? This Petrucha fell out with her friend, who happened to be a witch, and she came and told my grandmother that the witch had been stealing her cow's milk. In exchange for a tot of liquor, she advised my grandmother as follows: 'Tema! Around evening, start a fire in the oven, set a pot on a tripod, put in the strainer with hairs of a bat and these herbs that I'm giving you. Keep the door and the shutters well locked, and let no one in the house. If you're very frightened, keep Yachne-Sosye with you. When the pot begins to boil, you'll hear a knock on the door, and a voice calling, "Open, Tema, please open up for me," but don't say a word, because it will be the voice of the witch; she will be in pain, her belly will be aching, and she will beg you, sometimes in your husband's voice and sometimes in other voices. Be careful, Tema, don't listen to it, for God's sake, don't open the door.' And that's how it was, I remember as clearly as if it was today. The sun had set. The house was pitch-dark. I and my grandmother, may she rest in peace, were standing by the stove. The pot was sitting on the tripod over the fire. Just as the pot began to go 'Tyoch, tyoch,' there was a knocking at the door! My grandmother was trembling, her eye was fixed on me in terror, and she was biting her lip. My heart was pounding, 'Tyoch, tyoch!' Suddenly a voice exactly like my grandfather's could be heard from outside, pleading: 'Tema, open up for me! Listen, please, Tema, open up for me.' My grandmother bit her lips even harder, and laid a finger on them for me to keep quiet. The pot was boiling. Again came the imitation of my grandfather's voice, louder and louder, first pleading and then scolding. The damnable witch did all this with her deceitful tricks; her intestines must have been boiling with the pot. After a while, my grandfather's voice quieted down, and you could hear the grunting of a pig, the barking of a dog, the bleating of a goat, the meowing of a cat. Listen Sarah, I'll tell you something even better"—Lebtsiche suddenly interrupted herself, staring at the cat stretched out peacefully on the bench opposite her, flicking its tail and licking its front paws—"Do you hear? I feel uneasy about that cat of yours. I'm afraid he's a transmigration. . . . Scat!"

The cat was startled and in its attempt to flee fell into the pot of feathers, and emerged covered all over, looking like a very odd demon indeed. Terror in the house, screaming and chasing; the cat jumped onto the table, sprang onto the benches, with everyone giving chase. A regular pogrom against the wretched cat, poor thing!

From that moment on, all animals seemed to Shloymele to be transmigrations. A gander was no gander, a cat was no cat—a man was no man, for that matter. The whole world was nothing but a fantasy.

CHAPTER 8

Here, in the present world, Shloymele was a dunce, utterly ignorant of life, but in the world of his studies he was brilliant and well informed, a great scholar, familiar with texts that are today almost a mystery. Perfectly at home in the past, in his manner of speech, his gait, and all his concerns, he found there a busy whirl of activities: people arguing whether an egg laid on a holiday may be eaten; Levites making the rounds of the threshing-floors collecting tithes; priests coming in at sunset to eat their portions of the sacrifice; and ordinary Jews forking over Levitical tithes, priestly dues, large portions of their crops for the poor, and receiving forty lashes for every infraction of the law. Shloymele was quite busy in the world of the past, where his real life was lived.

One day, when Shloymele dropped in from that world like a guest to grab a bite at his parents' home, he was greeted by sounds of mourning and lamenting, as if someone had died. His mother was wringing her hands and weeping aloud. Dovidl and Edel, the two toddlers, were standing in a corner, howling at the sight of their mother crying. Leah, his older sister, was sitting miserably on the dairy-bench, hanging her head. As he took in the scene, Shloymele's own heart began to throb, his eyes filled with tears, and in a moment, he too was crying.

"Oi, an evil fate, a terrible misfortune!" Sarah lamented, beating her breast.

"Ma-ma, ma-ma!" the children wailed, rubbing their heads with their hands.

"Sniff, snni-iff!" sobbed Shloymele, the other-worldly sage, blowing his nose.

"Cry, Shloymele, cry!" his mother crooned when she noticed that he had come in, and placed her hands on his head. "Let our prayer come before you, our Father in heaven; collect the tears of innocent *cheder*-children, and have pity on us! Oi, they want to take poor, helpless Jewish children off to the schools!* What will become of us?"

"Help! help!" Shloymele screamed, bursting into tears under his mother's hands.

Shloymele the other-worldly had heard that in this world of ours, "they," that is, the Gentiles, have something known as schools. What they did there, he didn't know, but he had heard that they beat the pupils with straps. Now that he realized what his mother was crying about, that Jewish children were to be forced to go to these schools, his spirit failed him. He envisioned soldiers snatching him, laying him out, whipping him . . . and he howled in anticipated pain.

But his mother wasn't crying for the beatings; even in the *cheder* the strap got plenty of use. She was weeping over the very idea of sending Jewish children to the "schools"—the name itself was revolting. If, God forbid, the evil decree were to be carried out, it would mean the end of Judaism.

The whole town was in an uproar. Jews went about sighing and groaning, talking of nothing but the schools. It was rumored that a certain German Jew, a *maskil* by the name of Lilienthal, and his circle of "Berliners" were to blame.† Like their fellow Jews elsewhere, the Jews of Kapulie called meetings to weigh the problem, and decided to proclaim a public fast-day, to recite Psalms, to beg the dead to intercede with God for mercy. The poor *cheder*-teachers trembled for their jobs. The schools would destroy their livelihood, and unless God were to send a miracle, they would die of hunger and enter an early grave. Thus the *cheder*-teachers were particularly instrumental in stirring up public indignation, bringing their pupils from *cheder* to the crowded synagogues, where

*In 1842, by imperial decree, all Jewish schools, including *cheders* and yeshivas, were placed under government supervision and two years later it was announced that attendance in specially-established crown schools would be compulsory. These schools were to teach Russian, secular sciences, Hebrew and "religion, according to the holy writ." At first there were assurances that the reforms were not to be directed against the Jewish religion, but the real aim of the government was to Russify the Jews and "to erase the prejudices fostered in them by the study of Talmud."

†Max Lilienthal (1815–1882) was appointed by the Tsarist authorities to tour the major Jewish communities in order to persuade Russian Jews to accept the crown schools. For information on Lilienthal and the entire experiment, see *The Golden Tradition*, ed. Lucy Dawidowicz (New York, Holt, Rinehart, and Winston 1967), pp. 28-32, 148-153, and further references there.

day and night, men recited Psalms, wept, and fasted. Even the *cheder*-children fasted. Women went to the cemeteries to measure graves and pour out rivers of tears. It was a sorrowful summer! Even the few Gentiles in the shtetl were affected. The Gentiles and Jews lived peacefully together, depended on one another for their livelihoods, took an interest in one another's affairs, and shared each other's sorrows and joys. If there was a wedding in a Jewish family, Gentile friends would send gifts: a fatted hen, a few dozen eggs, a loaf of bread, a honeycomb, some fruits or vegetables, whatever they could afford, and at similar occasions the Jews did the same. It was therefore only natural that the general dejection of the Jewish community should affect the Gentiles, and make them wonder what the weeping was all about.

"Ritzka, do you know why our Jews are crying so much?"

"They're afraid the demon will get them."

"No, Ritzka, that can't be it. There are still two or three months before their Yom Kippur. Look, here comes Chaika. Let's ask her."

"Wait, Chaika! What are you so upset about? Why all this commotion?"

"Oi, veh, Mikita! A terrible thing . . . I'm in a hurry! Here comes Berke—ask him, he'll tell you," Chaye-Grune answers, rushing off to the cemetery.

"Stop, Berke, listen! What's up? What are the Jews crying about?"

"Oi, oi, my friends! This is a time of trouble for us. They're going to snatch our children away . . . into their schools!" Berke stopped and began to explain to the Gentiles in their own language as best he could about the schools, which, according to his description, were very strange institutions indeed. The Gentiles shook their heads sympathetically, crossed themselves, and spat three times over this unfortunate event.

The Jews fasted and rent the heavens with prayer and supplication, but at the same time they didn't stand by idly waiting for a miracle; they also employed the trusty old device of marrying off their children. It was a period of panic. The marriage brokers, God's own agents, spared no effort, laboring long and hard, out of pure devotion to the Jewish people, to arrange marriages between little boys and girls. Why? So that in the event, God forbid, that the decree of the schools came to pass, the entire Pale of Jewish settlement would be devoid of children; only householders would be found. To prevent fathers from demanding inflated bride-prices for their daughters, someone started a rumor to the effect that the girls were to be taken away for forced labor in the distant colonies. If Shloymele escaped whole, and was not married off during the panic, the hand of God must have been at work: Shloymele's predestined bride was simply not in town at the time, and no human device is of avail against God's decree. What other explanation could there be? His mother was very anxious, and even though his father grimaced in disgust at the very idea, in the end he would have gone along, because in such matters a woman's will is iron. Nor would Shloymele have objected, had things come to that; quite the contrary, he would have been delighted. First, why should he be worse off than all the other boys his age? Why should they have brides and not he? How he envied the boy who became a bridegroom! True, this bridegroom didn't yet have fuzz on his face, and still got whipped in *cheder* like all the others, but yet, he seemed to grow more manly, treating his playmates with condescension; after all, in a short time, he would be a father himself. Secondly, Shloymele was entranced by the very idea of having a bride. What a delightful thought: I have a bride . . . This bride is mine . . . . "I am my lover's and my lover is mine!" One should bear in mind that Shloymele was of that different world, a man of ancient Jerusalem, where marriage between children had been an everyday occurrence. Furthermore, he had been studying the Talmudic laws regulating marital relations from childhood, and knew the facts of life very well. On top of that, he had a powerful imagination, a poetic spark, and this spark sometimes burst into flame, scorching his heart in the process. . . .

However it may be, Shloymele didn't marry during that period, and it worked out for the best, for in due time the panic proved to have been unfounded. Boys were not forced to go to the schools, girls were not seized for labor in the colonies, *cheder* and *cheder*-teachers continued as before, nothing changed. To be sure, schools for Jews were established in some big cities, but no harm resulted: only a handful of pupils attended them, all children of the lowest class—hardly even people. Lilienthal too seems to have disappeared, and he and his gang were forgotten, as was the whole matter of the schools. Shloymele would not have heard further of them had it not been for the following incident:

One fine summer day, an old gray-haired Jew arrived in Kapulie, a short man with a belly and an affable face. Word got around that an important visitor was in town, "Reb Nochem of Rozev has come to say goodbye!" And everyone understood what that meant.

After Reb Nochem of Rozev, a widower, gave away his youngest daughter, he made up his mind to go to die in the land of Israel. But since a man, while waiting to die, must eat, and since a Jew, obliged to remarry, is in need of money, Reb Nochem did what other Jews do under similar circumstances—he spent several years wandering from town to town throughout the Jewish diaspora "to say goodbye" and collect donations, trying, if possible, to get promises of annual donations in perpetuity. This way of making a living by saying "goodbye" is regarded by Jews as a perfectly respectable one. A man who is going to the land of Israel to die is on a higher level than ordinary beggars, idlers, people whose houses have burnt down, and outranks even abandoned wives. Such a man is thought of as a candidate for Jerusalem, he already exudes the fragrance of the sacred land of Israel. Reb Nochem made the rounds for several years, and his labor was not, God forbid, in vain. Someone would invite him home for dinner, someone else for supper, and each would press a coin into his hand in parting. In return for this, Reb Nochem made various promises: he promised one man he'd pray at the grave of Rabbi Meir the miracle-worker, and another he'd send him some dirt from the land of Israel . . . nor did Reb Nochem neglect Kapulie, where he had acquaintances and a few distant relations. One fine summer day he came there to say goodbye.

On summer nights the people of Kapulie usually ate supper by moonlight, when there was a moon, and when there was none, they supped by the light of a penny candle. The meal was over with quickly, and then good night—to bed, though sometimes they did take a little air outdoors. But one beautiful moonlit summer night there was a change in this routine in Reb Chayim's house. The table was neatly set, and brass candlesticks were lit as if on a holiday. This was in honor of Reb Nochem of Rozev, whom Reb Chayim had invited home for supper. They sat long at the table talking about the Wailing Wall and the Cave of Machpela,* about the Mount of Olives and the Tomb of our mother Rachel and about other sacred ruins and tombs, concluding with a discussion of figs and dates and

---

*The Cave of Machpela at Hebron is popularly held to be the burial place of the patriarchs and their wives.

pomegranates, vines and grapes and carobs. Everyone at the table listened intently, eyes shining with delight. Reb Nahum told one story after another, as if he had just returned from the Holy Land where he had seen everything with his own eyes; his listeners looked upon him lovingly and respectfully, taking in every word. It seems so simple to say, the land of Israel, Jerusalem. It would seem to be a land like any other, a city like any other, the same earth, dirt, refuse, and mud as everywhere else—but no! It's somehow different. The difference can't be expressed in words; it's not substantial, but spiritual, you have to sense it in your heart.

From these exalted themes, the conversation moved to more mundane matters. After all, Reb Nochem had been around a little, saying goodbye to a goodly number of Jews, and so he had gotten to see and hear a good deal. In this part of the conversation, Vilna played the main role, as the most interesting city on earth. Reb Nochem spoke with pride, "ai, ai!" of its renowned rabbis, powerful leaders, and fantastically wealthy businessmen; of its tiny synagogues, yeshivas, and the poor boys who studied in them. Then he spoke with lowered voice, "oi, oi!" of the harlots that are to be found in an alley there, where pious people are afraid to walk at night. Finally, he inveighed against some people called "Berliners," "oh dear, may the Lord preserve us," the same Jews that were involved in the "schools," Lilienthal's gang: in the privacy of their own homes, unobserved by other people, they sat bare-headed and ate without washing. Their whole doctrine was "language" and rhyming verses in high-flown Hebrew. It was rumored that their most eminent leader ate candlewicks wrapped in bread, and stuck a tallow candle into his kasha before eating it. . . .* "Some creatures these are," Reb Nochem concluded with a sigh.

Shloymele could imagine the harlots that Reb Nochem had spoken of. They were probably versions of the evil "husks," the Liliths and Sirens about whom he had already heard many horrifying stories. The people of Vilna were certainly well advised to avoid those desolate alleys at night. But how could he understand the Berliners, who were neither demons nor spirits, but real, live Jews, bareheaded Jews who ate without washing. . . . Was it possible—Jews without hats? Eating without washing? Were the Berliners crazy, or merely insane? Didn't they know what awaited them in

*Eating "candlewicks with bread" is an expression signifying ostentatious heresy: the candle was made of non-kosher fat.

Gehenna: pitch, fire and brimstone, and whips made of red-hot iron! But future punishment aside, how was it possible to conceive of a Jew without a hat? Yet the authority for these stories was Reb Nochem, who was "saying goodbye," who was on his way to the Land of Israel, and such a man had to be believed. So Shloymele believed this story, and from then on the name Berliner signified for him a Jew without a hat, a Jew who doesn't wash, a Jew who eats wicks wrapped in bread.

CHAPTER 9

Shloymele was now eleven years old and having exhausted Lipe Ruvens's teaching, came under his father's tutelage. "Lilmod ule-lamed," to study and to teach others, particularly one's own sons, is a commandment of the Torah, and every Jew prays for the opportunity to fulfill it. Reb Chayim was punctilious in its observance, setting aside an hour or two each day, no matter how busy he was, to study Talmud with his two elder sons and their friends. He followed this custom from the time his sons left *cheder* until their weddings, continued it with his daughter Leah's husband and his friends for a while after the marriage, and with Shloymele now that his time had come. After the morning service they stayed in the synagogue, where his father would teach him a chapter or two of Mishna. After breakfast, Shloymele would sit at home in a quiet alcove studying the lesson his father had assigned him. Later in the day, or at night, whenever his father could break away from his affairs, he would recite this lesson to him. Sometimes his father even woke him before dawn and took him to the synagogue for an extra hour or two of study.

It was not easy for Shloymele to rise before daybreak out of a deep, sweet sleep; but once up and out of bed, he was exhilarated by the early walk to the synagogue, and the study hours before dawn. For the Jew, night is a time of marvelous imaginings. The workings of Divinity and the fascinating ancient legends move him to the very heart, melt him with feelings of holy warmth.

It is said that at midnight when a breeze blows from the north, the angels change watches in heaven. The north wind prods the angel Gabriel who utters six loud cries, and opens the judgment book to read aloud all that men have performed on earth that day. The wind goes on to nudge the rooster, who crows on earth just as Gabriel cries aloud in heaven. At that very moment, God descends through three-hundred-ninety heavens to stroll through Paradise in the company of the souls of the righteous. Groups of seraphim and cherubim run ahead singing:

> Lift up your heads, O ye gates!
> And be ye lifted up, ye everlasting doors,
> That the King of glory may come in!

The trees of Paradise sing too, offering Him their fragrant perfumes. Now the King of Glory has arrived—Hush! Angels stand ranked before Him, trembling and quaking in silence. Filled with compassion, God looks around at the souls of the righteous in Paradise, and shakes His head. Suddenly He lets out a great cry, and roars like a lion; He mourns and weeps for the destruction of His Temple, for the desolate city of Jerusalem, for Zion, His widow, and for His children, the Jews, who are in exile—and two hot tears fall from His eyes into the great ocean.

So does God weep in his heaven three times every night, and pious Jews, hearing His cry, are unable to sleep. They get up from their beds to say the *Tikkun Khatzot** prayers, and to pour out their souls before their merciful Father in heaven, feeling, at that moment, an extraordinary mixture of pleasure and pain.

Shloymele walks along the street before dawn. The town is deep in sleep, the moon and stars stand at their heavenly posts. It seems to him that there is a lot of activity up there: the light breeze that touches his face is the gentle north wind caressing the angels' wings, the same wind that in olden days brushed over the fiddle hanging above King David's bed, and played songs of divine sweetness; the tree rustling in the garden is a rustling tree in Paradise; the cock crowing is a herald of the angel Gabriel. If his head grows damp with dew it is from the tears of God, crying over His exiled

---

*Tikkun Khatzot: midnight prayers, including a confessional, Psalms 79, 102, 137, and dirges for the Temple. The custom of midnight prayer was instituted by kabbalist circles in Safed in the sixteenth century and was practised widely in Eastern Europe in the following centuries.

children. . . . Shloymele's emotions are heightened, his imagination is inflamed, his heart full of holy longings; once in the synagogue, he throws himself wholeheartedly into his studies, and sings out the lesson in a resounding tune.

After leaving the *cheder*, Shloymele found his life slowly changing. He was now somewhat freer to linger in the actual world. His mind became a little clearer; he looked around and noticed things that he had no doubt seen before, but which had looked different, or which had formerly won from him only a passing glance. Before, like a clay *golem*, he could stand and he could see but with no idea of where he stood or what he was seeing. As if the world in which he lived wasn't already narrow enough, he had restricted it further. Of all the streets in his little town, he knew only the street of the synagogue; of all its buildings, only the *cheder*, the study-house, and the synagogue; of all the people only the Jews, and not even all of them, but only those he met in his own study-house. That was world enough for him, and it never occurred to him to feel hemmed in. The ancient sages were right when they said that this world is only a passageway to the next; what difference should it make to a Jew, even a grown-up Jew with a beard, if the passageway was a bit cramped, and not very pretty? You hunch over and pretend not to notice, you put up with it during the short time you have to stay in this temporary home. If you really want to learn how to make do, look at the worm, who lives out his whole life in a clump of dirt and doesn't seem to mind. So who needs this world and all its pleasures?

Now, however, Shloymele began to look around like a man waking from sleep; the light dawned and everything seemed new, as if he were a freshly hatched chick. The town was perched on a high mountain. Besides the street of the synagogue, there were others, also inhabited, even some non-Jewish streets, that were perhaps neater and prettier (may God forgive his saying so!), with gardens, trees, and vegetable patches. The green valleys stretching into the distance offered a fine view of gardens, fields, and thickets of nut trees; ponds and marshes overgrown with grasses, reeds, and willows, with running springs, and swarms of wild geese and other marsh birds. Beyond the valleys were other mountains, fields, and forests, extending into the distance as far as the eye could see. Shloymele was entranced by the sight.

Still later, Shloymele became aware that the town in which he had been born and raised belonged to Count Wittgenstein, and that Jews were only tax-paying tenants; that the local Gentiles were respectable householders just like the Jews, perhaps even more so. From where, then, did the town's sanctity derive, and why was it called in Hebrew "The Holy Community of Kapulie?"* True, the market and the shops, the merchants and middlemen, the taverns and inns, were all Jewish; but the land, and the fields round about the town—all belonged to the Gentiles! There was proof of this in the nuts and blackberries which Jews with pots and jars came to the forest to pick, trembling lest "Esau" suddenly grab the pots from their hands and give them a good beating into the bargain. Any pleasure they may have had was ruined; the forest with its lovely trees and fragrant vegetation was only a source of terror. If a leaf fell to the ground, their hands flew to their throats in fear; if a bird chirped, their hearts pounded. Everyone intoned a silent prayer, as though he were alone in the desert. . . .

Shloymele also discovered that there were Jews who neglected the study of Talmud, who concerned themselves with quite other matters, and yet managed to live and prosper. He had thought that the whole world of Jews was dedicated only to study, and to finding clever new interpretations of sacred texts; that one Jew only wanted to know of the other: "Which tractate are you studying? How many pages have you learned?" But he saw that it wasn't so. At first he was pained by his discovery, but on further reflection he grew resigned, reasoning that even this kind of Jew must have some place in God's plans.

As for the source of these new insights, it was, of course, Satan, the Evil Impulse himself. Even a child knows that man has two impulses, one for good and one for evil, the only question being which is the more powerful in his nature, which is the more garrulous, the shrewder, the more calculating, which knows better how to ingratiate himself and to manipulate. Shloymele's acquaintance with his good and evil impulses began as soon as he was a little freer to break away from that other world and enter the real one. In that world, where there are teachers, assistants, overseers, and all kinds of guardians to instruct and direct, to implant their wisdom and

---

*Kehila Kedosha, or Holy Community, was a traditional formula used in religious documents when referring to a Jewish city or township.

morals in one's heart, there is no need for the tempters of good and evil. But Shloymele's very first step in this world revealed the nature of his Evil Impulse and foretold what would later become of him. . . .

Shloymele was a passionate boy. He had a poetic spark, which the Evil Impulse shrewdly fanned into a flame, arousing his love for the beauties of nature—a clever device for alienating him from that rigid, dusty world of learning. He approached Shloymele deviously, masking his cunning with pious words: "Boy! Lift up your eyes and admire the miracle of God's creation—the starry sky, the rainbow, the drops of dew sparkling on the grass in the garden. Hear God's voice in the thunder, lightning, and the storm wind, in the soft rustle of the breeze, and in the humming of the bees, beetles, and gnats!" And Shloymele gave in, interrupted his study to look at everything, exclaiming, "How lovely the world is!" As days went by, the Evil Impulse drew him out to the green fields and to the forests, thick with foliage: "Come my friend," it said to him. "Come take a walk with me!" And Shloymele sneaked out of his room and went out to greet the lovely world of nature like a bridegroom going out to greet his bride. The bride smiled at him, murmured from among the whispering sheaves of grain, beckoned to him in the waving boughs of trees and in shafts of light breaking through the forest thicket. She showed him her jewels and finery, enticed him to stretch out on a grassy carpet and rest his head on an embroidered pillow of moss, caressed him with a warm, gentle breeze, fondling the locks of his hair and kissing him, to the wondrous accompaniment of her lovely choir. The nightingale raised his magnificent voice in song, and the canary's chant was answered by a chorus of trills, chirps, and flowing melodious runs. From the meadow came the bleating of sheep, the neighing of horses, the lowing of cattle. Birds danced on the treetops, butterflies in all their colorful finery fluttered about in the sky, crickets and grasshoppers jumped in the tall grass. What joys the world had to offer! Shloymele was filled with emotion, his heart melted with the sheer joy of it all. Had his natural talents received the proper training, his emotions would have expressed themselves in poetry or drawing or music. But of these arts he knew nothing, he knew nothing but Bible and Talmud; so he would pour out his soul at such moments in joyous renditions of the Sabbath songs, and the psalms of hosanna and praise.

CHAPTER 10

Although nature may be foolishness, it is still a foolishness to be tolerated. The simple, pious denizens of the study-house are right in asserting that a Jew has no business wasting time on it, but something that is not fit for a grown-up Jew, who has a wife and children to support, may nevertheless be permissible for a boy. "Go ahead, son, take your walks outdoors with this so-called 'nature' of yours, loll about on the ground, lie back on the grass and admire a beetle, a ladybug, a bird! You're still just a foolish boy, after all. But remember there's a limit to everything. Don't forget, you little whippersnapper, that a Jewish boy has to study Torah. Remember that a Jewish boy should keep his mind on the Talmud. The problems of 'An Egg Laid on a Holiday,' and 'Marriage Contracts' are still with us." Had Shloymele kept his activities within reasonable limits, his walks could have been tolerated; but he wasn't careful, and sometimes spent so long in the fields that he was late for dinner. His father was too preoccupied to notice; business kept him from dining with his family except on Sabbath and holidays. As for his mother, she was busy with housekeeping. Once, when she did scold him and threatened to tell his father, Shloymele assumed an expression of innocence and said that he had spent the time studying in the women's gallery of the synagogue.

It was only after Shloymele had progressed quite far in idleness, in taking long walks, and in telling lies, that his Good Impulse awoke from its slumber and gave him a proper dressing down: "It's enough that you neglect Torah, and twiddle your thumbs all day, now you've become a liar too! And whom do you deceive? Your own mother, the mother who bore you! Gehenna is too good for the likes of you!"

Shloymele was in mortal dread of Gehenna, being well acquainted with the Jewish Hell from *The Chastising Rod** and other pietistic works. They described the seven types of hell-fire in which wretched sinners are fried, the furious destroying angels with their iron rods, and the streams of fire and brimstone, everything in

---

*The Chastising Rod (Shebet Musar) is a moralistic book by Elijah ben Abraham Shlomo Hacohen, written in 1726, stressing the punishments that await sinners.

exact detail, as if the authors had actually been there and seen it in person. Terrible, terrible was Gehenna—how could one escape its torture?

Shloymele did penance. He prayed and begged God for mercy, promising to abandon his evil ways and become a proper Jew, devoted only to Torah and utterly oblivious to the world.

But resolutions are more easily made than kept. If a man is unfortunate enough to have a sensitive nature or a taste for beauty, it cannot simply be brushed aside by an act of will. If, through Satan's evil offices, he takes pleasure in the material splendors of God's world, then books of pious admonitions cannot render them ugly and hateful, but may only increase his love for them, and attract his soul toward them like a magnet. The Evil Impulse assumes all kinds of lovely forms and shapes with which to lead a man astray—more than enough. "If you don't care for this, my friend, try something else. If you aren't satisfied with this, or with that or the other thing, Shloymele, here is Fradl—a fine and charming girl to tempt you."

Fradl was a young girl, about Shloymele's age. Her parents were respectable people, distant relatives of Reb Chayim, who had moved to Kapulie several years earlier. Fradl often came to play with the children in Reb Chayim's house, where her beauty and sweet disposition endeared her to everyone. At first Shloymele took no particular notice of her, she was just a girl called Fradl, but suddenly, out of nowhere, he was struck by her perfect loveliness—and he fell in love! There was a pounding in his heart, the blood coursed hotly through his body, his face flushed and paled in rapid succession. He yearned to gaze into her eyes, but—Ah, Lord of the World, Thou standest in the way! To look at the face of a woman is a sin, and he had sworn never to sin again! The Evil Impulse tried to make him break his vow by arguing that God relaxes the rules in cases of genuine romance, but Shloymele resisted with admirable stubborness. "No, I won't! You can't make me!" Just as he was saying this, he looked up, as if inadvertently, and got a glimpse of her, just a tiny glimpse; then he looked again, and then for a little longer, until gradually his fear of Heaven relaxed, leaving only his fear of man. He was now in terror of being seen; if even a single onlooker realized what was on his mind he would die of shame. Like a thief, he was afraid to look around, suspicious of everyone, fearful that someone might guess what was going on in his mind; he felt transparent, as if all his thoughts and feelings were visible from outside.

But his fears were in vain. Even had it been possible to see into his heart, no one would have had the least understanding of his thoughts. Love is not the kind of thing the Jewish mind can grasp. Love and lovers are not to be found among Jews, especially not in those days, and certainly not in a small town like Kapulie, and in a respectable family at that! "Charm is deceitful and beauty is vain," says the Bible, and romance doesn't last long either. To build one's family life and personal happiness on such a foundation is like building a house on chicken legs: "Today you are a blossoming rose, tomorrow you will wilt; today I lust for you, and tomorrow for someone else, so get lost." Marry and bring children into the world—that, according to Jewish belief, is God's command. You love your wife and honor her because she is your wife, mistress of your household and mother of your children, and you provide for them—that is the sacred duty to which a Jew devotes his whole life. That is the source of Israel's strength, the force for its survival, the support of our ancestors and ourselves in time of trouble. When life is dark and bitter, when a Jew's lot is nothing but misery, he finds light and joy in his own home with his wife and children. Love, that fragile soap-bubble that bursts at the slightest puff of wind, was unknown to our ancestors. And even among us moderns, it wouldn't occur to anyone that love might afflict a child. Kids are kids—boys, girls, what's the difference?

A grown-up, in Shloymele's situation, would have found it impossible to keep his secret. It would have shown in his face, his speech, his general behavior. Ordinary passion is a kind of fire, which consumes itself as it rages, afterwards turning to ashes and smoke. But Shloymele's love was pure, and sufficient unto itself; a spark of that divine fire that burned in the bush and was not consumed; a spiritual radiance, a longing after beauty: the beauty of the sky, red with dawn, when the morning star appears; the beauty of the budding rose; the beauty of young, red lips, of gentle smiles and warm glances when lovers' eyes meet. This love is the "eternal light" in the hearts of poets, those beloved of God, which inspires them to expression of prayer, or silent tears, poured out in the presence of God alone.

Who knows? It may have been as a reward for the purity of his love that Shloymele was protected by a miracle, and his secret was not revealed.

The Sabbath of Comfort after Tisha b'Av* is a traditional feast day for Jewish children of the shtetl. A week or even two weeks in advance, the children form groups and arrange to get together on that particular Sabbath to feast on whatever food they can collect, and one of them is elected to be in charge of the contributions. During the intervening period, each child brings whatever he can beg or steal. Everything is accepted, no questions asked. One brings a bit of cake, a green apple, a stolen carrot from the bunch put aside for carrot-pudding; another brings a large cucumber and half an egg saved from his lunch. A thin slice of bread, a radish, an onion, or a herring tail are also welcome.

On one such Sabbath of Comfort after the afternoon nap, sounds of a boisterous good time were heard in the street in front of Reb Chayim's house. Some of the boys and girls had black mustaches from the cooked blackberries they had eaten, while others had puffy cheeks and scratched noses as evidence that they had distinguished themselves in the inevitable battles among those dissatisfied with their portion. They have hands, thank God, and nails too, these children; and God certainly didn't shortchange the Jews when he gave out noses; so they did the natural thing—fought and scratched each other a little. But only a little, for the day is short, and there's a lot of playing to be done, and if not now, when?

Fradl was playing with the others. That day she was looking especially pretty, and Shloymele couldn't keep his eyes off her.

On a bench in front of the house, the housewives of the neighborhood sat together, among them Sarah, Fradl's mother Gitl, and the renowned Lebtsiche. They weren't idle, God forbid, but talked and talked, each one pouring out all that was in her heart. One enormous pregnant woman with yellow blotches on her cheeks complained of pressure on her abdomen, which she attributed to the Sabbath stew she had eaten at dinner. She was sweating profusely, and fanning herself with her apron, crying: "Oi, for a drink of cold water!" There was a spasmatic woman, yawning something awful, spitting and wiping her nose; and another, all skin and bone, and still hoarse from the Tisha b'Av prayers, who gasped and coughed as she struggled to speak to her neighbor, sticking out her tongue in a futile attempt to catch her breath. A fine-looking housewife with watery eyes without lashes was examining the scalp

*The mid-summer fast day of Tisha b'Av is followed by *Shabbes Nakhamu*, the Sabbath of Comfort, when the weekly portion read in the synagogues is the passage from Isaiah beginning, "Comfort ye, O my people. . . ."

of a child in her lap, consulting with her neighbors as to what salve would be best for it. Lebtsiche was so busy she didn't have a moment to spare. There were many women, after all, and she had to say a word to each and every one, and to spice her conversation with stories, with no pause for reflection. Besides, God gave her eyes as well, which wanted to do their own work—to look around in every direction so as not to miss anything going on before or behind. With so much to do, no wonder that Lebtsiche got her stories mixed up, and had to rely on the ability of each listener to untangle from the confusion whatever applied to herself:

"For God's sake, don't sit on top of me. I remember, when the preacher's tongue got caught in his throat, my grandfather, may he rest in peace, said, 'Be quiet, and don't try to force it out'. . . . When gas gives you pressure in the abdomen, God forbid, open your mouth and bring it up. 'The nose is a sewer pipe,' my grandmother used to say, may she rest in peace. Get hold of it and give it a good picking! Well, well, he's got hold of her! He chased her and got her, fine boy!"

This confused stream of words was addressed to the pregnant woman, to the woman wiping her nose, and to Shloymele chasing after Fradl, whom Lebtsiche had noticed as she spoke.

"Oi, Gitl, I can't stand it another minute!" Lebtsiche said, leaning toward Fradl's mother. "Your Fradl is so cute! You can't look at her face any more than you can look straight into the sun!"

"Don't give her the evil eye!" answered Gitl, breaking off her conversation with two other women.

"Tfoo, tfoo, tfoo," Lebtsiche spat three times, twisting her nose and gesturing at the spasmatic. "Just look at her yawn and spit! . . . When she would charm away the evil eye . . . my grandmother, I mean . . . I was such a pretty, chubby little girl—everyone used to chase after me. Then all of a sudden . . . Listen, Sarah—you must remember this," she interrupted herself abruptly, turning toward Shloymele's mother. "Look at your boy over there! He chases Fradl like a bull . . . what do you think? A nice match . . . may Yachne-Sosye give you a *mazl tov* soon! Remember my words."

"What nonsense, Yachne-Sosye! They're still children!"

"Come on, Sarah, you must remember what happened during the panic. How old do you think I was then, when I was married? My husband was about eight or nine years old, or maybe less—a little boy!"

"If Fradl had been around a few years ago, at the time of the panic over the schools, it might have been worth talking about. It probably wasn't meant to be, so let's not talk foolishness."

"Yachne-Sosye hasn't gone blind yet. . . . I see, I see!" The last four words were addressed to the woman with watery eyes, who paid Lebtsiche the same homage of attention as all the others, and pushed her child's head right under her nose for her opinion. Lebtsiche examined it like an expert, blowing on it gently, and launching into a long story related to the case, meanwhile letting the subject of Shloymele drop.

So Shloymele was saved by a miracle. Were it not for this story, Lebtsiche might have ruined him by her gossip, as she had once damaged the reputation of their household cat.

CHAPTER 11

You can imagine the appetite a boy has for "The Egg Laid on a Holiday" once the Evil Impulse has given him a taste of the pleasures of this world. Try to retrace your steps and return to that bygone age, to that strange, remote territory, when you see right in front of your eyes God's lovely beckoning landscape. Shloymele's mind was no longer given over with the same enthusiasm to the study of the Talmud. He continued to study his daily quota for his father, but as a duty to be gotten over with as quickly as possible so the rest of the day would be free for walking. He formed new habits and new friends, some on his level and some not—some younger, some older, it made no difference, as long as he enjoyed their company and felt at home in their presence.

On rainy, overcast days, when one tends to feel blue, Shloymele liked to go to the smithy and watch Isaac the blacksmith at his work. He would sit in a corner staring pensively into the dark interior. The patched leather bellows puffed hoarsely into the furnace, and with each puff, sparks leaped from the burning coals and danced in the air like demons. As Shloymele watched, the scene before him blended with the episode in the Bible in which Abraham sits miserably in the darkness. As he dozes off, the sun sets and just then a cloud appears, and a smoking furnace, with flames leaping outward. . . . The sparks flew up and Shloymele's imagination flew after them; all kinds of strange forms and faces seemed to dance among the sparks and scurry up the opposite wall. The forms kept shifting, melting into one another until at last Fradl's shining face appeared. He concentrated hard on her image, trying with all his might to get a clear look at her, until her face disappeared, and Isaac's took its place. The bellows creaked, and Isaac heaped coals on the fire to make it hotter; hurriedly he drew out of the flames a white-hot lump of iron, and using one hand to hold it on the anvil with his tongs, he hammered it with the other, while a stocky, broad-shouldered boy with a heavy hammer did the same from the other side. Isaac hammered once and the boy twice; Isaac turned the iron over, and the boy hammered it again, sending off a shower of sparks. There was plenty for Shloymele to see and much to hear in the smithy, since work goes better when it is accompanied by lively good-humored conversation, and there was no lack of talkers, thank God! Local townsfolk and people from outlying villages brought their blunt axe-blades, locks, a milk jug with a broken handle, horses to be shod, wagon wheels that needed new iron rims. . . . Isaac was a talkative person. He had an explanation for everything, and could always tell why something was this way and not otherwise. Why, for example, are the nostrils on the bottom of the nose, and not on top, when the upper air is purer and healthier than the lower air? He would raise the question earnestly, with furrowed brow, then, smilingly, provide his own answer: "It was clever of God to do it this way, so that rain drops don't run down into the nose." He would ask similar questions about the nature of the universe and God's conduct of the world, always providing an answer based on speculative research of his own, which demonstrated that so it had to be: God was right in whatever He did. The cat has sharp claws so it can climb up smooth walls. The horse has a tail so it can flick away flies from its back. Flies have wings so they can get away in a hurry. Isaac was not versed in Bible or Talmud, but this didn't prevent him from theorizing, or from acquiring the title of Isaac the Philosopher. Obviously, learning and thinking are two different things.

As fine as Isaac seemed six days a week in the smithy, expounding his theories in his torn leather apron, he was even more splendid on Sabbath eve and holidays in the synagogue courtyard. There he stood, in a silk caftan and a fur hat, like any well-to-do householder, lecturing to a circle of people, with one hand hooked in his sash. The circle grew bigger, drawing people as if by a magnet. The talk was first of vegetable stew, known as *tsimmis*, and an argument arose as to the meaning of the word; this led to a discussion of parsnips, in the course of which Isaac explained why parsnips lose their flavor after the very first thunder of the summer. Then he came around to nettles: why do nettles grow by themselves, although they are never sown? "Are you listening? It's precisely *because* they aren't sown that they grow by themselves. Just like fools. . . . Apparently God understands that the world needs them too. . . ." The bystanders enjoyed the monologue and laughed in amusement.

But the fun was at its best when Isaac and Leyzke, the town's other philosopher, engaged in debate. Leyzke was a village innkeeper who had moved to the town in his old age to be among Jews, pray in a synagogue, and observe God's law as He had decreed. Because of a blocked and slightly swollen nose, he wheezed heavily, and made a honking sound when he spoke; sometimes, when excited, he squeaked. Leyzke had some education, and had looked into the old Jewish philosophic books; he and Isaac were always arguing. Leyzke would call upon the authority of other philosophers: Aristotle, the authors of *The Shadow of the World, The Book of the Covenant,* * and the like; but he himself was not very inventive, and he had no opinions of his own. Isaac, on the other hand, knew nothing of Aristotle, but figured things out for himself, relying exclusively on his own powers of reasoning. Their most famous dispute was about cuppers' glasses: what makes the glasses stick to the patient's skin without falling off?

Leyzke said, "It works like this, gentlemen: the candlelight, shining into the glass, empties it, that is, the cup, of its air. Now, pay attention, gentlemen! It is an axiom, that nature abhors a vacuum; and since this is so, you hear, this being the case, the flesh is drawn to fill the empty space in the glass."

"Candlelight and emptiness-shmemptiness—what has that got to do with it?" Isaac smiled good-naturedly and grasped his beard. "And does Reb Leyzke think that the glass wasn't empty before the candle came along? Is air a substance? Prove it—just try lying down

* *The Shadow of the World* is a book of wisdom by the sixteenth-century Polish kabbalist, Mattathiah Delacruta; *The Book of the Covenant* is a compendium of medieval scholastic "natural philosophy."

and stretching out on air. You would fall, Reb Leyzke, you would fall and break your nose. And besides, what does it mean to say, 'the candle-light empties the glass of its air'?"

"I didn't make it up, the ancient sages said so!" Leyzke honked, a tinge of anger in his voice. "Aristotle says so, gentlemen, do you hear, Aristotle!"

"Oi-oi!" Isaac exclaimed. "Now he comes at me with Aristotle! And if Aristotle says so, so what? Is he suddenly a rabbi and a Talmudic authority?"

"But it says the same thing in Jewish books too, in our Jewish texts!" protested Leyzke, getting excited and beginning to squeak.

"All you know is what it says in some old book," Isaac replied calmly. "You're always running to your ancient authorities and letting them fight your battles for you. Now I've been standing in my smithy for a good many years, thank God. There's a fire burning there, a lot bigger than your candle, but nothing ever happens like what happens with the cupper's glass. How come?"

"Eh-eh, how can I talk to such a child?" said Leyzke resentfully, waving him off with a hand and walking away so as not to hear Isaac giving the crowd his own theory on the matter.

Isaac the blacksmith, a grown man, who supported his daughter and her scholarly husband, and who had already been presented by the couple with grandchildren, was in fact a child, a child such as you rarely find. After the scowling countenances of grown-ups, with their sighs and groans, their sour moralizing and lecturing, Isaac's friendly smiling face affected Shloymele like the bright sun emerging from behind dark clouds; his conversation and theories were as sweet to Shloymele as the stories and legends that sometimes follow a long and involved legal discussion in the Talmud. The Jewish child, who is expected to act like a full-fledged Jew before he has learned to walk, whose childhood flits by like a dream, leaving him a gloomy old man before his time, this child feels completely rejuvenated in the company of an affable adult who smiles, enchants him with stories, and acts very much like a child himself. But such grownup children are hard to find among us; their number is daily decreasing, and the time is not far off when they will disappear altogether. To Shloymele's good fortune, there were still two in the town in his time, Isaac the blacksmith and Hertzl Kailis the carpenter. Both had an influence on the boy, helping to keep alive in Shloymele's heart the spark of childhood.

Hertzl the carpenter was, like Isaac, a grown man with children. Like Isaac, he was thin and pale; but whereas Isaac was tall, Hertzl was short. Isaac was always calm and deliberate; he spoke in a scholar's unhurried, controlled monotone. But Hertzl was ebullient by nature; he got excited when he spoke and his voice would shift registers suddenly, ending in a shriek. He spoke in rapid, chopped phrases, finishing his sentences with a gesture or flick of the head. If anything displeased him he would explode, his every muscle seething and quivering. He had the volatile personality of a poet, and in fact it seemed as if there were trapped inside him an artist's spirit, restless as the mythical river Sambation,* desperately struggling to escape its prison and find expression in all kinds of handicrafts. He didn't practice carpentry simply to make a living, but for the pleasure of creating artifacts. He would laboriously decorate and ornament his productions, doing much more than was expected of him in order to make the work beautiful. . . . When he saw Lipe Ruvens's elaborate hanging for the Sukkah depicting all the animals and birds of Noah's ark, he immediately drew a series of pictures based on the Talmudic story of Rabbi Yossi,† who was standing in prayer amid the ruins of Jerusalem when he heard a voice from heaven cooing like a dove and saying: "Ah, me! I have destroyed my house and burned down my Temple and exiled my children among the nations!" The local connoisseurs couldn't get their fill of the picture, and praised it as being absolutely unique. The portrait of Rabbi Yossi was merely magnificent, but as for the dove, the cooing dove—words failed them.

Hertzl also played the fiddle. He didn't perform at weddings, because that was for the professionals, a Jewish musician named Feitl who played on weekdays and a Gentile musician named Kondrat who performed in the bride's home on the Sabbath before the wedding. Hertzl played at home whenever he felt like it, to please himself. Late of a summer's afternoon, when the cows had returned from pasture and lay, after milking, in the street; when yellow pillars of smoke rose lazily from the chimneys and women stood by their stoves cooking supper; when from somewhere in the distance came

*The legendary river Sambation is said to seethe with rocks six days of the week, resting only on the Sabbath.

†Reb Yossi Ben Khalafta, *Berachot* 3:1. This very popular Talmudic story is retold in many of the story collections, e.g., the *Mayse Bukh*, a book of Jewish tales and legends compiled in the sixteenth century.

the croaking of frogs, and insects whirred through the air—then Hertzl would pour out his soul in music, standing barefoot on the porch in front of his house, in his undershirt. Children with slices of bread and halves of boiled eggs in their hands gathered around him, stuffing their mouths, cocking their ears, gaping, and listening. He would sing along as he played, and amuse the children with his antics. He drew the bow across the strings and stopped abruptly, as if something were bothering him; another draw of the bow, and he was suddenly in a rage. No more fiddle, the performance was over. Hertzl was played out. And then the whole street reverberated with the sound of Hertzl's wild, drawn-out shriek. . . .

Hertzl had a vegetable garden and some fruit trees, which he had planted with his own hands. He was rumored to have a book of remedies, which had been passed down secretly in his family from father to son, containing descriptions of the properties of all the plants and herbs and their medicinal uses. Unfortunately, the family had been adjured with the most powerful oaths never to make use of it. Had it not been prohibited, Hertzl could have cured all the sick, and there would have been no more need of conjurers, peasant crones, or gypsies, with their spells and panaceas. In general, Hertzl's way of life was different from that of others in the town. His house never doubled as a tavern, as did the houses of his neighbors. In addition to the usual cows, he also had a pair of oxen, a horse, and a hired hand, a Gentile peasant named Trachim, whom he paid to work the fields he had inherited from his forebears. It goes without saying that he kept a dog too, the only Jewish dog in the whole town.

Only rarely did Hertzl come to the synagogue to pray. Not that he was a scoffer, God forbid, for he believed even in demons and spirits, and trembled in fear of them like any other Jew. So why didn't he go to synagogue? No particular reason; it just wasn't his way. If anyone else had missed so much as a single afternoon service, he would have had to answer to the whole town; but Hertzl could forego hundreds of services and no one ever complained. He was considered a kind of child, frivolous and immature. And besides, people were afraid of his shriek. When he did come to the synagogue, he would stand among the mischievous boys behind the pulpit, and stir up much talking, pushing, and shoving. The sexton would call for quiet, just for form's sake, and the fine citizens would pound on their reading stands crying, "Ei-ei!", their faces frozen in disgust.

Hertzl was everything that Shloymele needed. The two of them, years apart in age, shared many of the same feelings. The nameless dissatisfaction and longing in Shloymele's heart, which seemed to find no counterpart among the grown-ups of the town, laden as they were with troubles and responsibilities, were matched in Hertzl Kailis the carpenter. And as events were to show, the Evil Impulse could have found for Shloymele no better friend.

CHAPTER 12

Isaac the blacksmith and Hertzl the carpenter were considered respectable householders, a distinction which set them apart from the town's other craftsmen in the same way that some Jews in those days were set apart from their fellow-Jews because they had received a medal, or in later times because they had gained the privileged status of "citizen," or in our day because they have achieved the rank of "counsellor." At that time, government officials would pay such Jews the honor of eating fish at their houses on Sabbath, just as nowadays great ministers condescend to accept invitations to their banquets and even dance with their wives and daughters. Yes, miracles do happen: craftsmen become burghers, Jews become human beings. . . .

This is no idle metaphor! Craftsmen were about as despised by the Jews as the Jews were by Gentiles. Nowadays, craftsmen aren't actually hated; the general public treats them with all due respect and friendship, except for the high and mighty, who treat them with the same duplicity and deceit with which they treat everyone. There was a time, however, when craftsmen were badly abused, especially in places like Kapulie, where prestige depended on scholarship and lineage. Many a marriage was called off because of the discovery of a tailor or shoemaker in the pedigree of one of the parties. Among the better families, where pedigree was the most important consideration in arranging a match, all the rabbis, scholars, ritual slaughterers, cantors, and idlers from past generations would be dug up, and the craftsmen, if there happened to be any, buried. A tavern owner, innkeeper, storekeeper, or moneylender was also thought respectable; in fact they made excellent in-laws, and their opinion carried weight everywhere from the bathhouse to the synagogue. This was because hardly any other decent professions were open to the Jews, whereas these occupations could provide for the practitioner's own needs and sometimes for those of others as well—with a handout, a favor, or an influential word dropped in the right place. Their frequent business dealings with the rich, with noblemen, and government ministers, enabled such people to intercede for individual Jews or for the whole community in time of crisis. More than once, a community escaped disaster through the intervention of an innkeeper or moneylender (what is now called a banker). The village innkeeper's house was open to indigent guests, who were given food and drink and a handout as well. Innkeepers usually betrothed their daughters to the most promising yeshiva-boys. They were thus to their generation what the Israelite tribe of Zebulun was to the tribe of Issachar in olden times: Zebulun engaged in trade to support the tribe of Issachar, whose members were thereby freed to study Torah.

The pillars of the community kept the craftsmen in their places, and discriminated against them in many ways. A laborer was not permitted to wear a silk caftan or a fur hat on the Sabbath. In the study-house, his place was in the last row of benches behind the pulpit. If he was summoned to the Torah, the reader would call him by the name of "friend," instead of the usual appellation of "master"; then they would read only three verses, the absolute minimum, unless he had been called up for the reading of the curses in Leviticus and Deuteronomy, in which case the whole passage was read, despite its length, and its contents wholeheartedly dedicated to him. When a meeting of householders was held to discuss community affairs, he was never invited, and his opinion never asked. For any trifling act of insolence, he was scolded or slapped, and sometimes publicly flogged. His children were seized and turned over for military service in place of a rich man's sons.

Even by their own standards the Jewish craftsmen were a lowly group in those days. The way in which they learned their crafts was faulty from the start, with predictable consequences. An apprentice had to serve his master for several years, and act as maid to his master's wife; he did menial jobs around the house, and got slaps and beatings for his trouble at whim, learning more of beatings than he did of his craft. He then became an incompetent craftsman, bitter and unhappy. To brace himself a bit, he would begin to drink.

When his hands were free, he took pleasure in beating others, not excluding his wife. Woe to the child unlucky enough to be apprenticed to such a master when his time came. This was the lot of orphans, poor children, abandoned waifs who had never gone to *cheder*, never learned to read properly—the commonest sort.

Yet despite everything, as lowly as their station was, there were among the craftsmen many intelligent and sensitive men, and some good-hearted, jolly paupers.

No matter how dilapidated the craftsman's house may have appeared from the outside, it could be lively and gay inside, when work was in progress. Itzik the tailor stands, for example, with an iron in his hand, pressing a garment he has made. He launches into a marching tune, pounding the iron in time to the music, and all the workers sitting around the table, stitching rapidly, join in, each to the best of his ability, working up into a rousing chorus of "King on High" from the Rosh Hashana prayers. Then someone begins to mimic the gloomy chant of the wedding jester at the ceremony of the veiling of the bride. Some of the boys imitate the melancholy accompaniment of the instruments, others, the sobbing of the women. The caterwauling rises in a mournful crescendo, and then breaks into a wedding dance. The boys aren't allowed to interrupt their work, of course, so they execute the dance in their places. Instead of wedding gifts, one gives his neighbor a pinch, one knocks off another's hat, and the ceremony concludes with hearty cries of *mazl tov* all around. Then the tailor's wife sets before them a big pot of steaming potatoes cooked in the skins, and it would be worth the price of admission to see the dispatch with which the potatoes are peeled, tossed into their mouths, and swallowed. Masterful performance! No one in the world eats hot potatoes as fast as tailors' apprentices or their counterparts in other trades. This is a skill they've had plenty of opportunity to learn, more's the pity, for potatoes are their staple diet.

Often, they sing songs of their own composition which then spread among the people and became known as "folksongs." Traveling from village to village, their songs acquire many foreign words with half-Yiddish, half-Slavic endings. The content varies widely, but love is the common theme. A Jewish girl employed as a scullery maid, for example, dreams of her lover; weeping, she recalls the happy hours they passed, walking, like a pair of doves, in forest thickets or fields of grain. Or an ordinary girl wishes she had a husband, and her whole soul goes out to him, as a child stretches its hands to embrace the moon. There are songs of a bride complaining about her cross mother-in-law; a wretched orphan of his foster mother; and songs of Jewish army recruits bidding farewell to their loved ones before going off to the service, perhaps never to return. Husbands part from their wives and children; youngsters, wrapped in cloaks twice their size, are carried off in the arms of old soldiers as they cry to their parents and brothers and sisters. These "wretched little orphans" are borne, like fallen leaves blown by the wind, to the cold and distant north, far from civilization, to live among crude peasants, to tend pigs, and to die, God alone knows where; their parents will never even know whether to mourn over them. . . . Some of the songs are bitter attacks on the rich, the leaders of the community, and religious authorities, in which the artisans vent their resentment over the misery and suffering they have to endure.

Plainly, the craftsmen harbored a poetic spark that refused to be extinguished, and held on to the freshness of youth; this explains why they consorted with children and why they remain friendly to writers and poets to this very day.

Isaac the blacksmith and Hertzl the carpenter had their ancestors to thank for having escaped the fate of ordinary craftsmen. They were considered of a better class because they came from good families, and were related to the finest people in town. Their fathers, who were men of substance, had bequeathed them houses in the market, the most desirable location in the town, and good seats at the eastern wall of the synagogue. They both were neighbors of Reb Chayim, Isaac's house adjoining to the right, and Hertzl's house to the left. The three neighbors were on good terms, and visited each other on family occasions and on holidays. Isaac's son, Meir-Itze, a fine boy who was good at whittling toys and Purim noisemakers, attended the same *cheder* as Shloymele. Hertzl's son, Ben-Zion, was a friend of Shloymele's older brother, and Reb Chayim taught him together with his own son, free of charge, for an hour or two every day, when he could take the time from his business. It goes without saying that Isaac and Hertzl wore silk caftans and fur hats on Sabbaths and holidays. The question then is: how did these sons of important and respected fathers happen to become artisans? People said: "An evil spirit (God protect us!) got into them when they were children, kept them from studying Torah, and muddled their minds with foolishness. Children they were and children they remained. The evil spirit never stopped muttering and mumbling inside them, and what became of them in the end? Nothing—craftsmen! Still . . . they are different from the others—after all, they came from good family!"

It was to these childlike old men that Shloymele's Evil Impulse led him. This was the last stage in his voyage out of the world of the past.

CHAPTER 13

Shloymele was fond of both Isaac the blacksmith and Hertzl Kailis the carpenter, but in the case of Isaac, it was not for the man's personality or his theorizing so much as for the atmosphere of his smithy. Hertzl, on the other hand, won Shloymele's heart for what he was, with all his eccentricities and mannerisms. Hertzl Kailis was himself a kind of smithy, always glowing, burning with passionate fire.

Shloymele divided his free time between the smith and the carpenter, according to the weather and season. During the rainy, muddy autumn or on cold, windy days, when the darkening sky donned an ugly spotted cloak that looked as if it had been patched and repatched with dark black clouds—at such times, Shloymele was drawn to the smithy, where he would squeeze himself into a corner among the discarded tools, and look quietly, thoughtfully, about him. The bellows would puff, the coals burst into flame, the iron glow, and sparks fly—while Shloymele was transported to realms of fantasy. From the blazing coals in the furnace, black eyes peered out at him. The flame, thrown upwards by the bellows, became a ladder reaching to heaven, on which the sparks flitted up and down like angels. The clanging hammers on the glowing iron were the locks breaking on enchanted palaces, freeing princesses from their long sleep. All the princesses were lovely, but the most resplendent of all was his Fradl, radiant as the morning star. . . . In such miserable weather, Shloymele's body would come and sit in a corner of the smithy, while his spirit soared to warm and lovely realms, where all was in blossom, and wondrous visions abounded.

But when the weather was mild and lovely, the skies clear, the sun bright—he was drawn outside, as it seemed, by every fiber of his being. At such times, he felt a greater kinship with Hertzl Kailis than with anyone else in town; his household smelled of country, the rich aroma of fresh fields. Who ever heard of a Jew, and a prominent householder to boot, having poultry and cattle, a horse, and a Gentile named Trachim to work in the fields, and, to top it all off, a dog? How does a Jew, who isn't expected to know anything more of nature than the *etrog,* permit himself such foolishness as to plant fruit trees in his garden? How does a Jew, who need only attend to the market, the synagogue, and his nap on Sabbath afternoons, come to frolic like a child and go off on long hikes in the woods?

Shloymele was at home in Hertzl's house, and found a good friend in Hertzl's son, Ben-Zion, Reb Chayim's former pupil.

Ben-Zion combined the qualities of a city boy and a country boy. He had had some education, and knew how to make sense of a page of Talmud, but he had no taste for study, devoting his energies instead to house and field. He was a quiet, kind-hearted boy, who preferred action to words. He and Shloymele understood one another instinctively. On a blazing summer day, for example, Ben-Zion sits on the porch of his house. The dog lies prone at his feet, panting from the heat, raising its head from time to time to stick out its tongue and—flick!—capture a fly. Nearby squats the hen, the chirps of her chicks sounding from under her outstretched wings. The market is deserted, with not a soul in sight. The cows are in the field, the children in *cheder,* and the grown-ups yawning at home or in the shop, dying for a drink of cold water. A cat scampers up a wall, stops halfway, and looks around trying to decide whether to continue upward or descend again. At just that moment, Shloymele slips like a cat from the house, having prepared his day's quota of study for the lesson with his father. He is drawn outside by a stubborn yearning, and his eyes peer into the distance, to the point where the sky touches the green line formed by the crests of the tall trees. His gaze lands on Ben-Zion, and in a moment Shloymele is beside him. Not a word passes between them. Ben-Zion winks agreeably, sniffs, rises from his chair and sets out for the woods, with Shloymele right behind. They are off on a long hike.

On the way they stop off in the family barn to check on the freshly mown hay. The air on the threshing-floor is delightfully cool, and the sweet odor of hay permeates the barn. Without a word, the two friends throw themselves down on the hay to stretch their limbs. They lie back watching the swallows fly in and out, chirping as they approach their nests under the straw roof. Little yellow mouths of naked chicks, begging for bread, extend to them in greeting.

Leaving the barn, the two friends come upon a wide expanse, with cultivated fields of grain stretching in all directions. The view is like a painting: the blend of white and red of sprouting buckwheat in a golden frame of wheat; blue flowers peeping out from among the corn; and God's little creatures swarming and flying about with a cheery buzzing sound. Ben-Zion casts his eye with particular satisfaction over the field of oats belonging to his family, then moves off in a different direction with Shloymele still behind him. They are both red as beets, enjoying their outing in silence. In a meadow, where some hobbled horses are grazing, a bonfire has been lit under a great willow tree and there Trachim sits roasting potatoes, adding fresh twigs from time to time to make smoke that will stave off the mosquitoes. One of the horses, recognizing his owner, raises his head, and whinnies an equine welcome. Ben-Zion returns the greeting with a slap on the back, and after delivering instructions to Trachim, continues on his way, with Shloymele behind him, until they reach the deep recesses of the great forest.

From the moment Shloymele first met the forest, he was in awe of it. As a child he had heard dreadful stories about it; it was said to be inhabited by highwaymen, wolves, bears, demons, and evil spirits. . . . The first time Shloymele entered the forest with his friends, his heart pounded; he peered anxiously in all directions, raising his finger to his lips at the least sound of a rustling leaf: "Hush!" Much later, walking with Hertzl and Ben-Zion and their dog, he grew accustomed to the forest. If they happened to meet Gentiles, they would exchange pleasant greetings; the dogs would lick and sniff one another and they would all go their separate ways. Nor were demons a very serious threat, for they were afraid of Hertzl Kailis, who knew how to ward them off with a magic charm. He used to tell how once the demons started a whirlwind in the forest in order to steal a haystack, but he threw a knife into the whirlwind, pronounced a charm from a manuscript that had been passed down secretly from father to son in his family, and drove them away forever.

Shloymele pictures the forest as a living organism, a kind of society. Thousands upon thousands of trees stand together in one place, the old trees like grandfathers and great-grandfathers, the young like children. Each one seems to stand alone, but at root they are united and draw their nourishment from the same source. Whenever a light breeze blows, they all begin to whisper, each leaning over to hear what the other has to say. The same spirit moves each to have its say, nodding its head for emphasis. The slightest rustle aimed at one reverberates among them all. And when, as sometimes happens, a mighty blast of the angry north wind strikes, they all make a great din to proclaim their troubles to the world. The forest rages, like waves of the ocean, and every living creature within its borders scampers fearfully to his cave or hole.

Shloymele knows the forest and has come to understand its temperament; having seen its unleashed fury in the storm, he approaches it with some trepidation, even when it is tranquil, even when, like a kindly host, it invites him to enter and rest in its shade, setting before him a repast of gooseberries and blackberries and gathering its resident choir to sing him sweet melodies. After their walk in the open fields, he sits with his friend Ben-Zion under a tree heavy with foliage, listening and watching with a mixture of awe and delight.

From the forest the two friends return to town toward evening and slip unnoticed into the study-house, as if nothing had happened, there to finish their day with the afternoon prayers.

By observing Hertzl Kailis at his household chores, Shloymele learned to set up a similar routine for himself. Diligently he tended his vegetable patch in the back yard, weeding between the rows, hoeing the radishes, onions, and cucumbers, and examining the vegetables ten times a day to see if they were yet fully grown. . . . For the pigeons he now kept, he prepared nests of straw in the attic, and he also kept song birds in a cage. He set a hen to hatching eggs in a basket under his bed, checking frequently to see if the chicks had appeared. It so happened that a particularly handsome turkey-hen was in the house just then, and the children prevailed on their mother to keep it for breeding instead of slaughtering it for Passover. In time, the turkey laid and hatched a dozen eggs, and Shloymele undertook to care for the chicks.

No denying that he did his work faithfully, devoting a good bit more of his time and energy to the chicks than his parents would have wished.

"You hear," said Reb Chayim to his wife, addressing her, as he invariably did, in the Jewish fashion, simply as "you" instead of by her name, "the turkey business is all your doing. You had to have turkey chicks, and the result is that your son neglects his studies and thinks of nothing but turkeys all day long."

"Very nice, it's all my fault, he says," Sarah answered resentfully. "As if I wanted the turkeys! Everybody felt sorry for the mother turkey: let's keep her! And whenever anything happens they all come running to me. I tell you, as I'm a Jewish woman, tomorrow I'm going to send for the slaughterer and let him slaughter the mother along with the chicks, if that's what you want."

"Don't get so angry," Reb Chayim said, more gently. "You can't say a word to her without her getting angry. What do you want to kill those poor little chicks for? Pity dumb animals!"

"So what do you want with me?" protested Sarah, still looking peeved, "If you're so full of pity, what are you coming to me about? . . ."

"Nothing at all," smiled Reb Chayim apologetically, trying to placate her. "I'm only saying that he pays far too much attention to the turkeys, and that he spends altogether too much time out of doors."

"I don't know what you want!" Sarah cried with tears in her eyes. "He wants the child to be cooped up in the house all day long. I don't have the heart to keep him from looking at the sunlight. I'll tell you what: you're his father; why don't you sit and study with him from morning to night, and keep an eye on him."

"Alright, alright!" Reb Chayim poked his wife with his finger and smiled so good-humoredly that she finally returned the smile and all was forgiven.

Shloymele wanted to be like Hertzl in every way—in his handiwork too. He studied Hertzl's picture of Rabbi Yossi and the voice from heaven that cooed like a dove, and tried to do some drawing himself, but without any luck. To himself and to others his excuse was that he lacked the right tools: woodwork requires a sharp knife, while the one he had won in the raffle was made of soft lead, and was inadequate. For drawing, he needed red and green paints. Clearly, it wasn't his fault if the work was less than perfect. Luckily, he did have some skill at making paper lanterns, carving wooden spoons, and doing fancy calligraphy on letterheads, with complicated curlicues that ended in the shape of a bird.

CHAPTER 14

Shloymele's path up to this time may not have been strewn with roses, but neither was it unduly hard: a straight road at least, without obstacles or pitfalls. But from this point on, the road became ever more crooked and bumpy, and thick with brambles. It led up steep hills, down deep valleys, and across many a dangerous chasm. The first stumbling blocks were communal troubles, a series of disasters that plagued the town of Kapulie.

The economic mainstay of Kapulie, the source of its renown among the Jewish villages of Lithuania, was its "Astrakhan" industry, and particularly its manufacture of cloth for women's kerchiefs. Astrakhan was a heavy material of a dark green color, sold by the arshin. * It was used mainly for lining, and for making caftans for the poor. The archives of Kapulie nowhere explain how it came to be called Astrakhan. The kerchief material was a thin, bleached linen, in length and breadth about the size of a handkerchief, and it too was produced by the local weavers. The women would wrap this white turban over their hairnet in such a way that two corners fell over the nape of the neck , where they looked like a pair of blintzes, with a second, smaller "fan" alongside each fold. Around their turbaned head a kerchief would then be wound like hoops of a barrel, twisted into a knot on the forehead and the ends drawn back and tucked in on either side near the ears. On the heads of pious old ladies, this knot stood right in the middle of the forehead, like a man's phylactery; younger women wore it modishly off to one side. Wives of well-to-do men wore silk, cashmere, or Turkish kerchiefs on the Sabbath and holidays, and printed wool kerchiefs, known as apple-kerchiefs, on weekdays. A bridegroom's parents would send both kinds of kerchief to the bride before the wedding, while the bride's parents sent the groom a fur hat.

Such was the finery of our grandmothers!

The kerchief was always kept starched and ironed. The work of smoothing and ironing a kerchief was performed by two women working together, thus: the women would stand as far apart as the length of the kerchief allowed, holding an edge in each hand so that

*Arshin: a Russian measure of length, equal to twenty-eight inches.

the kerchief was stretched out lengthwise between them. Into the hollow thus formed, a large, smooth ball of glass or iron was placed. One of the women lifted her arms a bit and the ball rolled down from her side to her partner's; the second woman repeated the motion sending the ball right back. In this way, the ball rolled back and forth until the kerchief was smooth.

It was the greatest fun in the world to watch two women smoothing kerchiefs. They stood so seriously facing one another, raising their arms with a jerk of the shoulders, their stomachs protruding, and their heads cocked to one side; they would make faces and glare, exchange poisonous smiles and sarcastic cracks. Anyone who had the chance to watch them in action had no need of theater.

The kerchiefs were finished by Gentile weavers in their own homes, and local Jewish businessmen would buy them up for cash and spools of new thread, each businessman dealing regularly with his group of weavers. These businessmen were generally young husbands who were still living with their in-laws or who still had some cash left over from the dowry. Reb Chayim's married sons supported themselves in this way. The kerchiefs were then sold to the great merchants who distributed them throughout the cities of Lithuania. They were very popular and sold well, providing a good income for the many Jews of Kapulie whose livelihood they were.

Business went on in the same way for generations, until a government ordinance, the Clothing Decree forbade Jewish women to shave their heads, and required that Jews, including Jewish women, dress like Germans.

Mercifully, the decree had not yet come into force in Kapulie, where men still wore sidelocks and fur hats, and women still shaved and covered their heads with kerchiefs as before. But in other towns the situation was shameful. Jewish men were donning hats! Jewish women were replacing their kerchiefs with "Lithuanian bonnets"—a kind of rag, if you will. No kerchiefs meant no business; and no business meant nothing to eat. Kapulie was laid flat by the blow. Spinners, weavers, small and big businessmen—all were hit by the decree. The tavernkeepers suffered, because if the weaver can't afford bread, he can't afford a drink either. And if spinners, weavers, tradesmen and tavernkeepers can't make a living, then the storekeepers, craftsmen and laborers are also in trouble, because who can afford to give them business? A new crop of paupers and beggars came into being. Bankrupt householders became *cheder*-teachers to support their children, and *cheder*-teachers proliferated like weeds. Soon there were more teachers than pupils. Times were very bad, and when things go badly, people become ill-tempered too, bickering and fighting, each one trying to snatch a morsel out of the other's mouth. The erstwhile peace and quiet of Kapulie was now gone.

Reb Chayim was also affected by the collapse of the kerchief market, for his married sons lost their means of support. Then, a brother-in-law who dealt in linen thread went bankrupt and fled, abandoning wife and child, and leaving Reb Chayim no choice but to support them, though this put a great strain on his resources. His own business fell off too. He had been farming the meat tax, but since the townspeople were now eating much less meat, he suffered enormous losses. His family was no longer as comfortable as it had been, nor as amicable.

Shloymele began to taste the bitterness in life. The peacefulness of childhood was at an end.

Once trouble comes, it pours in from all sides. One fine summer day, during the dry season, a terrible fire broke out in Kapulie, destroying over half the houses in town, including the one that belonged to Fradl's family. Heaps of ashes lined the street and sooty chimneys protruded like gravestones in a cemetery. Hungry, ragged and homeless, people wandered about the streets like living corpses. Some rummaged through the heaps of rubble of their ruined homes looking for mementos of better times. The joy they displayed over a nail or a pot or some roasted potatoes found among the ashes was more depressing than the dumb misery of those other poor souls who merely sat about mournfully, hanging their heads.

Reb Chayim took Fradl's family into his own home. There wasn't enough room for them, and the crowding caused great inconvenience, but in the emergency the change was accepted by everyone, out of pity.

The only one who did not suffer was Shloymele; in fact, the situation rather pleased him. He was together with Fradl under one roof, and the less room there was, the better for him. Each day brought unlimited opportunities of meeting her, of gazing at her face, hearing her sweet voice, watching her bare arms while she worked, and all without any fear of discovery. Shloymele went out of his way to give Fradl's parents a hand however he could, fetching and carrying things simply to curry their favor. In hopes of pleasing them, he went every day with a wheelbarrow to their burnt down house just when Fradl was scavenging there. Silently he dug and searched, putting whatever he found in his wheelbarrow; and whatever Fradl found, he quietly took from her hand and added to the haul. When the wheelbarrow was full he pulled it home, flushed red as a beet and sweating with exertion, while Fradl helped by pushing from behind. In this way he dismantled a whole chimney and oven and carried the bricks home. The joy of a warrior returning triumphant from battle with booty of silver and gold did not surpass Shloymele's joy as he and Fradl reached home, pulling the wheelbarrow laden with bricks, bits of iron, and other odds and ends salvaged from the fire. The truth is bitter, but it must be told: this fire, this terrible affliction that caused suffering to so many people, brought Shloymele a good deal of pleasure. He was like an heir who makes a show of weeping at his father's death, but who secretly feels great satisfaction.

It was only later, when Shloymele himself got burned, so to speak, that he felt the pangs of sorrow. Fradl's parents, who had lost all hope of restoring their fortunes in Kapulie, moved to a distant town, taking their children with them. Shloymele was badly hurt by the separation. His very life seemed ruined.

CHAPTER 15

Like tidal waves, trials and sorrows of all kinds now swept over Kapulie. Luckily, its unlimited experience with all forms of disaster has taught tiny, pliant Israel how to bend like a reed when the great breakers sweep over, and how to raise its head upright once they have passed. Blessed is He who said: "Fear not, Israel . . . when thou passest through rivers, they will not sweep you away, and when thou walkest through fire, thou shalt not be burnt." A decree is enacted prohibiting the wearing of kerchiefs—no one would deny its disastrous consequences. But Jews can adapt to anything. They pull in their belts a bit, go hungry a bit, eat their hearts out a bit, and make do with a little less. A fire breaks out—true, a terrible misfor-

tune. But God is our Father, and Jews are merciful people. They
write letters, send out messengers, wait hopefully, and what
happens?—Nothing. The messengers, after all, are also flesh and
blood; they too have wives and children; they too have to eat. When
autumn comes, bringing cold and rain, making the outdoor life
impossible, the homeless slowly move into other people's homes
wherever a place can be found. And if there's not enough room for
everybody—no matter! At least all are together. An epidemic breaks
out and people die—so the rabbis proclaim a fast, and the people
recite Psalms. The poverty gets worse—so whoever is able, takes his
walking stick and knapsack and leaves. There's plenty of room in
God's world, in the region of Volhinia, for example, where teaching
is a good business. Jews pick themselves up and move. Does everything then seem to be going well?—A "papers" decree is enacted,
prohibiting anyone from teaching Torah unless he has a government permit, a piece of paper. Terrible! But Jews do what is necessary under the circumstances, and God is merciful, and the teaching goes on.

Thus did the people of Kapulie weather that bitter time.

In those days rumors of the colonies reached the town, as
though carried by the wind: the government was giving Jews land to
settle and cultivate. This rumor, as usual, rolled from mouth to
mouth like a ball of yarn, and grew entangled in so many versions
that in the end it was impossible to unravel. Where were they giving
land away? How were they giving it? To whom? It became the town's
only topic of conversation. Everywhere—in the market, in the study
house and its courtyard, knots of people stood arguing angrily.

"Come now, Reb Zelig," argues Chaikel the Lame, who is
committed heart and soul to the colonies. "Tell me, my philosopher, exactly what you mean when you say 'beh-beh'? And what is
signified, pray tell, by your 'et-et'? This offer, which is our only hope
for survival, can't be pooh-poohed so lightly."

"What should I say to you, Chaikel, what can I argue if you are,
with all due respect . . ." Reb Zelig replies with a frown, taking a
pinch of snuff, ". . . if you don't understand the true essence of
anything. They're giving away colonies! What does it mean, 'giving'?
Does anyone come to you for no good reason and say, 'Here you
are, Chaikel, go and be a nobleman'!? Et, a thousand times et!"

"I've been telling my Feibush exactly the same thing," inter-
jects a poor Jew of good family, "You think you're going to become a

noble, Feibush? Quite the opposite. It smells of peasant. Not only that, but they say that if you don't fulfill your quota of work in the fields, they send you straight to the army or to Siberia. Feibush, I say to him, you are a *cheder*-teacher, a *cheder*-teacher you will remain in this world, and in the next. So go back to your teaching, and don't get any wild ideas. The hands of Jacob are not the hands of Esau."

"No!" Someone's voice can be heard from a nearby circle. "We won't try any of the neighboring towns, not for all the money in the world. Better go to the distant provinces, Yakterinoslav or Chersun."

"Right!" other voices are heard chiming in. "But the money, where do we get the money. . . ."

"They're offering money! . . . There is money available! . . . Let's find out what Reb Chayim thinks about it! What does Reb Chayim say? Call a meeting, let's have an assembly!"

And at the meeting the matter of the colonies was explained as follows: Many of the thousands of Jews of White Russia who had been expelled from their villages had, in 1806, been granted their request to be settled on royal lands in the southern district of "New Russia" to work the land autonomously. They were assisted by royal decree and financing. In 1810, the government announced that no more Jews were to be sent to these colonies as the money set aside for that purpose was exhausted. Nine years later, Jews were once again granted permission to settle, but this time at their own expense. Four years later, further Jewish settlement was again forbidden. A law of 1835, renewed in 1847, granted the Jews permission to settle as farmers on royal lands anywhere inside of the Pale of Jewish settlement, especially in the districts of Yakterinoslav and Chersun, their expenses to be paid by the community out of the meat tax. And since it was a matter of community funds, the community had to think it over, and so it was tabled until a later meeting.

This later meeting and those that followed were fruitless, as usual. Money was needed, but the community had none; not only that, but it owed arrears in taxes which the government threatened to collect by force. The entire town fell into a depression. When would the troubles finally end? Behind the stove in the study house people talked about the coming of the Messiah, an event for which a new date had been announced by a certain prominent rabbi on the

basis of an obscure Biblical verse. The conversation brightened
their spirits for the moment, and their eyes flickered with new hope:
"Don't worry! God is God, and he will not let Israel perish!"

The pillars of the community met often to discuss the state of
affairs. They talked, weighed the issues back and forth, and
concluded, invariably, with a deep sigh, "Dear Lord, help us out of
this crisis."

It was a winter evening. Outdoors it was bitter cold, with a
moon so dazzling bright, you could string pearls by its light, as the
expression goes. In fact there seemed to be pearls shimmering on
the street, the reflection of twinkling stars on the silver white snow.
It was a lovely night, a glorious night, a night for lovers' walks—but
such pleasures were not meant for the Jews of Kapulie: the streets
were deserted, not a soul was about. Inside Reb Chayim's house it
was warm and bright. A lively flame crackled in the lamp; by the
warm oven, Reb Chayim and some of the prominent citizens were
sitting around a table, talking about community affairs.

All of a sudden the street door opened, and a cold draft of air
rolled in, settling like a cloud of steam over the room. There
followed a sound of footsteps, and a squeak, and then, from the
cloud of steam, the figure of a man emerged.

"Shimen!" they all exclaimed. "Welcome, Shimen!"

Shimen was a householder in his thirties, a shrewd, witty man,
cheerful even when things weren't going too well, and a favorite of
all the townspeople. When the rumor of the colonies reached Kapulie, he didn't waste energy on idle speculation like the others, but
immediately went to the regional capital and from there to the
provincial capital to find out exactly what the story was and what
had to be done.

Shimen returned their greetings, shook the bits of ice out of his
coat and beard, and stood by the fire to warm himself. The others
watched him affectionately until suddenly they all began to laugh
and point at his feet.

"What in the world is that, Shimen!"

"Bast-shoes," replied Shimen earnestly.

"Purim is still a long way off, and already you're masquerading,
you clown?" they said, continuing to laugh.

They had good reason to laugh. Bast-shoes—boots made of a
soft plant fiber, with long straps that wrapped around pieces of cloth
covering the lower leg from heel to knee—were worn by peasants,

people of the lowest classes in Lithuania. Even the most wretched pauper of a Jew would no more think of wearing these boots than he would think of eating pork. He would rather have his soles worn through, he would rather go barefoot in the snow. . . . There was no such thing as a Jew in bast-shoes, unless it be a wedding jester, a Purim-player, or a clown of sorts.

"I'm not masquerading," Shimen replied with a shrewd smile on his lips. "I actually am a peasant now. I decided to wear these boots to save myself the trouble of informing every single person in town and having an argument with them one by one. Here they are, my fellow Jews! Take one look! You can see for yourselves what I am, and let me alone."

"So that's it, Shimen—you're a colonist?" they responded, suddenly serious. "Tell us the whole story and give us the details."

Shimen didn't have to be asked twice. He explained every detail about the colonies, and every law thereunto appertaining, in his usual pithy manner. He also related what had happened to him and what he had gone through before finding a congenial group with whom to form a colony in the district of Chersun.

"But who's going to work the land?" one of the group asked. "Do you think that by putting on peasant boots you've become a peasant, Shimen? You have no experience at that kind of work!"

"Don't worry! Rashi* has provided for this emergency," answered Shimen with a smile, "The government is staffing the colonies with German instructors, who will teach us how it's done."

"Yes, that's all very well," someone else asked, "But what about money to start with? From the meat tax? How are we to raise 170 rubles per colonist from the meat tax? Impossible! The community hasn't got a penny, and its needs are pressing. So much is needed. . . ."

"You don't have to worry about a thing," Shimen cut him off. "I have a little money saved up; and while I was finding out about the colonies, I managed to pick up a small fee for acting as a marriage broker. I also figure on selling my household furniture; and if that doesn't bring in enough, I feel sure that you gentlemen will help out. What do you say, Reb Chayim?"

"I say that you're a fine man, Shimen! We need more like you,

*Rashi, Rabbi Shlomo Yitzkaki (1040–1105), author of the authoritative commentary on the Bible and Talmud, which is called by his name.

people with love of the soil, with courage, and independence—many more!"

Sarah brought refreshments to the table: cracklings, bagels, and wine, and begged them to eat.

"God willing," Shimen said, smiling, "Next year I'll send you a pair of geese from the colony. There, as the song goes,

> Food for all, and the bread is free—
> A goat for five pennies, a chicken for three. *

CHAPTER 16

Reb Chayim's business did very poorly that winter, and the expression on his face reflected his concern. Reb Chayim had always been a serious, pensive man; he kept to himself most of the time and rarely exchanged a word with the family. His appearance inspired respect. No matter what racket the children may have been making in the house, the instant their father appeared at the door they would fall silent and no one uttered a peep. Not that the household was kept in fear of him, as with some tyrannical fathers who like to let everyone know who's in charge—far from it! He wore a grave expression, but hardly ever an angry one. The wrinkles on his fine, high forehead were a sign of his deep concentration; the blaze in his eyes reflected only the light of the Torah on which he meditated. In fact, he was quite soft-hearted; the silence that greeted his appearance in the room pained him. If any member of the family suffered the slightest hurt, it tore his heart out. It was his wife who actually ran the household. Reb Chayim provided what was needed, and had no interest in household affairs beyond that. His only concerns were the business, the community, and his studies, for which certain hours were fixed. The household understood all this; everyone treasured and loved him, took pride in his wisdom, and accorded him respect.

*The author was fond of including folk songs and folktales in his writings. The complete text of this song about the colonies can be found found in his story, "Di alte mayse" (The Old Story), 1895.

But that winter, Reb Chayim underwent a great change. His usual calm, thoughtful expression was replaced by an angry one. When he paced back and forth in the room in his usual way, with his hands behind his back, he would stop at intervals, bite his lip, cast an irate glance about him, and tug at his beard, on which many gray hairs had suddenly appeared. Reb Chayim had aged prematurely. He was then no more than forty-two or forty-three years old.

It was the meat tax that aged him. Since the town had gone bankrupt, his business had fallen off, as people ate less and less meat. And on top of that, some people began to evade the tax by smuggling meat into the town from the outside. The ban of excommunication that applies in such cases did no good at all. Need is stronger than iron, as people say, and certainly stronger than a ban of excommunication. Poverty and hunger are serious matters, and after all, the meat tax was not decreed at Mount Sinai. The inspectors, whose job it was to ferret out such smuggled meat and seize it by force were hardly any help at all. There was continual complaining, dissatisfaction, curses and tears, bringing upon Reb Chayim hatred and resentment. For a while he managed somehow—his personality still commanded deference. But later, when it came out that Reb Chayim had stopped paying the installments on the meat tax, and had even lost money which he had borrowed for that purpose, his enemies began to talk behind his back and finally to raise an open scandal.

Reb Chayim was not about to give up; he was a shrewd man with a wide reputation, even among the local nobles, as an intelligent businessman, and he might have pulled through. But he was as proud as he was intelligent; he couldn't bear to be gossiped about by people who had once trembled at his glance. He lost his appetite, then his health, and finally his fighting spirit.

Reb Chayim was also deeply troubled by events concerning his daughter Leah, a fine girl, clever about the house, intelligent, and blessed with a strong character. As the eldest child she was second in command after her mother in household affairs, and adored by everyone. Reb Chayim married her off to a boy from a different town, and maintained them in his house. The husband came from good family, as befit Reb Chayim's station; he was a fine and well-mannered boy, and the whole family took a liking to him. Reb Chayim devoted a few hours a day to giving lessons to him and a few of his friends, also sons-in-law of good families. Among these boys, there were some who came from other, larger cities, and they were conspicuous in their clothing and behavior, so different from the Kapulie manner. This group stuck together, and sometimes behaved in "strange ways" which the townspeople viewed askance, giving rise to talk that they were "newfangled." What the people of Kapulie in those days meant by the expression "newfangled" would seem archaic nowadays, even by the standards of old-fashioned people. But the talk went on, and led to scandal, until finally the group broke up. At the same time, tension developed between Reb Chayim and his son-in-law, and mutual antagonism: in town gossip, this meant that Leah was having trouble with her husband. The couple were no longer happy together, and the boy was sent packing back to his parents; that winter Leah was divorced.

Leah's strong character enabled her to act as if nothing had happened. But Reb Chayim could feel she was wounded, heartbroken. He ached with compassion for her, and blamed himself for the sufferings of his daughter, whom he loved as a true father. Had Leah uttered a word of complaint, they would have talked it out, he might have consoled her and felt better for it. But Leah said nothing, and it was her silence that pained him most. Her unfaltering love and devotion were salt to his wounds.

Reb Chayim's health deteriorated, and the family became more and more anxious. They sensed that their mainstay was weakening, that one or two strong waves might topple him and hurl them all into the great abyss.

It was a hard, joyless winter. On Purim night, Reb Chayim sat at the table with his family, making a tremendous effort to look happy and celebrate the holiday in his traditional manner. A purse lay at his side, full of coins for the poor. A few came in, and Reb Chayim gave something to each of them, with a smile and a friendly word. Children of well-to-do families came with handkerchiefs, collecting for others—for a family that had lost its fortune and was suffering in secret, for a respectable pauper, for a widow with small orphans—and Reb Chayim contributed freely, sending along Purim refreshments as well. Religious functionaries came too—sextons, wedding musicians, bath-house workers, Purim-players—Reb Chayim treated them all to a glass of spirits and a donation.

Sarah, for her part, was busy preparing and receiving Purim gifts. Poor yeshiva-boys, children, and servant girls were bringing covered dishes from relatives, neighbors, and friends, and under the covers were different kinds of cookies: *hamantashen,* poppyseed cakes, sugar cookies in the shape of a fish, or with the name of a Purim character—Queen Esther or Vashti—in iced letters on top. Neatly arranged around these goodies, of which there were only one or two to a platter, was a circle of prunes or almonds or walnuts. Occasionally a platter held a herring pickled in vinegar and honey—this from a neighbor who preferred things simple and substantial.

While Sarah was busy rewarding the messengers for their trouble, and sending her thanks and good wishes to this one and that, the children attacked the food, casting hungry eyes over the little dainties that so teased the appetite. Exercising self-restraint, they rearranged them on the dishes to send them back again: a *hamantash* to the family that sent a poppyseed cake, a Zeresh to the one that sent a Vashti, a fig or red apple in exchange for an almond. Naturally, disagreements arose, and fights; slaps and pinches were exchanged, but no one even noticed such minor disturbances at a time of such major rejoicing.

Outwardly it seemed a Purim like any other, but if you looked closely, there was a difference. The poor who came were the same, but the handouts were smaller. In place of the many guests that used to pass a joyous evening at the Purim meal, only a few poor relatives showed up. Reb Chayim sang "The Rose of Jacob," * and the children chimed in, but the verve of former years was gone. In his singing, you could hear the tears of a suffering soul, and the melody of Lamentations. The "Rose of Jacob" had been plucked: still pretty to look at, colorful as ever, but without the juice of life, and about to wither. Reb Chayim did his best to bring it off. He turned to the poor relations and tried to console them: "Don't worry—one must hope, one must not lose spirit. Trust God to help!" But his speeches were forced; care was sucking away at Reb Chayim's heart like a leech. Sorrow and suffering were reflected in his eyes.

Sarah noticed this plainly, and her heart clenched. She went off into a corner, covered her face with her hands, and wept quietly.

Leah, who felt it every bit as strongly, understood her mother's emotion, but controlled herself and kept her place at the table. She looked pityingly at the children and gave them each some sugar

* *Shoshanas Yaakov,* The Rose of Jacob, is a traditional Purim Song.

cookies: "Let the poor little ones eat." But at night, in bed, the pillow was wet with her tears.

CHAPTER 17

It was a week after Purim. The sun as it peered down from the sky was friendly and mild, sending a gentle, warm breeze as a first notice to winter that its lease on earth was expired. Winter was acting the bad tenant, postponing its move from day to day with one excuse after another. During the daytime, in the presence of the sun, winter said its teary farewells, sending streams of water into the streets. "I'm going, I'm going. Just let me pack up my things, my poor snow, blackened with toil." But no sooner did the sun shut one eye and go to its nocturnal rest, than winter turned around, thumbing its nose, ice-cold as ever. Ultimately, however, these delaying tactics were of no avail. Winter was as good as gone, and no one had time to pay attention anyway. For the Jews, it was the "before Passover" period when closets and cupboards had to be opened, tables and benches taken into the street, and everything scrubbed, washed and cleansed.

Kapulie was busy as an anthill. Everyone had something to do in preparation for Passover. Children, housewives and husbands were running about the market among the wagons of grain, potatoes, eggs and vegetables that Esau, the man of the fields, brings to his brother Jacob, the man of the town. In the mill, hidden behind the town in the woods, the stones had already been scoured clean, and Jews were bringing their bags of grain to be ground for *matza*; everyone patiently waited his turn, even if he had to stay overnight at the mill, for the rule was first come first served. The *matza* bakers and their helpers were all ready for business: some to knead, others to pour, still others to roll the dough, to make the rows of holes, to put the dough in the oven, to take out the finished product, and to deliver it in huge baskets. Passover was everywhere—in the markets, in the houses, and even in the *cheder*, where children's voices could be heard studying the Song of Songs in the traditional melody that makes a Jew's heart melt.

In Reb Chayim's house, which had been the hub of activity in former years, the atmosphere was heavy, altogether unlike the eve of a holiday. Reb Chayim lay in his bed fully clothed, pillowing his head on his arms, with a distracted look on his face. He was pale as the wall, and his breath came heavily. Sarah sat, depressed, in the front room doing nothing, her eyes red with weeping. When any of the children made a sound, she motioned, "Quiet! Father is ill, keep quiet!" The children walked on tiptoe, squeezed themselves into corners, and watched gloomily in silence. Only Leah busied herself with housework. But she looked black as death, and avoided meeting anyone's eyes.

The door to the street opened noisily, and there entered ceremoniously a tall, solidly built, impressive-looking nobleman with finely pointed mustaches. Two lackeys followed him, one carrying a bag, the other a pipe with an amber mouthpiece.

The nobleman looked around at everybody in the room and stood a while in silence, with a dark expression on his face.

"Ah, noble sir!" Sarah cried, rising suddenly to greet the nobleman.

"*Pani Rabinowa!*"* the nobleman cried, visibly moved by the sight of tears in Sarah's eyes. "What's the matter?"

Sarah was sobbing too hard to answer. The nobleman left her to collect herself. He sat down at the big, colored table, twisting his mustaches, and his own eyes grew moist.

"Hey, Antosia! My pipe!"

Like arrows from a bow the two lackeys leaped to his service; one brought the long pipe stuffed with tobacco, and the other the fire-tools: a piece of steel, a flint, and a bit of wick. He struck a fire, and lit the tobacco in the pipe. The nobleman sucked at the pipe and ordered the servants to leave.

Jan, the noble of Va——tzitz, was a descendant of a Polish family that owned the towns around Kapulie. This property had been divided among several brothers. On Gentile holidays, and sometimes on Sundays, Jan would drive into town in a carriage at the head of his retinue, as did the other local nobles, and proceed straight to the church, which stood across from the row of houses in the marketplace. Services over, he would cross the marketplace on foot to Reb Chayim's house, where he spent some time settling his

---

* *Pani Rabinowa:* the Polish greeting, something like "Esteemed rabbi's wife."

affairs with artisans and shopkeepers, who would come there to meet him. He had a high regard for Reb Chayim, valued him for his shrewdness and honesty, and loved him as a true friend. Whenever he had a dispute with anyone, his invariable solution was: "To the rabbi!" Jan relied on Reb Chayim completely, confident that he would not deviate from justice by a hairsbreadth. And besides all this, he simply enjoyed chatting with Reb Chayim, who could speak Polish, and even write it tolerably well. He would tell the nobleman proverbs, parables, and Talmudic legends, which Jan enjoyed and praised to the skies. If Reb Chayim was occupied with other visitors, Jan wouldn't interrupt him, but make himself at home, and smoke his pipe while waiting for Reb Chayim to finish. Whatever others may say about friendship between the Poles and the Jews, it is a fact that Jan was a true friend to Reb Chayim. This was evidenced on numerous occasions, as it was now in his gloomy expression and in his moist eyes as Sarah told him how things stood with them, and about her husband's illness.

"Can I visit with him a little while?" Jan asked.

"I'll go and see," Sarah answered, "and if he's up, I'll tell him you're here."

A moment later Sarah ushered the nobleman into the room.

"What is this, *Pan* Rabbi?" Jan blurted, stopping momentarily by the door as he came in, forcing a smile and shaking his head as if in astonishment. "*Pan* Rabbi seems to have lost his will to fight! Where is his iron spirit? Where is his wisdom?"

"There are times when human wisdom is of no avail," Reb Chayim answered, managing a weak smile.

"But there is a God, who can always help, in any circumstance. Do I have to tell *Pan* Rabbi things that he knows better than I?" Jan said, taking a seat facing Reb Chayim. "I know—it's a bad business. But such a clever man can't be lost. Are there many Jews like *Pan* Rabbi?"

Jan spent about a quarter of an hour with Reb Chayim. Then he said goodbye, and with a heavy heart went to his carriage, which stood by the church.

The next afternoon a wagon arrived at Reb Chayim's house, and two servants brought in sacks of wheat and potatoes, chickens, and a pair of turkeys.

Reb Chayim's life flickered like a candle. His strength ebbed until he lay weak as a baby, unable to move. The family sank into a black mood. No one ate, drank, or slept. Relatives and close friends came by, each with words of comfort and suggested cures. A certain doctor from the region was brought in. He pronounced the name of the disease, wrote a prescription and accepted his fee, but he was no more effective than the local home remedies.

A week before Passover Reb Chayim spent a terrible night. He lay in a stupor, gasping for breath, his eyes closed, his mouth half open, his lips parched, his pulse weak. From his chest came a rasping sound, like the sound of sawing wood. From time to time he grimaced and heaved a sigh. Sarah bent over and talked to him, but it was like talking to the wall. He was unconscious, unaware of what was going on around him.

Sarah bowed her head and wept silently. Leah sat at his head, choked with tears; from time to time a tremor shook her whole body.

On a long bench by a dimly-burning tallow candle, Shloymele swayed over a miniature edition of the Psalms. A soft, fervent prayer and hot tears poured out to his gracious, merciful Father in Heaven, "O mercy! Have mercy, holy Father! O almighty God, perform a miracle, and spare me and those poor little children that lie there exhausted in the corner. O spare us, our Father! In exchange," he said to God in his heart, "I will do everything you ask, I will be your faithful servant." Shoymele prayed and bargained, and from time to time cast a glance over at his sick father, expecting that any minute God would perform a miracle and heal him. Ceaselessly, he went over the same psalms, and the same thoughts until—with a sudden leap of joy—he saw his mother beckon to Leah. Stroking the patient's feet, she said quietly and joyfully:

"He's sweating!"

"Um-m-m!" Shloymele continued mumbling, exerting himself to the utmost. "O God, dear God!"

It was late by now. The crowing of a neighbor's rooster sounded through the house. The patient lay almost hidden by a huge eider-down quilt. Sarah moved about on tip-toe tucking him in more soundly to make him sweat. Leah picked up the little children, who had fallen asleep on the hard bench, carried them to their beds, and told Shloymele to go to sleep.

Shloymele was tired, broken from the strain of his long vigil. His head was spinning, his eyelids stuck together. He threw himself, fully clothed, on his bed, and in a moment he was sound asleep.

Reb Chayim recovered his senses toward morning. He sat up suddenly with a tremendous effort, looked at his wife and daughter standing by him, and with a groan, raised his eyes upwards: "Oh God, father of the orphan, judge of the widow!. . ."

Sarah and Leah broke into bitter weeping. Reb Chayim collapsed full length on the bed, his throat rattled, and he died.

Shloymele had gone to bed with an easy mind, confident that his father had been spared. He awoke to find his father stretched out on the floor under a black cloth and himself orphaned. Sounds of weeping filled the house.

SOURCES

I. M. Weissenberg, *A Shtetl*: first appearance in literary supplement of *Der Veg*, Warsaw, 1906. Translated from *A Shtetl* (Warsaw: Ferlag Progress, 1911) by the editor.

David Bergelson, *At the Depot*: first appearance in book form, *Arum vagzal* (Warsaw, Ferlag Progress, 1909). Translated from the *Verk* (Works. Berlin: Ferlag Vostok, 1922) by the editor.

Joseph Opatoshu, *Romance of a Horse Thief*: first appearance of *Roman fun a ferd-ganev* in *Shriftn* (New York, 1912), Vol. I. Translated from *Ale Verk* (Complete Works. Vilna: Ferlag Kletzkin, 1928) by David G. Roskies.

S. Ansky (Rapoport), *Behind a Mask*. Translated from *Gezamlte shriftn* (Collected Works. Vilna-Warsaw-New York: Ferlag Ansky, 1928) by Abraham Igelfeld and the editor.

Mendele Mocher Sforim (Abramovitch), *Of Bygone Days*: most of the original text of *Shloyme reb khayims* appeared in *Der Yid*, Warsaw, 1899, nos. 1–19. Translated from first complete text of the work in Jubilee edition of *Ale verk* (Complete Works. Warsaw: Ferlag Mendele, 1911–13) by Raymond P. Sheindlin.